RYAN'S WOODS

RYAN'S WOODS

A SOUTH SIDE BOYHOOD
FIFTY YEARS AGO

PATRICK CREEVY

Introibo ad altare Dei—ad Deum qui laetificat juventutum meum
I will go unto the altar of God—to God who gives joy to my youth

BOOKS BY PATRICK CREEVY

Ryan's Woods
AMIKA PRESS

Tyrus
FORGE BOOKS

Lake Shore Drive
TOR BOOKS

First Edition   ISBN 13: 978-1-937484-11-8
AMIKA PRESS   Jay Amberg, President
53 W Jackson Blvd 660 Chicago IL 60604   847 920 8084
info@amikapress.com   Available for purchase on amikapress.com
Edited by John Manos. Cover art by Francie Bala & Natalie Phillips. Map by Susan Creevy. Designed and typeset by Sarah Koz. Body in 10.25/14.5 Iowan Old Style, designed by John Downer in 1990. Titles in Interstate, designed by Tobias Frere-Jones in 1993–4. Thanks to Nathan Matteson.

FOR
CAITLIN
CONNOR
FRANCIE
PAT
& BREE

CONTENTS

1   **SPRING OF SIXTH**
VAL PRIZER & SUSIE SHANNON

28   **END OF SIXTH**
THE HANGED-KID TREE

60   **EARLY SEVENTH**
BOTTOM OF THE NINTH IN THE DEAD END

87   **FALL OF SEVENTH**
FIRE IN THE WOODS

113   **WINTER OF SEVENTH**
THE ICE TREE

149   **WINTER OF SEVENTH**
GEORGE JOHNSON'S JL

179   **BETWEEN SEVENTH & EIGHTH**
THE FOURTH OF JULY, 1961

215   **FALL OF EIGHTH**
IN THE INVISIBLE CIRCLE

247   **FALL OF EIGHTH**
BLACK CADILLAC

269   **FALL OF EIGHTH**
THE FENCE & THE SCAR

291   **FALL OF EIGHTH**
"BYE"

311   **FALL OF EIGHTH**
LAST PLAY IN THE WOODS

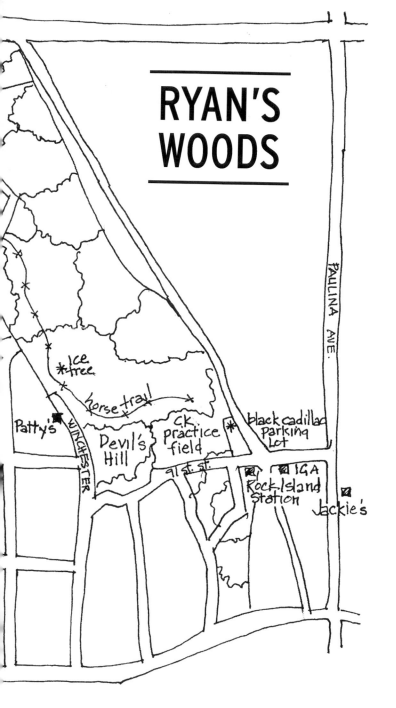

RYAN'S WOODS

PAULINA AVE.

*Ice
*tree

horse trail

Patty's

WINCHESTER

Devil's
Hill

C.K.
practice
field

91st st.

black cadillac
Parking
Lot

IGA

Rock-Island
Station

Jackie's

CHAPTER ONE

SPRING OF SIXTH

VAL PRIZER & SUSIE SHANNON

"Man, where d'ya get *that!*"

The first day of eighth-grade b-ball, one of the kids at my new school saw this scar on my right thigh and went kinda nuts. It's a bad one, all right, still purply and all sort of lumpy. "You shoulda seen the white goo, ya know, not just the blood but the guts when I did it. I'd a puked, but I was stuck up on this fence and I had to get off first. It was this fence prong that cut me, and it was stuck in me like half a finger deep. I was goin' nuts. But I pulled the prong outa the gooey stuff, slow, like taking out an arrowhead, and then sprung off that fence like a lunatic. Then you shoulda seen the blood. I mean, it was like a river."

I let out a few more facts then about my old life on the South Side, now that the scar got us going a little on my story (which starting up of things, a little blood and guts is always helpful for). Told 'em how down there I lived on the edge of a huge city forest preserve called Ryan's Woods, which was on the other side a the fence that I caught my thigh on. The fence was this nine-footer cyclone, for privacy and stuff, I said. Then we were talkin' for a while. And then I talked about Memorial Day and the Fourth of July and how all kinds of people would come for picnics, which even as I was saying it, I was wanting to pull the words back, 'cause the kid asks, "Colored?" Which wasn't like a shocker question, but it, for a bunch of reasons, I guess, sorta bugged me the way he said *"Colored?"* So I told him, "The music, on those huge picnic days, it was so cool, Rich. It would go on way into the dark, and I used to listen up in my room, lyin' in bed. Drums and saxophones, like pounding and blazing away all night. It was cooler than anything I ever heard in my life. I used t' just lie there and want it to keep goin' for a month."

And I've been thinking now, lyin' back in my new bedroom here up north, that it's been a month and then some since I moved here from the South Side. If I were sixteen, I could drive, go see Frankie and the gang, and maybe Patty...if I had the guts for going to see Patty. But I'm still four months short of fourteen, which is to say I'm goin' nowhere fast, while the days keep going nowhere fast, right along with me.

And I've been thinking like hour after hour tonight about the Dead End, which was out in front of our house on Hamilton. The Dead End. It was so cool—sort of like God stuck his thumb into The Woods just to clear out this place for us to play ball in. And, down at the end of it, there would be that cyclone fence again, only here it was stuck on top of this other major deal—I mean this four-foot concrete wall, which they put there so cars wouldn't go nosin' down into the ravine that cuts through The Woods there, just the other side of the fence. By the way, we had a way through the fence here into The Woods: a kind of rabbit hole we dug under the bottom cyclone prongs, past where the concrete stopped, very secret and cool. And blood brothers this rabbit hole made us, since we all got belly-ripped a time or two or three, shimmying head-down into it on our backs.

And was it not one perfect place to play ball in, the Dead End—at least if there weren't lovers parked down by the wall, makin' out. There'd be no cars coming—'cause it was a NO OUTLET—and there was that concrete wall and fence, which together was like a home-run fence in the majors, thirteen feet all told. But only Jackie Leonard ever got the thrill of sailing one over it. Frankie Malone and I would do the best we could to muscle the old rubber-coated out, but— truth compels me, or whatever that saying is—to say we never even came close. Jack, though, *believe it,* had a swing like a real ball player's. I swear they could've put a picture of it on a card, starting when he was like nine. Lefty, too, which is always so much sweeter. And it wasn't just all of us that Jackie was better than: it was all the Vanderkells too.

The Vanderkells. I swear, like a month and a half and I'm not caring about that stuff at all anymore. Vanderkell versus Christ the King. And you wanna know the real truth? Both sides had good guys, and neither side gave a single crap-ball about the religion part. It's just, you know, that you're gonna duke it out with what's not the same as you. And when it's their huge, humongous block of a school right smack across the street from your huge, humongous block of a school.... I mean the only natural thing is gonna be pretty much total war. But I couldn't care anymore about any of it, except to say this, which I'll always say about the toughest kid I ever knew: I'll be glad till the day I die that Jackie Leonard was on our side—and that like for every single day of the eight years before that one stupid second he died in (which wasn't Frankie's fault—no *way* it was), Jackie and I were true best friends.

But there was this day, about a year and a half ago, when I was alone, no JL, no friend with me, and I crossed the path of the number-one rat among the Vanderkells, Val Prizer (and between me and Prizer there was enough bad stuff so that I *won't* just be forgetting things or forgiving, not till I'm smart enough to see how a real, true rat is something besides a real, true rat).

It was at the mailbox near the end of the driveway of what everybody called Reed's Castle, the only house in the neighborhood bigger than Prizer's own house, which was across Hopkins Place from Reed's. But Reed's Castle was really, really beautiful, and Prizer's place was the spittin' image of Castle Dracula. I swear—it was like a mile high and all pointy and crooked, and it had the steepest drive-way I ever saw. It was like their driveway should have been illegal. And inside—get this—there were animal heads of like every kind there is, sticking out from every wall—be-cause Prizer's old man, who nobody ever laid eyes on, *ever,* was this famous big-game hunter. And no doubt about it, the guy put to death maybe every kind of creature that ever moved. I mean, picture a giraffe neck and head, I mean the whole—what?—eleven-foot deal?—stickin' out from over their fireplace, and then the seats around the fire, ever so nice and cozy, being the cut-off legs of elephants. Cut-off legs for chairs! What a pack a spooks those people were.

And where this punk Prizer got me was dead cold at the

Murder Place, the spot where, about a month before, a taxi went slamming into the mailbox—and not from any plain-old car accident but because a madman who was the cabby's passenger, just for kicks put two bullets in the back of the cabby's head (and any kid who hadn't seen the blood on the leaves from when they took out the dead guy wouldn't be able to say much about anything).

"EAT IT! EAT IT, you *PUNK!*" Those are words I won't be forgetting any time soon. The rat had me pinned against the new mailbox with the stick of this push broom he'd picked up at the end of Reed's drive. I'd seen him unscrewing the thing as I tried to sneak by, quick like. And how dumb was I? What would Val Prizer be unscrewing a broomstick for but to whack the livin' crap outa me with it? Not that the punk needed anything extra. He was old for our grade, born in like November of '47, which should have put him a grade ahead, but when he moved here from Arizona, or maybe it was Mars, they decided to start him late for some reason. But he'd a had me by about twenty pounds any-how. Not baby fat, either. It was that serious punk muscle of a kid who got the foghorn in his throat way before ev-erybody else, and zits, and even a few black hairs mixed in, even before he hit thirteen. You know the kinda guy. It's like he knows he's gonna be a fireplug midget in the long run, so he's gonna whomp the crap out of everybody while he's got the chance.

"EAT IT!" After he'd pinned me with the broomstick against the mailbox, he'd gotten one end of the stick un-der my right arm and he'd like pried me off my feet and slammed me to the ground. I got my arm free, but I felt the broomstick now shoved against the back a my neck and the ten tons of this guy like half on my back, as he held me down in the dirt, and half on my neck, where he shoved my face toward a pile of dog crap that lay right where the lunatic pumped the two bullets into the cabby's brains. "Eat the shit! You little chicken! Eat it, Collins! You're a fly! So eat shit like a fly!"

"You'll never make me! You'll never make me, Prizer, you punk! And someday...!"

"Someday! Someday *what!* Collins! What are you gonna do *some day!* Say it, Collins! Say it, you little chicken shit, so I can get really pissed at your chicken life! Call *me* a punk! You say what you're gonna do *some day!* You say it, *punk!*"

As he kept spewin' out his crap-balls, he kept jerking the stick down, over and over, hard as he could against my neck. And I mean it—it was like *total lunatic madman NUTS* how bad that rat wanted my face smeared into that crap pile, which some Vanderkell devil must've put there nice'n fresh because he *liked* Val Prizer and cabbies' getting their gray matter blown out by crazy men. My neck was shaking and my whole body was like on fire as I tried, with all I had, to keep the stinkin' dog dung off my face, pressing my neck back, just about blowing my veins out, though the pile and the stink were so close now I was afraid to open my mouth, thinking I *would* swallow the shit if I did! But I shouted, "You can't make me, Prizer, you punk! You can't make me do anything!"

"Oh yeah! I can make you do whatever I feel like, Collins! I can make you eat dog shit, you punk! So EAT IT! I say EAT IT! EAT IT right now!"

He threw the stick away and started with his two hands to try and grab the back of my head, so he could make it for dead-cold certain now my face'd be wearin' a shit beard. But—when he tossed the stick away—he lifted his weight enough off my back—just enough—so I could get my right foot pulled up. And I shoved with my right leg, and got him off me. Then I took off. I was running for my life, but—like an idiot, counting on my speed—I shouted back, "Some *day*, Prizer, I'm gonna kick your ass!"

Which of course cinched it. The big rat wouldn't be through with me now, not by a longshot. And, truth, how stupid and dumb could I be, thinking my speed was good enough to keep me outa the reach of Val Prizer. Was I nuts? The guy was just as quick as he was tough. And I didn't have any lead, just to Kearns's. So by about Bobby Stupnicki's, I felt against my thigh the first whack of that broomstick, which naturally he brought with him. I nearly peed my trou. I couldn't run another step. The pain was like spreading fire all up and down my leg. So I could only limp and hop. But I had to keep goin' because I could hear the whistle of a second one on its way. But what, really, was I gonna do? I was completely screwed. And *whack!* the second one caught me right on my calf, every bit as hard as the first one. I was screamin', "You punk! You punk, Prizer!" But already my nose was running and tears were falling. I was bawlin'—shit!—in front of Val Prizer. And I couldn't move. I could only scrunch down to my knees and grab my leg, which was on total fire from the two shots. Then there was this huge black shadow standing all over me. So what would it be now? Death?

"Say it again, *punk*, you're gonna do *what* to me some-day? Kick my *what?!*"

I was rippin' my sleeve over my eyes because of the stupid tears, and with my other hand I was holding my calf, and under my other arm I was hugging my thigh, tight. I figured he might crack apart my brains now like the cabby's, but I was blubbering, "You're a punk, Prizer! You're a punk. You can't make me..."

"Oh ho ho ho ho, I can make you all right, Collins! I can make you do anything I feel like. I can make you crawl. See! See how I've made you crawl on your punk-shit knees. And I can make you *kiss* my ass. Not kick my ass, Collins. Get it! But for now, my little fly, I just want you to *get up and start walkin'!*"

I felt the stick then poking me hard, right square in the back. And I couldn't believe how dumb I was or *nuts*, but I wasn't gonna do what this gigantic *punk* told me to do. I just scrunched up tighter into a ball, and was blubbering, "You can't make me..." But then I heard the stick rising....

"Oh *yeah!*"

And then I heard the stick coming down, whistling, so I exploded—and broke into a run. My leg could move again, sort of limpy like. And he didn't catch me right away, trying as hard as he was to whack me to death. So I made it all the way to Allens', our next-door neighbors', before I felt his hand gripping my shoulder, and then his forearm putting a choke hold around my neck. And his mouth in my ear, like he wanted to eat it.

"I have to ask you, Collins. Just *where* do you think you're going? You keep playin' games with me. *And I don't like that! Ya hear!*"

Before he strangled me, he threw me off, but he put himself between me and my house, and I couldn't get past him and his lunatic stick. He held it sideways out in front of him, and he backed me off from my house, back out into the street, with right-hand shoves and then left-hand shoves, steering me where he felt like. "Where ya *goin'*, Collins! Eh?! Where ya *goin' now!*" He was laughing with that frog voice of his as he kept backing me up and steering me, sh-ovin' me where he wanted. "Where ya *goin'*, punk, hunh! Tell me where you're *goin'!*

"I'm goin' wherever I wanna go, Prizer, you rat-face punk!"

"Oh, is that so? It must be you wanna go *this way,* then. And *this way* and *this way* and *this way!*"

He kept backing me up and steering me wherever he felt like, and I wanted to get around the lunatic into my house, but I couldn't pull it off. So I broke and ran the other way, along Mathis's yard toward Howland. Then I heard that insane stick again—and then *wham!*—one more time the fire on the back of my leg! And it stopped me again, dead. I grabbed my knee up to my chest and was hugging my thigh in both arms, hopping on one leg like the other was being blow torched. And Prizer wouldn't give me a second of time.

"You don't seem to *get* me, Collins. You're gonna go where *I say.* You're gonna do what *I say. And nothin' else. Ya get me!*" He began again then with his witch broom held sideways and shoving it at me righty, then lefty, to back me up. He wanted to corral me now down into the Dead End, where he could really murder me.

But right then and there, it happened. A true miracle! I swear I got a *true miracle,* just when that insane rat had me backing over the manhole cover that was our home plate. Susie Shannon! And, oh, man, I loved her for this one! Over his shoulders, I could see her. She was coming up the hill on Howland, her pony-tail hair bobbing, her school uni-form (which was like the cleanest, most beautiful thing I ever saw. White and blue. I swear—it made me think it was like a gift to see her), all beautiful as ever. She was com-ing home this way from the Academy of Our Lady, 'cause their bus would drop her off at Longwood and 87TH. Then she'd walk through The Woods down Longwood and then come up the hill on Howland. She was carrying her books like usual, the way girls do, like holding a baby.

And I was maybe even gonna shout, "Susie!"—things getting as bad as they were, which would've been deadly embarrassing. But I got spared. 'Cause Susie saw it all herself—the Rat King backing me down the slope now toward the Dead End wall, steering me with those righty and lefty broom shoves. She didn't need any explanations. She flung her books down right there on Mathis's lawn and came running faster than lightning.

"I've had about *enough* outa you, Collins! Ya little *shit face!* You and your little games. Tryin' to get *away from me* and workin' your smart little mouth about what you're gonna *do someday!* Who do you think you are, eh? Just who do you think you *are!*"

So Val-boy kept right on spewing. And wouldn't he start really foaming now as I started *not* moving where he wanted me to, but even standing my ground, knowing of course that the rat's time was juuust about up, which he didn't know 'cause he couldn't see Susie flyin' right at him. I even started like grinning, right in his whiskery-pimple puss, which threw him really off his rocker. "You crazy little punk shit you wipe that smile off your punk face or I'll crack your brain in two!"

"Oooh, you scare me, Prizer, you punk. You really scare me. Think you're so, so tough. You're nothin'. You're *nothin'*, you *punk!*"

"Why you little dirt crap shit, I'll knock your brain in two! I'll knock your head right off your skinny shit shoulders!"

He raised the stick like Mr. Hyde, I swear, right outa the movie, and was gonna bring it down on my skull to finish me—when he felt it get stuck!—like somebody put a spell on him from outa nowhere!—'cause Susie had it grabbed! She had it grabbed! I mean, it was so perfect I couldn't a planned it in a million years! "You *will not!*" she said. And there he was, kid a the famous Big-Game Spook, standing there like all his muscles had just croaked. All's he could do, trust me on this one, was turn around and see who told him what he *wasn't* gonna do. And now what he *was* gonna:

"You drop this stick *right now!* Do you hear me! You *drop it!* Or you'll be sorry, you *coward!*"

She had him so completely ambushed he couldn't hold that broomstick for a million bucks. So she just snagged it off him like nothin'. And there she was, her cheeks all flushed and beautiful, holding that stick like a spear. I swear she was to me the number-one most beautiful girl in the universe. Number one, no contest, not even close. Because think about it—who's more beautiful to a twelve-year old guy anyhow than a seventeen-year old girl who was like a complete legend in the neighborhood for her looks—and there she is, on top of it, standing with that brown-gold pony tail, her blouse cleaner white than anything, and that spear in her hand—and, in the bargain she's just sliced up my number-one enemy in the world and saved my life.

"Only a coward picks on smaller people, and with a stick. Do you hear me? Only a coward!"

Oh, man, I'll tell ya I was loving every word; or I can't even tell you, it was so cool. And now she started holding that stick like it had a very nasty disease. Like it was something *she'd* never need, that's for sure. And when she told that punk Prizer, "You should be completely ashamed of yourself," I swear if the grenade was there, I'd've fallen on it for her, dead cold like nothin'. I loved Susie Shannon with everything in me. Or if that wasn't what it was, then I wouldn't be able to say much about anything.

But of course Prizer wasn't through. He'd gotten over it that there'd been this miracle for me and was looking now for something to say or do. He started clenching his fists real hard—but you couldn't hit a girl. Not even Val Prizer could hit a girl. And she had those five years on him and that stick in her hands. So he couldn't tell how it would've turned out—which was a real stopper, for the only thing worse than having the word spread that you'd hit a girl, would be having the word spread that a girl had handed you your lunch (though he had this little problem already, *didn't* he...?). So the punk was frustrated. In fact raging. And with his brain kinda fried, not that he had much of a brain anyhow, he couldn't come up with anything but more spew. "Who died and made you boss, girlie. Think you're so great. And that's my *property*, that stick, so give it back."

"Oh, yes, I'm certain as can be, you could be trusted with it, sir. Just certain as can be."

"It's my *property*, whoever you are. You give it to me or you'll be sorry, I swear."

The big goof now started stepping toward her and then started reachin' in for the stick. And no doubt I was feeling safe because we had numbers against him (I wasn't dumb: we had a sure thing), but I wasn't kiddin' about how thankful I was feeling and what I'd do for Susie either. So I put myself between 'em and said, "You touch her, Prizer, and so help me, I'll..."

"You'll *what*, Collins, you pitiful little *punk*. You'll *what!*"

He was plenty glad, I could tell, to have *me* to work on again. But Susie was really sick now of this insane goof. She was gonna shut down the spew factory—closing time:

right now. "Never *mind* what he'll do or won't do. You leave him alone. And you listen to me. You don't have any business around here, mister. You just take your angry self away from here right now. And I mean *right now*, do you hear me?"

"I got ears, big shot girlie queen. But just who do you think you are, ordering me around. Just who do you think you are!"

"Never *mind* who I am. I'm sick of your questions and your mouth. I just want you gone. And if you don't go, I'll just send out a little shout for my brother, Mike, which, believe me, mister, you do *not* want me to do. Am I right, Kevin? I do believe this would be one sorry fellow here, if Mike Shannon were to appear right now."

Oh, man, this—believe it—was a very excellent call on Susie's part. This was one very, very excellent call. I mean, sorry? Prizer would wish he were a stuffed monkey on the old man's wall rather than see Mike Shannon coming his way, and to defend his sister. "Oh, man," I said, "you'd be one sorry *punk* then, Prizer."

"You *shut up*, Collins, you hear me! You *shut up*! And I'll tell you exactly what I'm gonna do to you, when your girl here and your Mike whoever-he-is aren't around. I'm gonna…"

"Oh no you *won't*, mister. You won't do anything. Not *one thing*." So Susie put her grip on the rat's future with me too (which grip I wasn't dumb enough to really believe in, though I stayed respectful of her). And Val-boy was once more ragin'.

"Oh yeah, girlie! You give me that stick! You give me my property! And I'll show you what I'll do!"

"Not a chance!" she shouted. "Do you hear me! Not one chance—ever!"

Prizer now pushed me out of his way and took a step again toward her, and he'd even gotten a paw on the stick (his 'property', only if all the broomsticks in the world belong to like evil spirits of the dark), and was trying to yank it from her. But she had another sweet move waitin' for him, all right. And it might just be the sweetest move I'll ever remember. I know I never saw one sweeter before or since in my life. For what did she do? Well, she starts by ripping the stick right back from the chump, like nothin'. Then—like a queen—she strolls over to our manhole-cover home plate, which wasn't one of those manhole covers with a bunch of iron bars and spaces between 'em, but one of those big huge iron circles with nothing but a small little notch-hole in it, a tiny little hole, juuuust big enough— oh yeah—for the end of a broomstick. And was it not perfection, the way Susie stood there now, fitting the end of Val-boy's broomstick *juuust* into that little notch-hole, and saying, "Wish your property farewell, mister whoever-you-are!"—and then letting the troll's weapon go—goodbye—down into the dark. Oh man! The perfection! And the sound!—the way that stick went clattering way down into the dark cave there, with this dark sound, if a sound can be, like, dark. And then finally, somewhere way way down there—splash!—into the liquid shit it goes.

What sweet justice! So beautiful! And there was Susie, brushing her hands, you know, sort of clappin' 'em three or four times against each other to dust 'em off, saying, "So there, mister whoever-you-are! *So! There!*"

But now wait! Wait! It wasn't finished! This wasn't it— for how about this?! She starts smiling now, bending forward a bit, and says real soft, "Of course we could continue. But then I'd have to shout the name of my brother, Mike, who, if you'll look two doors down towards the Dead End, happens to be coming out of our house right now, which makes me quite certain you *will* be on your way."

Oh, man! I know it sounds like a crock. I know it does. But one more cool little miracle was on its way, because, I swear it, there *was* Big Mike, all two hundred All-Conference-fullback pounds, coming out with a bucket and sponge to get started on the Shannon family Buick. And I couldn't help it. I mean, it was too much perfection all at one time. So I just started grinning. I couldn't wipe it off my face. And what in the whole world could Prizer do but scram, just exactly the way Susie told him.

Watching him turn tail, I might have felt a little sorry even for the Rat King (nah!), if my leg wasn't starting to kill me. But for that, I figured out a cure. I shouted, "Your books, Susie! Let me get 'em for you!" And sure enough when I took off at top speed, I was running right through my pain, making it go away. Then when I came back to her and handed her her books, and she smiled at me, her lips so soft and beautiful that I had a hard time breathing, I knew I was way, way outa the reach a the Rat King's tricks. And seeing her pony-tail hair (which I heard an old guy comin' outa church one time say to his old wife was "like honey in a jar") well, it made me love being younger, being just a month past twelve, like I was, with her seventeen. Because you know, girls her age look on guys my age, not like they're guys their age, I mean not like those class-A jerks, who just bug 'em, but sort of still like angels (instead of the devils that teachers try to make us out as). And I was feeling, even, that girls like Susie Shannon *made* punky kids my age into like really good guys or something, when they looked on us that way. But I couldn't get a word out. About as nervous as the time I caught the Host in the paten (and you shoulda seen my sorry fingers shaking then), I handed her her books. I wanted to say, "Truth is, Susie, I would die for you, if you were ever in trouble." But I could just barely get outa my choked throat, "Susie…you…really saved me."

She took her books up again, like a mom does a baby, and she smiled a smile about as gentle and nice as any smile even my mom had ever smiled at me. She said, in this incredible like soft way, "He's just a little older, Kevin. That's all. And someday soon. Someday very soon, he'll know he'd better let you be."

She knew I couldn't talk. So she just kept smiling. And then what? She reached out a hand, I swear it, and touched me, right on my cheek with the palm of her hand and her warm soft fingers. Then she smiled a good-bye smile that I could've died for, too, and turned toward her house, the last on Hamilton. The Shannons, I forgot to say, lived at the very end of the Dead End, their house right there on the edge of the ravine, looking right out at The Woods. But since I had this feeling now that like God was on their side, I got it why they weren't sort of spooked to live there.

I watched her just a few seconds as she went down the Dead End slope, then thought I'd better turn away, and not stare. I walked off toward Howland, trying to look like I had something to do, in case she and Mike were looking my way. Then I took the hill down out of sight and headed for Longwood, figuring I could retrace the steps Susie took from the bus on 87TH.

Down in The Woods, the big trees were just sort of starting to be green, you know, with that kind of lettuce-y color the little new leaves have, and the high-up branches were swinging all over the place in that kind of cool-warm breeze that you'll get in May. The stream in the ravine, which the City put foot-bridges across (and it was really neat now because if you looked to where the stream went winding off back into The Woods, you could see most of the bridges, going off in the distance, getting smaller and smaller)—this stream had a flagstone bed (my dad told me the stones were flagstones), and there were flagstone walls up its sides and flagstone paths all along it for walking. Very cool. And it was flowing now with like two feet of rain water, making all this noise over the stones. I knew that if I walked a side-path back toward Hamilton, I would come under the Shannons' house in just a few minutes; but I'd've died if Mike or Susie ever caught me spying on 'em.

I walked on down Longwood over the stream, which was making a really cool loud sound as it went tearin' through an under-the-street tunnel. And I had this thought that Longwood was okay because in her walk home, Susie would've had to clear out any possible demons and stuff (I swear, ya think stuff like this sometimes, when you walk The Woods). I thought, though, too, that it was pretty strange to be saved by a girl, no matter what age she was. I knew I couldn't tell Jackie, or Frankie, or any of my buds, Terry Thillens, or Bobby Stupnicki, or George Peterson, or Pete O'Connor. So I had a secret. But I smiled, thinking my secret was a real good laugher compared to that punk Prizer's, who'd gotten a full clipping from Susie. No need to worry about the word spreading among the Vanderkells! And as I came up to 87TH and then turned back again and headed home the way Susie had come home from the Academy bus, I felt all thankful again. And so incredibly glad still that I was like this un-jerky twelve-year old in Susie's eyes. I couldn't help it. It really got to me, like some kind of I don't know what, and I just started getting silvery eyes. Which made twice with the tears in one day! But this was all different from the snivel-shit that that rat Prizer had whacked me into—though FX Malone wouldn't've seen it that way. I saw Frank stay totally dry-eyed when his brother Tom knocked his jaw right outa the socket (and he looked like Frank, then, all right—as in en-stein!). But without Malone around, I wasn't ashamed of myself. So too bad—it felt good to still be a guy but a kind of an angel-kid too in the eyes of Susie Shannon. It felt so good—truth—that I couldn't believe how good it felt. And as I was wiping away these tears of happiness (an expression I never *got* before), I wondered if a girl my age could ever make me feel the same way.

At dinner not a first word—at all. No chance I was lettin' on about *anything* that happened during my day. But still it was like I wanted some way to get noticed; so I clammed up in this really weird way, just sort of staring and not saying anything, for a long time, which got everybody very, very bugged. "Why don't you *talk*, creepo." "Yeah, *talk!*" "Come on and *talk!*" "Why don't you *talk!*" That's what I was getting from my brother Johnny, who was ten then, and my sister Katie, she was nine, and my brother Dave, seven, and my sister Peggy, she'd be five. And even my twerpy little sister Annie, who was like three at that time, was going, "Yeah, creepo, why don't you *talk!*"

I didn't know which'd work better for getting my mom and dad into it. Just to keep staring? Or to try something guaranteed, like yellin' *"Shut up!"* to the punks. And isn't it kind of interesting how the words 'shut up' 'll get ya your ass kicked in a lot of families? But I have to say I was really liking that weird stare I had goin'. And yet my parents had not jumped in. So, for full-boat getting myself noticed, I had to go suicidal. And I thought I was being very cool in the way I did it. I didn't move my head. I just kept staring, full-boat zombie style, and then in a kind of whacko build-up, makin' my voice louder and louder, and like widening my eyes up t' the Jerry Colona point, I said, "Why don't you all just SHUUUT UUUUP!"

In no time, my mom. "Oh, my God, Bob, your son has lost whatever mind he had! Did you hear what just came out of that mouth! And look at him! Please!"

My dad? Well…. He didn't make any fast moves. No way. He'd take a little time, because what he was going for—one more time—was, naturally, terror. Slowwwwwwwly, he put his knife and fork down on his plate and then out on the table he set both his fists, like the heads of humongo sledge-hammers. And that would be my dad, who lets you know all right what Mike Shannon's gonna look like at thirty-five. Or now thirty-seven. He looked me square in the eye, which took care of the zombie thing, speed of light. Then, *not* good, not at *all* good for yours truly, he comes on with the slow, deep voice. "Would you, my friend, do me just one, little favor, and *explain* yourself, please."

Which of course worked. I was dead scared, even though I was very familiar with the man's style. But no way, not in front of my punky brothers and sisters. No way. I would not want to explain myself. Couldn't tell my mom and dad, even if all the little punks and punkettes weren't around and eating it all up. Couldn't even *think* about opening up myself to the parents. Crazy even playing with the notion, which of course was exactly what I *was* doing when I made all the effort to get my idiot self noticed. But that was a mistake I could fix: I kept clammed, though I really buried outa sight anything like that staring-zombie deal, not being the dumbest kid on this planet.

My dad had his face muscles kind of rippling. "No Tom

Malone stuff between you and Sister Armida, I hope."

This meant the time when Frank's insane brother had like an *answer* for the Armadillo. She gives him the old "Thomas Malone, you just make me *tired!*" And he says to her, "Well, Sister, you're wearin' me out pretty good, too." Which got us all laughing for about a month. But, Tom Malone, what a shit-for-brains. That *minute*, the Armadillo tees him up and place-kicks him, right through the uprights, CK to Vanderkell. And what it meant to end up over there was something we discussed a lot but could never quite picture. We couldn't figure out, either, how you could be as stupid as Tom Malone, though bro Frankie was never short of ideas.

But to my dad now I just gave out a goofy sort of play-ing-dumb look.

"Does that mean *no?*"

"Yes. I mean no. I'm gettin' along fine with Armida."

"Gett-*ing* along fine with *whom?*" My mom, fast as could be.

"Sorry. Sister Armida."

"Well," my dad said, "what do you *mean* then, buster, by talking to your brothers and sisters the way you did, and at the dinner table? Not that that garbage is acceptable *any-where, any*time."

"I don't know. No reason. Nothin'. They just kept *buggin'*, I mean bugging, me."

"And you weren't just asking for it, were you, with that little *Shock Theater* bit of yours?"

I gotta say I liked that my dad threw in the 'shock' thing. Very cool on his part. And even though it made no sense, I felt glad he *had* caught my zombie deal. And that Mom had, too, the way I hoped—don't ask me why. But I really wanted out of this tangle now! So, fast as for Susie's books, I went with trusty instinct, and started apologizing. "I don't know,"

I said. "Maybe I *was*.... Asking for it, I mean. And...I...I'm *sorry* for what I said. I...I just was gettin'...*getting* bugged at the pu.... At them, I mean. And I'm *sorry.*"

He was thinking, rubbing his hand up and down over his mouth, so ya could hear the whiskers. I took it as a good sign. And I was still alive and breathing.

But I wanted all the way out now. I couldn't, though, rush the next move: hurrying things could ruin the deal. So I eased now, very, very mousy-like into a..."But...please... may I be...excused?" I showed 'em my plate was clean. Then I lied cold and said I had a whole bunch of math. Then the old I'll-get-the-garbage-the-*minute*-I'm-through-with-homework promise. But this can bring on the we've-heard-that-a-thousand-times-before response. And ya never want your past record brought out. Never.

Giving it a last good whisker scrape, my dad lowered his hand back to the side of his plate. He waited, which again was very solid terror tactics. Then, "After you answer a question, my friend...you can go...*maybe.*" He looked at me hard—right smack in the eye. "Do you understand, Kevin, the meaning of the word *never?*"

I have to say I wasn't fond of this particular question. But what an idiot I would be to say, you know, like I *didn't* understand the word *never.* To try somethin' like "No, sir, I really don't understand that word. Perhaps you could explain it to me." That would be Tom-Malone dumb! (And even though you've probably got the idea already on that colossal brain-spastic, how about this: One time he says, talking about Frankie, "The kid is dumb. And when I say dumb, I mean D-U-M.") But never a day have I been in that mope's category, so I nodded and said, very mousy but clear, that yes, I understood the word *never.*

"Well," my dad said, "that's how often, my friend, I want you to use the language you used tonight. *Never.* That's how often. Do you understand that?"

Hoping I looked like the undisputed world-champion sorry person, I nodded again and moused out a "Yes. I understand."

"All right, then. Put your dishes in the sink, and you're excused—to do *homework.*"

So it worked! My bullshit worked! Which meant freedom! And I always had a very sweet situation waiting for me. Couldn't be sweeter for a thinker-type like myself. Because what I had was my own room. And in my room, I would be like fifty worlds away from the punks and punkettes. We had a three-storey house, and even if my brother Johnny was up on the third floor with me, his bed was out in the hall—private sort of, because away from the other goofs—but he had no door. Which I did. And behind that door was perfection. My room was kinda small, with a low ceiling, but I loved it; and, believe me, I was *up* there, like in a pueblo, with nothing beneath me, just the straight drop. I had a decently cool window, too, which didn't look south, to Allens' house—but north, to The Woods. Most nights I could follow the moon, which ya never quite know what it's gonna do, as it goes shinin' its way across The Woods.

I went running up the stairs like a sailor going to check from the crow's nest if the guy on deck shouting "Land!" wasn't full a crap. Because there was something I couldn't hold back anymore, though I hadn't admitted it to myself: I was nuts that night to get to my private lookout…and for the dark to come. Crazy for it because, between my window and The Woods, exactly high as mine, there was this one other window.

For forever, there was nothing between our house and Shannons' but a prairie. Then the Schwendrowskis came and built their house. But I didn't need to worry: it was just a one-storey place and so nothing more to me than a black shadow of roof way down below and outa my notice. The only thing between me and The Woods, still, was just the Shannons and that window, three storeys up, exactly like mine.

Before the day that I'm talking about here, I'd never been interested enough to wait for her. Maybe, even, I don't know, five months before, I couldn't've cared if I saw her, except that I didn't like to share my pueblo deal with anybody. But things had been changing (truth? I'd sort of lost it once or twice before now, catching that pony tail coming up the hill on Howland), and this night was just real different.

So I'd fed the lie about the math and made that phony take-out-the-garbage promise. Which promise I naturally forgot in under five seconds. So now there was time to kill; and, lying back on my bed, I killed it with goofy dreams. Like kindergarten stuff, to begin with. *My* dad, Val Prizer would say, could get a hundred men. And *my* dad, I would say, a thousand. *His* dad could get the Navy. But *my* dad the Army. *His* dad the Air Force. But *my* dad the Marines. And on and on as the two of us went at it like punky little six-year olds.

Don't ask me what I was doing with this pitiful simpy crap, which had me laughing at myself. But when I'd dropped my trou, I'd seen my leg was deep purple all right, in all three places—my skin looking like I just got slapped across the face. Or maybe the blood was ragin' pissed because all it could do was spread beneath the surface of my skin, and couldn't get out. Anyhow, it was a long time before I got past thinking of *some day* making Val Prizer my total slave. I laughed, too, thinking of the sap as whipped clean by a girl. There was a very sweet perfection in that one.

But after some time, eventually, I started thinking of my sprinting that day for Susie's books, of my being lucky enough to touch things she'd touched, and then to carry 'em to her—to save her trouble. I thought how I could wait for her every day now in The Woods, where she got off the bus from the Academy of Our Lady. That I could maybe hide behind the trees and move along without her knowing—but ready every second to protect her when she walked down Longwood alone—all ready to spring out like the miracle she'd been for me that day and be a miracle for her. Or—to pay her what I owed her—to give my neck for her if I had to. Only say the word.

It had gotten all dark, and the moonlight's silver was all over my bed. It was beautiful, and I felt so comfortable now, and thankful to Susie; and I didn't worry about myself at all, just her. I felt so much of these kinda things, even, that the silver in the eyes started coming again some, but of course it was that good kind. And when I wiped it away, I thought of how a couple of times I'd actually come up to my room to like pray that the BVM would appear to me, the way she'd appeared to other kids, even guys. One time I know I started with the silver eyes—so that's maybe why I thought about it now—I mean this time when I was sure that it was Mary, coming down with the white light when the moon was like half out of a cloud.

I hadn't looked yet. I was so comfortable and warm just lying there that I almost didn't want to look. But I wanted to. I had to. It like gripped on my bruises to move...but I got up now and put my face, so I wouldn't get caught, just at the side of my window. The moon was a huge full one, spreading silver all over The Woods; but, from the window at Shannons', a jillion-times-cooler light was shining. And I could see her. My heart went as crazy as it ever did in my life when I watched her. She was at her desk, studying, her one hand like holding her cheek and her other one turning the page of a book: it had to be one of those books that that day I'd gotten to touch. I looked for some time, and I knew that there was no way there could be in the world a more beautiful girl. Her hair was still up in her pony tail, and it was shining in the light from her lamp, like honey in a jar, all right. She wore still her short-sleeved, white uniform blouse, from the Academy. And everything about my day, all of it, made me feel sort of like I'd died and gone to heaven.

But the pain was comin' up too in my beaten leg when I knelt there; and as good as I felt, I felt somehow not good about spying on Susie Shannon. It had to be wrong. No getting around it. So I took myself away from the window and was lying back again on my bed. Then, after some time, the pains in my leg went down again, and the comfort came back, and I was feeling good to have stopped looking. But still, about one quadrillion times cooler than the moon was the light comin' out from her window. And I couldn't help it. I knew I shouldn't—I knew that—knew it—but I got up again on my knees and put my face to the side of my window again, to not get caught.

She wasn't studying anymore. She still sat at her desk, but her book was closed, and she was looking out her window, sort of staring at nothing. Then, after a time, she reached with her hand to what was holding her pony tail (and when she did this, it made me think I'd love to give her a gift of some girl thing, 'cause that would let her know

I cared about her, not about me). And then she took it out, whatever was holding her hair. Some seconds went by; then she kinda shook her head a little, and her hair started comin' down like crazy, all over her shoulders. She ran her fingers through it, both hands, two, three times, slowly, like she was thinking of something as she did it; then she reached for something in her drawer. It was a brush, I could see. Then she got up and walked to her closet door, which, I could see when she opened it, had a long mirror on its inside. And because she had her back to me now, I got careless. I couldn't help it. I couldn't stop. I came out all the way into my window and watched.

It was so beautiful, when she was standing in front of her mirror, the way she brushed her hair out smooth. It got me going crazy warm-like again, just thinking about her and what all I'd do for her. But now there was a new, different thing. It felt not just warm, but hot, all over me and all through me, and really good. So good. And I couldn't help it: I couldn't move. I watched her as she brushed and brushed her hair. And when she finally stopped, I still didn't move. I watched as she held the brush sort of against her heart and just looked at herself some time in her mirror. I wanted to whisper in her ear, to send over the words, "You are so beautiful, Susie Shannon, and so incredibly cool." But, even though her back was to me, I began to have a feeling. It seemed like she could sense I was watching her. Crazy, but it seemed like she could. And she must have, because slowly…as if she suspected something…she turned. And it was true: she *had* felt somehow my eyes on her back. And there I was. She didn't do anything; she just for some seconds stood still and looked over at me, holding the brush up against her like it was some sort of magic protection against me. Then she walked to her window, and she pulled down the shade.

I fell back on my bed in total shit pain. I didn't water up in my eyes or anything now, just clenched my fists because I was so ashamed. I knew I must be ugly as a million-year old devil to her: no angel little kid anymore. And that I'd never in my life anymore have feelings like the ones I'd had that day. Never. I clenched my fists so hard it was like I wanted to kill something. I imagined myself right in the face of Val Prizer. I imagined him saying he'd have my head cut off and stuffed and stuck on his lunatic old man's wall. And then I imagined myself knocking him down and shoving his face exactly where he'd wanted to shove mine, so he could eat it good.

CHAPTER TWO

END OF SIXTH

THE HANGED-KID TREE

So. Yeah. Bad stuff. Real bad stuff. But sometimes, lo and behold, things do happen. I mean, even when you think they never will, hours and days do pass sometimes, even weeks and months pass. And we kinda get past things, or some things. Of course, on things like turning the tables on a Prizer and serving him the shit, when you're out there where real people are, you're not quite as tough as when you're lyin' in bed thinking about how tough you are. So till school got out, figuring—I mean being dead positive—that I was completely out of miracles, I did something which wasn't dumb at all on my part. I walked home every day with Bobby Stupnicki. I mean Bobby, I don't think he ever, even in his room, thought about stompin' anybody. The guy never got ticked off. But then you always wondered...*what*...if *he* did. Oh, man, that would be one perfection of a butt-kicking. The boy is huge. And so, logical enough, I made it safe every day past Castle Dracula. I saw Prizer, plenty. But with Bobby and sometimes even Big Joe, Bobby's eighth-grade brother, right with me, the Rat couldn't do a thing except fire me the evil eye (which of course he did, about daily).

And up in the pueblo, though Susie Shannon kept her shade down all the time now when she studied, which did create like a regular official OH-NO for me (you know, when ya think back on something stupid or bad you did, maybe even a long time before, and like maybe right in the middle of the street, you go "OH NO!"), I was still sort of gettin' used to it without wanting to kill myself. And Susie's shade being down meant, too, I could look out my window without using a periscope or anything.

Then the best day of the year came. The forget-it, no-comparison best day: by which I mean school was *over*— and *OUT!* We'd have to face Mother Madeline next year in seventh, but we'd made it past sixth and the Armadillo. Even Malone, Francis Xavier, didn't flunk, which was a relief, because we were going for hotdogs at Malones' that night and then walking down to my house for an overnight (which we'd all planned 'cause we had something else very cool up our sleeves, too).

Not that it wasn't plenty tense, though, when Frankie opened his card. As he bent up together those little prongy gold things and opened that brown-yellow envelope, I was wondering where a flunked kid would end up *being?* I mean he wouldn't be with his friends anymore, and he couldn't really hang with the pitiful idiot punks in the grade behind him: that was an impossibility. So he was like nowhere. And I figured I might right now be standing next to a kid who'd be in exactly that spot the second he opened his card. But Frankie began grinning when he ran his eyes down the list of his grades. And then he broke out laughin' like a lunatic, which he is, because in every subject except art and music (which he always got A's in 'cause he can draw and sing like nobody I ever knew in my life, though he could care less about either of those things), he got the lowest possible grade you can get and not flunk. In everything! And this made him like especially proud in a very Malone kind of way, which is to say a way known only to the certifiable.

"Beat *that!*" he was screamin', when he showed us his final numbers. "The Armadillo couldn't hold me back. She was trying, but the stinkin' penguin couldn't do it! I stopped her cold!"

But Pete O'Connor wasn't gonna be impressed, or even polite. "Those grades just show she wanted to get rid of you, you jackanapes. She would have kept you back if you didn't drive her straight to the ledge. Who couldn't tell that?"

Pete's a good guy, but he never got in trouble in his life. Even in like fourth, he was living for the bookmobile library, which stops up near the fire station at 95TH. I mean he'd be bringin' back and then carrying out humongous wheelbarrows of books every two weeks and not just to show off. Believe me, he read the things. And he was very cool the way he'd get you to come with and try and get you reading stuff too. I gotta say that thanks to Pete I'm not as dumb as I could be. But Frankie, who wasn't ever going to any bookmobile, and who was like Pete's true natural enemy, called Pete a fairy on a daily basis. It was jealousy speaking, who couldn't tell that? And there was that time that Pete kind of shocked old FX with a very sharp left cross, which produced a fine-sized shiner, which Frankie had to wear for about a week and which made him lie right through his teeth and say he got it, that same day, from hitting the edge of the pool at Ridge Park (a pretty easy-to-see-through crock, as we all agreed).

So, like I say, natural enemies Malone and O'Connor were. And, that day, Frank had already jumped on Pete for having just one single conduct card for the whole year, and all clean, "like a cat's ass," while he had five, count 'em, ya simp, all stapled together and totally covered with SMA, SMA, SMA, SMA, SMA, SMA. As in Sister Mary Armida. It was kind of rough, get-your-goat stuff to Pete, especially when Frankie like flipped the deck of his cards under Pete's schnozz. But I had to laugh till I about leaked when Frankie said he always kept that pack of cards in his back pocket, so every time, just before he had to hand it over to the Armadillo, he could blow one on it.

But now, about the final grades and Pete's as much as saying Frankie didn't really pass, it was Frankie right back in Pete's kisser with, "Shut up, you goody-goody bookworm know-it-all suck-ass." And it was gonna maybe be fisticuffs for sure, which would've screwed up again the hotdogs at Malones' and our other very beautiful plans for the evening. But this was the kind of time when Jackie Leonard (who had this just slightly crook tooth in front, which was like, I don't know, somehow the sign of his incredible toughness but also cool when he smiled, or I should say warm)— I mean this was when Jackie would step right in. It's like he never one day had trouble pissin' laughing at Malone, no matter how lunatic insane Frankie got, and that he never didn't see, either, how cool a guy Pete O'Connor was, even if Peter never did do anything wrong (I mean the kid said 'jackanapes' because he thought 'jackass' was swearing, which non-swearing JL also thought was cool). 'Cause for Jackie, I mean, it was like Frankie was all of one thing, and Peter was all of this other thing, but Jack had enough of both things in him to get it that both things were cool, which I loved watching come into action.

And let me add in right now that I loved watching Jackie's butt-kickin' come into action, too, seeing as it saved my skin more than once or twice. Because, I mean, I wasn't the smallest kid in the class—that would be Terry Thillens, by a mile. But I wasn't anything more than average, believe me. So there were these times (which I gave one example of already, with the Rodent King, but there were others, which I'll tell ya about as we go along) when I needed help. And I've gotta say, too, that it makes me like laugh deep in my heart thinking about the help I got, sort of like with Jackie I was a little brother that his older brother actually loved way down into his guts. And I mean you just took one look at JL with that crook tooth and that tough-as-shit Irish face—and maybe a look down at his hammer fists—and you knew. I mean not even Bobby Stu could stop Jackie Leonard. No way.

But JL only used his toughness for good stuff. Period. And sure enough, right away, when Malone and O'Connor did start closin' in on each other, he said, "All right, let's break it up, you two world-class goofballs." And that's all it ever took.

Cool. Period. Cool. And (about that real situation I was in then with Prizer), it makes me really laugh thinking about the number of years that would pass before Val-boy would think I'll pin this Leonard kid down at the Murder Place here and serve him a plateful a dog crap. Which, let me add in, too, was the kind of stuff I loved to think about up in my room, when I thought about my friends, which was a lot. That, and stuff like, maybe I'd lie there and think how unaware of stuff I'd be without 'em—I mean, say, if I did something like just stayed up in my room and never came out. 'Cause if I had something in me which was, how can I say this one, *asleep* or something, they'd bring it out. Like Pete with me and books. Or Frankie with me and the love of the certifiably insane in all their adventures. And Jackie with *getting* stuff, like that good-behaved people aren't anywhere near as pain-in-the-ass as you might think: that they can even be very cool. And that bad-behaved people are so funny they make ya piss a lake, like Francis Xavier Malone, who isn't bad for real, so don't go thinking it. And I'd think, too, how it was my friends who put guts in me, if I could say I had any guts, or any honor. For instance, I knew I'd never cave to a pig-shit like Val Prizer, knowing I'd have to face my friends. And the final thing I liked thinking was how if I had like maybe a hundred friends teaching me, I'd get *all* the sleeping stuff in me waked up and I'd start really and truly to *get* stuff, which, along with the guts, would be perfection, though maybe you'd want to throw out the OH-NO's while you're at it.

Anyhow, after we all except Frank brought our report cards and stuff home, we were back around 92ND and Hoyne, just hangin' out after that last day, feeling great because we were free. It was all the usual suspects, which meant Jackie, and me, and Frank, and Pete, and Stu, and Terry Thillens, and George Peterson. Seventh graders all now. And if we were seventh graders, that meant that the guys just ahead of us would have to be kings of the school next year because guys like Big Joe Stupnicki, and Grady, and Murphy, and Saccitello, and Katie Luce's brother Mike, would be gone to high school. It didn't seem like those punks ahead of us, Mulroney, DeNiro, Donovan, Smythe, and those guys, were ready for zilch, let alone kingship.

But another year and *we'd* have the job, which really didn't seem real. Except I thought Bobby could be a Big Joe any day, which tells ya why I wasn't worried about Prizer, at least when I was walkin' home on Hamilton Ave. And like I know my own name, I knew that JL would be the best Christ the King ever saw in football *and* basketball. Already guys like Satch and Big Joe and those other guys goin' on to high-school wanted him in pick-up games at the Courts. And they called him 'Jack' and 'Jackie' and even 'JL', which was like a compliment and an honor never heard of.

But, anyhow, after we'd hung out, and had had a fine time doing nothing of value (as the Armadillo would put it) and Frankie'd made us laugh our royal heinies off (if he sort of scared the deep shit out of us too) by chucking his report card into an alley trash can, we finally headed to Malones' for the dogs. It wouldn't be like a bar-b-que or anything. It would just be Frankie's mom boiling the Oscar Mayers in a big spaghetti pot and doing her best to keep the psycho Malones out of her hair, which was like this very weird bleach yellow and always sort of hanging down and going weird directions while she walked around smoking and walked back to tip her ash into the triangle hole of the can of Schlitz she'd been drinking before she started working on the one she was drinking now. And one of the things that was most amazing to me was how Mrs. Malone had this voice that would like crack glass all the way down Leavitt to Sullivans' but not one kid in the Malone house paid the first crap-ball of attention to it. And they gave her shit you wouldn't believe. I mean, it was like you wouldn't be totally floored if even one of the little kids, even maybe Frank's sister Pepper, who was like three, told her to snarf a cup a snot, and DIE. It almost made you want to experiment with a little smart talk to her yourself, even though you liked Mrs. M like crazy. And I mean that would be the deal: when you were at Frank's house, you just sort of felt like trying stuff you'd never go for in maybe six lifetimes at home.

But—truth—no matter what you thought of doing, you stayed polite with a parent around. And so there we all were, sitting nicely around the table with Mrs. M, who sometimes you worried might catch on fire from her ash if she didn't go pretty quick for her Schlitz ash tray, which was kind of amusing, especially with Frankie makin' smart-ass fun of her and her not getting it. And we were havin' a good time, too, doctoring our dogs with ketchup and mustard that came out of those huge plastic bottles, which, like sixth graders still, we thought were extremely cool for a family to have. You know the kind, like at ballparks, 'cause Mr. Malone, who wasn't home very often but who was a really nice guy, I mean when he didn't lose it, worked for this concession company that even brought the ketchup and mustard to Comiskey.

'Course we were staying polite too because we didn't want to screw up those plans of ours, which we were getting closer and closer to putting into action. So it was please pass this and please pass that. Maybe we were elbowin' each other a little here and there, and like threatening to goose each other—and, when somebody cut one, we naturally had to go a little nuts, especially when we were trying to identify the dealer. But we were being good. We really were. But then this thing happened.

Mrs. M, who I should say has as her favorite word 'mortified', had just opened a new beer and taken her first sip out of it and lit up a new cigarette, and she was kind of smilin' and dreaming as she blew a stream of smoke up toward the ceiling. Then she smiled even wider, and kind of shook herself, and said she had something she wanted to show us—and she got up and went over to this covered-up bird cage that was standing by the window. I didn't think there was anything in the thing because no sound was coming out of it and because of course if there was a bird cage at Malones', no way there was going to be a bird in it. But when Mrs. M took off the cover, lo and behold, there was this black and really pretty huge and not fake bird sitting in there. But it looked like a crow. And I smiled, thinking that would be your Malone version of a parakeet. But then I thought, before I started making jokes in my head about the Malones and singing-birds, who that I ever knew in my life could sing better than Frankie? Answer was, not even his dad, who was the voice that everybody hoped would be there when the King's Chorus sang at the 11:30.

"It's a myna bird," Mrs. M said, "and it talks—better than a parrot." She was psyched up, and we could see she really wanted to show us all how this bird they had could talk. But when she tapped the cage and started saying stuff like "Hey, pretty boy," and other kinds of goofy stuff, like "Hal-A-Loooooooooya," the bird didn't do diddly. So then she started workin' harder because she really wanted now for their myna bird here to show us its stuff—you know, so she wouldn't look like a jerk, or for probably the hundredth time that day, be mortified. But nothin' doin'. Not a word...from the Malone bird. So then she started to get pretty well pissed at the dopey thing, and her voice was gettin' louder. And then when she was giving it another good and loud "HAL-A-LOOOOOOOOOYA," she lost her cigarette out of her lips and had to catch it off her blouse before there *was* a fire. Which got Frankie goin', all right.

He starts pointing at her from behind his hand, but obvious as could be, you know that way, and whispering, *"Shit for brains,"* loud enough so that she had to hear it. Which was the kinda thing we were all sort of used to, though still it always sort of whacked ya out. Jack, though, figuring, I know, that it would break things up some, asks Mrs. M if he could be excused to go to the washroom. And she seemed, right away, pretty glad too to be out of it all, 'cause right away she turned her back on the myna, which, clear enough, wasn't gonna do beans for her, and she smiled, and said, "Of course, Jack," and sat down again to her new Schlitz, though now she looked a little gloomy and started tappin' her ash kinda hard into her old empty, you know, like about fifty times when she only needed to once.

But then when Jack came back from the head, we were all just wolfing on our dogs again, especially Stu, and slugging down cokes, and eatin' chips and stuff, acting normal, even though Mrs. M hadn't quite come back to life. But then all of a sudden, and I mean this was more psycho than I can ever get across, the big ole crazy myna bird, outa nowhere, goes—DAMMIT TO HELL FRANKIE! DAMMIT TO HELL Frrrrrrr-RANK!—which was way-out-there too much for everybody, even JL, who fired full shots of cola right outa both barrels of his nose. And of course the louder we all start laughin'—and we were goin' completely nuts, choking and spraying coke—the more the goofy bird keeps going—DAMMIT TO HELL! DAMMIT FRANK! Frrrrrr-RANKIE! GOD DAMN YOU!—and I honest to God don't know how even Mrs. M couldn't go nuts laughing over this one. I mean ya gotta laugh at yourself when, ya know, you're more nailed than Jesus. But she didn't. And neither did Frank, who was like hanging his head embarrassed, which was really surprising, and which made it fairly weird, 'cause none of us could even come close to not splitting our guts. And the bird.... Well, Mr. Myna was gonna put Peterson and O'Connor in the hospital, 'cause there it would go again—DAMMIT TO HELL FRANK! DAMMIT TO HELL Frrrr-RANKIE! GOD DAMN YOU!

Finally, though, Mrs. M had had enough, and she goes up and puts the cover over the myna again, which shuts the idiot up. But George P, who you might say was as big an idiot, was still about completely out of control, and everybody was still breakin' out with laughs. So things kept getting sort of weirder—'cause at the same time we were bustin' with 'em, we were holding the laughs in, hard. And with one thing goin' one way in us and another thing going another way—you know how that is—it was like really *painful*. So I was plenty glad when, finally, after what was about a lifetime and a half, Jack said, "You know, Kev, if we wanna get to your house on time for your mom to take us to the movies, I think we better shove off."

Lucky for us, this worked, kind of like that last trick of Jack's. We could see that Mrs. M was definitely gonna go with it. And when she smiled (but looking still pretty miserable, too, so that she didn't ever have to say her like trademark word), we all got up and started picking up the paper plates. We tried to be civilized and to be careful with all the mustard and ketchup smears on the plates, and the poppy seeds from the buns rolling all over, and the half-empty dixie cups of coke, which we mostly drained before we tossed 'em with the plates into the grocery bag that Mrs. M held out for garbage. Then we all said thanks, polite as we could—George P, though, still needing a very solid gut-biff from Stu to choke him off. And we were at last heading out the back door, when Tom Malone, Frank's legendary D-U-M brother, you know, the one who got himself shit-canned to Vanderkell, starts coming up the back stairs.

It was kinda weird seeing him, 'cause Vanderkell wasn't even out yet and so he was in this completely different situation—like nobody in his family, or like any of his old friends. I mean it was very weird. But George P—naturally because it was really not the time for it now—decides to go nuts again, spazzing one more time over Mrs. M and the bird, which gets Tom going, 'cause naturally Tom thinks it's all about him. So Tom, who happens to be—did I forget to mention this?—an utter, complete, 100% purified anal canal, says to George, "What's your problem, you little round mound a shit," and he shoulder shoves George right into the stair rail. And *on THE spot,* Frankie just flies at his brother and fires a really wicked punch right into his chest, yelling at him, "Fuck you! Shovin' my friend! Fuck you!" It woulda meant no-kiddin' blood and guts, but we had JL and all of us, including 'Little Stu' Stupnicki. And Tom Malone had nobody. So all he could do was promise Frankie, very hard-guy and older-brother-like (I mean of the more usual older-brother kind, not like JL with yours truly): "You're DEAD."

But naturally Frankie'd heard that one about every hour on the hour for a straight twelve years, so we were kind of like back to normal when we hit the streets again. And then, before too long, Terry Thillens (which made it really funny 'cause, like I said, Terry's the littlest guy in our class by a mile and he never starts stuff) pipes up with a "DAMMIT TO HELL FRANKIE! DAMMIT TO HELL Frrr-RANK! GOD DAMN YOU!" And then everybody starts goin' nuts with it, even Jack, which after about a minute or so (but I think especially because Jackie put a soft headlock on Malone, ya know the kind that's meant to put a guy in a good mood, not get him ticked) even made Frankie break out laughing and start goin' nuts. So it was really getting close to okay again.

And it was also getting dark, which meant it was about time for our plan....

I need to say that that thing Jack said about the movies— it was a crock. And when I told it to *my* mom, I said *Mrs. M* was gonna drive us up to the Beverly. And when Frankie told it to *his* mom, he said *my mom* was gonna drive us. So we'd freed ourselves up for a good couple of hours, with everybody thinking the other person took us to the movies. And what we wanted to do was wait until it was good 'n' dark and then go to The Woods, because this really spooky and insane thing had just happened at a school right next to ours, called Little Flower, which got out a few days before we did. This kid our age, eleven, or twelve, a real goody-goody sort of kid, had gotten like the first bad report card of his life. And what did he do? Because his mom or dad yelled at him or something, he goes out to The Woods, and he climbs up a tree, and he takes off his belt—and he hangs himself. Dead. And I knew exactly which tree, because the next day I could see out my window where about fifty cops were walking all around it, looking to see if the kid had really done it to himself, which that night on the news they said he did: Suicide, not murder. And what our plan was, was to go out there in the dark and see if we had enough guts to sit under the tree.

Sneaking past my house wasn't too bad. 'Cause we were at the movies, right? So nobody was lookin' for us. And it was now officially dark, though the street lamp we used for first base in the Dead End gave us a bit of light to see our rabbit hole by. I went first, because the Dead End was my territory. And because O'Connor needed to be shown how to slide through, head first on his back, him not having been with us here before, at least through the hole. A couple guys needed to be there on the other side, too, to pull and stretch the fence up and out for Stu, who couldn't make it through without the extra room. So after he saw me show how, Pete got down on his back and started to make his way head first into the hole, which meant, dead certain, that Malone, just when O'Connor was totally helpless, halfway through the hole on his back, would initiate him with a very, very intense goose job, which of course he did till he had Pete laughing so hard he couldn't stop and was beggin' for mercy, crying, "OkayOkayOkayOkayWhateverYou WantOkayOkayOkayOkayI'llDoANYTHING...." And then Frankie: "Anything?" And then Pete:"OhYesYesYesYesYes ANYTHINGANYTHINGANYTHING." And of course all Frank wanted was for Pete to say, "I AM the fairy bookworm." And of course Pete told him "ANYTHINGBUTTHAT." But of course when you are had by the balls, you are *had* by the balls. So soon enough it was Pete: "OkayOkayOkayOkayOkayOkayIAMTHEFAIRYBOOKWORM." "Once more." "OkayOkayIAMTHEFAIRYBOOKWORM." "And once more." "IAMIAMIAMTHEFAIRYBOOKWORM." Which was so much funnier than shit that even Peter laughed—even after he was free and saw that his shirt was ripped and his belly good and pronged, which Jackie and I told him made him a full-fledged member of the Ryan's Woods Wild Men, which he liked and didn't even want to murder Malone for.

Then Pete and I held the fence for Stu. Then Jack came through. Then George P. Then Frankie. And then Terry, who, 'cause he was so little, had no sweat with it. But it was Terry who, when he stood up inside The Woods, with the laughing all over now, said what we were all thinking—which was—"It is *really* dark in here."

But there's somethin' about a plan that you've been perfecting for two days—and somethin' about just having the guts to go through with a thing. So we told Terry he was a chickenshit and that he couldn't back out now. There wasn't one of us, though, who wasn't wishing we'd never had *this* big idea. But, for whatever that crazy reason is that once ya start something, ya go through with it, there was no backing down. And for gettin' us into this one, I had to take a lot a blame, 'cause I had a pretty big hand in the original brainstorm. Also I was the smartguy who knew exactly where what we called the Hanged-Kid Tree was, so naturally I like found myself in the lead and had to act like I wasn't scared shitless, even when the first steps we took were a very weird kind of crackly, and loud, because we'd been standing frozen silent for some time.

"How'd they know it wasn't murder?" Terry like peeped, when we started headin' down into the ravine.

And then George P said, "'Cause he wasn't nude. When it's murder, the kid's always nude."

"What is wrong with you, Peterson, you whacko?" Stu said. "The kid's not always nude."

Which was a thing we argued about back and forth for a minute—but mostly because we were tryin' to make ourselves laugh, instead of bein' scared as we were. But I'd say it all pretty much backfired, 'cause the only laughs we had were that fakey hard kind that just shows you're coverin' somethin' up.

In the daytime, if we were on the high side, we'd have

jumped the gully. But no way at night, especially with the light from the street lamp now no good. So we carefully edged along the high, skinny ridge of flagstones instead, until we got to a foot bridge. Then across we went, Malone threatening to chuck Terry into the drink because he knew Terry was more scared now than ever—and because Frankie really enjoyed torture. Then up the other side of the ravine—because the Hanged-Kid Tree was up on the flat part of The Woods over the top of the other ridge. I thought I might just wanna take everybody to the wrong tree now, like maybe to save our lives. But, ya know, like I was saying, there's something about this kinda stuff that keeps ya goin', stupid as it is, toward stuff like the real tree; and when, up over that other ridge, finally I saw the true tree like this huge monster-shadow standing in the middle of this field, I started runnin' like an idiot, saying, "Come on! There it is!"

It was sort of, too, like I wasn't just the leader but the one-man show now in this spook fest, for even Jack and Stu were just taggin' along without a word. But then when Frankie said, "Holy shit, that tree looks like Armida," everybody started laughing that really hard scared laugh again. But it didn't work this time, either, too well. And when we came up near to the tree, which was this huge elm with a low fork, so we could see how the kid who hung himself could get up in it, we were all out of breath. Like no strength at all in anybody, which wasn't because we were running and laughin' but because, trust me, we were scared shitless.

Even when Frankie tried to be funny saying we could check out how many nude-lovin' murderers were close by if we just pantsed Peterson, nobody got too relaxed. But there, like a pack of idiots, we did it: we sat down like we were at a pow wow or something, all ready to smoke the peace pipe, right underneath where the dead kid had been swinging in the breeze, probably with his tongue stuck out and his eyeballs poppin'.

"I heard when ya get hung," George P said, "ya shit your pants first and than ya die with a full-fledged boner."

Stu let him know right away again that he was a total moron and we all looked at him like he was nuts all right. But we weren't really laughin' too hard—because it was very spooky, what we were doing, when ya sat and let it come at ya. And with the moon coming up now over the trees down near Longwood, it just got shadowier and creepier under this huge tree, even if we could see our faces better than when we were in the thicker trees by the ravine and weren't, like now, out in a field. So we just sort of sat there for a while, getting very spooked. I mean, not even Frankie was talkin'.

But after we relaxed a little, after about a couple more minutes, nobody having been hurt or kidnapped or murdered or strung up (although Frank, to torture Terry some more, did make like he had a snapped neck and stuck his tongue out extremely weird), Stu said, "The kid couldn't a possibly been normal. I mean what kinda idiot hangs himself 'cause of a report card? The only logical thing's he was an idiot."

But then, sort of quietly, Terry said, "I heard he did it to get revenge on his mom and dad."

Stu said that that was really stupid, too, "'Cause he's the one ended up dead."

But I asked 'm, "How'd ya like to be the parents of a kid who hung himself?" And everybody agreed maybe the kid got revenge on his mom and dad pretty good, like for*ever*, but that still his way was really stupid.

"Maybe," Jack said, "they said to him somethin' like 'We'd like to kill you for this.' You know, the report-card thing, just sayin' it the way parents say that stuff, and the kid took it seriously, thinking like his parents wanted him to die...."

"But that's so stupid," Pete said, "thinking your parents want you to die. Nobody thinks that."

"But maybe he did," Jack said, "you know, the way, with certain things, a kid starts thinking about 'em and then just gets crazy keepin' on thinking about 'em...." He stopped himself and started to laugh a little bit and said, "You know, like we got here 'cause we kept on thinkin' about it, and then did it...." But then he got back on the kid. "I mean," he said, "you know, the way a kid will keep on thinking about certain things till he gets really whacked out and then he believes 'em. And maybe he like was hatin' himself for something in the first place."

"Ya don't hate your*self*," Stu said, "that's not logical."

Then Frankie came in with a kind of goofy but pretty spooky voice, sayin', "Maybe they said to him, 'Go to hell, ya little bastard,' and he started thinking he *was* a little bastard and he was *supposed* to go to hell and he kept thinkin' it and thinkin' it until he *wanted* to go to hell—so he strung himself up in this tree right here, so, like on this very spot, right here where we're sitting, he could get the DEVIL to come MEET HIM!"

For a second nobody said anything to this total weirdness. And nobody wanted to start talking about the devil already, though we figured we'd probably get there soon enough. So George P said, "You're a complete idiot, Malone."

"And nobody's parents," Pete said, "ever wanted their kid to be damned to hell. So you're talking about something impossible."

I could hear the squawking of that goofy myna bird, though, about the second Pete said this one; and it was like really close to what Pete said was impossible, I mean a parent wanting their kid to be damned to hell. So I was embarrassed. And I think Jack was, too, 'cause I could see signs on his face. And I was hoping Frankie didn't get what we were gettin'. But, outa school, Frank Malone's not dumb, believe me. I wish he was dumb—dumb as a brick—when I think back.

But Pete threw in some really spooky stuff now, which changed the subject kinda. "Suicide," he said, "is the unpardonable sin. And the kid was five years past the age of reason. And it's a mortal, 'cause it's a kind of murder. That means the kid's in hell. Right now. Not even God can get 'm out."

"Shit," Terry said.

"For eternity," Pete said.

"And all for a report card," Stu said. "It proves what a total idiot the kid was."

Then Frankie jumps in sort of outa-the-blue really pissed off (though I could maybe guess now what was makin' him pissed, and I thought that what I was hoping wasn't true, was true; I mean about a parent telling their kid to go to hell—and I'm thinking, too, of Frankie's trash-canning his card and that in some weird way maybe like trash-canning your card and hanging yourself over a card aren't that far apart, like somewhere there might even be some weird crossroads where you'd never wanna go, but where if you did, you'd end up taking one road or the other, trash-canning your card or stringin' yourself up over it). "They wanna get ya to hate your own guts," Frankie said, "and if ya let 'em, you're a stupid idiot."

"Who wants to get ya to hate yer own guts?" Pete said.

"Lots a assholes."

"Like who?"

"Like your parents, and like the penguins, and lots a assholes."

Then Pete, a little pissed off, too, says, "I'll bet it was completely the kid's fault. If he thought he was supposed to hate his own guts and go kill himself, how do ya blame his parents for him being such a lamebrain. He's the one who's responsible."

Then Frankie jumped right back. "I'll bet, O'Connor, you never in your life thought your mom or your dad were assholes, or were tryin' to get ya to hate your own guts. I'll bet you never one time did, which shows how stupid you are."

"D'ya ever think, Malone," Pete said, not backin' down, as he wouldn't, and not liking anybody to say shit about his mom and dad, as who would, "that if your mom and dad are fouled up, then like just about nothing *isn't* fouled up. And if nothing *isn't* fouled up...."

"Then everything *is* fouled up, including you. Yeah, I thought that. And at least I'm not like you bozos, who might someday go and do what the jerk here did, 'cause somebody told ya *you're baaaaaaaad*—and you *belieeeeeeeved 'em*."

This was comin' out to be another fairly creepy thing to say, which Frankie realized right in the middle of saying it, so he'd turned his voice that kinda extra-weird way again and then he started starin' at Terry again, just for a little extra-special torture, making one more time like his neck was snapped and giving it the insane stuck-out tongue, like he wouldn't be satisfied now till Terry had nightmares for the rest of his life.

So Jack made a secret face to Frank to cut out the shit.

He didn't wanna shut him up, but just for 'm to let Terry be. Frankie naturally didn't want to let Terry be, but he started to anyhow, turning his attention instead back to Pete, who told him he was an idiot to think that any one of us there, except maybe Frank himself, was as dumb as the hanged kid.

"And you're completely stupid, too, Malone, for thinking nobody knows what's fouled up except you."

"And you're completely stupid, O'Connor, for thinkin' everything somebody tells ya is the truth, like we were gonna fry in hell that time we stole the Trojans outa Rexall if we didn't get to confession before we died. Don't lie. I heard you say that, about five minutes after you nearly died laughin', holding a rubber on the end of your nose and blowin' it up, which was the only funny thing you ever did in your born days."

Everybody laughed now, no matter where we were, 'cause we all could remember Pete holding the rubber over his nose and breathing into it like a balloon, which maybe *was* the only thing he ever did wrong. And it was so funny. But now Frank, feeling better 'cause everybody was laughin', even Pete for a minute, said something maybe insaner than any, even, of his other psycho stuff. "Okay," he said. "I gotta tell you guys somethin'. Truth. Total truth. When I like swipe somethin', like outa Rexall, like candy or rubbers or stuff—I get a boner."

And with that one, everybody went totally nuts. We were laughing so hard it didn't matter at all, for a second anyhow, that we were in about as creepy a spot as you could be in. The moon was like coming up bigger and spookier than ever, so you'd normally a figured werewolf any second now. And there we are laughin' our butts off 'cause

Malone is so completely out of his mind.

"You are the stupidest idiot I ever met," Stu said. "I mean it, Malone, not one thing you ever said in your life's made sense. Not one thing."

But naturally Frankie took that as a compliment, knowing Stu didn't want to fight but wanted kind of to keep hearin' more of his insane stuff, which he had lots of. "And when I ditch," he said, "I sort of hang out where I can see everybody gettin' ready to go into school. And as the time keeps gettin' closer and closer to go into school but I keep not going in and planning not to, my wiener keeps growin' like I was watching B Bardot gettin' more and more and more nude and crude. And when the bell rings and the doors close, I've got another whoppin' bone-meat."

We couldn't stop laughin' now. This stuff was so funny and crazy. But then Peterson tops it all by pulling out his wiener, right then and there, and sayin', "More whoppin' than THIS!"—'cause he had a boner on it! And I gotta give George P credit, because it's very difficult to be more nuts than Malone, but he sorta did it here. Then of course we all start whippin' out, except Terry because he was still like just a little boy at the time—when some of us, anyhow, had some pubies comin' in and thought we were cool. Then we started to get rid of all that Coke in a humongous piss fest, cross-firing with each other, whippin' Lash Larues at each other. Even Terry was joining in now. And it's too bad we didn't have a fire, so we'd had to have pissed it out with a seven-man brotherhood, though Stu migtha been able to handle a pretty big blaze all by himself.

But then when we went back under the tree ('cause we couldn't clear out and go to my house yet, 'cause the movie wouldn't a been over, as Pete, who never went anywhere without his watch, let us know) and when we looked around, we saw there wasn't seven anymore, but only six of us. And would it not be Malone who disappeared. And of course we all figured he was pulling a trick and was in earshot, so we started askin' stuff like would we miss him if he'd been maybe axe-murdered?—"No." "No, I don't think so." "No, not really." "No way." "No, I'm pretty sure not one person in the entire universe would give a single, solitary crap-ball if the axe went in his nose and came out his crack." Then all of a sudden there was this loud noise up above us, like there was some big animal in the tree. But it wasn't an animal; it was a Malone, and he'd climbed up to about a fifteen-foot limb, and now he'd let himself drop so he was hanging there by one arm, dangling so much like a hanged kid, with his neck bent funny and his feet swinging but lookin' dead, that he scared the pure, complete turd factor out of us, 'cause we couldn't see it was by his arm at first. O'Connor was so scared he like about started crying right on the spot. But then Frankie, while he's still dangling there, starts talkin' like a ghost, saying, "I huuuuung myself.... So I could get the huuuuuugest bone-meat.... Of aaaaaaall TIME…!"

Then it was like all of us sayin' "YOU IDIOT!" at exactly the same instant. But when he came down, Pete even told 'm he was glad it wasn't true he'd done it, which got Pete a "You're a dope." Then we killed more time talking, saying stuff like parents and the penguins *had* maybe to come up with really scary stuff like hell, 'cause otherwise people might do things like steal stuff all the time. And like ya'd never do anything you were told, if there weren't punishments. Or do anything at all. Frankie, who of course hated every word we were saying now, said he was always gonna do just the stuff that gave him a rod. And nothing but. But we were all together on him now, and this got us saying stuff like then all you'd ever do would be leave school instead of go and you'd end up dumber than dog shit. And that there was lots of stuff that isn't any fun but you gotta do it. Which got Frankie to say, "Yeah, like the dumb dope who went and hung himself: that wasn't any fun, but he did it." Which got Pete to say, "'Cause he wanted an erection." So we were going back and forth, saying stuff, then, like doing good things could make ya feel good, even if somebody made ya feel so lousy that ya wanted to kill yourself. I remembered the time I started going every morning to six o'clock mass, getting up in the dark and going to pray for my grandfather's soul, so he could get out of Purgatory faster (and it was only logical that's where he was, because my grandfather, who was way too funny to have gone straight to heaven, still wouldn't have died with a mortal unconfessed). And there was Armida with all the other nuns, 'cause they always went to the six. And one day it was raining, and Armida came up and tapped my shoulder as I was about to head home after mass, and she gave me her umbrella and smiled at me, like really really nice (and hold on—she's got like this actually really pretty face), and she told me I was blessed for praying for my grandfather—and I told everybody how it scared me even to touch a penguin's umbrella, but that I felt like incredibly good for a long time after. But it wasn't just Frank who told me I was a sucker for falling for this kinda junk. And then we were wondering if there was anybody besides a nun or your parents or maybe God who could make ya feel good again if ya ever got as screwed up as the kid who'd hung himself.

But right then Pete, who sorta just knew when to do it,

checked his watch, and he said, "If we don't go now, they'll start wondering where we've been." So we told Frankie that if he was getting any kind of a rod over not comin' in on time, that he'd have to stuff it back wherever a boner goes, which was a question we'd thought about one time when we were guessing what's inside a girl's tits. So then it was back across the open field and back down into the ravine—and, if it was a whole lot spookier lookin' down by the stream now because of the moonlight, we still were feeling very cool about our big plan, nobody having gotten murdered or kidnapped or having had a stripped-nude job done on him of any kind.

But there's something about getting really close to pulling something off. Ya get specially nervous toward the end, feeling suddenly like there's no way you're gonna make it to the finish line okay. Like it couldn't really be possible that you would. So we were pretty jumpy crossing the stream, and then really nervous stepping back along the flagstone ridge. And then when we started back up the other side of the ravine toward the rabbit hole, sure enough, 'cause ya know this is gonna happen, we started hearin' something. It couldn't a been Frank, either, 'cause now he was with us. We thought it was steps. We were getting very sure that it was steps and that someone was coming our way. So it was crazy how we scrambled up the hill toward our hole, to stay ahead of those steps. But then we thought we'd be dead anyhow, 'cause how could we all get through the hole fast enough?

We let Terry go first 'cause he was about to shit a brick (which of course woulda been one of your smaller-type bricks). And then George P, who ripped his shirt shimmy-in' backwards up the hole 'cause he was spazzed too. And then Frank, 'cause we needed somebody who knew how to hold the fence for Stu. And then Stu, even though he was so slow goin' back up, 'cause ya had to like grab his arms and yank 'm on the one side and push his feet and legs on the other. And we managed to rip up Stu's shirt pretty good, too. And then Pete, who had to have Frankie and Stu pull 'm, though there was no goose job now (even though it couldn't a been a more perfect occasion, 'cause sure enough some-body heard those steps again, and goosing and terror go together like a horse and carriage). And shit Jesus if those steps weren't coming up the hill toward the hole! And of course I should've been the last one to go 'cause it was my territory and more than anybody else's, my big idea. But Jackie pushed me up before him, 'cause what chance would I have alone against a maniac? And I got through somehow, even if I tore my shirt and pronged myself, too, no matter how many times I'd come back up through that hole. Then it was JL, quick as a cat, even though he was scared too.

Then of course, safe on the other side, we started biff-ing each other and laughing—and accusing each other of being the LIAR who said there was some stupid sounds in the first place. Because when we listened now, on the safe side, we couldn't hear a thing. And then everybody start-ed calling everybody else a total chickenshit. And George P was even a little pissed about rippin' his shirt for noth-ing, although actually we thought it was cool with about all of us ripped again. But then—truth, and no lie—some man, so it couldn't a been Frankie, shouted out, "HEY, YOU KIDS!" And whoever it was, *was* close! So we took off like batshit outa hell toward my house, not looking back till we were all the way up out of the Dead End. It coulda been Mr. Mathis, I told everybody. Or Mr. Shannon. Or Mike Shannon. Somebody who lived along The Woods and wondered what all the racket was at the fence.

"Or it coulda been a maniac."

"Or that dead kid, come back to haunt the place."

"Or THE DEVILLL!"

"Shit," Terry said, "I knew we'd get back to him."

And Terry said this in a way that was really funny because like really serious, so we all started laughin' and slugging each other again and stuff. But then it was time, Pete said, with another look at his watch, to let my mom know we were there. So we brushed the dirt off ourselves. And the four of us with ripped shirts tucked 'em in tight and practiced holding our arms kind of over our bellies and stuff, to hide the rips. And then we practiced talking about the movie, which was *The Magnificent Seven,* which we'd all seen like three times, though now George P was naturally pretending to be confused and to get stuff all wrong. And Frankie said, "You morons, the movie was *And God Created Woman,* starring BB. Didn't you *know* that?" And for about a minute, he had us scared a couple a different ways on that one, 'cause we'd be screwed if we didn't know what the movie was about, and more screwed if we did. But then he started laughing and calling us sobsister dopewads, so I rang the bell.

And we pulled it off. We got up to the third floor and my perfecto-private little crow's nest without having to answer too many questions and without my mom saying anything about the shirts. I don't think she was stupid, though, about the way we were holding our arms crossed over our bellies—you know, like old fat guys with beer guts, trying to look like they're wise instead of just lardos, especially 'cause there were four of us doing it. So I'm pretty sure she maybe just wanted to get rid of us, which wouldn't be surprising. But still the fact was, we made it, and got the door closed behind us, which was all that counted. And we were psyched to go back over stuff, which we did for a long time, calling each other on the truth, but also making up stuff, and still guessing about stuff like who it was who said, "HEY, YOU KIDS!"—which made us think that maybe we did hear footsteps, and that no place in the world were ya ever safe and home free, which got us back to the devil again for a while, and how he could see everything and hear everything and go right through anything he wanted and how his face looked, which we all agreed was maybe handsome sometimes on the outside but always ugly as a dead guy's guts, worms included, on the inside. And then we thought again about what, besides his being a complete idiot, could make a kid hate his own guts enough to hang himself—which got us back to if there'd be anybody besides maybe God who could help ya feel okay enough again if ya ever got that screwed up. And it was right about then that—blink—Susie Shannon's light came on across the way, and I was thanking God the shade was down, so nobody noticed it even, other than me (talk about OH-NO's you might need help gettin' out of).

But the subject of girls came up, because Frankie said Bardot could make him feel good enough to do anything. Which got us asking everything, to if he'd kill somebody for BB, or if he'd break a baby's neck for BB, or if he'd eat sheist for BB, or if he'd eat a cup of boogers for BB, or drink a cup of spit for BB, or tell God to eat sheist, or tell Armida to eat sheist, or tell his parents to eat sheist, or tell Stenham to eat sheist.

This last question was from Terry, and instead of the

goofy "In two shakes of a kangaroo's ass," which every-body was getting on the other questions, even the God one, it got Terry a headlock of the nearly-piss-ya-off kind. Which told us naturally, no, he wouldn't ask Stenham to eat sheist. But that Frankie Malone had a thing for Mary Stenham we knew from the way he tackled her whenever there was snow on the ground and pulled her hair when-ever there wasn't. At Devil's and Suicide, the hills in The Woods where ya go sledding in the winter, he told us he even got a feel off her. We reminded him, though, there was nothing there to feel. But now when Jack untangled Frank's headlock on Terry, Frankie got back for all the hoots he was getting by hooting right my way.

"And what about you and Conlon! Wooo-ooo! Wooo-ooo! What about you and Conlon, Kevvy Boy! Unhhh! What about it!"

This kinda shook me, first off, because Frankie didn't ever pick me out of a crowd to go after. And there he was, pick-in' me out. And then it turned out he wasn't alone. They all started in, razzing me about Patty Conlon. And it was funny, 'cause—truth—I didn't have then any crush on Pat-ty or anything, at least as far as I knew. I'd be nice to her. And I'd tell these idiots to shut up if they ever said any-thing bad about her, which there was nothing to say, and they knew it, she being not just the smartest but the most beautiful girl in our class, as well as the coolest. Maybe they said stuff just to see how pissed I'd get and have me tell 'em to SHUT UP. I don't know. But now they had me turning red—I gotta admit it—AS A BEET—and they re-ally let me have it.

"Woooo-oooo! Woooo-oooo!" "Oh yeah!" "Isn't he cute when he blushes!" "Oh yeah!" "Wooo-oooo!" "Hey, somebody's in luuuuuuv!" "Woooo-ooo!"

I couldn't a done the first thing with either Jackie or Stu, so logically I jumped Malone and at the same time got a headlock on O'Connor. But then Peterson starts goosin' me. And then O'Connor and Malone get the best of me and start holding my arms while George P keeps on goosin' the crap out of me and makin' me beg for mercy. I swear they had me worse than Frankie had Pete under the fence, because sure enough even Jackie and Stu joined in and started holding down my legs. So naturally, under complete torture, I confessed I was in love with Patty Conlon and that I'd marry her tomorrow, and that she could make me eat sheist whenever she wanted to, and eat a cup of boogers, and drink a cup of spit, and that I blew one on Armida's umbrella, which was equally as unpardonable as suicide, and never told anybody.

But, then, maybe it was because they'd gotten me so good that we were all worn out with disgusting stuff and kind of in the mood for something different—you know how that goes—that lo and behold we actually started talking, after maybe a little more time passed, about how cool certain of the girls in our class were. And how beautiful. And it felt really good for a change, which was weird, trust me, I mean not just to talk about how stupid they were. And I know we all felt the same good feeling, except maybe Frankie, who had a way of not coming over to the soft side real easy. Of course, no way on earth I was gonna tell these maniacs about those weird silvery eyes I had the day Susie saved me. And her light was still on anyhow, so her name was NOT gonna come up. But there we were, still letting ourselves talk all this un-disgusting and praising stuff about our girls, no swear words thrown in, which still felt incredibly good,

for all its weirdness. And when one guy would say something, then that made it easier for the next guy. And it was
very cool and was feeling amazing, as if like all of a sudden
on the spot we got, you know, older, and less stupid. And
there was this thing that I let out, which was how I did go
pretty seriously nuts this time when I heard Patty sing the
Pange Lingua (which if you're not Catholic, it's about Communion, and the Last Supper, and the body and the blood.
And it's maybe the most beautiful hymn the Church has),
and I said how I was goin' nuts watching Patty in the procession, with her head bowed, holding her hymnal in her
hands, listening to her.

Then of course Frankie, 'cause he knows, I swear it, all
the Latin to the hymns, starts singing some completely
whacked out version of the *Pange Lingua*. It was goofier than
Biondi doin' *On Top of a Pizza*. But I have to say I loved how
hard O'Connor was splittin' his guts, even if this whole
deal pretty royally screwed up my warm thoughts on Patty.
But then Jack, and I mean this is the kind of stuff Jackie'd
do, if I haven't gotten the picture across—he asks FX to
sing it straight. And there's nobody all the way up to the
BVM that Frankie wouldn't a just called a pathetic dope, or
'sobsister', which I might've said was one of his words. But
I swear to God, when JL asked 'm that, and it was kind of
in the way we'd been talking, you know, feeling older and
less stupid, and with it making us all happy, Frankie didn't
tell Jackie to kiss his ass. I don't know, either, if like the
Paulist Choir means anything to you, but it's boys picked
out for having the best voices in the whole city of Chicago,
and until he quit it, Frankie was in it, and like did solos, I
mean like at Holy Name cathedral. So, ya get me? And now
he just sort of stops with the goofy thing. And then, after

like a moment or so of silence, which made us not know *what* the kid was gonna do, he starts with the real thing. I mean, don't get me wrong, he didn't really go into it or anything. It was just this quick, like, fifteen-second shot, sort of up to the *pretiosi*. But there was Frankie's voice, if only for fifteen seconds, still beyond killer, doing for real the *Pange Lingua*, which you can trust was a singing that I'll never not remember.

And I mean forget the Armadillo, or Mr. and Mrs. M, or anybody, the cops who'll arrest Frankie someday—I wish Mary Stenham had been there. Because it was that cool, and not stupid. And I swear, it was like we all (naturally without saying so) kept thinking so all night, as we kept going over stuff, our day having been cooler than all get out after all. Then as one by one my friends all fell asleep and I was last, I thought how cool it was to have 'em all up there with me, in the pueblo. I leaned up even and looked at their faces and felt how great it was—all the stuff they'd gotten to wake up in me, each one of 'em something cool at one time or another, and now, like this thing with Patty. But I felt, too, with the moonlight the only light, Susie having gone off a long time ago to sleep, that, yeah, if I stayed forever in this room and never knew these guys, I'd be a pretty sorry soul all right—but that this was my place, and that I got things here in a way that not even Jackie could understand. Sort of the way I was awake now, and they were all asleep.

CHAPTER THREE

EARLY SEVENTH

BOTTOM OF THE NINTH IN THE DEAD END

And, I don't know, I mean, having, the way I did that night, cool feelings about what's the coolest stuff—maybe that's what yours truly is good at, though I can't see this becoming like a real job for life or anything. But maybe, no matter what, ya gotta think you're sort of excellent at something, you know, so you'll give your most psyched-up shot to whatever that something is, 'cause you're proud of your excellence. Then again, maybe it's not true. I mean about psychin' yourself up thinking you're specially good at something. JL was the best ballplayer I ever saw (and that includes baseball, basketball, and football), and he didn't think beans about any of it. It was all like total nothin' to him. And, believe me, this always struck me as the extreme of cool. So like I mean, there's psych and then there's don't-think-anything-about-it psych. But then, about the stuff Jackie would do, I *did* think about it. 'Cause if the guy who does cool stuff doesn't see how great it is, or ever say word one, there's gotta be *somebody* who gets the picture, and puts the word out. Doesn't there? I know God gets the picture, like nobody, and that He's like totally got the word, forever. But I'm talking about down here, and stuff Jackie did on earth before he died. But his dying is something…I can't even think about that day. You don't know.…

I mean, to get off that for good.… There was this great time the next September.… It was this completely fine day, and, though we were locked back up in the Big House again, which is to say CK (with Mother 'Mad' being every bit as psycho a warden as the Armadillo), we for some strange parent-teacher kind of reason, got let out at noon. It was maybe a Wednesday. And it just so happened that it was the day Ted Williams was playing his last game at Fenway. And they were gonna have the game on Chicago radio, even though the Bosox were playin' Baltimore. This was the kind of stuff that Pete O'Connor was always up on. It was what Pete was best at—having the coolest info. Only Peter, like I say, could get a little annoying about what he knew, doing stuff like hittin' Frank Malone with Frankie's having no info on jack point anything (outside of on BB, of course, and what it was like to go to the Capri Theater and take in a skin flick, which Frankie had actually done—and then provided us some *amazing* info on, which he couldn't a made up). Which if it was pretty much the dead truth about Frankie, I mean his being info-free, still meant O'Connor was gonna get called a serious, know-it-all fairy punk—and so forth, including biffs and borderline real fisticuffs.

But even the two natural enemies shut their yappers up when Williams stepped up in the eighth. Because this had to be it. It figured sure to be Williams's last at bat in Boston, which, word was, he'd make his last at bat ever, 'cause WHY would he go to New York to play his final game? I mean, only a supreme, off-the-map bozo would blame him for picking Fenway over Yankee Stadium.

Anyhow, there was this big elm in my front yard, and we had the transistor propped against it, 'cause the tree was right there next to our home-plate sewer, which I hope still holds Val-boy's broomstick in it for serious bad luck to the rat. And when Williams stepped up, we stopped our game, and we sort of made a huddle around the radio at the tree. O'Connor, Mr. Fact Man, laying the stats out, said Williams'd probably take a base-on-balls, even now. But this made us all, not just Frankie, tell Peter to SHUT UP! We all did, though, pray hard, fingers crossed, for a sweet one in the zone. And one came, but Williams whiffed on it. "Shit on a stick!" George P said. But now, I swear, we all started getting this feeling—that there was gonna be another pitch to hit and that Williams really and truly *was* gonna murder it. I mean, it was this really strange feeling, and like all of us truly had it—so we were almost tipping over, listening as tight and quiet as we possibly could to the transistor.

Which I'll always remember, the way we were listening and leaning, and how the announcer was taking us through the wind-up, and the pitch. And how the guy on Baltimore (and you'll have to ask Peter for his name) sends another one in there and because he's Ted Williams, this time Williams gets all of it! Every last bit of it! BANG! And it's going, going, GONE! Holy SHIT! I mean how does a guy pull miracles like that off! It was so incredibly cool, like the Babe callin' the shot, only nothing about it that couldn't be called a complete and total truth! And we were all, Pete too, goin' fully nuts, jumping up and down, and dancing around all over the place, playing some kind of goofball ring-around the tree. It's funny how it works, you know, like ya hit the shot yourself. And there was also that spooky-cool, answered-prayers kind of feeling, too. But right then, when we finally calmed down a little, I looked over and saw JL, just sort of grinning. And I knew. The City could come by and move the Dead End wall back another thirty full paces and that rubber-coated was still goin' over, the next time Jack stepped up. Which makes me a deep kind of happy saying it, 'cause I guess Jackie makes me feel like I hit that shot of his too. But for a strange reason it makes me feel great, too, knowing, and saying, Jackie was Jackie, and I was just me.

I can't remember the situation. It was just a pick-up, horse-around game, which'll have, though, for me, always a little of the Fenway center-field wall in it in my memory. And like I said, our wall was only for dreaming about for the rest of us, who, truth, got our home runs only when we knocked one into what George P named the Screw Yew, which was this kind of octopus-like prickly bush in Shannon's front yard that swallowed for good maybe twenty rubber-coateds that I can remember. But you never knew if yours wouldn't get found; so when you hit one in there, you still had to scitter quick around the bags and hope not to get your butt nailed. No slow trot comin' home, in other words. And no dignity. But Jackie didn't need any Screw Yew.

And what it was, I swear, was kind of like Ted Williams came right through the transistor into JL It's not like Jackie was trying to one-up the guy. It was like he was the same kind of guy, with the same kind of picture-book lefty swing—and like the one guy put the other guy in the exact same mood. Only Williams—is he, or is he not, a chip-on-the-shoulder, crabapple jerk, great as he is, or was? But, like I've been sayin', Jack was none of that. Or maybe he did have somethin' raging down in—even though he never showed it. I don't know. How can you say exactly what makes a guy's miracles happen? or the way he lives happen? I know Jackie had pride. That I'm very sure of. And I'm sure of this, too: when he got his pitch, that sorry ball was tagged as clean and hard as any I ever saw in the Dead End, except one (which I'll tell about in a minute) and that we had to cross the ravine stream and go a nice way up the far ridge to get the thing back. So talk about your high-quality kind of getting waked up. There's JL going after something inside himself 'cause of, not just anybody, but Ted Williams. Which, now that I think about it, makes ya think about people's thinking about, I don't know, maybe Jesus Christ and the Apostles and stuff. Or the martyrs and the saints. Which brings up that double feeling again. I mean, that, you feel like something inside you could shoot for that—and that like on the other hand you're psyched, too, thinking, whoa, is that ever supernatural.

Of course naturally Malone had to try something to out-do JL's shot, which is cool and funny, too. So when Frankie gets up and hits a pretty solid poke himself, which got all the way through and was rolling downhill to the wall, he pulls up at second when he could have easily taken three. And so what was this? This pulling up stuff? I mean instantly suspicion was everywhere, with our first thought being like Malone had maybe some side bet against his own team or something. But Frankie points to his shoe like he's gotta tie it, and he kneels down at second, and then stands up. So, okay, we figured the untied shoe was *maybe* the reason he stopped. And the game was ready to go again, with FX standing there on second base, which was this pretty-good-sized flat rock we kept over near the fence till game times. It was a flagstone, so maybe one the City forgot to use down along the ravine.

But then when Terry Thillens is about half-way through his windup, all of a sudden it's, "Hey, guys! Get a load a this shit! Time out! Time! Time! Look what I found stuck here to the bottom of the rock!"

And what was it Frankie found—stuck to the bottom of the rock—but a twenty-dollar bill! Of course the first thing we did when we ran up to look at it was to see if it was counterfeit or something. Or some other pathetic crap like maybe Monopoly money. But the twenty was real. So logically we had to figure out, now, where Frankie stole it from. But he swore to us he didn't—and that he really found it there, stuck on the bottom of the rock, just sort of pokin' out its nose by a quarter inch or so. "I swear on my grandma's grave!"

"How about on your grandpa's nuts?" Terry asked him.

And naturally Frankie had no problem swearing on his grandpa's nuts. Or as he put it, on the old bastard's humongous scro-tissimo, which he swore in the summer hung down and dragged on the ground, which made George P say he knew exactly how the old bastard felt, which made Stu biff Peterson so hard he fell over. And then it was, 'cause we weren't at all sure yet about this so-called *finding*—did Frankie swear on…. How about on his mother's tits? And how about on Armida's tits? And how about on Mother Mad's tits (which Stu said were actually fairly mana nu-atchee)? and then on Father Harmon's chestnuts? (which idea, too, Frank naturally one-upped, sayin' he swore on Father Harmon's tits, which he described as very, very tasty, as well as humongous, which of course kind of stopped us for a second). But then JL asks him the serious, final question, which is did he swear on STENHAM'S tits. And of course he did. But then like everybody at once goes "WHAT TITS!" Ya know, like we just dead proved that that twenty did *not* come from the bottom of that rock.

"Screw you, you Mexican-hairless dinks. Just because you don't have good luck finding beautiful green stuff right under your noses."

"Ya mean like this?" George P asked, which was pretty perfect, 'cause it just so happened GP had right then an extremely green and juicy boog on the end of his finger, which even made Frankie laugh a shit brick, though of course he just told George to shut up and eat that thing before it got cold.

Then he said, "Juuust because"—(though he was still laughin' at George P)—"juuust because the good luck is allllll mine, ya gotta be jealous, jealous, jealous, jealous. Ya oughta be ashamed of yourselves, which I'm sure O'Connor already is, 'cause he always is."

Then naturally he takes the twenty and snaps it out straight in front of our faces, and then folds it real slow, gives it a juicy kiss, and puts it in his pocket. And this whole thing Stu was pretty much startin' to fall for, only he couldn't figure out how it got allowed that such an idiot as Malone would ever get to find a twenty. "It doesn't make sense," he said. "It just isn't logical when somebody dumber than Behan finds a twenty." Which I need to explain was about the time when Cathy Behan read 'Arkansas' in her Social Studies book as *"Arkanzess"* and the Armadillo says, "It's Arkansas, Miss Behan," and Behan comes all confident back at her with, "It says *Arkanzess* in my book," which no matter all the A's she was always getting, made Behan a card-carrying dope for life.

But, truth to tell, none of us (except one) could really figure out what Frankie had pulled, and we were starting sort of to buy it, too. But then it was—sort of slow and quiet—"Did ya get a big, fat *erection* over this one, too, Malone?"—coming—you guessed it—from Pete O'Connor, who wondered did Malone have any more bills in his SHOE, which we all knew right away, when Frankie kind of moped and frowned, meant his little jig was up. And of course Pete was feeling he pulled off a very solid triumph. But I have to say there was a little weird moment of sort of like true sadness that came over Frankie, which I could see, or get a feeling of, when he didn't say anything other than O'Connor could go off and yank for awhile on his wazoo. Which, by the way, Frankie's coming by the money, I knew now, we'd never know the story of, even though I have no doubt it was not a normal story and would have been really funny as crap to hear about, and which he couldn't have not leaked out sooner or later.

And I don't know what it is about the couple of times I'd seen Frank Malone get mopey. I don't know—they kinda made me mad, or sad myself, for some reason. I mean, we all need to pull off our tricks and plans—maybe not all the time, but *enough* times, if ya know what I mean. And including, even, the outsmart-everybody kind of tricky little tricks. I don't know. It's like ya have to weigh *enough* pounds, at least at some point. Or have *enough* something or other to keep ya from gettin' beat down, so then you can get on to other things besides thinkin' of getting beat down, and then you're psyched up. And Frankie, well, it kinda makes me mad even right now, thinking about him getting his goony balloon popped here, or not getting to lie in bed that night with, ya know, sort of a cool, devilly grin on his kisser. And I wish I could go see that insane criminal. Nobody on the North Side here is making me laugh that hard yet. And there's stuff I want to talk to him about, though it's not about anything I'm sayin' right now.

But I *was* saying, about that *other* huge four-bagger JL hit, 'cause, talk about trottin' coolly on home, what a total, and complete, and killer beauty that one was. And I think there'll probably be some time in my life when I won't really know which one came first, the one on the Ted Williams day or this one, because they so much remind me of each other, and help me think over the cool and happy stuff about JL.

So I'm gonna talk about this ball game, which was early in 7TH, too, around World Series time. And we were all down in the Dead End, the seven of us plus Keater Phillips, having a game of four a side, when, up over the hill on Pleasant, comes a sight *not* pleasant, which would be the Vanderkells, and no other than the son of the Big-Game Spook leading 'em like they were a flying wedge. There was Stanley Entemann too and Marlon Pateo (who roll-blocked me so hard in this football game we played later that fall that I thought maybe I'd come down, you know, like some cartoon character, stuck with my head about a foot into the dirt, kicking my legs around and tryin' to find ground in the air), and Pete Fox, their pretty incredible qb in that game (*whew*...was Pete Fox good), and guys like Johnny Gibbons, who I egged one time, don't ask me why, while he was riding his bike down 91ST, minding his own business. I don't know. I mean, you know how it is with an egg: if you have one in your hand, and right there you also have a Gibbons, you have got to fire off that egg. And is it not true that with a nice fresh egg, maybe just 'cause of the sweet feel of it, you score with her *every single time*. And they had other guys, too, like Mick Tweedie and Johnny Shakespeare, who said if anybody ever called him a poet he'd beat the livin' shit out of 'm right then and there. Which of course meant nobody ever called him anything *but* 'Poet', even though, as Frankie put it sort of like a poet himself, the kid was dumber than a dead dog's dingleberries.

And it turned out, in fact, that this Vanderkell wedge was made out of exactly eight guys, just like us: so enough for an eight-on-eight ball game, or maybe the real World War III. But we weren't dumb. We put JL out front and then Bobby Stu (who by the way was, I'd call it, permanently calm in such situations because he knew he had zero reason to be scared of anybody in Beverly but his brother, Big Joe, who by the way was smart enough to let Bobby be, which I think explains why Stu never once walked around pissed at stuff, thank goodness for that). And then behind Stu was Frankie. And then me. And then Pete. And then behind me and Pete, it was George P and Keater Phillips. And then Terry.

And now, right up to us, comes this not Cavalcade of Stars but Flying Wedge of Punks, with that shit Prizer looking first and sort of only at me, very weird-like, or trying to be real killer, as if he wanted to say, "You put out word one, Collins, about you and me and that girl and that stick and that sewer hole and I'll cut your sorry little pecker off and hang it stuffed over the fireplace at Castle Dracula…where we drink the blood." And after he lays out this hocker, all hard-guy style, hangin' out the drip, he's still looking only at me when he says, "Christ the King can count its luck. We'd be teachin' ya a lesson or two about this game you're tryin' to play, if we had our gloves."

But now I've gotta confess it that, when he said this, I was feeling pretty much relieved, figuring, and hoping, that there wouldn't be too much more of anything at all. And that with Pateo and Entemann there, too, Malone wouldn't do anything overly suicidal, which you know he was just itching to do. And so they'd just leave and we could keep our honor the easy, sort of soft and smiley way (like just dreaming, up in your room).

But right then, Jack steps out, and he says, cool as somebody it's so hard to believe could *ever* die, "When we're up, you can use our gloves."

And do I need to say any more now about how somebody else can put guts in ya? And let me add another thing: Ya never know, until ya take action, what all can happen. I mean, I could actually tell now, because of the way Jack said what he said, that Prizer was taking some quick backward steps in his guts and heart. Amazing. Who'd've known that could ever happen? But of course Prizer *had* to stay now. And all of 'em had to stay. And we had to play. No getting out of it for anybody now, though there were some bullshit questions about how many lefty and righty gloves we had, sort of like what'll it be? wrestling or boxing? You know, the kind a bull when two guys just wanna stall and not begin a fight.

But this fight was gonna begin, which meant it wouldn't be Terry Thillens pitching: it would be Jack Leonard. And it meant we'd see if somebody at Schwendrowskis' was home so we could borrow Doc Schwendrowski's catcher's mask and chest protector, which the Doc, who was like a famous semi-pro ballplayer in his day, cut to size for his kid, Gene (who was already out of high school now), and let us use if we played fast pitch, which the way things were going, had to happen now. And it turned out the Doc himself was home and that he'd be setting his chair up in his picture window to watch us play, which was another thing that put something in ya or woke up in ya something that could be very cool and sort of like guts—somebody like the Doc watching.

Of course we didn't have a backstop in the street, so when we went fast pitch, some guys on the batting team had to always back up the pitching team's catcher, so the ball wouldn't go rolling half-way up Hamilton if one got away. But George P was a very decent catcher and Marlon Pateo was an even better one; and with Jack pitchin' for us and Pete Fox for them (with maybe like seven Little-League no-hitters between the two of 'em), there weren't many pitches that got away, believe me. Which was also cool 'cause without a lot of stupid shaggin', and wasting time, the game got to be all business. In fact the Doc got enough interested so that about the end of the third, he bagged the window seat and brought out a lawn chair and set it up in his driveway so he could take things in better. In fact he even started umpiring, which was very kind of official and cool, just yanking his thumb or criss-crossing his arms from his chair, which calls we all started looking to as the word. Even when the Doc barked one time at Frankie for lining a shot a little too close to that picture window, things never got goof-around-like, which was cool and kept getting cooler, 'cause, well, you know how it is when a game is serious. How it makes every move of your body and mind cool—and makes you feel that you might be a kid, but, where you are then, you're not a kid.

Of course there's a lotta stuff you're never gonna remember. But there's other stuff ya never forget, for whatever the reason. Like for me one thing was the way from behind the plate George P was givin' it to the Rat King whenever Prizer

came up. And I mean George has got a mind like he oughta become a professional comedian for his life job—unless
maybe he like says so much funny stuff before he's twenty
that he won't have any left. But he gives ya the impression
that it doesn't work that way. And of course the catcher has
a sort of right to give a little more than just the usual shit
to guys, because that's a normal part of the game. Which
means that what he says shouldn't start WWIII or anything,
unless he really crosses over the line, which a George Peterson isn't going to be a Frank Malone enough to do.

So there was George (funny-pudgy like Smokey Burgess
anyhow), mumbling away behind the plate, which is very
hilarious the way he does it, like it's this steady flow of
never-stopping bs, givin' grief even to guys like Pateo and
Entemann and Fox. And then eventually up comes Val-
boy, ever so hard. And, hold on, I gotta say right here that
last NIGHT, I swear t'God, I had this dream that I was that
cabby, and that Prizer was that madman in my cab, and
that right at the Murder Spot he was gonna put a bullet
in the back of my skull and turn my brain into just like
splattered gray guts and blood, when just in time I woke
up. But *screw* that shitface, like I was saying, I mean about
George P, I mean, he starts on Prizer for being Popeye the
Sailor, which gives ya a sort of perfect idea of the punk's
body. And then when Jackie blows one by him, it's where's
that can a spinach when he needs it, which George can do
in this Popeye voice that's kill-you perfection and which it
seems now like he's been saving all his life for this exact
situation with Prizer, because it was so completely perfect
for it. And then when strike two comes, it's like even more
insane Popeye-goin'-nuts stuff. And then when it's strike
three, 'cause that's what it was gonna be, nothing clearer,

believe me—it's like lunatic Popeye spazzin' his brains out about where's me spinach and blamin' Olive Oil and calling her the number one skank at Vanderkell because she didn't bring that can a spinach. I don't know if ya had to be there. But, trust me, it *was* perfect.

And maybe you know how it is, sometimes, with real muscle-y guys and baseball. I mean that they might be able to beat the livin' shit outa *you,* but they can't much beat the shit outa the ball. Which I have to say was the same with Stu, too. Funny how that goes. I mean—that fact about Jimmie Foxx—that he was so strong he could for real twist the cover off a ball. I mean with his bare hands. That's the kind of strong Stu is, I swear. But the other part of Jimmie Foxx he just doesn't have. And neither, believe me, does that pissed-off-insane King of the Rats, who would try so raging hard at the plate that he'd about pop his neck zits every time, but couldn't hit the ball for his life, and especially with JL moving him out, and in, and up, and down.

Or if the punk did manage by some black-magic trick to get a piece of the thing, the ball didn't go much of anywhere. Like his time up in the fourth, after he'd already struck out in his first appearance (looking of course like a total moronic jag), and he hits this extremely freaky, weird, spinning pop-up about half way out to Jack, and when the rubber-coated hits the concrete, the thing backspins right back *at* Prizer and almost knocks his block off. Only he luckily ducks and the ball takes off backwards past all the Vanderkell back-stop guys and back down Hamilton like a line shot in reverse, which, get this, Prizer decides to run on! Like it was fair. And of course he's being such an extremely pitiful idiot 'cause he knows that this backward thing is the best thing he's gonna get off Jack Leonard for the day, or for the rest of his sorry life. So he's tearing down toward first and screamin' "It was up-the-middle fair! It was fair! It was fair!" But—and this is another thing I think I'll forever remember—Doc Schwendrowski, who's started that umpiring by now, says out of his lawn chair, like he was St. Peter giving the final scoring on Prizer's life: "It was a FOUL BALL."

Of course, too, the next pitch after that, Prizer strikes out one more time, very, very pathetic-like, getting all twisted up like a lunatic pretzel. So in the sixth, when he comes up for his third appearance, he's *dead* raging. And he's especially raging, too, I'm sure, at Jack because Jackie's just cool and friendly, like it's no special pleasure to him to whip your sorry butt, and yet whip your sorry butt he does. And of course he's raging too at George P, special catcher's rights to be sayin' what he's saying, or not. And naturally, on his part, GP is now asking for an outfielder's glove in case he has to peel off backward for a deep, deep 'backshot' by the 'Prize', which is what he's calling Prizer now.

And I was out playing third, and I couldn't even start to help it. I mean nothing could be as perfect as when Susie Shannon grabbed Prizer's witch stick, but I gotta say this was even wickeder and funnier. And, I mean, there that muscle-y, whiskery-pimply Rat King was, standing right at the same sewer with a stick in his paws, sort of, and my memories, come on, *had* to be mixing in with all that GP was saying. So of course I was seriously bustin' inside my glove.

But I wasn't the one saying anything, at least out loud, and I had my glove completely over my mouth. And even like Pateo and Entemann and Fox were bustin', which was somehow kind of cool, ya know, sharing the laughs with your enemies. So it was weird when Prizer fires off some very serious rage in nobody else's direction but mine: "You SHUT

UP, Collins! You SHUT YOUR MOUTH, YOU PUNK!"

I mean everybody had to know there was something weird goin' on between us. Ya couldn't not. But the Doc was there, and he came in real quick with an official-like, "Hey, mister, just play the game!" Which I was loving, even though it scared me for the future, when, you know, I might run into Prizer all by myself, which always seemed then like a day that had to come.

I need to put in here too, though, that something extremely cool had been happening. This game was so good and tight and serious, with the score at the end of seven only 1-1 (Pete Fox in the top of the fifth having actually gotten an honest double after Entemann walked; and Keater Phillips in the bottom getting a scabby single that Jack followed with a shot off the Dead-End cyclone)—such a, like, weirdly once-in-a-lifetime ball game that old Mr. Allen, our next-door neighbor actually started watching seriously, too. And he came over from his house and just plunked himself on *our* steps for a better view, which was tremendously weird. Only my mom didn't kick him off, which, to say the least, would not be her style; instead, she brought him some lemonade, which would be exactly her style. But it was like weird and cool having Mr. Allen there, with lemonade on *our* porch, like this was a game at a park that you paid to get into. And my punk brothers Johnny and Dave were out, too. But they weren't acting like morons, which is something that never happened in all of life or history before. They were just sitting there with Mr. Allen, with lemonades too. And even our across-the-street neighbor, Mr. Mathis, stopped washing his car to watch, who I always was pretty sure wanted to rip out our guts for the time we put a pretty serious dent in his

Caddy (which, though, was nothing compared to what the high school punks would do when they, just for the kicks of it, would rip their cars across his grass, which was one of those painful two-ways-at-once kinda things, 'cause it sorta made ya giggle and sorta made ya sick to your stomach at the same time—and I'm thinking how Frankie might naturally give this little stunt a go when he gets that age, but I'm hoping he won't). Even Mr. Mathis was out there, and he even shut off his hose and stuck his sponge in his bucket. So, like I said, this was a game.

But of course there was no swearing now, or, like, battossing or bullshit, because the adults were out there. But the no swearing was part of the coolness, too, and another of the things that meant that stuff from that day was gonna get remembered for always. So you didn't want to screw things up with idiot behavior that might be kind of cool if the adults weren't out, but was really stupid if they were. But when the Doc tells Prizer to just *PLAY*, and calls him *MISTER*, I could sense something could be coming right now, adults or not. And of course underneath it all, it was me that his brain was raging about.

Of course, too, Jackie was gonna once more whiff the jerk, because a Ted Williams our fantastic, fabulous Muscle Boy was the complete opposite of, believe me. And it didn't take long this time, either. George P, naturally, after the Doc's coming in with the reprimand isn't gonna *really* still smart-ass it up. But then he couldn't help himself completely, so he just starts sort of humming, you know, a little on the loud side, the Popeye hornpipe song, while Jackie is moving Prizer *this* way and *that* way with his curve ball and fast ball, bang, bang. And it was too perfect, and funny. I mean, ya know how funnier than shit cruelty can be. And

I'm pretty sure like even Pateo and Entemann and Fox and the rest of 'em had to be like humming in their heads the old "I live in a garbage can" and "I eat all the junk" and "I smell like a skunk" as George was humming that cartoon Popeye tune, and the Rat King was goin' down.

And when, sure enough, he goes down all the way, even right after the Doc's reprimand, and with old Mr. Allen out there and Mr. Mathis, the goofy spook goes ahead and roars out "GOD DAMN FUCKING *SHIT!*" and like whips the bat into one of Mr. Mathis's bushes, making the leaves fly and actually like cracking a branch or something. I mean how insane do ya get? And right away I'm feeling like even the Vanderkell guys must be full, dead embarrassed. Or, actually, it was like nobody really knew *what* to do. It was that bad. And I was especially glad my mom wasn't out, 'cause what kind of feeling would that have caused in everybody, not just me. But finally the Doc comes over. And ya don't think he's gonna really give it hard to some kid who's not his kid, but you're still scared. And, whoa, check that one, the Doc *does* come on strong. I mean, with a real healthy shot of anger going, he says, "If you want to come around this neighborhood again, sonny, you better start cleaning out your filthy mouth." And then he makes the kid go get that bat, which by the way got kinda tangled in the bush, so Prizer has to spend some time (which would be every-second-is-a-million-years time, which most kids know about from, you know, times they got punished in front of a thousand people, which one time or another happens to everybody) diggin' it outa there. And then Doc makes the kid go say he was sorry to Mr. Mathis. "Go on," he says, "Mr. Mathis is right there. Go on. You go over and say it." Which the kid did do.

So it was a bad dog gettin' whipped real hard here. Not that I care. For what does the jerk do now, with the Vanderkells taking the field again (after his royal, supreme, pretz-ified K), but head right for *me*, like there was nobody else on the whole earth for him to be pissed at, which was a situation that was starting to wear out my nerves, with, like I say, the amount I was already thinking about the day to come. And he whispers, in this voice that coulda maybe passed for Charlie Starkweather's when he was showing off for his psychopath-ified girlfriend, "Some *day*, Collins, I'm gonna fucking kill you."

I wished to God the Stu-ball had heard that one and gotten killer-pissed for the first time in his life. Or Jackie had heard, even better. But no such luck. Our incredibly cool game didn't get blown, though, for all Prizer's Dracularian moron-ism. So on we went, right smack, you guessed it, into the ultimate classic situation (which is another reason why I'm telling this), with the home team batting in the bottom of the ninth, and the score tied, and two out. Actually, truth to tell, I think it was one out. But—doesn't it just sorta work this way, at least with stuff you don't forget: There would be Jack Leonard at the plate, givin' a little touch with his bat to the old sewer grate, and Pete Fox on the mound, with Pete Fox being no sorry chump like that guy who served it up to Ted Williams, whatever his name was.

I need to put in one more thing, too, which is to say that none other than Mike Shannon had come out there now also, standing in the Schwendrowskis' driveway next to the Doc, looking like the toughest kid ever to go to high school, even though he was a really nice guy. And needless to say I've been avoiding the subject of Susie, sort of like my own brain's version of her pulling down the shade on me on a permanent basis. But Susie, thank goodness, had by then left for her first year at St. Mary's in South Bend. And I figured, too, that the fact Mike didn't seem to hate my guts meant probably Susie didn't blab on me or anything. I sure hoped so, anyhow. 'Cause even though it's natural for an OH-NO to be there *for years,* you'd never want to be famous for it for even a second.

But Mike's bein' there, trust this one, too, meant we were getting watched by the best athlete by a mile of all the older guys. And this was how ya really made a name for yourself—showing a famous older guy like this that you could do it, whatever it was. I nabbed a kind of tough one-bouncer by Entemann while Mike was definitely looking, and the good feeling in my stomach can come back, even right now, if I think about that stab. But now it was Jackie against Fox, and everybody was looking, 'cause Mike and those old guys weren't dumb about what the real deal was. The Doc even got up off his lawn chair, and he and Mike came up closer. And can't ya see it, the two of 'em standing there kinda with their arms crossed over their chests. And Mr. Allen got up and joined 'em, though he was kind of a bent-over old guy, but this was cool, too. Even my mom came out and was watching, sitting there on our steps. And Johnny and Dave *still* had their insane yappers shut and were sitting there with my mom. And Mr. Mathis still hadn't gone back to his hose.

And now, as JL steps in, Marlon Pateo starts the "Hey batteh hey batteh no batteh no batteh" hum, which if it ever does any good anyhow, sure wasn't going to do it now. Jackie wouldn't hear this kind of stupid noise ever. But then Pete Fox wasn't going to be caring if he did, either. Way too much of a situation for bullshit. And I watched the Rat King backing up to the Dead-End wall where, you know, he would have murdered me if he could have. And I was kind of laughing inside, thinking, a lot of good it was going to do him if Jackie did what I was beginning very much to feel he was gonna do.

But how's this for a weird one? I was beginning to feel a little sad thinking how it really *was* going to happen. How Pete Fox and the Vanderkells were truly in for it now. I must be nuts or something. I mean, seriously, why would I feel sad for anybody that had anything to do with Val Prizer, no matter that we shared a few snickers at the punk's expense. Because let me tell ya now, no surprise, there *was* a later time when it was just the two of us and that promise, you know, that Susie Shannon made me about it being only a matter of time till he'd let me be? It hadn't come true yet. So, fact is, I should've been not too sad, for my own sake, if the rat cracked open his skull against the Dead-End wall and croaked.

But now the Doc all of a sudden, though it seemed totally natural, started calling not just the safes or outs but the balls and strikes too. "Outside. Ball one," he said as Fox's first pitch was away. And it was very cool the way the Doc said it, kind of quiet-like and unexcited, right after the ball made the loudest WHAP into the catcher's mitt we'd heard all day by a mile. And the same with the next pitch, which the Doc called "Strike one," it being low but not too low, which however Jackie let go because of course he was looking for one right at the belt and he had the patience to wait because he was good enough to have it. I mean even against Fox he was, which none of the rest of us could be thinking of doing. But Pete Fox was not one bit stupid (even though it was our thinking that the reason some of these Vanderkell guys were so tough was that they must've flunked like three times and were really like fifteen in 7TH grade). And, like I said, no dummy whatsoever, Fox goes right back low again, but not too low, and a little outside, but not too outside. Of course most of our guys thought it was a ball. But the Doc didn't think so, which meant it was strike two. And though nobody swore out loud, I think some of our guys were swearing pretty good inside (which I leave it to you to figure out how I knew about). But not Jackie. He didn't look like he was swearing anywhere.

He just touched the bat a little tap to the sewer grate, and got ready. And Pete Fox got ready, though I was starting to feel kinda sorry for him again now, because this would be something *he'd* remember, and which I was pretty sure he was gonna want to cold forget it. But as he started into his windup, we all got ready. The Doc was ready to make a call. Mike Shannon was ready to give the big nod of recognition to JL or to Pete Fox. My brothers, but this wasn't all that goofy, were up and running down toward the elm and they started to yell for Jack. And we all started to yell for Jack. And the Vanderkells were now all humming with Pateo. So the noise was roarin' like crazy on both sides. And Pete Fox starts now rocking forward, slow, and now rocking slow back, going into his wind-up, feeling maybe real good already 'cause he's got those two strikes and he's thinkin' maybe Jackie's gotta be scared. But for how long's Pete Fox gonna feel good? I'm thinking, as he turns his body and starts to whip himself into his delivery, which is a real sweet one, that Pete Fox won't be feeling good for too much longer.

And now in it comes, and you bet it's the one Jackie's

been waiting for. Not low. Not outside. No way. It was right over the heart. So, like somebody said, good things come to those who wait. And was he ready for it when it came? Oh, man, was he ever! Just the sound! You know that sound. It was like louder even than all that screaming and chatter. And then it was like when they fire off a gun to shut everybody up and get silence. That's how the crack a that bat came, and shut everybody up. And you know that way a pitcher almost snaps his neck, turning to see if the ball really's gonna go as far as he's afraid it's gonna go? Sometimes they just don't look back at all, 'cause they know so dead cold. But Fox had like this insane hope, which was weird to see a guy like that be so pathetic. And I mean that ball was hit so hard that there was still no noise 'cause nobody could talk for a second or two. If it had been straight on a line, it'd a gone through the cyclone by blowing a hole in it. But it was high and dead center and so far gone that anybody'd a had to laugh at that idiot Prizer, who jumps up now like a muscle-y monkey onto the concrete barrier and starts climbing the chain-link like he's gonna snag the shot before it says good-bye and game over.

But Val-boy was about fifty feet too short. Which when the ball cleared like that, everybody starts goin' fully nuts. The adults, even Mr. Mathis, are even clapping like crazy, and cheering. And Mike Shannon is there smiling and clapping and saying out loud to Jackie as he rounds second, "Good job, Jack Leonard. Good job." And I'm thinking this is as cool a thing as I've ever been there for in my whole life (to say nothing of our just now knocking Vanderkell's block off). And my brothers are out there and grabbing Jackie as he's rounding third. And yet I didn't really blame the idiots, and wasn't totally ashamed of 'em, which felt funny itself.

But wouldn't ya know—and I gotta say I couldn't help looking down to the Dead End even with all the incredible psych, and with Jackie doing the sweet trot home—there would be Prizer, all monkey-muscled, high up on the fence still, and no doubt raging like that Vanderkell Satan that put that handy little dog-crap pile by the Murder Spot. And what the punk does is he takes Keater Phillips's glove, which was the one he was loaned. And like it's his, he takes it and hand-grenades it hard as he can over the cyclone, just for the shit of doing it. But also of course 'cause he's gotta be the largest sorehead in the universe.

Not to say that any of the Vanderkells came like close to friendly in the handing back of the gloves. They all just like automatically dropped 'em on the street, even Pateo with the Doc's stuff, which was a hard move, no doubt. And, without saying anything except a hard-spewy sort of "Next time," they took off, flying-wedging their way back up (not so) Pleasant. And I knew that without the adults still there, things might've gone differently after that game, or I was pretty sure, even with both Jackie and Bobby Stu there, 'cause a blast like that is an automatic bad-blood creator.

And now for another pretty bad-taste-in-the-mouth kind of thing, there was Keater's glove over the fence, which Keater didn't know had happened. And I mean, I didn't want to seem like a special noticer of the guy, but I told everybody what Prizer had done. Which of course got Frankie goin', who says, "Who'd give a shit if somebody killed that asswipe. You could like take him out and bury him in The Woods and nobody would go lookin' for him. God wouldn't give a shit about him."

"Francis Xavier Malone," George P says, sounding to perfection now like Mother Mad, which is another voice he can do, "How many times must the Church remind you: God gives a shit about everybody."

Which was another beauty. And it made me think if ya can crack jokes about God, you really oughta be a pro comedian for life. And Frankie was laughin' pretty hard again, though, through his last giggles, he told Peterson to zip his yap.

Anyhow, besides Keater's glove, we had to go down and get the ball, which we all gave some royal crap to JL about— ya know, the kind that ya smile when ya give it. And we all, except Pete, kinda like went to JL at the same time, "What an asshole you are!" when we found that ball *WAY* up the hill on the other side of the ravine. Which of course any idiot knows is like the highest praise, I mean calling a guy an asshole in just the right way. And we found Keater's glove, too, without any trouble, with me being the one who spotted it.

But that brought back the subject of what humongous assholes, of the true kind, the Vanderkells all were, and not just Prizer, who we all agreed, though, was the undisputed king of the anuses. And, as we came back into the Dead End and were walking back up the slope, we started talking and thinking about that "Next time," which would most likely be the 7TH-grade CK-Vanderkell football game, that fall. And of course there was some baloney in how tough we were talkin', with our pretty cool triumph making us kind of dizzy, like we could never lose again. And then, sitting under the big elm at my house, we all went on with it and started goin' on and on about the game, which we all played better in than maybe we ever played, truth to tell. And after a while we were kind of like not giving the usual crap to each other. So it got like to be a really cool kind of satisfied feeling. And I threw out a weird one, which I had people sort of used to about me, which was, "It was like somebody was playing a transistor while that game was goin' on, and every time ya did something, it was like you were doing it with a cool song comin' over the radio." Which didn't make everybody bust, and got a few nods. Terry. And Keater. Naturally Malone made the puke sign, you know like he was chuckin' into his hand. Frankie never, though, gave me a really hard time.

But, then, after we'd been sitting around the tree for a pretty good time, and we'd about taken as much satisfaction from our very cool triumph as we could, we started thinking the other way. Terry said, "Of course next time they just might kick our butts." And if our confidence weren't pretty much half a crock, we all woulda gone, "Nah." Or, "No way." Or called Terry a "twerpy little crap-ball." But there was always something about stuff Terry said, which, like I've said, was comin' out of his being the smallest of us. But somehow, just for that fact, he was saying what we all were thinking. I don't know if that makes sense. But I know there were times when I wanted to tell Terry to shut up because he was saying, out loud, stuff that I was trying inside myself to get to shut up. And sure enough, a few guys, like Keater and even George P, started chirping in now with "Yeah. I hope it wasn't just fun while it lasted," and stuff like that. And this was definitely foulin' up the good feelings, because it was about time for everybody to head home for dinner and this would have been maybe the last thing we were saying to each other on one of the reddest of red-letter days of all time.

But now JL was just standin' there, with that tough-kid's face, showing a little of that crook tooth in his grin, and he says, "Next time, we'll beat 'em again." And then he smiled a little more. And these words of JL, not any of our turnin'-chicken stuff, were the actual last ones any of us said.

And that night, as I was lying in bed up in the pueblo, watching the moon take a sail over the black night-time leaves in The Woods, I thought about Jackie's words, and about the way he said 'em. And about how they put the guts back in us again, which they did. And about how, as I was thinking about our guts going this way, and then that way, how things can go either way. I mean, look at that kid who hung himself. Things just started headin' the wrong way in his head and he couldn't stop 'em. And, like I was saying, you gotta have *enough*—like enough solid good stuff that's happened to you, or somebody puttin' enough solid guts in ya, or gettin' enough to come out in ya, so ya can stop things. I mean hold things solid without fallin' back, when things might wanna go the wrong way in your heart or your guts. And so then you might even walk home past all the numerous killer-cruel punks and right through any supposed Day of Doom and just slap off the dust and grin like JL, who, like I say, reached the point of coolness in his life where he didn't even feel the need to take credit, after he'd really done somethin'. Which seems to me, now that I've really seen it, to be like the number-one first and maybe last step to not being un-cool in this life. But then I'd say ya gotta after all be somethin', too, not just see something.

I was thinking all these things that night, lying back on my bed. And then, like for hours, something was telling me that it would be pretty much pure psych to talk to a girl named Patty Conlon about all this stuff, if I had the guts for *that*, which of course I didn't.

CHAPTER FOUR

FALL OF SEVENTH

FIRE IN THE WOODS

Later that fall, which was of 1960, there was this bunch of things that happened. They didn't all happen on the same day. But they always go together in my head for some reason, so I'm just gonna pretend they did happen on the same day, even if it seems like, no way, not that much stuff could happen on one and the same day. And they happened in The Woods, which is pretty much the place I'm talking about stuff happening here, because sometimes things just seem to have a lot more psych if they happened there. Like this time I was walking home from JL's house over on Paulina, which is a whole *other* time, not one of the ones I'm gonna talk about, but which just sort of came to me now (though I won't pretend *it* happened on that same day, too, 'cause that many things would really be too much). Anyhow, there were these black, cindery paths that ran mostly along the edges but sometimes through The Woods, and you could walk 'em for a good long way, like for miles, 'cause they all connected. But ya never knew why they were there. At least I didn't till this time, when I was maybe a fourth grader, and I was coming home from Jackie's and it was this foggy day. And I was walking down a part of the black, cindery path where it ran out from the parking lot just kitty-corner from the Rock Island station, which parking lot, I swear to God now, I must be wanting to kill myself if I start mentioning. 'Cause it makes me not want to talk about any times. Ever. But I swear it's like I'm gravitating to it.

But, piss on it, I can't just like shut up for the rest of my life. So I'm not stopping. I'm not gonna stop just because.... I'm not. And 'cause I can dodge stuff I really need to dodge. So, like I was saying, I was on that part of the black, cindery path that ran along there, and I'd been heading along into The Woods pretty good now. And it was like this really foggy afternoon. And like I said, I was maybe a fourth grader, so I was past the time when your parents have to tell ya that ghosts aren't real—and maybe ya start then writing ghost stories, which I liked to do then, to make the ghosts as real and as scary as ya can all over again, which is kind of interesting when ya think about it. No sooner are the ghosts out of your life than you're psyched to get 'em back again (of course now you're the one in charge of what the ghosts do, you being the one writing the story). Anyhow, I was on that black, cindery path, crunchin' along, and it was a very, very cool kind of spooky fall afternoon, with the fog. Perfect for like a ghost story. And out of the fog, just ahead of me, comin' right at me, is this white horse. I mean a real horse, right there in the city, and it was huge and powerful, which just about made me flip, 'cause I never knew the path was for horse riding, as many thousand times as I walked there. And it musta been that the horse riding was from different times and was about going outa business completely, because I never saw a horse on the path again, which means it was the only one I ever did see. But there it was this day, with this lady on it, and who knows, maybe the last horse to go down that path, ever. And the lady had those boots to her knees and that black kind of cap, which I think has metal in it. And another cool thing was that the lady seemed very beautiful to me, too, with blonde hair that looked so pretty coming out from under that black, metal cap, which was for me, I think, the first time ever that I really cared about how a lady looked. But I felt pretty much like a complete idiot when I waved and she just stared ahead and kept riding, not waving back. And I had to get outa the way, but I was still close enough to feel the ground about shaking when that huge horse went by, breathing this sort of double chimney of smoke out his nose and with smoke coming off his back and him diggin' some serious footprints into those black cinders. And I could smell him like I was at a horse barn, which I have been; and I could hear the leather of her boots on the leather of the stirrups, which she was sort of hunchin' up and down from as she went riding along. And there was all kind of jingly stuff, too. And the big white horse seemed to like sway a bit with his butt swinging kind of sideways, and then his head rose way up, as they moved off past me into the fog and then disappeared. But the lady still seemed beautiful on that huge thing, even if maybe a little out of control of it and not un-nervous enough to wave or smile. All of which I'm mentioning just because it was a cool thing that happened in The Woods, which wouldn't have been as cool, I don't think, if it happened any place else.

And yeah, I'm gravitating, I guess. I don't know. But what am I supposed to do—'cause if I'm talking about the good things and they happen to come close to the place Jackie died, I can't like back off and gag myself completely, 'cause the whole place I'm talking about in Beverly (86TH to 96TH, Western to Paulina) is only about a square mile or so, so how can good and bad things not be close? So even if I do feel like some kind of—I don't know—guy going back to the scene of the crime, or something, let me say it, that there was this field right next to that parking lot across from the Rock Island station. And now, about this field, I'm gonna talk about this one other time, this time even before the horse time (and who cares if it's still *another* time, I'll get back to those times I said I've sort of bunched up)—I mean this time, in like maybe *third* grade, when Jackie and I met at the field there, which is in The Woods and that parking lot is, too, right at The Woods entry, on the far south end, off 91ST.

It was just the two of us that day, such little punks, and we thought we'd try and look like big-time pro football players. So we stuffed our shoulders with like some old towels and stuff because we didn't have shoulder pads yet. But we had these dippy little cheapo plastic helmets. And we put down some sticks and stuff for yard markers, thinking we were very cool. And we just punted this white football we had, because it was supposed to be cool to have the white kind they played night games with. And we kept on just punting to each other (you can guess how far, 'cause this was from a time when there wasn't even any difference yet between what I could do and what Jackie could do) and we were just running back the punts against each other, and tackling each other, all afternoon, for hours. Which is like something I'll never forget, because it was so much fun, just the two of us, thinking we were cool, and hard guys, with the towels stuffed in our shoulders, and our dippy helmets. I remember perfectly Jackie's was a bright red one and mine was white with a blue stripe. And the way I see this time now, even though it stays always so clear, is like I was taking a movie of it from up high in a helicopter, or something, and the time gets smaller and farther away as the helicopter peels off and flies away.

And there you go. Good times. And what do they do but make me feel incredibly sad. So. Shit. Maybe shit for a long time to come. But I gotta get to stuff. So let me now get finally to that bunch of things, which happened that fall in seventh, after the Ted Williams day and the day we, which is to say Jackie, whipped the Vanderkells in the Dead End.

First of all, it was fall but the day I'm talking about (or squeezing things together into) wasn't foggy. It was real dry and sunny, almost like it was still summer, and yet not the kind of day you're ever gonna sweat much on, 'cause it was fall. It must have been a Saturday, because I don't remember school or mass, or it being like Columbus Day or anything, though it would have been maybe just a little past that. It was the seven of us plus David Flynn. 'The Pin'—he was so skinny he might've had a hard time even in a fight with Terry, so he wouldn't have been much help in any war with the Vanderkells. Anyhow, we of course goosed the livin' sheist out of him as he went through the rabbit hole, and it would be Pete O'Connor, naturally, who would be the main goossage artist and whose idea it was, not that somebody else wasn't gonna come up with it, needless to say, Frankie being there. And Frankie later, to make a bit of a poem out of it, though this was also fact: He burned

Flynn's ass with a magnifying glass.

I need to say, too, that these days when we crossed the ravine, we pretty much always would stay clear of the Hanged-Kid Tree. But we liked to go to this big like house without walls that they had out there in the fields up over the other side of the ravine. I mean it was just like a big roof, with a concrete floor where people who came for picnics could go if it rained, I guess. But I know the colored people liked to set up their bands there, too, and have big dances on that huge floor. But this day, it was quiet as could be, the way noisy places 'll get when there's nobody around making noise at all. Which made a cool kind of mood.

Of course we weren't gonna start acting like we were in church, or anything. Because if we had a full-time job it was, naturally, goofin' off and being idiots—except for those times when, you know, things got cool and serious, the way I've said. Anyhow, we were all under that big roof, sitting at a picnic table, and Frankie, with this jackknife he had, into one of the log kind of columns holding up the big roof, was carving the words 'Eat Fuck'. Which words of course didn't make any sense—no surprise—but which FX said, for carving, were still "one full shitload better than 'Fuck You' or 'Eat Shit'," which were a nice and unfriendly kind of swear terms but still too normal for him to be wasting his valuable and precious time on. This made sense, sort of. But with his little carved term, FX was talking about something that was still stupid because it just wasn't possible. And if we kind of agreed it made probably as much sense as 'Fuck You', which doesn't make any, if you think about it, we still said you can't *eat* an *action*. Which got us into stuff that's possible and stuff that's impossible. Which got us talking about God.

And forget about making a square circle, after a while we were wondering what all God could eat and not be grossed out by it. And then, I'd say just to get him riled, Malone asks Pete if God could eat the entire human race, blood, guts, and all, and not be grossed out. Frankie, though, even though it sounds like it, wasn't an atheist, which he proved by splitting Poet Shakespeare's lip when the 'Poet' announced he was a full-boat atheist and so were his old man and old lady, which for us dead cold proved the completely out-of-this-world weirdness of Vanderkell and made us think maybe a whole school could get fried in Hades. But back to the point—could He? Could God eat everybody and not think twice about it?

"The answer's 'yes'," Pete said. "But that question is the kind that lets ya know there are questions just too stupid and too disgusting to answer. It's a Malone question. And it would make God puke."

"So God can puke?" Frankie asked, right back.

"Of course He can puke," Pete said.

"I'd say He's pukin' right now," Stu said.

And normally the person who said that, which came out so funny, would get biffed off his pins, but it was Stu. So we went on to other stuff.

"God is omnipotent," Pete said, "which means all-powerful."

"And you are homo-ipotent," Frankie said, "which means all fairy all the time."

But, miracle of miracles, no fight broke out. And Pete didn't even much notice and didn't even ask Frankie what dictionary for bozos he found that one in, which I was dead positive was coming. Instead he just sort of ignored him and went on with, "God is also omniscient, which means He knows everything. And eternal. And infinite, which means he can be anywhere He wants, anytime He wants."

"Sort of like Earl Torgeson," George P threw in.

And when we all said, "What's *that* supposed to mean?" George P goes on about how Torgy could stretch so far for a throw he'd have like one foot at CK and the other at Barnabas, which was like he was in two places *simultaneously*—which last word he threw in, because (speaking of things that appear impossible) GP is not a total idiot.

But then Terry, before GP could say anything else, all kinda angry, whispers, *"Piss on* Torgy." Which is explained by Terry's being the only Cubs fan outa six hundred and ten kids at CK—but which was funnier than crap, too, with that little voice of his and the all-ticked-off whisper, which sounded kind of like a garter snake trying to hiss. So we didn't start whomping on him the way we usually did over Sox-Cubs.

And then we started thinking about God again. And we were thinking what we would do if *we* were omnipotent, what kinda things we'd go for.

"I know what O'Connor would go for," Frankie said.

But Stu got Frankie in this no-way-out-of-it bearhug, and if Malone started yapping somethin' that Stu didn't like, Stu put on the big squeeze, which meant we could talk for a second and get something going.

"I'd make the Russians and the Chinese into like not-jags," JL said, "so we wouldn't be worrying about any World War III."

"Yeah," George P said. "Enough with the duckin' under the desks just to practice kissin' our butt-factor good-bye."

"No way," Frankie said (by permission of Stu). "Last time we ducked, I got to look up Cosgrove's...aaagghhh..." (permission of Stu denied).

I myself was thinking, of course, if I were omnipotent, of what I'd do about that punk Prizer. Or about how I'd at least speed up time if what Susie Shannon said was true. I mean about me being big enough someday to handle that f'ing rat, who had that special threat goin' on me now, promising *not* to let me be, at all, forever and ever amen. But sometimes when you're with your friends, which I guess I've showed ya, you're ashamed of talking about little problems like that, even if like all the time, in your head, you have the feeling that Val Prizer's waiting somewhere in the weeds to kick the shit out of nobody on earth but you (I mean, sort of like you went to a fortune teller who said in a way so spooky you couldn't get it out of your head, "Death has picked the exact place and time when you two will meet, and the hour is fast approaching."). So I said, "I'd like to be able to put myself in any place I wanted or any time I wanted just by sayin' so."

"Where would'ya go first?" Pete asked, in this way that showed he actually really gave a crap-ball, which was cool, and just like Pete. So I was glad when Stu shut up Malone, who had just started to say something about my picking Patty's house to go to—if I had the power, or the guts. And maybe he was gonna say something about Patty herself, something plain stupid, to tick me off, which *would have* ticked me off. So I was really glad Stu shut the idiot up. Though I have to say Frankie must've guessed, all right, how much I wanted to get up the guts to go see Patty some quiet afternoon, which fact I'd be dead before I would've let anybody know, but which visit I think I would have traded even for what I said I wanted, which was, "The year 1, when Jesus was born. Or maybe the year 33, when he died. I'd like to have been there when he rose from the dead."

And on the spot, with that one, Frankie was starting to let out one big insane yap. But Stu strangled 'm, just about as fast. So it came out "What BULLSH…" which became a really funny expression we used for a while.

But it was so funny, too—and I've gotta give Pete credit because I think he actually meant it to be funny—the way Pete just said, "Thank you, Stu," in this like normal, businessy voice, not even looking up, which made Frankie's getting sort of strangled and buried all at the same time really funny, not that it wouldn't have been anyhow. And Pete's joke dead guaranteed, 'cause it was so hilarious, that we'd all act now like we wouldn't give a crap-ball if FX Malone keeled over and croaked right in our kissers, but we'd just go on in businessy voices, which Pete did. "But d'ya remember, Kev," he said, "what Jesus said to St. Thomas about needing to stick his hands in the holes and stuff? Maybe there's stuff you're not supposed to know, but just believe."

"FAHHCK…ING…BULLSH…."

And like I said, on I was gonna go completely calm and quiet, while Frankie was very hilariously losing his life. I said, "I know you're right about that, Pete. I was only *thinking* if I were all-powerful, which maybe we're not supposed to even be thinking, even for fun. I mean maybe we're not supposed to be all-powerful so we won't know everything and be able to go anywhere we want, 'cause then we'll like have to count on somebody besides ourself, I mean up above us, for all the stuff we need."

"FAAHHUUHHHUUHHUUHHUUHH…."

"Yes *indeed*," Terry said. And now with this 'indeed' of Terry's, we were of course all goin' completely nuts inside. And then the little guy, not even busting at all, starts going on with the perfect businessy thing, too, while Stu was—

and I mean it, he wouldn't have been sweatin' even if it'd been mid-July!—doing that Jimmie Foxx cover-of-a-baseball thing, all right, to Malone's body. And like I've said, not to change the subject too much, Terry would say stuff that we were all afraid of because he was a little guy but, for the same reason, also stuff that we all hoped for, only a little more intense because it meant more to him, being little like he was. "I think," he said, "that like God *does* make it so ya need Him, so you'll *figure out* what a good guy He is. Otherwise ya wouldn't."

But now the Pin...pipes in. Not to keep making poems about the guy. And I gotta say the Pin (and I'm not just saying this because he wasn't ever part of our gang at all) was a rather completely nauseating sort of human. I mean the only thing not bone skinny about the scuzz—and I know you're gonna think I'm gonna say his braunschweiger—but I'm not—'cause it was his nose, which was so big we actually started calling him Noser once in a while, even though Noser O'Reilly already had that name, for reasons that, trust me, would be obvious to anybody in the universe. And even though we were like outa sixth now and into seventh, there were like always still these extremely nasty deposits around the Pin's nostrils, which ya could see fairly far up into, even though they were always about half clogged.

But anyhow the Pin, like I said, pipes in. And of course he would always *say* stuff, too, that was disgusting, which of course we all did, ourselves, a lot—but with him it was like never funny and like there was some brain-connection between his mouth and what he called all the time his 'inflamed adenoids' (which Frankie said a specialist discovered somewhere far, far up the Pin's bodily sewage canal). Or maybe when your reputation is I AM DISGUSTING, you pretty much settle on being disgusting all the way around, or ya figure it's what gets ya attention or something, and you make every single one of your sayings disgusting too. Anyhow, what he says (sort of pickin' up in his un-funny way from Frankie on the subject of God) is, "If I was all-powerful I'd like have eleven extra mouths, with like ten times the normal teeth in each one, and nine extra stomachs, all huge, so I could eat as much as I wanted, and like twenty eyeballs in the back of my head or maybe ten thousand all over my body so nobody would ever be able to sneak up on me, and I'd be like invisible so I could spy on all the fat and disgusting people and break in on them when they were taking dumps, and I'd like scare people all the time, or maybe I'd just like wipe out the world so I could have it all to myself and like drive down highways without anybody getting in my way, ever, or just walk into banks and just grab up as much money as I needed, whenever I wanted."

Which of course nobody on earth needed *The Twilight Zone* to know was a dream for supreme morons. I mean this all-the-money-but-nobody-alive-but-you dream is maybe *the* dream that turns on the red light for idiot. But George P, just to prove it, started humming the theme song from the *Zone*. And then we all just told the Pin to SHUT UP, 'cause, as usual, he was making us just a little bit ill.

Then guys started saying stuff like if they were all-powerful, they'd have a hundred-and-five mile per hour fastball; and a perfect curve, one that broke three feet at the very last split second; and that they'd be able to run the hundred in eight and a half seconds; and the mile in three and a half minutes; and they'd be able to lift a thousand pounds; and they'd be able to swim the English Channel and back again, underwater; and that they'd hit sixty-five homers, or a hundred homers. And all that kinda stuff.

Then to somebody who said one of those things, George P asks a good question, which I'm positive he could do all the time if he didn't every single time prefer to ask an idiotic one. "In other words," he said, "if you were all-powerful, you'd go ahead and make yourself only sort of powerful instead?"

And then JL says, "Actually it does make ya think, I mean about what the fun would be if you were all-powerful. It's like it wouldn't be so great after all, 'cause it would be boring, and you wouldn't care. So maybe if ya had your three wishes, you wouldn't want to make that one of 'em. Same as living forever."

Of course now, knowing what I know, that's something I don't want to remember. I mean Jackie saying that stuff about life forever. But at the time I said, "But you do live forever, in heaven." Which I'm glad now that I said.

"In heaven, you see God. That's why it's never boring," Pete said. "You're forever part of the Mystical Body."

"Sounds VERY FAHHHKING BOR...."

"Thank you, Stu," Pete said, once more in this way that was still so funny. "But let's ask Mr. Malone what he would do if he were all-powerful."

"I'd make out with Bardot non-stop."

And of course we asked Frankie if that meant every second of every minute of every hour of every day of every week of every month of every year of every decade of every century for all time and forever. And of course he said it did. And we asked him wouldn't he get bored. And of course he said no. But then we started guessing about Bardot's feelings. And of course we said Malone'd have a bit of a problem because Bardot would blow her brains out after the first one billionth of a second. To which he said, "You wish!"

And then we were all just sort of sitting there, doing nothing, you know, throwing rocks at trees and stuff, waiting for something to happen. Which then suddenly it did, 'cause outa nowhere the Pin just starts screaming complete bloody murder. And he jumps up and starts running around like an idiot on fire, which, lo and behold, is what he was. And it was really especially funny because like his butt was smokin' and he was leaving a trail like a fighter plane goin' down in flames, only he was whacking his own tail to try to put himself out, which we were hoping wouldn't happen right away.

"What's he doin' on fire?" Stu wanted to know.

"I think he like just started burning," Frankie said.

"What an idiot," Stu said.

And it was like so funny watchin' the Pin tearing around in circles and trailing smoke, we almost didn't say—but we finally did say—"Stop, drop, and roll, jag-off!"—which was close to but not exactly the same as the name of a chapter in the Red Cross safety book we had to read. Which he finally woke up and did, but not before he had like a wallet-sized smoking hole in the back of his trou, which still kept smokin' for a little while, much to our satisfaction. And of course we went back and forth for a while on whether it was possible or impossible that there was a butt anyhow inside the Pin's trou, which most of us agreed was *not* possible. But then Stu said, "He's gotta saw off the logs from somewhere." Which was logical and got us on all the possible places the Pin could saw off those probably very nasty logs of his from, which of course Malone said, forget all the other places that we guessed, like his ear holes and mouth and those monster nose holes of his, it had to be "his colostomy bag," which Frankie said if we were too dumb to have heard of, he wasn't going to explain it, and which even stumped Pete.

But then we began to think there might be somebody responsible for the Pin's goin' up in flames, because ya just don't all-of-a-sudden, lo and behold, start burning. But the magnifying glass we hadn't seen. And, as it turns out, Frankie had been workin' it from about four feet. So we knew ya can't use matches over a distance unless you either throw 'em, which wouldn't much work in this case, and like no way anyhow without a lotta tries—or, secondly, you have to hold the match right at the place. And so even Pete, 'cause we couldn't get past the idea of matches, couldn't figure how to hang this one on Frankie—though naturally he was wrackin' his brains to figure a way. So we just gave it up and figured that the truth, which meant exactly how Malone did it, would come out sooner or later.

And with that, it became time to do some roaming around. And so we headed back down into the ravine and started walking along the creek on the flagstone walkway, not the Longwood but the Leavitt way. And like I said, it was a day when you'd never be cold a second and you'd probably never sweat a second either. So we were feelin' good, and the trees were already turning, and colored leaves were all over the place, so I was in a specially good mood, but it wouldn't be everybody who would get what I was feeling and I didn't want right now to start up any particular private conversation. So we just kinda kept goin', walking here and there along the flagstone walkway and then back across the ravine on one of the bridges, when all of a sudden George P shouts out, "Holy shit, I think I just saw a nude guy!"

To which Frankie goes, "If wishes were kisses."

But GP was dead serious. "I swear t' God, you jags. And I mean like a *man,* not a kid. See! Right over there! Holy shit, there he is! See him!"

He was pointing up into the thick trees up about behind the Allens' house, which would mean really close to behind my house. And sure as shit we saw this guy there, and he was a man, and he was full nude. He was standing straight up and lookin' our way, as George P whispered very, very quietly, "with all three eyes." But he must not a seen us, because he didn't do anything like he was even embarrassed. I mean like to start givin' us at least the shine-on-harvest moon instead of the flying furry squirrel. And he didn't reach for some kind of weapon to blow us off the face of the earth, either. He just stood there. Dick first. With like, get this, a half a rod on.

And even Frankie was scared this time. Because this time we were talkin' about a psycho who was really and truly there, although it felt like we had to be dreamin' this psychopath up. And it's funny how it is when ya freeze. You could call it curiosity, if you wanted to tell pretty much of a huge lie. But it's not just that you're scared shitless either, though we were. It's more like you want to stick around to get killed, or something weird like that. Anyhow, we didn't run yet. We just sort of stuck. I mean just sort of stood there lookin' at the guy, who was maybe not even a hundred feet from us, but still he didn't seem to see us. And we were so stuck we didn't make any noise, not even Frankie, who ordinarily when it was absolutely and completely the time for real silence would like try to cut one or something.

And then—holy shit again!—we all saw that the guy wasn't by himself! And nobody could figure this insane stuff out at all, no more than why the guy would be there nude in the first place. Not that we were asking any out-loud questions. Because we weren't so funny now, the way we were when we just *thought* about a madman in the Woods. Though maybe some of us were asking inside ourselves if the other person was some kid who was going to be strangled or knifed or something. And we couldn't tell if it was a guy or a girl, this other person. We were all looking hard, but we couldn't tell. We could just see a back without a shirt on. Later Terry said it was maybe the two of 'em were Adam and Eve. And we were so screwed up by seeing this stuff that I swear for a minute or two we were thinking maybe it *was* Adam and Eve (with our throwing in ideas, too, of OH-NO, where's a fig leaf for the entire human race!). Even Pete the Fact Man didn't go *Nah,* it can't be them. But the other person was sitting on the ground and wasn't facing us, so we didn't know—man, woman, or kid.

Later, when we were able to think it through, we came up with every idea under the sun, like from it was Satan and the Hanged Kid, to it was Father Harmon and B Bardot. Frankie of course said he didn't remember O'Connor still being there with us, and even though we all swore Pete was there the whole time, Frank said that didn't prove a thing, when you're talking about somebody homo-ipotent.

But now the guy did see us. Holy shit! I mean he was lookin' right at us, and we knew he could see us, even if he didn't bother to cover up that half-boner he had. He just like wiped his mouth with the back of his hand, like he was some insane cannibal about ready for dessert after a nice hearty meal. And then like he smiled. Holy SHIT, was it weird! And then he took this spook-ya, quick, fake-out step toward us! like he was gonna run us all down and do a huge, nude, cannibalistic grab on us! Holy Jesus, Mary, and Joseph!

And like Stu—I mean Robert Stephen Stupnicki—was outa there so fast he even beat Jack, who also was wasting about no time whatsoever lookin' out for stragglers, which would be primarily George P, who truth to tell would get all-day STOMPED by Smokey Burgess in the fifty.

"Wait up! Wait up, guys! Wait up!"

Pitiful George P. It was so hilarious, hearin' him. And I mean he only caught up with us because this PATHETIC, simpo cry for help of his made us laugh so hard we either had to hold up for him or piss lakes in our trou.

And I'm not makin' any of this up about the nude guy or about anything I'm saying, except—truth—there was the Nude-Guy day and there was the magnifying-glass day, which second day, I guess you'd say, had its chapter one and chapter two. And where Frankie (naturally not satisfied with just a sort of normal stunt like setting the Pin on fire) used the magnifying glass for the second time, I mean *on* the magnifying-glass day—that happened in a slightly different place than where I'm gonna put it now, which is right back where the Nude Guy was. Don't ask me the reason for this movin' stuff around, which I can't say more about except that I pretty much do it in my head that way. And I don't know why I'm talking, anyway, about all this fiddling with times and stuff—but it's because I sort of feel, too, like I should be honest with ya, even though I know I could easily fool ya.

Anyhow, sort of the same way as with the Hanged Kid tree, we got pretty soon a completely insane idea. And by that I mean, *I* got an insane idea again. I don't know what's with me—but—it was me who said, meaning to where we saw the Nude Guy, "Let's go back." And just about the exact same time we agreed that that was the dumbest idea anybody ever had, and Stu was wondering if I wasn't like Malone's first cousin, we all said, "Yeah, let's go back."

And once we stopped laughin' and hitting each other, Frank workin' Terry over pretty good (first because that was normal, and second because Terry actually said, "Then again, we could *not* go back")—right after that, we started sneakin' back, quiet as could be. This time, though, Frankie did pop off a little magical-fruit toot, because of course he could conjure 'em like a prestidigitator. And this got us laughing so insanely hard—even Pete about peed his drawers—and hitting each other so much, that we almost had to call the deal off. But you know what I said about deals like this. Once ya begin 'em, you tend to keep on going with 'em to the finish, no matter how dumb.

So we started sneakin' on again, with me being sort of the leader. Not to say that I wasn't getting called, not a leader, but a jag by everybody from JL on down. But on we went, nonetheless. And it wasn't too long before we were turning the bend, which on the other side of it would be the Nude Guy Hill. Which might or might not have on it, the Nude Guy himself.

"You guys," Frankie whispered, "O'Connor just told me if we're goin' in, he wants us to go in completely, you guessed it, nude."

But this was so scary and serious—I mean there could be a murderer right around the corner—we didn't have time for the usual Malone stuff. And we didn't even threaten to pants him, which of course every so often was necessary. I mean when he went too far over the line. We didn't throw him, either, into the creek bed, which no way we wouldn't have done if there'd been water in it. And like nobody was laughing.

And, still, around that corner, we went. And around... the...corner...oh, shit, here we go.... SHIIIT!

But there was no Nude Guy. He was gone, as far as we could see. Which ya take a moment to believe. And then ya don't know if you're disappointed or not. And then ya start thinking how tough you are. So even though we'd just seen like this naked cannibal with a half-boner, we started running up the slope like we had the guts that even if he was there we'd show him who was gonna die and make us BOSS. But WHOA SHIT! there the lunatic was! Or at least it had to be him, because there was a dressed guy not too much past where the Nude Guy had been. And wouldn't I be the big-shot Mr. Leader who got us into this one! And there we were, still chargin' up the hill 'cause I hadn't called RETREEEEEEEAT!

But I put on the brakes before we died. And I'm sure you can see that one, with several idiots slammin' into me like in a pile-up and falling all over me. But I managed to get another look, too, before we scrambled up like crazy and took off the hell outa there. And it wasn't so much that I was lookin' at the *guy*. He was just this dressed guy now with his back to us, if that wasn't scary enough. But what I really was lookin' at was the other person, who was dressed now too. Not that I could see. I couldn't see. Not if it was man, woman, or kid. But that was maybe what made stuff happen, my not being able to see, 'cause in like a split second I started thinking all kinds of weird bad stuff, like it was my mom, or her sister, Gerry, or it was Susie Shannon, or it was Patty, or it *was* a guy, or it was a kid, and the kid was a guy, and like somebody I knew, and like the Nude Guy was gonna kill him, or WHOA shit! who knows what else. Actually I couldn't have thought all that at the time.

But when I thought of it all later, it seemed like I had *already* thought it—like right when I was there. And when I was doing this thinking it out, up in my room, I mean it was like all this gross stuff that I didn't want to think but I kept on thinking, almost like I wanted to kill myself but almost like it was fun to think horrible stuff. And weird stuff, like my mom and that weird guy, or some friend of mine, the kind of stuff that if it was true would really flip ya ass over elbow. I don't know if somebody could explain that to me. And I don't know if I'd want t' hear 'm if he could. But I would, I guess, wanna hear him while I was all the time tellin' him to SHUT UP! Sort of like how you'd be so curious if somebody really did know the day you were gonna die. Or if they knew exactly *how* you were gonna bite the dust.

Later, when we all were guessing about the second person, when we got past the goofy shit, which naturally took awhile, somebody said he thought he saw like a girl in a ponytail. And Pete said that even if the girl didn't try to fight the guy off, it would be statutory rape—"if she was less than seventeen and the guy…. I mean if he…."

"Nailed her," Frankie said, sort of polite, like he was trying to be helpful.

But even Frank didn't think he was true funny on that one. And after he said that, and nobody laughed, he shut himself up. And the statutory rape thing, which Terry imagined like the guy doing to a girl in our class, made us actually sort of seriously agree that God could puke, and sort of wore us out on the subject, or made us quiet, the way certain stuff will.

Not, though, to say that Frankie was through for the day, because later we went back to that place one more time (but you know now I'm takin' the two chapters of the magnifying glass day and wrappin' 'em around the Nude Guy day and putting everything in the exact same spot). And still the sun was, that day, shining warm and bright—so if an idiot still wanted to use a magnifying glass, he still could. And what we did was we poked around right on the spot where the Nude Guy and the other person had been. And yeah, right then and there, Frankie does haul out the glass—and he does use it, and what he set on fire this time, while we were guessing everything under the sun about what the Nude Guy and the other person had gotten all nude for, wasn't the Pin's pants or Terry's pants or Pete's pants, which is the burning order you'd expect Malone to go in, but one of the leaves that had fallen from the big elms there, which we now saw happening ('cause of course ultimately—ya like me using that one?—FX wanted people to know about his stunts). And no sooner were we jumpin' all over him, saying, "So THAT'S how ya did it!" and even starting to agree with the Pin, sort of, that Frankie oughta do something like pay for his pants, or at least say he was sorry—no sooner than this, we found ourselves in the middle of a circle of fire.

I swear to God, it was like that fast. Like no time. And before ya knew it, the flames were starting to jump into some bigger leaf piles and were rising way up high, about as tall as we were. We didn't know what to do. It wasn't like we were gonna get caught in the circle and burned alive, 'cause you could find places where the flames hadn't gone up too high and you could jump out from the circle of fire, which we all did. But we didn't know whether to stay or to run. And of course there were people, whose names I'm not now gonna say (meaning it wasn't just the Pin), saying we *had* to run for it 'cause there was nothing else we could do. And if we stayed, they were screaming, we'd just get caught and have our lunches handed to us, for like EVER. And the whole time, the fire was spreading out faster and going higher now while we were doing nothing except yelling about it.

Somebody yelled, "Let's run to your house, Kev! Call the Fire Station! Not say our names!" Then somebody else just yelled, "We don't have a chance! We don't! I'm tellin' ya, we don't!" And a couple of the other guys started yelling their asses off at Frankie that he was the biggest, most irresponsible jag on earth, and they weren't at all kidding. You know, they were screaming it like they really *hated his guts* for this one, and they like weren't going to be changing their minds anytime before they died.

Then a couple of us started stomping out the fire with our feet where we could. But it seemed like almost completely useless. So we were really about ready to jam our fingers down hard on the panic button. Believe me, we were! But then Jack, who if you've been following me, I mean if you've gotten what I'm saying at all, you can guess was NOT one of the ones who said stuff like let's clear outa here or let's call from Collins's house or who started ranking for dead real on Frankie Malone. What Jack was doing was putting his brain onto the problem, the whole time we weren't. And now what he did was he ripped his fall jacket off, which luckily we all had, and he started to whap out the flames with it, and it sort of worked 'cause the flames that ya didn't kill and that jumped away, ya could get to jump the way you wanted 'em to. I mean not out to new leaves but back inside the circle, although sometimes ya had to footstomp one that escaped 'cause you fanned it out rather than in. And with your jacket ya killed a lot more than you ever could with your foot. So right away then, seeing this sort of worked, Jackie started goin' like crazy to get the job done, not even looking at us but telling us to get our jackets off and spread out around the circle of fire and get to work. And, like not as dumb as we looked, we listened to what he said. And, like following orders from a general at Normandy or something, we all started going at it like crazy men, even the one or two or three who'd most wanted to take off, whose names I'm not going to say. And there was no going after Malone anymore, 'cause we all had a job right here and now. And it was one serious, no-goofing-off job, you can believe that. 'Cause wouldn't it have been one serious OH-NO to be known as the guys who burned down Ryan's Woods.

And if we did burn down The Woods, I'd sure be keeping it a to-the-grave secret, like a robbery or a murder. So you can tell from that I'm talking about it that we eventually got the job done. Of course Frankie was the one who put the final stomp on the final flame with all this pride and satisfaction like he wasn't the one responsible for the fire in the first place, which almost got Stu pissed for the first time in his life, but he just called Malone an idiot and an a.h. instead, only in this really not-kidding way that let Frankie know he was dead serious, not like normal—I mean just goofin' around.

To which Frankie gave Stu a look like if he could take him on and kick his ass to hell and gone, he would. And I mean he was just as serious as Stu, about this responsibility gettin' hung on him. Only it was impossible that this was gonna go anywhere, Stu being Stu and Frank being Frank. That's just the way things are. But there was like this feeling now that was weird, like the one that would come to me when Frankie got so mopey (even, that time, over that myna bird). I mean, ordinarily when we did stuff that like got us close to getting killed, once we got out of it, we'd start laughin' our butts off and thinking it was one of the coolest things that ever happened. And it like made us even closer friends and stuff. But this was different. Even when George P said, as we were standing there in this black, smoking circle, "We could call this place the Pin's Trou," nobody busted out.

And if anybody, including me, was thankful at least for the good move JL made and got us all into, nobody was saying the word. It was just sort of time to get outa there and get home, which we did, everybody going off his separate ways once we got back up through the rabbit hole.

And for a pretty long time after that, even though I was feeling free as a bird up in my window with Susie Shannon gone off to college at St. Mary's, I'd look out at night at that spot where we'd seen all that stuff with that insane grinning nude cannibal, and with the second person, whoever it was, and whatever it was, male, female, adult, or kid— and I thought of all those kinds of possibilities that scared ya so much you didn't know shit from a sandbag. I mean stuff that like scared ya so much ya didn't know your own name. So ya stop thinking it and ya get your mind to shut up. But then you get bored, so you start thinking it again. And then when I'd get all worked up, I'd start thinking of this red glow starting up. Because, as you know, I would put the fire from the magnifying glass in the same place as all that other stuff. And I'd think of the bright red glow then shooting up into a flame, as quick and outa control as the flames that shot up on the magnifying-glass day. And then of the whole of The Woods catching on fire. And then of men out there fighting the fire, hundreds of 'em, like you see in movies of forest fires, with yellow helmets. And of maybe like a firefighter getting killed by a huge burning tree. And of the whole thing getting on the news for like weeks and weeks, it being like a world-famous murder case. And I'd feel so guilty and scared it was very seriously like I did kill somebody.

CHAPTER FIVE

WINTER OF SEVENTH

THE ICE TREE

Not that you'd keep a seventh-grade class picture anyhow. But we didn't even have one, and I won't be there when they take the graduation picture for eighth. But I'm thinking now about faces and stuff. And I mean, here I am talking about all these guys and I haven't told you much about what they looked like, which I think makes it harder to work up your thoughts about 'em. Anyhow, I told you Jackie had that crook tooth, the one front one kind of lapped a little over the other. And he had kind of sandy hair, like his dad. And the kind of voice and laugh they call husky, which his dad has too, but which doesn't make you think they have a cold but instead that they could kick your ass. And I mean, Mr. Leonard, he's this incredibly nice guy who at dinner at Leonards' always talks to ya really kindly and like he's really interested in your life and stuff, with the way he asks ya questions and listens to your answers. And he's got this smile all the time that you'd call, I guess, quiet. But I mean if you ever, say, were driving behind Mr. Leonard and you started honking and getting all pissed off and then you jumped out of the car and then he got out of his car, and you took one look at his face, which is the kind of face that makes you say to yourself, for some reason, maybe because of like muscles right *in* the face, "Okay, now look at his forearms." Which you do, and then you say, "Oh, shit, what did I get myself into now." Which was exactly Jackie, you know, like right down to the forearms and face, too, which all goes along, or went along, with the husky voice and the crook tooth.

And then Frankie, I know you wanna know what that criminal looks like. Well, he's got real dark hair and a real Irish face with pale skin and dark eyebrows and blue-as-shit eyes, which brings up Bobby Stu, who has a total Polish face with blonde hair and blonde eyebrows and blue-as-shit eyes. And if the two of 'em were on Notre Dame, Frankie would be the qb and you'd know why they called them the Fighting Irish, all right. But Bobby of course would be the humongo tackle who reminded you for like the thousandth time that the Fighting Irish wouldn't be shit if it weren't for their Polish linemen. And George P, like I say, is Forrest 'Smokey' Burgess, only slower, with a pie face and you can throw in a pie body, too, and thick, real wiry-curly reddish brown hair that you'd be tempted, like, to scrub a frying pan with (which we did once). And Terry, like I say, is the opposite end of the size world from Stu. And he's got a very kind of handsome face, the way little guys will, like Alan Ladd. Only something tells me Terry won't be needing any elevator shoes when all's said and done. And Pete O'Connor. Peter's another dark-haired Irish kid. Only he's taller and skinnier than Francis X, and he's got a scar on his face from when he ran through a glass door in sixth and they had to spend about five hours pickin' glass out of his face but the scar's faded out pretty much now and doesn't look bad at all. But of course about once a day Frankie would say, "Hey, dopewad! Look out for that glass door!" So if the scar fades out, you know, as long as Malone has a say-so, the memory won't.

And speaking of scars, I was just now looking at that snaky one on my thigh. I'd say it's permanent, for sure. I mean—no doubt about it—when a war comes up, which it probably will, it's my 'Identifying Scar' for the army. I should throw in, too, I guess, that I've got green eyes and like average brown hair, and I'm pretty much average size. But I'm looking at my leg here, too. And it's getting bigger. And my dad doesn't call me 'Bones' as much as he used to, which may mean something…that only time will tell, eh? And I'm getting taller, definitely, I mean, like maybe you could say right before my own eyes. But somebody tell me this one, 'cause I don't know—when you've got a scar that's for life, does it grow with the rest of your leg? I don't know.

And not that any of this growing was there on time for my next one-on-one meeting with you know who, which, don't worry, I'll talk about. But that particular little rumble with the shitface King of all Punks, in which, I might as well admit it, I caught my ever-livin' lunch, actually happened on one of the best days—I think I'd rank it in like a tie for the second-best day of my not-too-long-so-far life, which day, don't worry about this either, I'll also talk about, along with some other stuff, like the one it's tied with, and also the first of best days.

And about another certain happening that I've kinda kept

hanging, which keeping it hanging I thought would be a cool move, I mean the aftermath of that stuff about JL saying that the 'next time' we ran into the Vanderkells would be just like the last time we met 'em—you know, when we were sitting around triumphing after that supremely cool ball game in the Dead End? Well, it happened pretty much exactly the way Jackie said, which fact now, just saying it, gives me chills ('cause for one reason, prophecies are extremely cool) but...*shit*...what amazing total *shit-ness* how this can happen to me so quick.... Like in no time I'm sore in my throat...like I've been bawlin'...in no time, sometimes...when I think about JL.... And it's like I get tired, like I've run ten miles or something.

But let me just say it. It was a football game, this 'next time', and we set it up kind of like a private duel, 'cause we don't play in the same sports leagues as the Vanderkells. It was the Saturday after Thanksgiving. And we set it up for The Woods, in a field over near the Leavitt Dead End, which field I'll talk about later, too. And I'll make it simple, which is that they couldn't come close to stopping Jack. I mean he had 'em chasing him one way, and then the other way, and then some new other way, but always the wrong way. It was like he had those punks totally and completely on a string—I mean with him being the one deciding on everything that was gonna happen. Not even Myron Pateo, who I told ya about that roll block he put on me and who is one tough—I would say punk, but you don't call Pateo a punk—so I'll say bastard—not even Pateo could find JL. None of 'em could find him. Not Entemann, not Fox, and not you-know-who.

But Jackie found them, all right, every time they tried something, old stuff or new. And you know what I mean when I say certain tackles have a certain sound to 'em? I mean Jackie would all-out flatten those punks. And if they were ever dumb enough to try the middle, which for a very good reason, named Stu, they weren't very often dumb enough to do, they'd get pancaked there, too, every single time.

But that's gotta be a bit of a lie, I guess, 'cause, truth, the final was 21-14. So they had to be getting their way some of the time, the score proves. But I already talked about one game, and there's this other that I'm gonna talk about, too. So I won't bore you with details. It's just that there it was, happening the way Jack said it would, if it was just by one touchdown or not. Which makes me think how maybe you're kind of always secretly prophesying stuff. And— like I was saying about havin' enough of this or that kind of good thing in your life—you always hope enough of your secret little good prophecies will come true. So deep down you'll believe things will pretty much work out in your future, or enough of the time. I mean maybe even Frankie, if he didn't have some pretty bad stuff to work out, which maybe he will work out, could feel maybe enough of a difference coming out of some great wish-came-true days; even *one* could do it maybe, if it was good enough. But the thing you're afraid of is some kind of bad day that could, you know what I mean, be bad enough—which is a subject I'm gonna change for now.

And—I've been meaning to say this—I'm not like such a simpy admire admire admire guy—the way I probably sound sometimes. I can admit to a little jealousy, the old green monster in me. And I'll say stuff to myself now, now that I'm, you know, filling out before my own eyes—stuff like maybe things wouldn't always have been the way they

were, with JL on top of the ladder. Up north here, I'm starting to make stuff go for me in basketball in like this way
that I maybe never thought I could, not that I'm any hotshot, trust me. But things change, like my legs, and my arms.
And maybe after time, Jack Leonard wouldn't have been so
different from everybody, 'cause guys would have caught up,
which—funny isn't it?—is a thought that makes me feel like
shit, too, or right away really incredibly sad. 'Cause—and
it's not so hard to figure out—I don't think you'll ever get
past it, not if you lived to a hundred and twenty, if, when
you were a beat-up-able little punk, whose life could kind of
be confident, or not, depending, there was somebody who
stood up for you, every single time, with ass-kickin' power.

I mean, for just one of those for instances, there was
this time in fifth when I came out of the IGA across the
tracks from the Rock Island and I had a stack of baseball
cards I just bought and was opening a pack to get at the
gum, which was always my real goal (unlike Pete, who naturally traded his gum for cards every time and had maybe two thousand cards, none of them bent). And when I
had my gum unwrapped and was just about to pop it in—I
mean I could smell it and taste the powdery sugar on it—
there was this hand that swiped it right out of the jaws of
victory. And who it was, was one of three Ethelreda guys
(Ethelreda was the parish across the tracks east from CK).
And this kid was tough. And the two kids with him were
tough, in the way kids from other places always seem like
to be tough as shit. And the kid was laughin' and holding
his mouth open and holding the gum in his open mouth
without yet shutting down his choppers on it. And I had
enough guts or stupidity to call him something, I can't remember what, for the sake of honor. And then the three

of 'em started going, "Shut up!" "Yeah, shut up!" "Shut your yap!" all back and forth like they were singing *Frere Jacques* or *Row Row Row Your Boat*—when Jackie comes out of the IGA with, you know, a Mars Bar or a Peter Paul or something. And maybe you know what I mean when I say there's sayings that some people can pull off and some people can't? Well, I was saying something like, "Hand over the gum, you punk." Which was normal. And the kid was saying, "Make me, twerp." Which was normal. Then Jackie comes up and slips his Mars Bar or his Peter Paul in his pocket, and, like stepping right up to the kid, says, "Give him the gum." Which was normal, too, only there was that kind of husky voice and some feeling, like immediately, that the big-time shit was gonna fly. And the kid says, "Who do you think *you* are?" Which was normal, only he's instantly down now to about half as tough as he was an instant ago. And then Jackie says, "Go ahead and hit me and find out." Which would be exactly what I mean by one of those sayings that some people can pull off and some people can't.

And I don't know what all it was like for this kid to go from the top of the mountain to like Death Valley, all in one instant. But the kid was fallin' fast. So as proof that honor can make you do some really dumb stuff, he puts the gum on his tongue like he's giving himself the Holy Eucharist, and then starts sort of slobbo-chompin'. And then he does it—he flings a punch out at JL. Of course the other two are acting like they wanna see a fair fight, so they're not getting in it (which I leave you to decide the real reason for).

And to make a long story short, Jackie never hit the kid. He just tackled him and drove his butt down onto the parkway and then rolled him over face down and then got the old uncle-arm up behind the kid's back and then jacked it up—a little higher and a little higher. Only he wasn't saying, "Say Uncle." He was sayin', "Spit it out! Spit it out!" And then he jacked the kid's arm up his back again. And again. Until out came the gum, sort of like the classic white flag, only pink with teeth marks, and covered with punk saliva. Then JL let the kid up and told him and the other two Punketeers to get, you know, permanently lost and not come back across our path at any future time, ever. Or as the missal puts it, *per omnia saecula saeculorum*.

Then after that, JL and I were laughin' because—what did we win? Because who'd ever eat an Ethelreda kid's ABC gum? Which got us laughing our butts off thinking of all the things we'd eat before we ate that. Which I won't go into except to say we kept thinkin' up stuff till we laughed so hard we about cried. But then, when it was time for us to split, it kind of just suddenly hit me and I stopped laughin' and just kind of sincerely said, "Thanks, Jackie." Then he gave me the old crook-toothed smile and he gave me a soft tap-fist on the shoulder and said, "Any time, Kev. I mean it. *Any* time—ever."

But like I say, it of course happened. I mean that I finally did run into Val Prizer with nobody else in the world around, and no miracles coming my way. And like I say, it was on a day when one of the greatest things that ever happened to me, happened.

But, even though the event with the Rat happened second, let me get the bad shit out of the way first. Isn't that how we usually like to do it? Anyhow, it was in the snow, this bad-shit time, about two weeks after that 'next time' football game. So the memory was nice and fresh in Prizer's mind, if that's what you call what he's got upstairs. And needless to say, he'd been like a walking penalty for unsportsmanlike conduct during that game and after it, too, screamin' at his own guys, throwing his helmet down and almost breaking it when Jackie scored one time (which time the Rat K had to look all over the field for his j-strap 'cause Jackie faked him out if it so bad that even the Big-Game Spook'd a probably laughed); and then when the idiot Rat K face-masked Frankie Malone so bad he almost ripped Frank's head off (which, by the way, led FX into one of the most insane retaliation attacks I've ever seen, like really scary, though it wasn't getting him anywhere, when Big Joe Stupnicki, who was reffing the game with Entemann's brother for the Vanderkell side, broke it up); and, like I said, after the game, too, when our friendly Rat K kept yellin' about how the clock was wrong (even though it was Entemann's brother who kept it) and how there *had* to be more time and what a cheat the whole thing was and what a screw job and what an asshole everybody in the whole world was, and especially, though he had to mumble this one so low that not even his best buddy, who would be Satan, could hear it, what an asshole Big Joe Stupnicki was, because of course Big Joe had told our muscle-y, mustachy idiot that if he didn't keep his mouth clean and watch his actions, he was outa the game, like it or not.

But Val Prizer is plenty tough all right. No denying that. And playing middle linebacker for 'em, he did a pretty serious slam job on somebody or other, just about every play. And of course a couple of times after he just slammed *me*, through the earhole in my helmet, he repeated his little promise to me.

SO—when I was making my way through the snow, that time about two weeks later, heading home (as it turns out, it was on that trail that I never saw another horse on), I figured it was some seriously deep shit I was in, when I looked up and saw somebody up ahead of me, when I was just about half way between Devil's Hill and Longwood, which is to say the middle of nowhere.

And you know, speaking of prophecies, how I said that like (no matter what good things were happening) I figured just about all the time, those days, that Prizer was waiting for me somewhere. It's funny how ya get that feeling, so bad. And then when it happens, the feeling that, well, *here it is,* which like goes down to the very bottom of your guts. And there's that second truth, which I'll say again. I mean that if it's true that doing something really cool can make ya think positive for a long, long time—so it goes the opposite way if ya get the serious shit beat out of ya, even if it's only one time. But then let me throw in a third truth, which I know about, which is I think that we have a thing in our brain that gets us to make some kind of a nnnnnnnnnnnnnnnnnnnnnnnn-sound in our head till the bad memory, whatever it is, shuts up enough for us to keep on feelin' ok.

But there I was, knowing *here it is,* 'cause for that crazy reason that we keep on goin' ahead even if it looks bad, I kept on walking until there was no doubt about it. Prizer. And, like I say, nobody else around. Just dead winter. And it was gonna be dead me, no doubt. I felt, even, like if I shouted for somebody, it would just bring on a snow even deeper than the one on the ground—and that I'd be found frozen dead in it. But ya have that thing, like it's your pathway home and nobody has a right to stop ya from using it. And then there's that other thing—that somewhere your friends are watching, and your dad, and Mike Shannon. And that Patty Conlon is watching, which is a feeling that for reasons

I'll talk about, I had real, real bad, thinking Patty wouldn't think too much of a pitiful little chickenshit, which if ya operated and opened me up, you'd find sometimes inside there (and sometimes maybe inside everybody).

So on I went, for honor and idiot-hood. And didn't that shitface just make it like some scene out of a movie. I mean, it looked like he was tryin' out for the part of leading jag-off in some hoody punk movie—'cause there he was with this like hard-guy leather jacket that he's got and smoking, 'cause naturally he was smokin' by now, which I'm sure is why he was in The Woods, hiding out from his mom (but only her, 'cause as far as the Big-Game Spook was around to do anything about the butts, old Val, any time the feeling struck him, could maybe like make a pyramid out of all those chopped-off elephants' legs, climb the thing, and blow smoke up the nose of the family's giraffe head). And the way he said, when like an idiot I kept on walking right toward him, "Well...well...well. WHAT have we here." I swear t' God, he said that, just like some third-string, trying-to-be-a-hard-guy punk *actor*. And then naturally he flicks his butt like he was trying to break the world butt-flicking record.

Shit. Did ya ever just wanna say FUCK YOU. I mean spit it through your teeth so wicked ferocious that it was like you *shot* the guy you were aimin' it at. Well, that's how I felt; so I fired away. "FUCK YOU!" Which of course was pure suicide. But, I mean it, something about that fact of him blocking my pathway home suddenly really set off the lunatic in me. Also I knew there wasn't gonna be any discussions, just maybe a few spew words before the shit-kicking got started. Something about all that stuff like out of a movie made me know we were going straight to the next scene.

But it was like it was Pearl Harbor, believe me. No spewy warning, like I expected, or anything. Just a flying tackle and I found myself slammed before I knew it against this dead-branchy wintery tree that seemed like specially ice hard, and like a broken prong out of it jammed and ripped the back of my head, and I was like already shit beat before I could even say *kiss my ass*. And then he like goes Jack-the-Ripper insane, whip-lashin' like fifty madman gut punches into me while he had me stood up and half knocked cold against that tree. I mean he had me like choked at the collar with one hand, and the other was hammering me with those fifty whip punches in the gut, which a few of 'em got me clean, so I was like ready to puke out some maybe blood-colored guts.

And I couldn't do much more than like gag out somethin' about who did he think he was, tryin' to stop me from going where I want. But like I said, that crazy man didn't even go through any even of the little torturings or spew stuff about who's in charge of who in this world, and all the usual who's gonna make who do what. He just, without a word, roundhouses me in the side of my head, which like before ya know it makes me see the real stars, you know what I mean? Like we've all had it happen when it's real *stars*, with all those colors, and we all know it's not just anything, but a sort of once-or-twice-in-a-lifetime cream job that gets the true stars to shine.

So there I was—BANG!—knocked clean off that hard-as-hell, wintery ice tree and slammed into the snow, face down. And before I could start up again with my stuff about it being my right to walk my pathway home.... I mean I couldn't even gurgle any shit out before, still completely like silent, he's on me and he's got the back of my head in his two hands, the way he wanted to with the dog crap. And—no time for anything I mighta had t'say, anyhow—he's got my face shoved down in that snow so hard and so deep that I figure I'm gonna see my life pass before my eyes like they say drowning guys do. And he's not even saying anything. No triumphing whoop-de-doo spew. Nothin'. Just holding my face buried down deep in the snow, like he wants to make sure my life *does* pass before my eyes. I swear t'God. It was like he was waiting for just that. And I did. I got all goofy and limp as shit, and it was like I was gonna hear somebody say, "Okay, time to show 'm his life." But all that happened was just Prizer finally jumped off me so I could lift my head out of the snow but then him wasting no time in this no-words-just-dead-silence thing he had goin' and kicking me total-madman style, like hell t' pay, right in my side, with the toe of his boot, and then one last time with the heel on my back, like a sledgehammer, before he just walked off. No spew. No nothin'. But not like he was scared he mighta killed me. More like he was in his mind clapping his hands together the way Susie Shannon clapped hers when she put that forever-, and I mean FOREVER-COOL and perfected move on him at the sewer hole. And he never did say anything. He just looked back and laughed. And like when I was staggering up finally and I looked down that dead-white trail through the ice trees as he was walking off, I saw him light up a butt as like the last scene in his little punk movie, which he knew I was sitting in the theater watching, all by myself.

And I swear t'God I've wondered hard if it would be a mortal if I killed that guy. I swear t'God I've thought it. Did ya ever go through some dead serious revenge stuff in your head? I mean did you ever really get stuck on it bad, like it was something you could go over in your head for maybe a million years without getting bored for one billionth of a second? I suppose I should go to confession about it, 'cause maybe it's a mortal just thinking some of the stuff I thought for a while there. But I got some sweet revenge anyhow, and that was thanks to JL, too, in like this extremely cool and strange way, 'cause, which time I'll talk about too, I promise, one time after he died, Jackie Leonard appeared to me.

But I suppose you're laughing now, 'cause I told you this Satanic thing at the Ice Tree happened on like one of the best days of my life so far. Or maybe you forgot I said that. Anyhow, I need to tell ya that I was a delivery boy for the *Southtown Economist,* which meant that on Wednesdays after school I had my paper route and on Sunday mornings earlier than all get out. Then the first Monday of every month, you had to do your own collections, too, which was a way the paper made it so their boys could get a little extra each month, with tips. But to show you what a genius I was, I would take my tips and pay the bill for the people who weren't home when I collected, which, after my dad set me straight, I made the mistake of telling Francis Xavier Malone about, who said he'd had a *Southtown* route once, too, but which nobody knew about, because it was the only thing he ever quit faster than Cub Scouts. "But," he said, "I still made more dough than THE NUMBER-ONE BUTT HOLE CHUMP SUCKER THIS SIDE OF CHINATOWN!" Which I figured might become my name for a while but which fortunately, and I guess you could say unfortunately, too, had too many words in it for people to remember.

Anyhow, the incredible thing—though it never worked out that she was there when I rang the bell for collections—was that lo and behold, one of the houses on my route was

Patty Conlon's. But like I say, she was never there, 'cause wouldn't ya know it and just my luck, on Mondays and Wednesdays she had dancing. And who was there, was her dad, who was this very old man. I mean he was like twenty years older than her mom, who was the oldest mom of anybody in our class of ninety-three kids. He was like over sixty when Patty was born, and she was an only child; so when I came to collect, with her off at dancing, which by the way was just one more thing she beat the world at, the Conlons' house was about the quietest place on earth. And I'd ring the bell and I'd be scared shitless but I'd be praying please just this one time no dancing just this one time no dancing please God I'll like be good even to the punks and punkettes if it's just please this one time no dancing. And then like in that quiet, after about an hour, there'd be footsteps. And then—one more time—it wouldn't be Patty—but this old, old man. But he was maybe the nicest guy who ever was, old Mr. Conlon.

I mean it. It was unbelievable. "Kevin Collins!" he'd say, "come on in, my good man." And then he'd wink at me, and he'd say, kind of whispery, "Are ya hungry?" And then he'd like go off to the kitchen and he'd get me a Hershey Bar or one of these incredible brownies that he'd get from these Carmelite nuns someplace and then sometimes he'd invite me in and the two of us would sit there and maybe have a glass of milk and one of those brownies, which were so out of this world. And I mean, I don't know if you've ever like loved somebody and then been in her house when she wasn't there? I mean, whoa, it's like something I cannot describe, how much you're kind of going crazy with loving her. And on top of it, her house was so quiet and peaceful, with her dad this old, old guy who was about maybe the kindest man who ever was and him treating me as if I was his own, I'd guess you'd say grandkid—which gave me the picture on how cool he must have been to Patty, and her mom, too, who was once or twice there but most times at her job as a college teacher at the U of C. Then the dead-cold-buckle-your-knees deal—I mean the kind of thing that makes you *hurt* it gets to you so bad: on the wall where the stairs went up toward her room (which would be for me the most private pathway in the world), there were a bunch of family pictures—but there was this one of Patty, up on her toes doing some ballet move, holding her hands in a circle in front of her like there was somebody invisible she was hugging, and with her head turned to ya, kind of over her shoulder. No. I mean I cannot tell you about the serious *pain* I felt, feeling so good looking at that picture, in like the quietest house ever, even when I'd see the real Patty every day at school, which was already putting a very, very steady ache on my entire being.

But then…. I mean I don't like to talk about this stuff because it makes me so sad. So I'll say it fast. Old Mr. Conlon…he died one day. They said he hadn't been well for a long time, from some disease in his blood (which, let me put in, never got him to act even one time like he felt sorry for himself), and that one day he just died. And I don't want to talk about it, that's all. So I'm going to go straight on to another thing, which was a Saturday when we were playing some no-equipment tackle football in the snow in the Priests' Yard at CK.

So—we were playing this game of snow tackle. And then it came time for confessions, which was something we always went to, even if it suspended a game for a while, and not just because we wanted to compare penances, which of course we would always do, Frankie naturally receiving some very incredible shit, every single time. Though when he told us one time that Fr. McCarthy told him to just go out and shoot himself, we wrote that off as a crock, not that we didn't, you know, do the usual, which would be talk about starting a collection so we could get poor Frankie the gun and the bullets he needed and asking him what kind of gun he liked best, though by this time we were in these kind of all-serious and caring voices calling it a *rod*, and did he want a gold-studded leather holster for his *rod*, and would he like maybe a bandallero for the bullets, and Terry thought maybe a sombrero, too, for style, because it would be no expenses spared for our dear, dear friend and we'd be ever so glad to help all we could when it came to his blowin' his brains out the way God wanted him to, with what we were calling now the God-rod, and all the usual kind of bullshit that guys just keep coming up with, till hell freezes over, out of who knows where. I mean guys like George P could come up with this kind of stuff to beat Einstein.

Anyhow, like I say, it came time for confessions. Before we head off, though, Malone's gotta wizz, so he whips it out and right in the Priests' Yard snow writes a nice bubbly-yellow FRANK. Which is stuff you just don't do. Or of course you do do, but NOT in the Priests' Yard, unless you're insane. But need I say more. Anyhow, he adds that if he'd had a beer (which he hadn't in his life yet, as far as I knew) he would've written the full FRANK MALONE, which got Stu to say, "As if it was gonna be some other FRANK." But anyhow, this gets us to start asking what if he had two beers and then three beers. And the stuff naturally gets crazier and crazier 'cause if there's anybody that rivals George P at this kind of stuff, it is Francis X—who then starts say-

ing what he could piss-write with a whole six-pack in 'm
and then a case in 'm, and a keg ('cause of course he does
know all the ways you *buy* beer in). And naturally it got
more and more to be the kind of thing that if Fr. McCarthy
did tell him to go out and blow out his brains for, it would
be perfectly logical. And I can't remember really how it all
went, except of course for BB's playing a major role, but
when he got to what he could piss-write with a whole keg
in him, it was like all one sentence. And this kind of thing
was one of the thousand or so things Malone was famous
for at CK because one time when Mother Mad gave him a
thousand-word punishment composition on the way Jesus
taught us responsibility and self-discipline, he got her back
by making it all one big thousand-word sentence, which
all of us went over and were laughing, goin' *holy shit* over,
and which we told him would be suicide if he handed it
in, while of course we were saying, too, it would be a real
shame if he didn't. But on the whole-beer-keg-in-'m thing,
I'll never forget the very final words he said he'd piss in the
Priest's Yard snow, which were, "And if you've got any myna
birds—before you *pluck* 'em, *FUCK* 'em—signed FRANCIS
XAVIER MALONE." I mean I promise for the rest of my
life if I ever think of the Priests' Yard with snow on it, I'll
be seeing that little kind of poem of Frankie's, written in
bright yellow.

But the reason I mentioned this day was that it was
the Saturday after Patty's dad died; and when all us goofs
went into church, and, you know, in the quiet, the goofing
off stopped, which is an extremely cool feeling, there she
would be. Patty Conlon. With her scarf pulled up for her
head-covering and her head bowed down, praying. George
P did sort of knuckle-punch me, you know, in that spot in

the upper arm where a knuckle-punch works best, but all this kind of stuff stopped really fast because every goof I was with (and you pretty much know 'em by now) knew Patty was there praying for her dad.

And it was a good thing, actually, that I was with the idiots because I was about ready to, I don't know, start trembling and fall over or something. I mean with the quiet, and with the sadness that Patty was feeling over her dad, who was so great to me, inviting me in for stuff even in like his last days. And seeing her there praying. I mean, when I saw Patty anywhere these days, even when she was happy, which you can believe was her normal way, it was enough to send some sort of insane, aching kind of warm thing all through me.

And yet it was pretty much bad luck, too, my being stuck with all these, you know, goofballs. But Pete O'Connor led the charge to the confession line, and that got everybody kind of in order. And by some miracle, nobody went out of his way to make me feel stupid for putting myself last, though I'm dead positive they all knew I just wanted to get as much of the feeling of her being there as I could get. And it worked out, with Frankie's taking the usual eternity to get his sins told, that when I was through, the time had just about come for Benediction. And when I came out of the confessional, and looked, Patty was still there. Which meant for sure she was staying for Benediction, which, if you ask me, is one of the coolest things that ever happens in church, and not just because it's short. Lots of times we'd all stay for it, even though that put off the game a bit more, because Benediction was so cool, and spooky beautiful, and short but in a way that kind of left ya stunned.

In my confession, I'd told Father Garvey the usual about

my sins of now and again torturing and terrorizing the punks and punkettes; and he asked me some pretty reasonable stuff about did I ever think, if I laid any kind of mean stuff on too thick, that it could hurt their confidence or feelings about themselves and make 'em feel pissed (he said angry) in a not good way. You know, and would I like it if I got the same thing from somebody bigger. So I felt honest contrition there. And I told him about my swearing, which I was truly sorry for, too—I mean for the bad part, which is if ya ever get even slightly close to what Prizer did with Doc Schwendrowski—but which I was glad he didn't make me promise to give up the good part, because, I don't know…. I mean, sort of the way you smile all the time to show you're a nice cooperative kind of guy, and to let people know you're with 'em rather than against 'em, which is cool, I think you swear all the time to make sure you never get like gooey nice and become a dead lame simp. He got me to think, though, about how, as he put it, you can demean yourself pretty bad, along with people and things around you, with language.

And, for me, it always feels good, and warm, to go to confession and later to like chew over thoughts like the ones Fr. G put in me. And when I came out and saw all the morons were gone but Patty was still there, I knew I was staying for Benediction, too, even though it meant I'd miss what Frankie had to say about his penance, which wasn't, naturally, going to be three Hail Mary's and a Glory Be (which all the rest of us got) unless, maybe, Father gave him for practice a quick-emergency penance, say for like if he'd finished his last cigarette and the firing squad was gettin' itchy to finish 'm off.

And there's not a whole lot more to say. You'd a had to've

been there, I guess. But I was feeling this thing in my head about how I had no right to kneel too close to where Patty was and yet because I like really knew her dad (though I'd never said a word to her about that, and she didn't to me either, even though I figure he had to've talked to her about me) I thought *maybe* I could kneel a little bit close. And I had this like incredible desire to hear her sing the *O Salutaris Hostia,* which if you're not Catholic is this hymn about asking God to help us 'cause our enemies are kind of breathing right down our neck (which I hoped I wasn't, I mean down hers), and then asking God, too, for endless days in heaven. And I wanted even more (because there's something extremely cool about not just saying something, but chanting it) to hear Fr. McCarthy go, in that long, echo-y way, *Panem de caelo praestitisti eis,* and sort of in the dark because the lights always seem to be down low at Benediction, and with the incredible beautiful gold of the monstrance there, firing out like a kind of miniature sun right there in the darkness, and the church pretty much otherwise totally quiet, except for the altar boy clacking the censer. And then hear, not the crowd, but, somehow, if I could, just Patty chanting back, in her girl's voice, *Omne delecta-mentum in se habentem,* which if you're not Catholic is about how all the sweetness in the world is in the bread of God.

So I kind of gutsed it out and got myself close enough but not so I'd look, if I got caught, like some idiot who didn't care about her privacy or that her dad died five days ago. And I did—I heard her both sing the hymn and chant the prayer, in that beautiful voice she has, which I was like insane to hear—I mean so much that I hurt my fingers crossing 'em. And that's it. That's all I'll say, except that, because the feeling was so good I felt like I'd maybe stolen it,

I hightailed it out of there and got back to the snow game before, I think, Patty could really tell how close I'd knelt to her. But then I think she had to know. I don't know.

And I won't go into what all that the idiots had to say about my being late getting back to the game. Except to say, I got a lot of ribs and biffs and a lot of Kevvy boy's in love, Wooo-ooo, Wooo-ooo, with even JL joinin' in.

But then about a week later I had this thing. 'Cause it came time again for my *Southtown* collections. And of course you know, don't ya, that it was that same day that I later got the shit beat out of me by you know who. But as part of my job, of course, I was supposed to collect at Conlons'. And the first thing I thought, with Mr. Conlon just put in the grave, was not only did I not shiv a git (which was one of our cooler sayings) what Malone would say, I'd go blast it right in his ears that, *yeah,* I took my tips from other people and paid the bill for the Conlons and left them alone. And I was like really fist-clenching positive of this, too, because of course I thought that going up to that door and ringing the bell and waiting and then *not* seeing Mr. Conlon, that it would have, like, so much sorrow for me now. It would be…. I don't know. I mean, I could see myself just waiting there for those sounds inside the door. Minutes and minutes. And then the sounds never coming, because that's what it was when somebody died. The quiet behind the door just turned into like complete silence. And no matter how long you waited, the lights inside would always stay dark.

So I wouldn't go. I just thought stuff like at least Mr. Conlon made it till he was old…though he had a daughter who was only just goin' on thirteen, the way I was then, too—I mean more now than just twelve and a half.

But. There was this thing. A thing Patty and I had in

common, which I haven't said yet. *Her* house, too, was right on The Woods, on this short little half-block stretch of Winchester that runs north a bit off 91ST and dead ends even before 90TH. And 90TH doesn't even go through there anyhow, 'cause around there it's all just The Woods, with all the cross-streets cut off. This little stretch has The Woods, too, all along the east side of it. So it's really, really quiet. No cars going through because of the no outlet and no houses all along the side that the Conlons' house looks over at, just trees in a forest. So it's sort of like a secret street, especially in the deep snow.

But what I would always do, because there was no cyclone fence there, would be to go to Conlons', which for some reason even more than the chocolate, I'd save for last on my route, and then cut through The Woods to that horse trail that I mighta seen the last horse on, a few years back, and then head home. So even though I wanted nothing to do with going up to a door where there wouldn't be this incredibly friendly old man anymore, I did go ahead and make my way down the Conlons' street, so I could take my usual cut home through The Woods, which I loved in the snow, that is, if there weren't any smokin' punks in there trying to star in some shitty hood movie.

And it psyched me, thinking how I could pay the Conlons' bill and leave them alone. I was thinking, too, because it gave me a cool feeling, even though it was a completely moronic idea, that I'd keep the paper route until we were all dead and gone, and keep the system going so that the Conlons *as long as Kevin Collins was their paper boy* would never pay for a *Southtown Economist* (of course now I did start smiling hard, and then chuckling, thinking what Frankie would think of that sappy moronism, and of how maybe tomorrow

I'd let him know I'd thought this stuff, so he could go nuts with jokes, even though they'd be at my expense, which you might've guessed I liked to do). But now I looked up, you know, from my black rubber boots, the kind with the clips that we all wore all winter, which clips I'd been studying hard for some reason—and I saw that, at Conlons', in an upstairs room, there was a light on (one I'd never seen before on collection day, or delivery days, either), and one downstairs, in what I knew was their kitchen.

I had instantly then about a billion feelings going through me. For starters, looking at lights in upstairs windows was enough to knock my eyes back down to my boots, for good. Throw in, too, that the only reason I would've had for ringing the Conlons' bell would be like as a debt collector, right after Mr. Conlon passed away. So I had this *I'd-rather-be-dead* sort of multi-powerful OH-NO comin' at me from several directions. But my mind was like instantly raging with schemes on the off chance that, today, there'd be no dancing. And when your head, or maybe it's your guts, or heart, or all three teamed up, they're in the like *I've-gotta-have-this* gear, it's amazing how they come up with stuff, or maybe more how (no matter about the OH-NO's and the *I'd-rather-be-dead* stuff) they get ya to *do* the stuff they come up with.

Which in my case here was go with the odds that Mrs. Conlon will be there and that she'll be the one who answers the door and then you can just say to her something like you just want to say thanks for all the chocolate and stuff and that you're very sorry that Mr. Conlon passed away—and then, buster, you're gonna have to hope you can get the words out because, right while you're saying them, there will be Patty coming down from her room to see who's there, not knowing it's you, but now sort of having to come and say hello and catch you in the act of being thought-ful, not like the average jerk your age and not like any debt collector, which you will be dead before you ever act like. And while I was thinking this and was as sick-nervous as I've ever been, I could hear every stupid clack-jingle of my boot buckles—and that's because I wasn't just thinking but moving—right up to the door, with that whole-body feeling of I can't believe I'm doing this but here I am doing it—and all because there was still that raging in the head-guts-heart, which will bring you right up the front walk of a girl's house and put your finger on the bell and holy-shit *ring* it for ya. Which it did!

But now there would be that quiet again, even though there were those lights on. And some time passing, before a sound came. But then there was the sound, and some-body coming. So, that heart-head-guts in me was getting my speech all ready. And with the sound of the door now unlocking and the handle turning, I was really revvin' up, I mean, so bad that I'd have probably blurted out my speech so cold-clumsy-fast that I might as well have gone on ahead then and asked for every last red penny of the bill-money and reminded Mrs. Conlon that oh, *by the way*, Mr. Conlon was always my most *generous* tipper (which he was, by a mile). But when the door opened, it wasn't Mrs. Conlon.

So I was an idiot. 'Cause sure enough, it was *her*, or as much of her as she let out from the door, which was pretty much just her face, because you know the way girls are at doors, keeping them pulled over them sort of like a blan-ket, and just peeping out, even when it's not cold.

And it's funny how even though I'd prayed a million times a minute, all those times before, that it would be Patty who opened the door, I was always glad, like as if somebody just stopped me from committing a crime or something, when it was old Mr. Conlon instead. And now when it *was* Patty there, or as much of her as I could see (which by the way was like this special picture of her face, which looked so pretty that it took me right up to whole new kinds of idiot-ness), I was about sure I'd robbed the Evergreen Bank and shot Mr. White, who was the guard there and this incredibly nice guy and the husband of my kindergarten teacher.

"Patty, who is it?"

I think we were both pretty much glad to hear somebody else, because we hadn't said anything yet. And I know Patty was glad because it gave her a chance to like skedaddle away from the door and go off and whisper stuff to her mom ('cause of course there was no *way* she could answer her mom's question out loud). And I know I was glad because she hadn't slammed the door in my face, although I thought I oughta close it a little on me 'cause it was really cold out, which I was starting to really feel now in like my lower back and my neck and my butt. And I thought I might've detected like a little pee in my drawers, which of course would ice up on me the way Pin Flynn's entire leg did this time Frankie unloaded on him. The Pin didn't even know he'd been hosed till Frankie had like already reholstered. And then the way the pee froze, the Pin's pants looked sort of like a banana-popsicle wrapper with freezer burn.

But now it was Mrs. Conlon at the door, and, even though Mr. Conlon just died, she invited me in, the way Mr. C would, which was kind of amazing to me, that she could be that nice now, and cool. And she said, "Take off your boots and coat, Kevin. I told Patty to look for a Hershey bar, so maybe you'll go back in the kitchen and see if she's found it."

Right away then, I started with my speech about how I

just came to say I was sorry and all. But I wasn't very far into it when she put her finger to her lips. And she had in her hand already the five-dollar bill that Mr. Conlon would always give me on the two-dollar charge for the month. And lickety-split she put the five in my hand, in that warm way sometimes people will shake your hand with both their hands. And they were so warm and nice, her hands, especially on mine, which were pretty much freezing cold 'cause I was just using my pockets that day, no gloves. And when I started with my speech again, she smiled at me in this really incredible nice way and put her finger up to her lips again; so I just sort of shut up, and put the money in my pocket.

But now Patty was standing in the kitchen door, so there I still was, saying stuff like I really oughta be going. But then when Mrs. Conlon just said, "Sshhh," kinda loud even, I really gave it up. And though I kept up with a few, last goofy looks, and I was pretty sure it was a miracle I didn't fall on my butt, I foot-pried off my boots, the way you get good at, so your shoes don't come off inside. Then I took off my stocking cap, which I stuffed in my sleeve as I was taking off my coat, which when I got out of it I gave to Mrs. Conlon. Then I slammed down my hair, or at least I hope I did, from the weird like electrical stuff it does when ya take off a stocking cap.

And it's so crazy, you know, how you sort of by instinct do all that stuff, I mean, saying ya gotta go when you not only don't have to go but you wanna stay more than breathe. But then if you're lucky, there's somebody there who knows you're bull-shittin' and doesn't pay any attention to you. And because I had exactly that luck, I found myself in this really pretty unbelievable situation, sitting with Patty Conlon, just the two of us, in her kitchen—with my pants dry, after all, and I hope with my hair not looking like some guy's they forgot to shave before they electrocuted him. And it was quiet again, the way Conlons' always was (and I mean, if ya can say this, even the lights at Conlons' were quiet), because Mrs. Conlon was gone off already, to read one of her books for college teaching, which I think Patty sneaks a read of maybe fairly often because she's the only one in the class who nails higher test scores on reading than Pete O'Connor.

I guess ya'd say Patty has light brown hair, though some people might call it blonde. And nobody would forget her eyes were blue or how beautiful they were. Or how she always kind of looked like she was blushing a little 'cause she has this fair skin but always some rosy color in her cheeks, which dead kills me, believe me. As it was killing me right then, believe that, too. But neither of us had said the first word yet, and that was getting officially weird. She wasn't, though, completely acting like she was only doing what her mom had, you know, forced on her, which you'd naturally expect from a girl in a situation like this.

So I tried sort of the first words that came into my head. "I saw you at confession last Saturday." And immediately I thought what a jerk I was because this might look like I was trying to make her cry or something, with some kind of cheap shot. And then I was thinking, too, that this was like way too *big* a thing to say, which you can't get into. But, then, speaking of big things, isn't it nuts how you can see somebody a thousand straight days, at like school, but then you see them at something different, like the grocery store, and it's for some reason this really huge deal. That is if you give a sh…. I mean if you care, or something, who the person is.

But she didn't do anything sad or try to be cool. She just went with the plural, which I considered normal for a girl. "I saw you guys," she said. "I think Peterson and Malone and Leonard and Stupnicki."

"Terry, too," I said. "Thillens, I mean. And Pete O'Connor. We sort of go most Saturdays, you know, 'cause we're right there, either in the Priests' Yard or playing ball at Vanderkell. So we go over."

"We go mostly Friday evenings," she said. "I mean the girls. But maybe we don't go quite once a week."

"Maybe guys need to go more than girls," I said, you know, sort of bein' funny just a bit, if you can call that funny, which it'd never in a million years pass for if I was with the idiots.

But in a situation like this you're not looking for major comedy. 'Cause there's this weird thing going, like you don't wanna become *friends* with the girl you're insane over, yukkin' it up and backslapping and that kind of bullsh (which was still a word we were using). It's much more like you wanna grin, kinda sly like, rather than laugh out loud. So, trust me, I did go full nuts inside, when, over my saying that thing about guys needing more confession than girls, she sort of just grinned a little and said, "Probably so."

But like another thing that you have to keep from happening is going oooh I love you or won't you please please *please* be my girlfriend or any other pathetic puke material. So I wasn't gonna be such a goof as to ask her did she like Benediction and singing the *O Salutaris Hostia* or the fact that I knelt so close to her that we could've been a duet. I just sort of upside-down grinned, I mean like frown-smiled in a way that said, sort of dippy funny-ish, *Yeah, well, girls aren't such angels either, as far as I can tell.*

And then we were both semi-smiling at each other, but

not in any way like *Gee, aren't we gonna be great buddy-ol' pals*. But then after our not saying anything again for like an hour (which was really just a few seconds or so, which I'm sure you know), she was gonna like just slam the Hershey bar on me, all wrapped still; and like that was gonna be it, because, well, that was gonna be it. So she did, she just, not smiling anymore, sort of table-slid the Hershey over to me, kind of like yeah she *was* just doing what her mom made her do. But we were both still sitting, sort of on two sides at one of the table's corners, which beat very solidly, believe me, something like her at one end and me at the other. And thanks to that old raging guts-heart-brain of mine, which I already owed maybe ten jillion bucks, I came up outa nowhere with this pure inspiration. I like tapped on the Hershey, so she'd know what I meant, and I said, "How do you break 'em?"

So now there we were, comparing ways of breaking a Hershey. And, you know, sort of fako arguing like we really shave a git. I was saying, which was true, that I liked to start on one end and take out a row at a time and then bite off a square at a time out of the row. She was saying she liked to break off a single square at a time, and of course adding that her way was way, *way* better than mine. But it was all fako, you know, the sort of stuff that you do because being too agreeable would still for some reason wreck the whole deal—and also 'cause for some reason you're kinda chickenshit about everything, especially like showing you gave a shit.

"But," I said, "I'll bet anything you can't break off your single square perfectly clean."

"How much?"

"Half the Hershey, which I believe your mom gave to me."

"Deal."

And trust me, I loved the way she said that. But of course we didn't shake hands. I just sort of slid the Hershey back her way, and she with her eyes not on me, just on the Hershey, took it and started to work on the wrapper. But this turned out to be this amazing thing, too, just watching her hands, which of course I'd seen every day at school, but now opening the Hershey wrapper. It was like that see-somebody-at-the-grocery-store thing. And of course I thought I was pretty well screwed on the bet when I saw how like incredibly graceful and coordinated her fingers were, like Fr. McCarthy's at the *Lavabo,* with the towel. But then there was nothing in the universe I wanted to do more than lose the fako-stupid bet and share the Hershey bar with her.

Of course when she said her square was clean, I argued with her that she was full of it (which *it,* we all know rhymes with.... But, speaking again of not demeaning, it's also cool when you don't swear with girls, you know, like you don't with the Doc. Of course—and you know how they do this—whenever the girls at school would turn to us and go "Sshh!" Frankie would always quickly say "it," which believe me was always perfect). But now Patty settles our argument to her liking by just popping the square into her mouth, which when she's there eating the chocolate in front of me, smiley, all bratty and stuff, drives me nuts about forty-seven jillion different ways. Take that, Wonder Bread. But then because I'm just not gonna be out of inspirations this day, I throw some bullsh at her about how she has a guest at her house, and I start like fako clearing my throat and nodding my head back at the Hershey. And then she like groans like it's the number one agony since Jesus under the INRI (which George P said his dad said stood for Iron Nails Ran In), but she breaks off a square for me. And where's she gonna put it when my heart-brain-guts has my hand open out on the table. I mean she did her job, which naturally was to act like she'd just been shot in the guts with some kind of flaming arrow, but I got the chocolate right where I wanted it.

Then we got kind of like cool with it all. I mean the sharing of the Hershey. And of course I'm loving the nice and slow one-square-at-a-time method now, though I could never in a million years say something royally puked-out like, while I was winking at her or something puke-ish, I sure do agree now that one-square-at-a-time is the world's best system. But of course this is actually what I'm thinkin'. And she of course can't get out of it. So there we were, one square at a time, working our way nice and slow through that chocolate bar. And we started talking about school and stuff, dumb stuff, but it was cool. It was nothing, though, compared to this incredibly cool thing about just eating some kind of food with somebody. I don't know. I mean with her breaking off a piece for me, and giving it to me. And the two of us actually like havin' a little meal together. It was like that see-somebody-at-the-grocery thing again— but you add to it that for some reason, don't ask me what it is, you feel like you shouldn't act like a jerk *at all* when you're sharing some food together like that, even if it's just a chocolate bar. It's sort of like you're really glad, the way they say you'll be grateful later in life about piano lessons, that your mom and dad taught you manners. Or sort of like it's another one of those things where you grow up twenty years in ten seconds, and it's fun and feels really good, sort of like your body all of a sudden got really light, and warm, or something. And we had sort of a cool little generosity fight over how I thought she should get the last square and she thought I should get it. So we just sort of left it sitting there in the shiny foil, which is something I'm positive I won't forget (which up in the pueblo once, I should say too, I made that square into a circle, same way as I made the tin foil into a paten).

But then all of a sudden it hit me like going into some silence where you'd never hear sound again, even though you weren't deaf, that Patty would never in her life see her dad again—and that, inside, she must be about sadder than anyone I'd ever known in the world. Then maybe it was the way we both got all quiet again, I don't know. Or maybe she just flat-out read my mind. But what she said was, "My dad told me how much you like chocolate." And then, like the second after she said this, her lips started shaking, like really bad. I mean really bad. And she was crying. And if it had been anybody else in the entire world, maybe even another girl in our class, or maybe even Frankie, I'd have like reached over and hugged her, or him. But it was the same as when we couldn't shake on the bet. So I was glad when she stopped pretty much right away, out of pride I'd say—and good for her—'cause I felt sort of ashamed of myself for not helping her with anything more than keeping my trap shut.

I told her then that I better go. And I hope my heart-brain-guts, which had been so smart about everything else, found out for me the right way to send those words across, along with some invisible feelings. And maybe it did, because she was like really nice and fought back to be smiling again, which pride I knew, that very second, was one of those things that woke up in me some other whole new sleeping thing, some really good sleeping thing. And she walked me to the door, too, and while I was jackin' on my boots, she got me my coat, all of which was very cool. Then while I dressed up, she stayed there, which was cool, too. And when I'm about to go, she asks me, "Why did you come today? Today's Tuesday. You usually come Mondays."

And a million things were going through my head like I oughta just lie and say because I hoped and prayed you'd be here if I came on Tuesday. But the truth was I thought it *was* Monday, 'cause as it turns out, the day before was the 8TH of December, which we got off for the Immaculate Conception but we all went to Mass for the obligation, so I musta thought it was Sunday or something, and that today was Monday. So all I did was make a dumb mistake. But I didn't want to say that, because I had this total premonition that something very good was coming if I didn't play it nonchalant-like and say *I don't know, I thought it was Monday.* So I just sort of stood there and smiled like an idiot. And then as I'm walking out the door and looking back on somebody who I'm pretty sure is the saddest girl in the world, just standing by herself there in the hall of that quiet house, she says, "On Mondays and Wednesdays, I have dancing."

Which I played it cool at (as if I didn't know) and then nodded at, and then left. But which I was going absolutely nuts out of my mind at, because it had to be her cool way of saying, *So come again on a Tuesday, okay.* And for that, and every other reason I've talked about, until I got half way home in The Woods, and even after the shit beating at the Ice Tree, this was the number-one best day in my life up to that point.

Up in the pueblo I felt this, with no doubts, even though I had to put an old towel under my head so blood wouldn't get all over my pillow, because from that prong on the Ice Tree I got the kind of gash you only hope your hair will be able to grow back over. I luckily didn't have any lump showing from the roundhouse to my skull. But I had the greeny purple again, too, from where Prizer booted me with all his might in the side. And I probably had like the name of his boot tattooed on my back, too. So there I was, all right, at love-and-revenge Riverview, riding the roller coaster— and I mean The Bobbs—between goin' nuts with my love for Patty and going nuts with my total hatred for Val Prizer, who I wouldn't care if I heard that a semi rolled over on. But Patty was so cool she made me think a lot more of her than him, at least if you're talking about quality, not quantity.

I got spared that night having to explain my broken head to my mom and dad, because they were out and Mary Clare, our sitter, was cool with me keeping my hat on while me and the punks ate pizza. In the morning, too, I slipped off early to the 7:15, which I'd just do sometimes, of course with the parents having no objections. Of course I never said to them how the truth was I liked to slip off to an occasional weekday mass because it was absolutely and completely and perfectly punk free. Anyhow, I was gone before anybody saw the gash, and the bleeding had stopped, and I had it cleaned up pretty much with a shower and a real like easy washing of my hair. So nobody noticed, really, till there was a bit of cap swipin' on the way home and I got whacked a bit by Scotty McKinnon, who didn't mean anything by it, and I started bleeding again.

Naturally, though, I was walking home that day with Bobby Stu, and a little later (I swear t' God it was right about at the Murder Spot) Stu saw me get blood on my hand when I reached up under my cap to check the damage. It sort of spooked him some, I guess, because he was like instant-ly really kind of worried about me, 'cause there was pretty much blood, and really wet and red. And I guess it was just the way he acted—I mean so kind of worried. I don't know. But I broke a rule. When he asked me what happened—after I made him swear he'd tell nobody else—I told him about that shit-faced rat punk, the whole deal, even the thing there, at the Murder Spot, which made 'Little Stu' go kind of weird silent all the rest of the way to his house.

And then this really cool thing happened (and it hap-pened every day after that for some time), which, like my time in the quiet kitchen with Patty, helped me get my mind a bit more off Prizer when I was up in the pueblo—though it was still a pretty solid ride on the Bobbs up there, night af-ter night. I mean what happened was, when we got to Stu's house, which was almost a block before mine and where he'd usually leave me and go in, he didn't go in. He didn't say a single word. He just let me keep on walking home. But when I got to my house, I looked back—and there was Bobby, still out there, and then giving me this kinda wave, to let me know he'd been lookin' after me.

CHAPTER SIX

WINTER OF SEVENTH

GEORGE JOHNSON'S JL

There was this time a little later that winter, and my mom and dad were out for dinner, because it was Friday. So we had Mary Clare again, and she was being a real ace, because she had the entire brainless trust—I mean Johnny, Katie, Dave, Peggy, and Annie—pretty much locked away in Mom and Dad's room, watching *The Wizard of Oz,* which I'll admit is extremely cool (and does that movie kind of get into your dreams, the way it gets into mine sometimes?). But I'd seen it twice. So I was downstairs in the tv room, where I wanted to be anyhow because on the *Friday Night Fights* the main event featured Henry Hank, and Henry was by about a hundred miles my favorite heavyweight.

The snow was falling deep in this huge storm. And the tv screen was the only light I had on in the tv room, so I could really see the blizzard outside, especially because in the back yard we had this spotlight shining, which lit up the coming-down flakes (or I should say coming-down-and-then-blowing-up-and-around-and-then-coming-back-down-heavy-again flakes)—and our spotlight had 'em lit up the way, you know, a street lamp lights up snowflakes, which is so cool and beautiful it makes you walk backwards after you've passed the lamp, so you can keep looking back at the light and the lit-up flakes and the dark all around the light. I love nights like this. And I loved Henry Hank. So I was in the mood, all right, when on came the old "Brought to you by Gillette Blue Blades!" and the old "Na *NA* Na! na na *Na* na na!"

And there was this really comfortable blanket we had. It was this kinda worn-down, brown-and-white checked thing called an afghan. I loved that, too, and I had it wrapped all up over my shoulders with my hands sort of clipping it under my chin. And still no punks; so it was still cool. *Laudamus te,* Mary Clare. And *Adoramus te.* And *Glorificamus te.* And when at last it was Henry in the ring, with all the handshakes out of the way and the bell finally rung and him circling with his opponent, or should I say about-to-be victim, I was already ready, with my grip tightened on that blanket and my palms startin' to sweat and my mind imagining me making jabs with my left, jabs with my left, jabs with my left, all the while gettin' ready my righthand bomb. For when it was Henry Hank in the ring, that meant only one thing: somebody, and not Henry, was any minute now gonna be goin' down for good. Lights OUT!

Oh, man, how my dad and I loved Henry Hank. I don't know if you know Henry. But I'm talking about him this way because he seems to have disappeared and you don't hear about him anymore, which I don't like to talk about. But he was a like blackasnight colored guy, and sort of lean for a heavyweight, but tall—a kind of Abe Lincoln kind of guy, who made you know it was dead true, all right, when you heard he could take every man in town—and who made you think, too, like he had to have the deepest voice you ever heard, and humongo hands. I mean hands so big they'd make you laugh they scared ya so much, which for some reason, the being scared, can make ya laugh like that.

And when was it comin'? When was it comin'? Any second now. Any second. No way not. So I was gripping the corners of the afghan tighter and tighter under my chin. And diggin' my fingertips like really hard into my palms. Left jab. Left jab. Left jab. Henry didn't have to mess much with bobbing and weaving. No way. He just waited, and let his opponent move. Let that pitiful *sucker* do all the dancing. And dancing. Until he made that one false dance step, yes. Until then, Henry waited—and jabbed. And jabbed. Left. And left. Waiting. And waiting. Until....

"Oh YES! Oh, *YES*, Henry! *YES!* YYYES! THERE IT IS—THE RIGHT!"

I know I was screamin' something like this when it happened. I mean that lightning, onepunch, righthand *finito*: the full SO-LONG, PARDNER! And the thrill, which came with the complete terrorization. "OH YES! YYYESS!" And that I was like laughing with happiness, screamin', standing with the afghan spread out like wings now over my shoulders, triumphing, raising my hands, thinkin' like I was right inside Henry, who had his hands raised and was walking the ring, triumphing the way boxers do.

And that I was walking around, too, and hollering, with my hands raised—when I heard the whistling of the storm come right in the house—because the front door opened. It was my mom and dad, come home from dinner. And when

I saw my dad, I hollered, "Aw, Dad, shoot, you JUST missed it! Henry Hank! It was incredible! One punch! BAM! The usual! He's so incredible! I love the guy!"

My mom just sort of, you know, shook her head with fako disgust, 'cause if she acted like she thought guys were disgusting over boxing, the truth was she really just thought we were stupid (which I bet about a million bucks Patty does, too). But she wasn't gonna be coming in and joining my little party. She headed up, kind of fako grossed out but smiling, saying, "Good night, *boys.*" Dad, though, came over and into the tv room and sat with me and asked me for the blow by blow of the knockout as the Gillette song came back on. And it was so cool, in that sort of gray light from the tv, with me getting ready my right-hand bomber—jabbing, jabbing, jabbing—and being there with my dad, with the old Na *NA* Na...comin' back on—so that it was like to very cool music that *BAM,* I landed the killer.

It had been primo packing that day. So naturally we had sort of a snowball World War III after we got outa the Big House, which you know is CK. And I was feeling all kind of warmed up from telling my dad about the knockout. So when he was kind of then just standing there, lookin' out the window at all the snow in the yard and The Woods and all the flakes still coming down, I started to tell him about the day's military action, which wasn't, this time, against the Vanderkells, unless you can call Tom Malone a Vanderkell.

It started in front of Jim Callahan's, and Callahan was a friend of Tom Malone's before bro Tom, as Frankie put it, became the Moron Without a Country, which name my dad loved because he laughs at all the stuff of Frankie's that I tell him (which'd be about one one trillionth of it). And he gets a kick out of hearing about all my friends, which is very cool. So I think you're gettin' it, the two sides of my dad, which two sides would be normal for a parent: There's my dad with like rules and terror tactics, and then there's my dad who loves the fun of life and me along with it. Anyhow, Callahan's is next door to the Priests' Yard, and that's where the war began. And it was one of those like full-scale operations with all kinds of charges and retreats, which I was telling my dad about, and I was saying how cool it is charging older guys even if you know you'll be retreating your butt (of course I didn't put it that way) as soon as you like hit the wall of those guys. And the barrages, which are when you each make about five snowballs and then everybody starts just hurling them high up in the air so they'll come down about where the enemy is located, and you don't figure you'll get all that lucky but like maybe one or two from your gang's will come down right on top of somebody's head, which is perfect, 'cause it's so funny and it pisses the guy off so much.

Anyhow, we'd been, about as you'd expect, retreating more than chargin', so we were backed up now to the tennis-court skating rink at 91ST and Hamilton—and then Terry T, still our littlest guy by far, with this absolutely perfect shot, knocks Tom Malone's cap right off his head. I mean the shot was perfect, and it was like Three-Stooges hilarious. And then when the Moron Without a Country, who thinks he's such a killer, was running down Terry to murder him, JL—and I told my dad (who I'm pretty sure I get my admiration feelings from, too, 'cause all the time you'll catch him saying really good things about people, like it warmed him up all over)—I told him that *nobody*, not one person at CK, had an arm like Jackie, and that JL nailed Thomas M right in the neck. "You know," I said, "right in that spot where the snow goes down inside your jacket and shirt, down your belly, down your back, and makes you freeze all over?"

My dad knew the spot. Big as he was then, he told me he'd had his face washed plenty of times, when he was little, by his big brothers, who liked to serve him the occasional snow sandwich for his health.

Of course I always cringed a bit when he said stuff like that his big brothers could be pretty scary sometimes, figuring he was trying to set me straight about me and the punks and punkettes. But he was still smiling. "So now," I said, "Tom Malone turns and goes the other way and starts chasing JL. But then George P goes, in like this perfect impersonation he's got of the Armadillo (I said Sister Armida) that we hadn't even heard yet! 'Thomas Malone, you're just making me tired—*once again.*' Which is incredible, it's so funny, especially 'cause it's kind of cruel in its perfection, not that Tom Malone hasn't had a time of it, like for years, with George P's rotundness. And now George P is getting him back, which is fun, too, 'cause it's only justice. So the jerk turns again and starts chasing George P, wanting to kill *him* now. So everybody's laughing, and bombs-away-ing on Tom Malone too! And it's so funny, because he's like gorilla-pissed now (I said really ticked off) and royally spazzing at the universe. But he was about to catch George P. And, unnh, that would not have been so funny, Dad. Believe me. But Frankie…and you're wondering where he's been, right?"

My dad smiled a big smile now, so it was like he was giving me the okay to make a fairly full Frankie report.

"Well, Frankie," I said, "he'd normally never in a million years miss a bombardment of his brother. Naturally. But he'd been working on this wicked, wicked iceball—that he'd started at this slush puddle. And now he had it ready to go. And Frankie's crazy, so of course he lets it go, full mortar shot, at a car. And BAM! he lays it right on this big black Cadillac! It sounded like an A-bomb went off! So everybody takes off, running for their lives. I saw Tom Malone leaving George P alone, which was good, and everybody scattering. I think it was an old guy in the car, so I'm guessing nobody got caught. There's no catchin' Frankie, anyhow; he's way too fast. And even less chance with Jackie. And I'm sure George P probably flipped home, you know, grabbin' and holding on to a car bumper and sliding down the street, which is the way he travels in the winter. And he's the best at it, so maybe it's a gift God gave him because otherwise he doesn't exactly motivate over the hill, if ya know what I mean. And Terry always gets away, too, by taking off through backyards and stuff, 'cause he's an expert on getting over backyard fences and through gates and stuff. So when I got clear, I didn't worry about anybody. I just came home."

About when I finished sayin' this, I heard our front door open, and then close: It was Mary Clare slippin' on out to her car. My dad turned for a second to wave, then began lookin' out our picture window again at the snow. He'd been smiling, like I said. But now he starts kinda really smiling and shaking his head, and then just slightly nodding it. 'Cause as it turns out there were these coincidences that like clicked in his mind now and led him to a story, or I should say two stories, when I said that after the snowball war and then Frankie's iceball, I'd headed for home.

"Did I ever tell you, Kev," he asked, "about George Johnson?"

I told him no, I hadn't ever heard that name, and asked who George Johnson was. He smiled again then and kind of like asked me to sit down on the couch, and then he sat with me, which was cool. Actually, very cool, because you had the strong feeling that some very cool things were about to follow.

"Well," he said, "your telling me about the iceball…and about Henry Hank, it all makes me think of George Johnson, who was a great, great guy, who lived with us for a number of years on Constance. He was a colored man, who worked for Papa down at Western Medical, and he could fix anything."

Then he, I mean my dad, starts telling me about stuff like the boiler and typewriters and adding machines. And like tarring the roof. And fixing the electricity. And fixing old printing presses and all kinds of stuff that George Johnson fixed. And then he says to me, "You get the picture, I think, eh?"

I got the picture—and, ya know what, I got the story beneath the picture, too. And, I mean, let me put in that, besides the shut-up rule, my dad has some very serious rules about other words. He's let it be known, like they say, in no uncertain terms, that if any of us ever says the word 'nigger', for instance—not just in our house, but anywhere in the universe—he'll consider that not just wrong but sickening to death on top of it. And the story beneath the picture—that I got—and that was put in there for me to get—was that anything a white guy can do, a colored guy can do too. And that the way for me to like get that fact forever was by seeing George Johnson, up on the roof, or with his eye on some adding machine or a printing press or something hard to figure out—and then, you know, me just getting it from that picture what a great guy George Johnson was.

And my dad said that Papa, who was my grandfather, loved George Johnson not just because of the way he could depend on him to do anything, and do it right—but because

George was a gentleman, too, and no phony.

Anyhow, the story goes that the house on Constance, which was where my dad lived when he was growing up, had about ten thousand things that Papa, who was a businessman, didn't have time to fix, not that he could have fixed 'em anyhow, my dad said. And when it got to the falling-apart point, and George had just about everything that wasn't workin' at Western Medical working again, Papa sent him out to Constance. It was supposed to be only a month or so. But things just sort of grew from where they started into something bigger. And my dad said Nana, my grandmother, loved George, and so did everybody at the house. And like there was never not going to be something for him to fix there, because it was this threestorey house with a big yard and a garden and three cars, which George was a mechanic and could fix, too. So Papa made him an offer, which was how about working at the house for the same salary as at Western, but, if George wanted to fix himself up a bedroom in the basement, where there was a bathroom already there, he could throw in a free place to live and he could use the third car sometimes.

But this got me kind of curious about something. So I asked my dad, "Didn't he have family? I mean, people he lived with?"

And my dad said, "None that anyone knew of…not that he spoke about, anyhow."

So the story goes that George came and set himself up in the basement, and lived with my dad's family, and he just sort of did stuff, which my dad said again that there was plenty for him to do, and he had this sort of apartment in the basement, which, the apartment, even had a kind of door lamp at the door.

"That's so cool," I said, about the stuff about the apartment with the door lamp. "Is George Johnson still alive? I'd love to have him build me an apartment like that. That'd be so cool."

"Well," my dad said, "I'm not sure where George would be now, Kev, or if he's still alive." Then he said, "But let me tell you what happened one night. It was a night just like tonight. Or it must have been just evening because I was maybe a year younger than you, and I was still out on the street. Anyhow, it was great packing, just like today, and your telling me about Frankie Malone made me think of how that day I was the exact same kind of jerk as Frankie, because there I was, packing an iceball. I was all by myself, but I just felt like making one. It was one of those great nights when there's no sidewalks left, or paths, and everything's just white and you can see the big flakes still coming down around the street lamps."

Of course those aren't the exact words my dad said. But close enough. And telling this story, I'll try to fake like I'm him because it's cool to have him in it, the way he was. And I won't be fakin' the details, trust me. Anyhow, I was nodding up a storm because it was so cool thinking of my dad as exactly like me, a kid only a little bit younger, on a great night, and walkin' with his iceball, which in my mind I was making one of for myself now, too, and could imagine it in my hands, getting smoother and harder-heavier, and becoming just about *perfecto*. And I was feeling that feeling, you know, when you've got something like a perfect iceball in your hand: I mean the feeling that you've just gotta do somethin' *bad* with it.

"Well," my dad said, "there was this car, and maybe it was a Cadillac. It was big, and moving slow, sort of trudging down the street, which didn't even have ruts; it was just all deep white. So what a target. There was no way I could miss, and I had this thing in my hands."

"So ya couldn't help it...."

My dad smiled. "Well, yes. I couldn't help it. But there's a lesson in this I hope you'll understand."

I nodded, to be agreeable, but I was a lot more excited about the bomb that I knew was coming. "But what happened?" I asked.

"Well, the inevitable."

He kind of hesitated, thinking maybe he needed to use another word (which I remember pretty exactly, the way he stopped). But I nodded, letting him know I knew that one (which I did). And I coulda said I was *feeling* the inevitable-ness, too, with an imaginary iceball in my mind, and all hot (if ice can be hot) in my hand.

"I had my weapon perfect," my dad said. "And this car kept coming. Slow. Big. I thought he'd get stuck. But he kept coming. And then he passed me. I let him get by about twenty feet, I guess, and then went into my stretch wind-up. I guess he was maybe fifty feet then when I let go. And it was a couldn't-miss shot, but I really got him good. Just like Frankie, I lofted it as high as I could, for the old aerial-bombshell effect. And BAM! I got him right down on the middle of his roof. He must've thought he'd been shot at or something. It was like an explosion. I hid fast behind a tree then to see what he'd do. And then I got scared when I saw the car stop. It was skidding, because the guy had slammed on his brakes. I was scared when I saw that, but I stayed one more second to see what he'd do. Then I saw him jump out and slam his door so hard I thought I'd hear the windowglass break. I was scared to death—because, when he came out from behind his door, the guy, I could see, was a huge guy, and not any old guy, bad luck for me. I didn't know whether to run or stay hidden behind the tree. Then I saw him start coming my way. So I broke running. I was too scared to look back. But I did. I looked back, and I saw him coming. He was running, too, right after me. And he was this huge, raging guy, who looked like he wanted to break my neck and kill me. I didn't know where to run to or hide, and the snow was so deep I couldn't get moving fast. It was like a bad nightmare, and I was so scared. I didn't want to go home because I didn't want Papa to know what I'd done. But I was so scared, I couldn't think of anything else. So I just started running as fast as I could for home, which was about a block. And this guy was only maybe fifty feet behind me. And he kept coming. I couldn't believe he didn't just give up, because he'd left his car, maybe even still running, right there in the middle of the street. But he kept coming. And now he started shouting at me and telling me he was gonna kill me. 'You little rat! I'm gonna wring your stinkin' little neck!' He was shouting things like this, and I was so scared, I almost couldn't run. My legs were shaking so badly, and the snow was so deep. But I had to keep going. I started shouting for Dick and Tom, hoping they'd come out and save me. But nobody heard me, and this guy kept getting closer. I don't know if I was ever as scared in Germany or France. I swear it, Kev. I don't think I ever was. But I kept running, even though now this guy was really breathing right down my neck. I remember when I got to the stairs at the house I slipped and fell and had to drag myself up in a second and was afraid I couldn't, but I did, and that with this guy right at our house now I was up and working at the door, begging it, and praying for it to open. But it wasn't an easy door. And this guy was coming right up our sidewalk now. And he was huge and so mad he was crazy, telling me he was gonna kill me. I know I was crying, 'Open! Open! Please open!' as I was pressing down on the thumb latch. And I swear this guy was right on the stairs when it finally clicked down and I got the door open. I jumped in the house in complete terror. And I slammed the door shut behind me, right as this guy came up. I dug my heel in at the base of the door as I whipped off my glove and started to hook up the latch lock. But sure as can be, this guy was beginning to push on the door. He was that crazy. He was going to smash right into our house to get me. So that tells you what kind of guy I'm talking about, if you haven't been able to tell already. But I managed to get the latch hooked. I couldn't, though, keep the door from opening as this guy forced back my foot and he was maybe about to rip the latch right off. And through the crack at the door, he was shouting, 'I'm gonna get you, kid! I'm gonna get you! You miserable little rat! I'm gonna break your stinkin' neck!'

"I was screaming at the top of my lungs for Tom and Dick and for my dad to come and save me. But they weren't home. Nobody in the family was. But then I saw the door to the basement fly open and George come running out. 'George! George!' I shouted, 'save me from this guy! He wants to kill me! He says he's gonna kill me!'

"George Johnson, Kev, was no small man himself, and he was one tough customer. But this guy at the door was huge. But George wasn't scared, not a bit. He took me under his left arm, and held me, to protect me. And then he did something I thought was crazy! He undid the latch! And sure enough this guy breaks in, right into our house, shouting 'I want that kid!' Then he sees George, holding me safe; and like a real scum, and you could tell now he was a lowclass bum, he says, 'You get outa my way, you piece a dirt nigger! I want that kid!' Then George, he didn't ask any questions like 'What did the boy do?' Or ask me, 'What did you do, Bobby, to make this man so angry?' None of that, for which I'm grateful to this day. He just held me tighter—and I held him as tight, Kevin, as I've ever held onto anybody in my life, believe me. And he reached then with his right hand into his jacket and pulled something out. I couldn't see yet what it was. I just heard that huge crazy madman inside our house shouting, 'Get outa my way, you black bastard! I want that kid!' Then I saw George take his right hand, with whatever it had in it, and put it up in front of the man's face and as he held me tighter and the crazy man shouted again, 'I want that kid! I WANT THAT KID, NIGGER!' George, out of his closed hand, right in the man's face, clicked open a switchblade knife, and he said, cool and quiet as could be, 'Not this kid, you don't.'"

"Oh, man!" I said, "Oh WOW! I can't believe that!"

"It's completely true," my dad said, in a way that made it clear he hadn't done any exaggerating—and that, in like a thumping in his heart, he still felt how true it was. "And you should have seen that big guy back off, Kev. I'd like to say he stumbled and fell going back—right on his backside. Or that he started whimpering and begging for his life and apologizing to George for his filthy, rotten mouth. But he just backed off. And left. And I'm sure of this. It wasn't just the knife, which was scary enough, but the way George said it—'Not this kid, you don't.' The way he said that was so powerful but just as quiet and calm as it was powerful. I love to hear it in my mind. I try to say it over in my mind to this day, sometimes. And I like to think it would have been enough to do the job, even if the knife hadn't been there."

I asked, "Did the guy ever come back, or call Papa or anything?"

"Nothing," my dad said. "Never saw the car or the guy again. The deal was done. And I never told anybody that story. Never told Tom or Dick or Papa or Nana. Nobody. Not until now."

So of course even more now I was loving this story down to the death, and maybe too because I was thinking that if you ever had a fully grown-up Prizer bustin' into your private property and threatening kids and callin' you filthy names that a switch-blade might be just the thing.

My dad looked at me then and was smiling, in this cool way. He put his left arm around me, and he like held me tight and gave me a bit of a Dutch rub. And this was all so cool, too, that I felt like maybe it wasn't happening. Then he sat away a bit and looked at me again. And he said, "But the story I really wanted to tell you, Kev, about George—and I guess the snow and then sweet Henry together made me think about him—was another one—about a time maybe five months later, because I know it was a warm, warm night...."

And so now I was getting ready for a *really* great story. But I'm suddenly thinking now—I mean while I'm telling you all this stuff—about black Cadillacs, because, speaking of inevitable-ness, maybe I can't avoid these cars or something...which is like a statement I guess now I've gotta make sense of for ya, before I'm through. But not now. And like I'm thinking too again of Henry Hank, who I was sure would be champ someday—but then like I say he just disappeared somewhere (so maybe some time when I didn't know it, somebody stopped him in the ring, which pretty much breaks my heart). And now about George Johnson, too, but at a different time, a month or so later, when I asked my dad what ever happened to him after he stopped that guy with the blade, because I never met him at Papa and Nana's.

We were in the tv room again. And I could see that my dad really kind of hated telling me—that he would rather have not, I guess you could say *hurt* the stories of the man that he'd told me on that night of the snow storm. Or wrecked the perfect-ness. But he said, "I'm afraid he got a little crazy, Kev. Such a good and fine man, George Johnson. I'll never forget him. I never will. But he got kind of crazy. He used not to come up from the basement for long stretches of time. He was a proud man. Maybe it was strange for him living in the basement of a white family's house, all alone. No place truly his, after maybe too much of a hard early life, about which we never knew. I'm afraid I just can't say. But in the end, after maybe four years with us, he started going long times without coming up. And finally Papa had to go down. And when he did, he found George with a gun. He had a pistol. And Papa found him with it in his lap, just sort of looking at it, and spinning the chamber, which was loaded. I don't know what all got said between them. It wasn't till a long time later that Papa told me about this. I just know that the next day George Johnson was gone, and that nobody ever heard from him again."

And I don't know why I'm putting this stuff in here now, about what came later. But when my dad told me about things being maybe too much for George, and the gun, I remember I just sort of swallowed hard and how painful it was in my throat and that I ripped my sleeve hard over my eyes. Which, because, like I say, certain feelings of the shit variety sometimes come on in no time, I'm doing again, now. And it's because, too, I'm thinking of Sweet Henry on top of it. And of Jackie. And Frankie. And black Cadillacs. But let me get off these kind of things, which I'll explain some time, now that I owe it to ya, I'm sure.

And let me get back to that "warm, warm night," the one my dad had been talking about, I mean when it was just the two of us sittin' there, with the big snowflakes going all up and down in the wind—and my dad said to me, "Well, one day, George Johnson asked for the car—because there was a special occasion."

There was still the sound on the tv set, and my dad got up from the couch and turned the sound down to nothing, but kept the screen on for the light. "This occasion was really special," he said, as he sat back down with me, "and extra-special for me, because I was the only one George invited."

He told me then how George, the day before, had asked him down into his basement apartment, inside, past the door lamp, and laid out two tickets on a table and said to him that he wanted him to come with him, the next night, to see (and my dad would like try to sound like George) "a reeeeal fighta—a no foolin' fighta"—that George said was gonna be the best there was. And then George pointed to the tickets, all smiling and stuff, and he asked my dad just where he thought those tickets were going to put the two of them.

My dad said he was so wound up at the thought of going to a for-real prize fight, he didn't care if it was the last row, which he thought might be the case, 'cause of George's being a colored man. But what he heard was that it was gonna be the first row! And George was saying stuff like they'd be so close my dad would need to do some duckin' and bobbin' himself. And he kept repeating that stuff about this fighter, saying that my dad—and he was callin' him *son*—was really gonna see something special and true, all right. That he was going to see the *reeeeal one*. And that my dad could believe *that!*

My dad said that in his room way up at the top of the house (which was cool, too, that he had a pueblo when he was a kid), he didn't sleep, he was so crazy excited. And that he even had tears in his eyes sometimes (which reminded me of some of the silvery eyes I told you about, with the reminder feeling extremely cool) thinking about how George chose him and how George had saved his life already and never leaked a word to anybody about it. He said he was mad thinking George might have been suckered by somebody about the first row and thinking that it would make George sad and embarrassed when he found out the tickets really were for the last row. But as it turned out, George was right as could be—and like my dad that next night would be the only white face in this gym with over maybe a thousand colored men—and right where he could put his chin on the canvas.

"I was the only kid, too," he said. "So I have no idea how George talked Papa into letting me go. But times were different then, Kevin. And Papa trusted George and knew him to be a good man, a real gentleman, the way I told you. And Papa believed in seeing what life's all about, too, since, well, you know how I told you Papa left home himself at fourteen to find his fortune. That was one of the great things about Papa—he knew that what people think is bad for ya is often good for ya. So there I was, off with George, front seat in the Oldsmobile, and the top down, with Papa sending us off, unbeknownst to Nana, I'm sure.

"And we drove right on down and into the all-colored neighborhood on Indiana Avenue. If we ever went anywhere near there with Nana, Kev, it was always lock the locks. But now it was top down in the summertime. And George was so proud. He had on a white suit with this red handkerchief and this fancy straw hat. And he'd trimmed his mustache, and his face was all filled with excitement, and handsome. And George was a very goodlooking man, about forty years old then, and in great shape from all the hard work he'd done. Not an ounce of fat on him and a good set of muscles and shiny teeth and smile and eyes, the kind colored men have. And then all of a sudden he was waving at people, at friends, which I was sort of surprised to see he had. But he didn't forget for a second that he had this kid with him, too. *Bobby,* he'd say, tapping me on the shoulder, smiling—and then he'd tell me again that I was going to *See the one. See the one.* One time he said, 'Ah mean, Bobby, what's you gonna see, son, is the *powah 'n the glowrih.'"*

Which last words I remember exactly, and how I got the feeling that my dad said 'em pretty much exactly the way George Johnson did, because of the way I've tried to get the sound right myself.

Then my dad told me that even though he was like only eleven, he wasn't too young to get it that George Johnson was takin' him out that night to see something really great, not just in any man, but in a colored man. Nor to get it, either, that George picked him because he saved his skin that time so he trusted that my dad's heart would be like all thankful, which would lead to his seeing things in a good way. And that he also trusted my dad because my dad never breathed a word about the knife. And my dad said how he thought he was being brought into something really good and powerful and how he loved George Johnson for bringin' him into it.

And I was for sure loving my dad for bringing *me* into it, too. And really gettin' wound up myself. So I asked him, "Was George Johnson right, Dad? Was the fighter really great?" And this is something I won't ever forget. I mean my dad, sort of swallowing back this choke-up in his voice, which I'd never seen, ever, and then saying, I mean even whispery, 'cause I swear, it was hard for him, "You better believe George Johnson was right. You better believe it."

Then he cleared his throat, real hard, and after a second he was okay again and stuff. And then I had the afghan ready again to be spread like wings! And I was starting to jump and shouting, "Oh wow! What was his name?! What was his name! Have I ever heard of him?!" I was gettin' like crazy to hear the fighter's name. But now my dad only smiled and said, "We'll come to that. We'll come to it."

Then he told me about the allcolored gym, which he said was really just an old kind of emptied-out warehouse building with all these bleacher seats, at 26TH and Indiana, but which went crazy that night with more excitement than any he'd felt in any stadium he's ever been in. He said then he actually wasn't the only white face, at least outside, for the guy taking the tickets was white and there were white policemen in squad cars and paddy waggons here and there circling the place.

"I guess," he said, "they were afraid of riots, maybe guns and knives. But I wasn't afraid at all. Everybody was great to me, Kev. And *in*side I *was* the only white, believe me. It was all colored men, packed shoulder to shoulder on those bleacher benches, which went way up around the ring—all the way up to the rafters."

Then he pictured it all for me, with like pitchers of beer gettin' passed down about every row and poured into big paper cups for all these guys laughin' and smoking cigars. But he said again how they were great to him. And how they said, as he and George made their way closer and closer to the ring, down to that front row, "Make room for this little boy! Make room there!" And how when George told them he brought my dad to see "the real thing!" they said, "Oh yessuh, son. You 'gon see it tonight! You gon'see it tooonight!" And like how in that first row, they would laugh and slap their knees or put a hand on his shoulder—as they stood up and got out of his way and George's way as they were movin' down toward their ringside seats. My dad was thinking that maybe it was that he was so young, but he said he felt no bad feeling from any of them—but instead that they were like glad to see a young white kid getting schooled, up close, in something that he oughta know about them, a thing that they were really proud of. "And by up close," my dad said then, "I mean *up close*: right in the middle, dead even with the overhead lamp, and *ringside.*"

He told me now how George told him there were gonna be "some little fellas" up first. And that they were real fast. And good. But that they weren't quite the same as the heavyweights. And that George told him not to get discouraged and think he like lied to him. And not to get bored. "Cause the real thing…it's comin'."

My dad laughed then. He said, "Bored! I don't know if I've ever been less bored in my life." Then he told me about those middleweight prelims, and how he never had seen speed and power like that. Never. And how it was terrifying. "I don't know," he said, "if it was the lesson that George wanted me to learn that night, but one thing I learned for sure, and it's a good thing *to* learn, is that there are guys who can kill you with their bare hands. That's what you learn," he said, "when you're up real close, from all the smacking and the thuds of the punches and all the sweat and the flying blood. It was amazing. But, Kevin," he said, "George was right. It was nothing compared to watching the heavyweights."

Then my dad said how there was this break, after the prelims. And he pictured it for me how all these lights went on besides the lamp over center ring. And how people were movin' out and about. But he said he and George stayed put because George wasn't a beer drinker, and that George bought him a hotdog and a coke and a candy bar right there at the seat, and how it was cool eating a hotdog there with George and drinking a coke, the two of them with food in their mouths kind of grinning at each other. But then how time kept passing after they finished, and how George was getting a little fidgety after a while. My dad was thinkin' George might be still afraid he was bored or disappointed, which my dad said was a pretty good laugher. But then the crowd started getting fidgety, too. Then after a while, when the seats were all packed again, this stomping started, and it got really loud on those bleacher planks. Then all the extra lights went out and a cheer went up. But then the lights came back on, and this booing started. Then, pretty quick, the booing was like workin' up to an official roar, and the stomping was gettin' louder and louder. But then finally the extra lights went out for good, and only that one center lamp was left on, over the ring. Still, though, no signs of the heavyweight fighters. So the stomping kept up, and the booing. The place was goin' crazy, my dad said. And some of the guys were laughing. But some weren't. My dad said George wasn't. That he was like serious as could be. And he and my dad couldn't stomp, because their feet were on the concrete floor. But George sort of rocked back and forth on his hands, and once or twice yelled, kind of nervous and angry, "Let's make it happen! C'mon! Let's make it happen!"

And it was kind of funny 'cause my dad said even as much as this whole thing meant a lot to him, to George Johnson it meant *a lot* more—but there my dad said he was, feeling pretty stupid, goin', too, "Yeah, let's make it happen!"

And I smiled because it was cool of my dad telling me about how he felt so sort of kid-like embarrassed and stupid. But this story was really gettin' to me and it was gettin' to him telling it. So we didn't start like smiling up any kind of storm or anything, or Dutch rubbing.

And then he told me more about all that crazy yelling. And like nervousness and anger. But then how this spotlight came on, and how it was incredible when it did. And how the gym went absolutely crazy with hollers and cheers. And how the stomping became like thunder. Then he said the spotlight, after like wandering around the whole place, came to focus on this doorway, because coming out of it right then was the biggest, toughest looking guy my dad had ever seen. Oh, man, he was thinkin': *This* is a heavyweight. He said the guy was black as Henry Hank, but bigger, much bigger. That there were more muscles on this guy's body than he'd ever seen on anyone, truth to tell. And he wasn't wearing any robe, so you could see every one of 'em. And he came trottin' in throwing practice punches, which my dad thought were even faster than the ones the middleweights threw and with arms like bigger than their legs. And he said he was screamin', "Oh wow, George, he will be the best! He will be!"

But then he said George Johnson wasn't cheering, or even looking at this giant guy now trottin' down into the ring across from them. George's eyes were back on the door. And there my dad was, shouting about the giant guy, stuff like, "George, he looks like the greatest fighter there ever was!" But George was keeping his eyes on the door, and he was saying in this voice all kind of nervous, and quiet, "That ain't him."

Which of course had my dad goin' crazy, and now me too. And then he said George wasn't alone. That the crowd was clappin' and clappin' hard for the giant now up in the ring, but everybody's eyes were turning back to the door. My dad couldn't believe that a bigger man could come out of that door. He couldn't believe it. But now he like began to expect it, as the stomping started up again, and became louder and louder every second. My dad said he thought the bleachers were gonna come down. That he was like afraid for the guys in the middle. That they might get crushed by the guys on top. But that the stomping still got louder. Until finally that door opened, and it stopped. My dad said there were still crazy cheers, so the place didn't go all quiet. But when the stomping stopped, it seemed like it did. Then out of the open door came this hooded man, slow, not throwin' big punches, just little jabs, and then trotting a slow kind of trot. George, my dad said, was kind of just gripping his fists and whispering *Yes.* So my dad knew this hooded man was his man. But my dad was worried, sort of the way he'd been about the seats, only worse, because George Johnson's man didn't seem as big as the other man at all. The hooded robe covered up his body, but my dad didn't expect, that when George's man took the robe off, that he'd be seeing anything like what he'd seen in the giant guy, who was up now waiting in the ring, sort of glaring, working his feet, punching his two fists together in front of his chest.

Then my dad said the cheering got all quiet, too, as George's man came up to the ring and stepped up into his corner. My dad looked back and forth from George's man to his opponent. And he kept lookin' back and forth, and he couldn't believe now that George's man had a chance. Then he took off his hooded robe, and my dad like knew. There was no way. George Johnson's man was big, plenty big, a heavyweight all right, and in great shape. But there was no way. It was impossible that he could beat the giant he was gonna face. But then George grabbed my dad's arm with one hand, when they were about to sit for the start of things, and he pointed with his other hand to his man. And what George said, the way my dad put it just like him, was "Bobby, you take a good look, son, 'cause you gonna be proud one day you seen him so close."

Of course I was goin' so crazy now listening to my dad that my hands were like sweatin' like mad, holding the afghan. But I kept my mouth shut.

And then my dad said there was something in him that didn't like to hear George talk like this about his man. He was worried for George, that he'd get so embarrassed. But he tried to fake it as best he could that he was excited and all enthusiastic about his man. Then the bell rang. And right from the start it looked real bad. The huge muscleman came on like some sort of black tornado. He was firing four punches to George's man's one. And they were punches, my dad said, and what George's man was throwin' was really sorry, harmless junk. And right away the crowd didn't like what it was seeing, which was not much of a fight. They weren't like cheering for the big man, but already they were startin' to boo George's man, who for sure didn't look like much now. And when they came over to George and my dad's side, and were bangin' it out right against the ropes so my dad could hear every one of those smacks of the leather on the skin—and my dad swore to me they were so close he got sprayed by the sweat—all George's man did was sort of duck and back up into the ropes and, you know, take the punches with both gloves up around his face for protection and his elbows sort of tucked in to cover his gut.

But my dad said George wasn't booing. He was whispering, with his fists all clenched, saying stuff like, "Come on, son. Come on, you the one. You the one." And he was so intense he sort of like lost sight of my dad. And my dad almost didn't want to look at what was goin' on in the ring, so he just sort of stared at George for a while, sort of way out there where he was now. And he could see that George's like whole heart was inside of his man, who was losing, and getting booed. Or it was more like he was doing nothing at all, and gettin' booed for that—and shamed. My dad said he thought it looked so bad that like this might be the most painful night of his life, instead of the best, if things went the way they looked like they were going.

He said all he could do when the bell rang for the end of the first round was try to keep fakin' like he had some confidence. But he was afraid it wouldn't be too convincing, so he was hoping George wouldn't even look at him. And he didn't, much. He was too wound up in his worry about his man. Then shouts started coming from more than one guy in those first rows—shouts coming right at George's man, from those colored men, who were calling him *nig-*

ger—colored guys calling him *nigger*—and askin' him stuff like if he wanted to *be somebody* or if he just came there to *lay down and die*. And it didn't let up, them calling him *nigger* and now telling him all he did was come to *lay down and die*. And my dad said they called him *boy* now and told him to go on home. And that it was rough—real rough, words like that coming from his own people. And that I could believe it that George was feeling the pain.

And the second round turned out no different. George's man still didn't throw much of anything, or move much. He just sort of moped around with his two hands up and his elbows tucked in—and got himself booed and mocked, only now even worse than before, because the crowd was gettin' really angry. The place seemed to be getting even dangerous and ready to go into maybe some kind of riot. My dad said he thought if there'd been chairs instead of bleachers, some of 'em would have been thrown by now. One guy down the row from him and George, who'd been so nice to my dad, chucked a full cup of beer on George's man when he leaned back against the ropes on their side. And all those mocking guys, colored men, calling him *boy* and *nigger*. My dad said he wanted to die for George, he felt so bad, like they were calling George those names, shaming him right in front of the white kid he'd brought along to see the real thing. But my dad, too, felt sort of bad for everybody, because nobody wanted the giant guy to win. They didn't care about him, my dad could tell that. But it looked like the giant was not only gonna win, but score a dead-cold knockout, and any second now. My dad said he really felt weird, too, like George was a million miles away and that if things went the way they were going, it was gonna be the strangest kind of ride home ever.

Then the bell rang ending the second round, but now the booing and the bad catcalls didn't stop. It all got worse, right through to the call bell. And George, my dad said, just went into this whispering sort of thing, like a prayer, saying stuff like "You come on now, son. You come on now. Don't you make no liah outa me, heah. Don't you make no liah outa me." Then it was like my dad was getting even more scared, figuring this thing might sooner rather than later get pretty crazy and those white cops and more might be needed, because people were raging a little bit more all the time. And those colored men calling a colored man *nigger*. My dad said he thought they had to be feeling a pretty strange feeling for that to happen. But he said he wasn't too young to get it that this showed how much they cared about this fight. So he felt sorry and embarrassed.

But then that call bell for the third sounded, and at least George's man answered the call. It was still just more of the same, though. No punches to speak of, just his covering up mostly and backin' away and looking like he didn't care. And from the crowd, even crazier catcallin' and booing, 'cause nobody cared beans what the giant did, and everybody was crazy furious at George's man. And my dad was praying that George's man wouldn't get knocked out, which he was sure, though, was going to happen. And he was really feelin' now a little too far away from those police and was gettin' full scared that George *was* forgetting he had him with him.

But then, my dad said, as the fight started comin' their way, something different suddenly happened. Something VERY different. George's man, instead of just falling back into the ropes, doing nothin', like shocked the whole crowd with this all-of-a-sudden, lightning move to get outside the huge guy. My dad said it was amazing. The quickness of the move sent this sort of lightning bolt through every guy there and shut 'em all up, and before you knew it, it was the big man backin' fast toward the ropes—and right toward my dad and George. Then—BAM—so *amazing*—the one who'd done nothin', not a thing all night, with this power and speed that my dad said were completely unbelievable, shot out this left to the body. My dad said he could never describe it. It was like you were thinking that that left hand was gonna go right through the giant's guts and come out his back. My dad was right there. He could hear the groan of the big guy, like the guy'd been hit with a spear. My dad couldn't believe what he was seeing, and hearing. And in just one more second, the real, real thing came, all right. The right-hand bomber, like nothin' my dad said he'll ever see again. And it was over. And the sound of that knockout punch—my dad said he couldn't believe his ears. It was different from every other sound he'd heard that night. Middleweights—nothin'. Then he saw the legs of that giant, who he didn't think could lose to anybody on the earth, start shakin', and going out of control completely. And then there he was falling, comin' down right onto my dad, only the ropes held him and he hit the canvas right before my dad's face, with his head hung over the ring side and the blood comin' from both his nostrils and out of his mouth.

Then my dad saw George's man standing over him, seeming ten times taller than any giant. And the crowd went crazy. All those booing voices went absolutely crazy with cheers. No more disappointment. No more raging. Everybody was cheering to take the roof off that place, as the referee started his count. My dad was right there, with that giant's head hung right into his lap. And the giant was dead cold OUT unconscious. My dad was scared stiff. But the crowd was insane with happiness. They began suddenly rocking together, like chanting all in unison, and not any word like *nigger* now. Then it was eight! nine! *ten!* and the referee's crossing the giant out. The crowd then went crazy all at once with this huge roar. But my dad was glad to see a trainer come with salts. Glad to see that big guy shake his head and come back to life when he smelled 'em. Then he could cheer, too, not so scared anymore. And as he started roaring and cheering, he felt himself all of a sudden picked up in the air. It was George Johnson, and he was huggin' my dad and dancing with him in the air, sayin' stuff like "Didn't ah tell you, Bobby! Didn't I say true, son!" And as like way out there as he'd been, he now turned to my dad and held him tight in his arms, and said, "Didn't I tell you true, son, 'bout my man! My man, Bobby, he gon' be champyon a the worl' some day!" And my dad said George hugged him tight the way he'd hugged George that time George saved his skin. And George said, 'He gon' be champyon a the worl', and it comin' soon, Bobby! It comin' soon!'"

I couldn't even start to believe what I'd been hearing. I was like so torn up, and ripping that afghan over my eyes. And I could see my dad was so torn up, too. And it was again like hard for him to go on. But then he got it out, kinda whispery again, "Oh no," he said, all kinda choked up, "not anymore. It wasn't any angry words that crowd was chanting anymore. No insults now. It was 'JOE! JOE! JOE!' And George Johnson as he held me tight was chanting 'JOE! JOE!' For Joe was his name, Kevin. Joe Louis. And he was the greatest fighter who ever lived."

CHAPTER SEVEN

BETWEEN SEVENTH & EIGHTH

THE FOURTH OF JULY, 1961

It was the Fourth of July, I know that for sure, when I told Jackie the story about Joe Louis, which got to him exactly the way it got to me. Which is to say so hard it made you feel like you were goin' full crazy, seein' every guy in that gym, hearing 'em chanting the name for their absolute life, and seein' with your actual eyes the greatest fighter who ever lived, not even close to a lie. We were up in the pueblo, 'cause Jack was staying all night. And Frankie was there too. But I waited till Frank fell asleep to tell Jackie both the Joe Louis story and that other one about the ice ball and the Cadillac and the switch-blade, which got to JL, too, so hard, the way it got to me, with both of us practicing a thousand times then, "Not this kid, you don't." Sometimes we said all the words in the same way. And sometimes we put a special emphasis on the 'this.' And the Fourth had been this incredible day: another of those remember-it-forever days, which

I'll talk about and which will explain maybe why I waited till Frankie was asleep to tell JL all about George Johnson.

But first, 'cause you know me, always mixing together the cool and the certifiable, I've got to tell you about something Frankie pulled (which word 'pulled', I can't help it, makes me start laughing about the thousand or so different uses, all about of course the same subject, that George P could get out of it).

It was in the spring, and two things I'd say were about equal. That is, how tired Francis X was getting of school and how tired school was getting of Francis X, which two things had a way of chasing each other around in a faster and faster circle, if ya know what I mean. So Frankie had—not a pocketful of miracles—but, as George P put this one too, "a pocketful of SMM." Which means a stapled stack of conduct cards so thick and with so many initials of Sister Mary Madeline on 'em that Frankie could like start flipping 'em and he'd get this really spooky cartoon-movie going where it was blurry at first and the initials were moving and then it turned into just one big solid SMM, which movie of course Malone said he'd talked about with Marvin from *Shock Theater*, who according to FX, wanted it bad.

But I'd have to say that not any of us, even Pete, got along with SMM all that well. Until the day she says to the Pin, "Mr. Flynn, you dis-*GUST* me." Which made us respect her a lot more. But it shows you how much Frankie hated her guts that he couldn't even give her special credit for this one. "Who in the universe," he said, "wouldn't say the exact same thing?"

"Peter Damien," Pete said, kind of chuckling. "He spent his life among the lepers."

"What a moron," Stu said.

"He was a saint," Pete said, already headed back to being serious, 'cause he just couldn't stay goofy for more than a second or two.

But now Frankie, pretty much just for disagreeableness' sake, I'd say, 'cause as far as I know he had nothing against 'em personally, says, "F the lepers." And George P says, "No way, *you* F the lepers." And then of course we all start wondering who in the universe would, to use an expression we were using those days, *nail* a leper. Because even Pete agreed, not saying the word of course, that working with lepers was one thing, nailing them quite another. And we all agreed that Peter Damien, no matter what other crazy stuff he might have done with lepers, probably never once like really nailed one good.

But then, sort of just knowing they were disgusting, but not any real detail, we sort of had to ask, "What exactly is a leper, anyhow?"

"Leprosy," Pete said, "is a disease that eats your flesh away." And you could tell he loved this knowledge, from the satisfied way he said it. And then he said, "I've seen pictures in a book, with people with half a face eaten off."

Stu naturally wanted to know if there was anyone in the book with half a braunschweiger eaten off. And then we all wanted to know if leprosy in guys maybe starts with your braunschweiger, or finishes with your braunschweiger. But then we went on and thought about leprosy of the brain. And if you had a partially eaten-up brain, about the kind of thoughts you'd have, which we decided would be mostly nauseating thoughts about guts and torn off body parts and nuclear-war stuff with people's eyes melting and skin hanging like Michelangelo's self-portrait in the *Last Judgment,* which we saw in this art book we had in sixth, and then of guys getting scalped, which we saw in this even cooler painting of Custer's Last Stand that Frankie's dad had in their basement, where he set up a bar for his parties. And then we had a leprosy-thought contest, which George P won with some incredibly disgusting stuff about people with leprosy makin' out with each other and not making any solid contact because every place they touched or kissed would turn out to be just this crust that broke open into this hole of like nuclear-bomb-powered halitosis and green and red boogery puss.

"So what does leprosy have to do with religion?" Jackie asked. "It's like all over the Bible."

Pete said it was just the main disease at the time, so that's why it was in there.

But then Jack said, "Maybe because it's like the main disease of all time is why it's in there."

Which I ranked as a far cooler idea, so I went with it; and then everybody went with it, except Pete, who told us that knowing things was better than makin' up stuff, which made Frankie say, all agreeably, that for instance it was good to know for an absolute fact that Pete was a moron, instead of bein' unfair and makin' up untrue stories about him.

But then Jackie said it was cool how, by touching it and stuff, Jesus cured leprosy wherever he saw it. And this sort of shut us all up for a while because, well, that's just what happens when you start talking about something like the miracles of Jesus (which made me think for a second, too, I remember this perfectly, about the word 'guts', which means of course blood and guts but also means courage; and about how Jesus with the good kind of guts could cure people who were getting eaten up and turned into the gross-out kind).

But then we tried to decide if even Jesus could cure the Pin, with Jackie saying he could, and of course George P saying he could but would most likely decline, and Frankie saying he couldn't. And then like back and forth we went with all the usual moronisms that we practice all the time and then have to stifle when we're trying to impress girls, because girls are like obliged to act like they think guys are nauseating idiots, which if they didn't have to do, I'm sure girls would be coming up with a lot of really funny moronic stuff themselves—but then how cute or pretty or beautiful would we think they were? (I put this in because it was the kind of stuff JL and I would talk about. You could talk about knowledge-stuff with Pete, but Pete didn't really know all that much about life yet. For instance I could never tell Pete how incredibly good it felt for me not to be an idiot around Patty. Whereas Jackie not only understood, he let me know how actually cool he thought that was.)

But let me get to this thing that Frankie pulled (and don't think what you're thinking), which thing I don't want to build up too much because it's really pretty simple. I mean what he did was just disappear. There we were in class, and there was SMM up at the board putting up some math problem—and Frankie just jumps out the classroom window. I mean it wasn't like suicide. We were on the first floor. And it was this hot day, so the window was open wide. And with SMM's back turned to him, Frankie just makes this move like a cat, hang jumps out the window, springs off the wall, and cuts out running. Which made us think about how many centuries would pass before we'd even think of something that certifiable, let alone do it ('cause it really was kind of a suicide). And it of course had me laughing harder than I ever laughed in my entire life, but it had me like really kinda sick, too, because I could care less about the Moron Without a Country, but if his brother Frankie got shit-canned, I don't know. I mean I didn't know what that would make me feel, besides that like part of me got ripped out.

"And what *exactly* explains all the commotion?"

Sister Mad hadn't gotten it yet what happened, but it didn't take her long because naturally when she turned around she looked straight to Frankie's desk for the source of the trouble.

"And where *IS* he!?"

"He busted out," Johnny Higgins said.

"What he means, Sister," Mary Beth O'Brien said, in this really sickening, simp-shit way, "is that he jumped out the window."

"He *WHAT!*"

And of course the way she said that let everybody know that in the history of the universe, with the one exception of his older brother, there'd never been a kid more insane.

"He really pulled a Maloner this time, I guess," George P said now. Which of course got us all laughing till we about wizzed.

But, for sure, SMM wasn't in any tolerating mood over this little move of Frankie's, at all. "If you value your *existence* any more than that sorry little *scoundrel* does his," she said, in a more pissed way than I'd ever seen in her (and this penguin could rage, trust me) "you'll find a fast way to keep your giggling selves *silent.*"

Then, with that, she takes off out of the room. I mean like *running*, which scared the batshit out of us. And then we all began figuring where she ran to. The girls were saying stuff like the Principal's Office and to call the Truant Officer and to call his parents. And we were saying stuff like to call the FBI, and the College of Cardinals, and the Pope. Then, in one of the few good moments of his life, the Pin says where SMM went was, "To get the screw."

Of course it was a race to say, "Who's the lucky guy?"— which George P won, not only because he was fastest but because he thought to say *caballero* instead of 'guy', which made Terry laugh harder than I've ever seen him laugh, but which was grossing out the girls off the map. But then Pete adds the knowledge-factor, saying, "The screw is an instrument of torture."

"That's not what I heard," George P says.

But then the Pin says, "You heard wrong."

And with the Pin you're always torn, because you wanna like pants him right on the spot—but then you don't—as Frankie says, "for fear of the unknown." And this was his little moment, so we let him go on.

"The screw is this machine that you tie the prisoner's arms to and legs to and you turn this wheel and it starts pulling the prisoner's arms and legs right out of their sockets and then you get him to confess to anything, and to say anything you want him to say, and do anything you want him to do, and eat anything you want him to eat, like puke or shit...."

"You're a twerp, Flynn."

And this was so funny because it was Terry who said it. And everybody was laughing, so the Pin shut up, though he was all pissed off now. And I swear that guy lives all day long in the place our bad dreams come from.

But now SMM comes back, and of course she's gotta put on the exact right act. I mean to close the door just right; to use the just-right voice; to get back to business just right, after scaring the shit out of us just right—because we were in really new territory with Frankie's move (or as Pete later called it, his 'defenestration', which we thought of as our coolest term since 'colostomy bag', which we'd been putting to all kinds of uses, though we still had no clue what it meant). So SMM closes the door very firm-like and then stands there like she's made out of wood (which was something we later took bets on—and had Terry half-believing, at least about her left leg). And then she comes on with the soft voice and all these soft expressions—to let us know—in so many words—that while Francis X Malone was hereby de-testiculated, and would be waiting in hell for that little bird that came by only every million years to like just brush its wing against the steel ball big as the sun, and when the bird had worn down the steel ball—*then* his suffering in hell was *just beginning*—we, because we would never do such a thing as he did, were all safe.

"I suggest, however, that you give the most serious consideration to the error of Mr. Malone's ways. He will pay a price. He will pay a *heavy* price, as will anyone else showing a similar sense of *adventure.*"

And there you were. After the we're-safe stuff, she of course hits us with the *but-not-that-safe* stuff. And I kind of had fun watching her moves, which I pretty much predicted, new territory or not, not that these moves didn't still sort of chill me straight down to the bone, and get me thinking that jumping out a school window could maybe actually be a mortal.

But it didn't happen—I mean Frankie's getting excommunicated. I think the reason being that the shit-canning of Tom Malone was maybe all that Mrs. M (who was doing a lot of Schlitz-y sort of mortified whimpering these days) could take, and she begged the Sisters of Mercy for some of their best stuff. I would mention Mr. M, but he'd sort of disappeared himself to the middle of nowhere, for some time now.

So there we were (Frankie being let back after about a week of being nowhere, like his old man), asking FX what the FAAAGH got into him.

"Other than the usual," Stu said.

And Malone, acting for fun like he's offended, says, "And what exactly is that supposed to mean?"

So we told him stupidity, mostly. "And let's not forget," Stu said, "that he's extremely fucked up." And we all agreed that we should never, ever forget that. No. And so there we were, kind of back to normal. And of course we talked about the size of the wad-bone Frankie had to've had before he jumped, knowing what happened to him generally before he took action. And Frankie told us that's exactly why he did it. His roderigo was getting so big, he said, he was afraid he'd knock a school wall down if he stayed inside.

"I'm sure," Pete said, "that's exactly what you told Sister Catherine."

"Fuckin' A," Frankie said, "and she thanked me for being so considerate."

Which made even Pete laugh. And we were all goin' nuts, of course askin' Frankie stuff like if he had to explain the term 'roderigo' to Sister Catherine, which of course he said no he did not, which made us laugh even harder because of course he said this, too, in this goonball serious way. But I have to say, as I've been sort of saying, there was always, even before Frankie jumped, or JL died, something that kinda worried me about Frankie. And you were always laughing when it came to FX Malone, but always sort of wondering where this is gonna go. Which has something to do with why I waited till Frankie was asleep to tell Jackie the stories about George Johnson, which waiting I'll explain more later.

But there's some more school stuff, now that I'm on it; and it's about Patty, so it's cool—and to me, extremely cool. And I should say about her, first, that even though she's maybe the only person I ever met who's flat-out smarter than Peter O'Connor, she had a very high tolerance for our stupidity. I mean she only every once in a great while acted like it made her want to chuck. And now and again she would be wearing what I detected as a slight shit-eatin' grin, which of course I loved her for, along with the way she—I mean even better than that ballet picture on her wall, which still knocked me over every time I saw it—the way she *was*.

But I gotta let ya know I hadn't had any luck by showing up at her house for my *Southtown* collections on Tuesday, and by that I mean she wasn't there the next two times, which threw me off, making me think she must've hated my guts, or something, or at least gone through some severe OH-NO's about the Hershey bar incident, and maybe the way she talked about her dad and her lip trembled so bad, even though she worked it down so quick, with that pride that I will not be forgetting. But isn't it funny, I mean, how we sort of grab on to thoughts like that—I mean being sure that the person we're flipped over is *not* flippin' over us—so that if one billion straight people in a row came up to us and said there were regular reports coming in that she was flipping her brains out over us, we would still one billion times, go *bullsh*. And I mean I, like crazy, don't wanna go reporting all my simpy little sob stories. But it was like my heart and brain had a twenty-four-hour-a-day charlie horse over this. Which is another fact of life I'd love to have explained to me about flippin' out over somebody— I mean all that shit pain—and the pain's being like just a snap of your finger away from the best feelings you've ever had, and vice versa.

And I'd think stuff, like, is it because there's a *word* called 'heartache' that all of a sudden I've got one—I mean like right down to the actual ache. Or is it that words don't make stuff happen, they just sort of wait out there for us to get to where they are. And I was thinking, too, about why I never said word one to Patty and she never said word one to me. So it was like we never ate jack-point beans together, let alone a Hershey bar (with the exception of one square). And we never sat around the corner of her kitchen table. And the subject of her dad never came up. And she never had her lips going all trembly in front of me, after which she sucked it up. And she never did all that stuff standing in her door, both lettin' me in and saying good-bye, looking both times like the most beautiful girl, I swear, on earth, even though she was only then goin' on thirteen, which by the time I'm gonna talk about now she'd come to, with me not too far behind her.

But now that I'm on to like my age, and miserable things, I've gotta throw in that it's been, with the time that's passed since I've been talkin' about all this stuff, more than five full months since I've seen Frankie or Pete or Stu or any of those kids I moved away from, so I'm pretty much thinking I might really not see any of them ever again, which includes Patty. And, yeah, I've actually made it to fourteen now, because another April 12TH has passed, which is my birthday. But a lot of good it's gonna do me. And I swear, I think it would already feel weird if I like saw them again—

I mean like even now. Don't ask me why. It just would, I think. Which is weird, and for shit. But it's true. No matter what, though—there's one thing I'll never, ever forget as long as I live, or wherever I end up in my life. And that's that, as sure as I'm a righty, Mary Patricia Conlon is a southpaw.

Of course you always know who the lefties are because of the whacked out way that they have to hold their pens when they write. And Patty (though when she wrote, she didn't like squint and stick her tongue out and bite it and all that stuff, the way a lot of lefties do) was no exception. She had that old corkscrew thing going, and her writing was kinda for shit, I've got to say. Only her answers were always so off-the-map excellent it made you even want maybe to imitate her corkscrew writing style. Sort of the way you wanted to walk a little bow-legged in the hopes that that might make you as fast as JL, who was a little bit of that (the way great college and pro halfbacks a lot of the time are) and who was as fast on his feet as Patty was in her brain, which is saying something for both of them.

Anyhow, I already knew Patty was lefty, but I came to know this fact even better. And did I say that Sister Mad was a little bit easily piss-off-able? Well, let me change that to the SMM was the nicest nun since like Claire of Sienna or Teresa of Avilon or Margaret Mary Alicoque (which last one we made up some poems about, which I won't say anything about, except that they probably cost us the plenary, which is too long to explain if you're not Catholic). Because, anyhow, what did Sister Mary Madeline decide to do one day but take our desks and connect them in these rows so that each row was sort of like one long connected table. And I was always glad my name is Collins because that came right before Conlon, as in Patricia, in all my classes, which made me think that God was on my side or something. But it always meant Patty just sat behind me, which wasn't perfect, though it meant I could smell the soap she used (which is another thing I'm pretty sure I'll remember till my final hour on the planet).

But what happened now was, Patty got moved up right next to me. And I was righty…and she was lefty. And our desks, like I say, were connected.

I can't say really what led up to it the first time it happened. I'd like to think that the two of us were sort of workin' on it in silence, moving our forearms sort of like the hands of a clock, which you can't see moving, but when you look up again, sure enough—they're there. And I mean, too, you're sittin' there, like in *your life,* and you've not been touched and you've not been touched and you've not been touched, like for years and years and years. Or your whole life so far. And then all of a sudden you've been touched. I mean it's like something you could write an entire book about. But then ya think, "I've been touched" wouldn't make much of a book. It could be the point, though.

And I mean it wasn't just Holy Shit, We Have Contact!— and then nothing, just like some accidental bump, and then excuse me, and then no more. No way. It was like once my right forearm somehow all of a sudden came up against her left forearm, neither one of us got all proud and faked it like we were grossed out or embarrassed. We just stayed there, forearm touching forearm. And then it was like this discovery that we could do this and SMM wouldn't know. And then it was like the best thing on the face of the earth, because we started doing it every day. But get this. We never said the first word to each other about it. We just did it, without even looking at each other, letting our forearms kind of just move over like clock hands, till the time said, "Oh *shit* does this feel good."

Of course, if I was like an eighty-year-old guy and never did see Patty again, but after sixty-seven years somebody, like down in Florida, told me that that eighty-year-old woman over there used to live just south of 91ST on Winchester, where the street sort of tucks into Ryan's Woods, second house from the end, and her name was Patty, used to be Conlon, I know this: I could go over to her and ask her if she would please like not belt me or anything and then just set my right forearm against her left one, and she—I know it—would say, "Kevin Collins."

Of course I didn't throw in for JL all that bullsh about sixty-seven years from now down in Florida, which has just been coming to me lately. But that Fourth of July night in the pueblo, and now I double-checked to see if Frankie was ko'd, I did tell Jackie—not just about Joe Louis and stuff, but about Patty and me and the forearms, and that though I didn't have any luck those two times in my *Southtown* collections, I still stuck with the Tuesdays (which the *Southtown* never even noticed), and since then she'd been there. And I said how I for some reason really loved it that she never said anything stupid like she *liked* me but that she sort of quietly, in this really cool way, told me that those times she wasn't there, she had to be at special dance things she hadn't known about. And it was so extremely cool, for some reason, I told Jackie, just sitting there in her kitchen, talking with her about nothing, and still neither one of us ever having said word one, even in the kitchen, about how we kept ourselves touched together every day at school. And Jackie told me some secret stuff about him and Katie Luce, who he was flipped over. Namely that he'd kissed her. And of course I asked him—more than once? And he said no. But then I asked him—cheek or lips? And he smiled, gettin' all red over that tough but handsome-like mug of his—and said, "Lips." And was it like a shit kiss or a good one? And he smiled again and said, "A good one." Okay, whoa shit, so was it for like five seconds, or four seconds, or three seconds, or two seconds, or one second? And now he got a really big smile, like he was almost too embarrassed to talk, but he said, "About four seconds." And what could we do then, with something that good, except start laughin', and, you know, knuckle-pronging each other on the arm.

We talked about other stuff that night, too, which I'll talk about. But the reason that I waited till Frankie was asleep is because that day was one of those days they plastered the NO PARKING signs on all the trees down Hamilton and Longwood and Leavitt and any street that bordered on The Woods because they didn't want people who'd come to picnic for the Fourth, which means one hundred percent colored people, to be walking around the streets, but to do their parking in The Woods' parking lot south of 87TH. But that doesn't all the way explain my waiting till Frankie fell asleep to tell the stories, does it.

Well, what happened was the three of us, I mean Jackie and me and Frankie were playing '500' in the Dead End, just sort of screwin' off, hitting flies and grounders and stuff, and all of a sudden Frankie, who's playing deep while JL was hitting, slams down his glove and shouts out, "Say 'black eyes' backwards!"

Jackie and I didn't know what was up at first, but then we could see there were like three or four colored kids up against the fence in Shannons' yard, you know, kind of staring through with their fingers all hooked into the cyclone's wires. And naturally the first thing we did was what white kids do when they see colored kids, even if ya love Joe Louis beyond to-death, which is get scared there might be a rumble and somebody might get like knifed or shot. But then we got over that, and tossed our gloves and the rubber-coated and the bat up on my lawn, and just went down to see what was up. And like three of the colored kids were just sort of standing there and kind of smiling and laughing, but there was this one kid who was shouting, "Say 'I'm white trash'!"

And there was Frankie—big surprise—goin' nuts and raging, sort of like that time he went nuts on the Rat King in the football game (though truth to tell, Frankie had about a daily insanity attack, either with his beloved brother who, you may recall, that one time knocked his jaw right out of its socket, and Frankenstein-ed him, or with Pete, or with somebody)—and Frankie keeps yelling back at this one colored kid, "Say 'black eyes' backwards!"

And the kid's goin' full and complete spastic himself, shouting, "Say 'I'm white trash'!"

And now Jackie and I are down there, and we're looking pretty dopey. But so are these three colored kids who are not spazzing. And we're looking at them, and they're looking at us like "Hey, you got your spaz and we've got our spaz." And I've gotta say it was actually cool, even while Frankie and this kid are in full spaz-out to be like sharing a non-spaz-out with colored kids who didn't want the Third World War any more than me and Jackie.

But now Frankie and this kid are like both their fingers full on the atomic button. And they're like climbing the fence to wipe each other off the face of the earth. And they're screamin' now "Say 'I'm white trash'!" and "Say 'black eyes' backwards!" And now they're right up at the top of the fence, screaming in each other's faces. And the kid changes it now, and like right in Frankie's eyes says, "You're a mother*fucker!*" Which of course would be the number-one favorite colored swear-term. And it is an outstanding term, no doubt, good maybe for even like a cool decade of the rosary. But I have to figure there isn't a single kid in the universe who wouldn't say, "Sorry, Mom, I love ya, and I hope you'll understand. But it's the leper I'm gonna nail."

But what does Frankie do—instead of maybe "Eat fuck!" or something really imaginative like "Chew my colostomy bag!" which would have set the kid back, I'm sure of that—instead of anything that, you know, would do us some credit, Frankie just shouts back, *"You're* a motherfucker!"

But then it was kind of interesting, because, well, Frankie's using that term seemed to be something that he had like all the right experience for, like he was right in there with this colored kid he was goin' nuts with, the two of them up at the top of that nine-foot cyclone looking like Cagney at his most gonzo, calling each other *Motherfucker!* then spelling it out in detail with stuff like *You love to fuck your mother, you motherfucker!* And *Eat shit, you motherfucker!* And *You eat your mother's shit, you motherfucker!* Which last one I don't know what it would have done to the colored kid's mom, but I could see Mrs. M taking a full Schlitz and maybe shaking the crap out of it and shootin' it.

But then like the five of us, I mean the three non-spazzing colored kids and JL and me, we all started saying *Break it up, Break it up, Break it up.* And just like Frankie wasn't ranked the toughest of the three of us, their spaz wasn't ranked the toughest of the four of them—you could tell by the way the kid came down when this one kid among them (callin' him a sorry-ass motherfucker) told him to fucking cool it and get his sorry ass off the fucking fence, sort of the way Frankie came down when JL, in more white-kid talk, told Frankie to get off the fence or he'd have to wipe the shit out of him. And then this other interesting thing happened, which is that both Frankie and the colored kid he'd had the *motherfucker* contest with, once they were down off the fence, both in like the exact same way started telling their friends to eat shit, and in the exact same way, I swear it, kind of whipped their arms and shoulders away when you tried to touch 'em and calm 'em down and stuff. And then in the exact same way they both fired off a couple of parting *fuck you* and *eat shit* shots, not at each other, but at their friends, and then took off. I mean it was like the two of them, I swear, were gonna go meet up somewhere and start up a special organization of their own, which of course would have been something like the National Association for the Advancement of Raging People.

So there the two of them went. And there the rest of us were: the peacemakers. But I've gotta say that when you're a peacemaker, you always sort of suspect something about yourself. And it's that you might not be so much one of the children of God as you are a chickenshit. And there's something about what I could call maybe the 'NAARP' that makes you think it might actually be kind of a cool club, where ya have it out, but at least you're not fako keeping it in.

But then something very cool did happen for us peacemakers. And that is that we started like talking through the fence, you know, for a while there, about the two madman MF's, and having kind of a contest about who was crazier, their MF or our MF, with both sides showing like a serious shitload of confidence, which got us all laughing, both sides. Which, like the second it started happening, you were thinking you wouldn't forget this, ever. I mean this conversation through the nine-foot cyclone. But of course (and this was something, too, that seemed to be part of the remember-it-forever stuff) it was like we were trying to visit each other through the glass at Joliet, or something.

But then Jackie just says, "Hey, come on over here." And he goes over to the rabbit hole, and he starts kicking away these leaves that we sometimes had there to cover the hole up. And I gotta say I had a thought, for a second there, like maybe we shouldn't be showing these guys this hole, 'cause who knows what they might use it for, and like how many of their friends they might show it to, and how we might be like walking for the rest of our lives because there'd be no more bikes in Beverly. But JL doesn't give a crap-ball about any of that stuff. He just slides on through like nothin'. And there he is, standing on the other side of the fence, him and the colored guys. And this would be one of those classic JL moves—I mean, one that got ya past the chickenshit inside ya. So there I was, too, like nothin', zippin' through the rabbit hole, which made me feel all of a sudden very cool, like I lost a lead weight out of my gut, or out of my head or something.

Of course this was our territory, so we started showing 'em all the cool stuff we knew, including (because it was broad daylight) the Hanged-Kid Tree. Which Jackie and I had to tell them wasn't something white kids do like every day. I mean hang themselves. And then all five of us were laughing 'cause we all, after the colored kids started it, started calling that kid "one crazy motherfucker." And then we all started calling everything around us some kind of motherfucker, and it had us all laughing up a very major, almost pee-your-drawers storm, which turned out to be a cool way to get started when you're in situations like the one we were all in there. And I asked, kind of settin' somebody up to be part of a comedy team, what's the word for when everything becomes one word and all you do is keep on laughing. And this really funny, kind of chubby colored kid, named Toby (who was also the one who was their toughest), jumped all over it and said that would have to be a motherfuckin' mother*FUCKER*. And so there we were, all five of us laughin' our total butts off, like throwing out all the words there ever were and starting all over again with all the different ways we all could say motherfucker.

Anyhow, we still hadn't worn this one out and were still all laughin' our butts off, when we ran into Toby's mother and family, who were like just a half dozen out of about ten thousand colored people there in The Woods, which was strange, because it was our woods, really, but it kept feeling cool, and like we wouldn't forget it. And Toby's mother was this really nice lady, who said, "Lord be praised, boy, who you got here? You gon' introduce me?"

And it was funny, 'cause like Toby was the only name we knew and they didn't know either of our names, and naturally we all started bustin' now at the same time because we're all like imagining Toby (who puts on, you can trust me, the look that would give us this idea) saying, you know, to his mom, that these were two motherfuckers from over that nine-foot motherfucker over there.

But now JL gets Toby out of it, even though everybody's still laughing—'cause, out of somewhere, he finds a straight face, and he says, "I'm Jack Leonard, pleased to meet you." And then I said, "I'm Kevin Collins, pleased to meet you." Not that this saying of our names didn't still get some good, kind of out-of-control laughs.

And then she said, "Well, I'm Laetitia, and I'm verih pleased to meet y'all. And I hope you boys'll stay for supper and have some of my fried chicken."

Of course neither Jackie or me had ever heard a name like Laetitia (which I found out later from my mom how to spell and that it was a name from like the beginning of America, and that like lots of white women had had it back then). And later I was wondering if there was ever a St. Laetitia because, even though I've always thought this was bullshit, because is there a St. Wendell? or a St. Ira? which were my grandfathers' names—but if your name isn't a canonized person's name, it's supposed to be you can't be baptized. But Jackie and I were saying later that night in the pueblo, anyhow, that we were glad there was baptism of desire, which, to explain, means if you're not Catholic (And how about the three colored kids, even livin' their whole lives in Chicago, had never even heard of Catholics! I shit you not!), you don't have to worry about dying unbaptized. All you have to do is *want to be* what Christ wants you to be, which is something you don't even have to know who Christ is, to know. Which (besides being a very cool doctrine, keeping like jillions of people out of hell) makes you think about coming up with the idea of something, or maybe you'd say the feeling of it, and like doing this all by yourself, when you haven't seen like any examples, which is pretty weird and cool, too—though like I've been saying, it's lucky for you if you have friends to show you stuff and bring stuff out in ya, which is probably why there's religions—I mean 'cause there's lots of examples and stuff in 'em, so it's easier for ya 'cause you don't have to go it completely on your own.

Anyhow, JL and I were a little worried that if we didn't get home to dinner (which meant to my house, 'cause Jackie was staying over), they'd be worried about us. Not that it would be the first time I, or friends of mine and me, didn't show up for dinner. So, truth, they wouldn't be calling the police about any missing persons. And she was so cool, Toby's mom, and we didn't want to hurt her feelings. And the colored kids were like being very cool, too. Because, I mean, I think we all were keeping on with thinking, in this kind of cool and spooky way, that this would be something we'd *all* remember. And Jackie and I later agreed that it would have been worth even getting into a fairly hefty amount of shit for. The two of us, too, understood the words 'fried chicken.' And the kids were throwing in other words we knew, like 'corn on the cob.' And then some weird ones we hadn't heard, but they said we'd love the *stuff*, which they called 'soul food', once we had it in our mouths. And then it got like we couldn't say no, not that we wanted to. So we just smiled and said, "Okay."

Then Jackie and me and Toby and Franklin and Theodore (which was kind of weird that they didn't just call him Ted—but it was extremely cool, though, for some reason, when we all told each other our names and got 'em straight, and even I'd say overused 'em a little in the excitement, 'cause we were like so much *wanting* to use them—the saying of names having this opposite but equally cool kind of happiness from jokin' up everything into one single word)—then we had to kill time, because it was only about four, and dinner, though they said supper, kind of like kids from the country, wasn't till six.

But (and it was still so weird but somehow so cool, which surprised ya it didn't piss ya off, to see people from like *not* your territory suddenly *in* your territory making like completely psyched-up use out of it) there was a softball game, sixteen-inch, getting started over the way, and it wasn't the kids, but the men, who were pickin' up teams. So there was like a lot of psych spreading around, and the five of us were there for it in no time. And then like this sort of cool coincidence happened because there were fifteen men out there ready to play but all the rest of the men were like cooking and horsin' around and stuff or just wanting to watch and not wanting to play, so for softball they needed five more, and there we were, not too completely punky, all of us at around thirteen, to fill in. And Toby's right out with the "We'll play!" Which got an *okay*, which was pretty incredible. And then it was like right away all the colored men were treating Jackie and me maybe the same way the colored men treated my dad when he was with George Johnson. You know, sort of like going out of their way to be cool and make you feel welcome, which I swear made me play better in the game, right down to stuff like the rhythm when I threw. And Jackie—well, he was always Jackie when it came to ball playing, as you'll see.

But it was so cool. I mean there might have been those men who didn't want to play, but there was just about everybody who wanted to be there. And just like that, it was becoming like a huge event, with the base lines about covered with people, like in pictures of old times in baseball, where there was no park but the crowd was all kind of formed around like a park, with guys in derby hats and ladies in bloomers and stuff. Of course I don't need to say the colored people weren't wearing those things. But, which is weird, even the guys were wearing some pretty weirdo-colorful stuff. And sure there was goofin' off (and some of it ranking right up there with George P's kind of total hi-lariousness, only there were a couple of times too that the people were laughing their butts off, and, I gotta be honest, I didn't think it was *that* funny—I don't know, maybe there's something wrong with me). But the goofing off was from the guys who ya could tell hadn't played much baseball and they were just trying to cover it up that they stunk. But there was only a couple like that. And the rest were ready for serious baseball action.

And you know me. I love a cool game, especially when it becomes like a really serious cool game, the kind that all of a sudden out of nowhere makes you feel grown up in a cool way. And this one was one of those. Of course, with six-teen-inch there's gonna be a ton of runs. So what you hope is that both teams score 'em. And that's what happened. The final was like seventeen to sixteen. But it was like all this stuff I really love to keep my eye on that was cool, too.

I mean the first time I came up, it was like they all wanted to let me know I was probably gonna get on base because when they threw the ball around they started dropping it and stuff, which was an act, but it was to be friendly. Because, like I was saying, there was like all this friendliness to the white kids. Which could actually be a game-wrecker. But there was like this really cool, serious question in the air, too, which was, can these white kids do shit in base-ball? And I gotta say I was a little ready to prove something because they played me really shallow, and this was after, the inning before, they'd played Toby deep (I forgot to say they put me on one team with Toby and Franklin, and JL on the other team with Theodore). But they didn't know me, and they knew Toby, who was like I said chubby, but then so was the Babe—and I mean Toby could knock the livin' crap outa the ball. But they came way in for me, even though, like I said, they made it pretty clear they might just bungle anything I hit. So it was like he maybe can't do shit but we're not gonna make him feel bad. And at that point, first pitch I mean, I smacked one right on the nose, down the left-field line and got a clean two out of it. And then it was like whoa shit the boy can play, and all the ladies on the side were laughin' and they found out my name and were calling out "Kev-in! Kev-in!" and the men on the side were giving shit to the other team and laughing their butts off, and the other team was going, "Whoo-ee! We ain't gon' make that mistake agin!" And it was like they were happy, laughing about it, that the answer to that big question in the air was that I wasn't shit. And I had this cool feeling like I was gonna play great that day, because of the way the ladies and all the guys on the side had gotten those laughs going, and said my name, and that they wouldn't be playing me in any more, or bungling the ball.

And then with JL it was, totally predictable to me, like up six notches. Because of course (even though I warned 'em), his first time up, JL gets everybody really laughing when he takes one over their—I mean our—right fielder's head and then does his slightly bow-legged blue streak around the bags for a stand-up home run. And I won't go into it all, but what happens then is that they got serious about this white kid (who it was real clear was so tough that colored guys would want him on their team, any time). And what they do is take their best guy and move him to right field next time JL comes up, 'cause of course he's lefty and you generally put your sorriest guy in right, almost everybody being righty—but then when that one lefty comes up...maybe a switch? So it was like real respect—I mean, when they *did* a switch for Jackie. And of course they were showing this pretty strong desire not to get beat.

But JL gets hits anyway, I mean every time up, I swear. And then it comes to the last inning, which as you know is JL's territory. And there's a man on first, which means a single won't get him home. And maybe not even a double. And that best guy, the guy who's shifted to right, is ready to stop JL, come hell or high water, from knocking the guy on first on home, 'cause the score is tied and one run will give them the lead. And JL's gonna back down about as much as he's, well—gonna back down, which is zero. And in comes the pitch, after a lot of cool fakes from our pitcher, which needless to say didn't fake out Jackie, who rips one high and deep. And it gets our right fielder motoring back. And it was like beautiful, watching that ball, and watching our guy, who was so good, and so fast—I mean fast like a man, goin' all OUT, with his shirt all rippling in the wind from his speed. But no sir. That ball was so tagged it got juuust past the fingertips of, I mean, the fastest-running outfielder I ever saw. And then there was JL, tearin' around all the bags, and then givin' them, as he crossed home, a two-run lead. And all the colored ladies and girls are goin' nuts. And all the colored men are goin', "Whooo-weee!" and laughing and givin' shit to our team. But it all was like the coolest thing ever, because even our outfielder was laughing, shaking his head all serious but kind of really comical (and not to spoil a good time, but you can compare him to Val Prizer in the same situation) saying, "Whoo-weee! That boy can PLAY!" And I was like seriously happy, even though we'd just fallen behind by two in the top of the last, which it turned out we came back from in the bottom and took the game by one, which was really cool, too. And it was like all just good, with everybody psyched and respectful and happy. I mean it was great.

But, then, there I was, too, suddenly thinking about the NAARP, 'cause it occurred to me I hadn't seen even one time that kid who spazzed with FX at the cyclone, and of course we hadn't seen Frankie. And I was thinking about how the game we just played was easily as cool as any having it out ever was. And where we were going now was for fried chicken (and I mean everybody, not just Toby's mom, was all around us and inviting us now, 'cause things were that cool, with all the tests of how good we were being passed with such flying colors). While Frankie and that kid were *where* and with *what?*

These are the kind of things I might think about for a while. But because by then it was dinner, or supper time (and I was thinking, they don't call it the Last Dinner, *do* they?), I only had time now to reach the conclusion that wherever those two were, they were probably, besides being super-hungry, still pissed. And what I was seeing now was so much food that I was sure it had to be a stretch or something that colored people were totally poor—except for the fact that they drank RC cola, which, though, I gotta say, is not as shit as reported. And that the food was out of this world, even though, you know, no matter where you go, when it's not home, you're going to think what *is* that stuff?—and with these guys, outside the chicken and corn on the cob, it was really weird stuff. But Jackie and I went with *Don't ask, just eat it,* which paid off, trust me.

So, even though it was getting dark and people at home would be getting worried and there we were with ten thousand colored people, in The Woods, in the dark, Jackie and I just kept going with this great time we were having.

And you maybe remember I talked about a building out in The Woods, you know, the one with no walls, just a big roof—that one where Frankie smoked up the Pin's trou with the magnifying glass, and where he was carving that special term of his on the column of it, which wouldn't now, though, get noticed, 'cause it was mixed with a jillion other carved words there, there being something about people wanting to carve words on a wooden pole. And that I was saying how places where sometimes there's tons of people, like a church, how quiet they get when there's no one around. Which this building in The Woods was usually like, big time. But now there *were* tons of people there. And it was the total opposite. I mean, it was like a Solemn High Mass when it's extremely good—with the three priests and the church packed and the music either like the most beautiful Latin hymns, or maybe *Holy God We Praise Thy Name*, and everybody singing to sort of shake the thunder down and the gold of the monstrance rising up in the incense smoke as cool as at Benediction. Only now what was gold were the saxophones.

And *shit* was it cool. Especially with the sound of the drums, too. And the way we got to see, 'cause there were more people gathered round for the music and dancing than even for the baseball, was we climbed up into the rafters, me and Jackie and Toby and Franklin and Theodore. And we didn't even do moronic stuff like spit watermelon seeds or anything. We just sort of, you could maybe say, went to a High Mass of Desire. 'Cause when that first saxophone broke out, the sound was as cool as the priest chanting out *Introibo ad altare dei*—and you whispering, if you're an altar boy, *Ad deum qui laetificat juventutum meum*. Which if you're not Catholic starts the mass and means, "I will go unto the altar of God—to God, who gives joy to my youth."

Of course it kept creeping in, the feeling that we better get home or get our butts kicked. But still we kept staying, even though it was real dark now. And the way the place was lit was with these torches, so it stayed all lit up under that big outdoor roof. And people danced non-stop, which was kind of weird to see men dance. Because if you're white, you don't see your dad dance unless it's at a wedding, which you generally don't get invited to. And like I say the shining gold saxophones—beautiful as like monstrances in church—but the complete opposite of quiet, believe me. And like all these torches where it would usually be totally dark. And all these colored girls in white dresses, some with really, really red roses pinned on 'em, so pretty. And the men dancin' like all get out, and really good at it. All of this like put it really solid in your brain, the memory of it all. So that maybe whenever in the future you heard great drums, or the break-out of a horn, your mind would go right back, and all the other feelings would come back, too, which is so forever-cool.

Still, though, time came. We had to get movin' or like my mom and dad *would* think we weren't just screwin' around somewhere but were dead. And there *would* be cops out or something insane, lookin' for missing persons. So one time when the band took a rest, we kind of agreed, Jackie and me, that it was time to go. And that was another thing, you know, saying good-bye to guys you knew you'd never see again in your entire life, but guys you'd had this thing with. But I think probably we were all, too, thinking maybe it's okay that this is ending before something uncool happened (because eventually something uncool will happen, no matter what the situation). And yet there was this thing—I mean, that because there'd been zero uncoolness, we'd be able to make use of this time forever, when people said stupid crap about colored people, or, for them, white people.

And, then, it was like Jackie and me, we already made use of what we knew, right after we said good-bye (which, I'd guess you'd say 'cause our good feelings *reminded* us, we made sure included to Laetitia)—because once we got away from the torch lights and were heading back over toward the ravine and then down, it got really dark as shit, really fast. And there we were in a woods full of about total darkness, with ten thousand colored people—but it was like bring on the Hanged Kid and the Nude Guy and whatever else you've got, because we don't give a crap-ball. We aren't scared. I mean it was this really incredible feeling of having *no* scared-to-deathness in ya, no matter that it was in The Woods, and on the Fourth of July, or how dark it was.

And when we zipped through the rabbit hole, we were like laughing and happy as clams could be, when all of a sudden, like out of nowhere from behind us, when we were heading back to the street, comes this "AAARRRGHHH!" And of course it brought us right back down again to you can be scared shitless. And we just started running, 'cause yeah, we were in no time back enough to normal. But then we heard this laughing. And then we knew exactly who we'd been had by, which of course would be Francis Malone.

First thing we had to do then was roll the kid pretty good, which he was extremely lucky didn't include the goossage royale, because, you know, it pisses ya off to be scared, especially after you so completely weren't. And then of course we want to know where he's been all this time. And it wasn't hanging at home, he said. And it wasn't hanging by the fence all day. And it wasn't hanging at Stenham's. So then I asked him, because maybe like my head was making up some kind of a story, if he'd been hanging with that colored kid he went face to face with at the fence, 'cause we hadn't seen that kid in The Woods. And Frankie told me I could boff myself for that little idea. Which actually made me laugh, you know, with a so-much-for-that-story kind of laugh. But then our dear Frank got suddenly all just sort of pissed off, so we never did find out where he'd been hanging. And we just sort of settled on nowhere.

Naturally we lied to my mom, saying we just lost track of time and then, for dinner, bought ourselves hotdogs at Darby's BBQ—and that we were really sorry, which of course was also, as it mostly is, a crock. And I can't say why I didn't get killed—maybe 'cause my friends were around. My mom just said she'd speak to me later, which she did, actually, and which was when I gave her the straight dope and she told me about the name Laetitia. But Frankie didn't figure we'd get food in The Woods, so wherever he'd been, he'd just sort of starved there, which meant he was sort of waiting to eat big at my house. So later on we had to sneak down and get him some chow. Or not really sneak, because with Malone my mom kind of expects a continuous feed, since, no matter what, Frankie's like insane with a bottomless starvation and hunger.

And then later, you know, when we were up in the pueblo, we told Frankie a little bit about our night. 'Cause like the saxophones were still playing and stuff. But you could tell he didn't want to hear a first word about it. So we let up, not to stick it to him and make him feel bad. But still, I don't know why, I was like still makin' up that story in my head about Frankie and that kid; and I was coming up with this ending like they'd turn out to be friends who actually kept seeing each other, instead of the way Jackie and me would be with Toby and Franklin and Theodore. And it was like my head was really believing this wouldn't be a bullshit story. And I thought it would be especially cool if you made it so like the two of 'em came close a couple of times to murderin' each other, before they became real and honest friends. But what it turned out to be was, we just sort of talked about other stuff until, you know, the saxophones were all quiet and gone, and the shade-pulled-over-it light over at Shannons' ('cause now Susie, speaking of remember-it-forever stuff, was home for the summer) got turned out. And, even though I was sort of suspicious that Frankie might be fakin' he was asleep—and wanting to get in on what I was saying—I'm about a hundred percent sure he really was asleep when I started to tell Jackie the stories about my dad, and George Johnson, and the iceball and the Cadillac and Joe Louis.

It's funny, though. I felt sort of sneaky and chickenshit, waiting till Frankie was out cold, to tell those stories. I mean it was like guaranteeing it that I'd get a good audience. But then if I told the stories to Francis X, too, it would be like I was trying to preach some kind of a sermon to him. Which was a thought that puked me out, 'cause it was like Frankie was way too cool for that. And so were the stories.

JL, like I said, went nuts over both of 'em (though I don't know why, but I left out the stuff about when George Johnson had the loaded gun). The stories of course came out of the day we'd had, and then they led back to our day, which ended up with our talking about baptism of desire and stuff. Which dead guaranteed that Frankie was now ko'd (and does the word 'okay' come from its being the opposite of 'ko'd'?), because there'd have been some funny bullsh out of the kid over baptism of desire, no doubt, you know, about what he was desiring, or something. So then it was safe to talk about Katie Luce and Patty. And Jackie and I did that till it was like really late and The Woods were for a long time totally quiet, so it was like a church again, when it's empty.

Then I did something that I'd never done with anybody but Bobby Stu. That is, I told Jackie about the Rat King, the whole deal. And because I like wanted Jackie to really love Bobby Stu, which of course he did already, I told him about Bobby watchin' out for me, every single solitary day for a long time afterwards.

And it really kills me, I mean just thinking of the way Jackie said it, about Bobby, which was just in this great, kind of quiet way he had, which you always have to combine with his being the toughest kid any of us ever knew, by a mile. "I love that kid," he said.

I sort of chuckled a little and said, "Me, too. Believe it." Which of course was the obvious thing to say for a laugh, in this case.

Then Jackie smiles the crook-toother, which I can see in the moonlight. And then he brings up another thing. "How about Stu-ball and the math, do you believe that kid?"

Which I should explain by saying Bobby got this score in the national math test which was the highest in the whole school, eighth-graders included. I mean he even beat Patty on this one, and by a poke. And there's Jackie and me like laughin' our butts off thinking about the big guy being some kind of a mathematical genius (which actually didn't totally shock us 'cause Bobby would generally be like bored as shit all day in school until like a really, really tough math problem came up, and then bang, there he'd be, and, you know, we were starting to think it couldn't be luck, not *that* many times).

We got sort of satisfied-quiet then, after chuckling and thinking about Bobby the genius. And the moon now, I remember, was all spooky bright. And of course it was the middle of summer, so we had the window open wide. And a really great, sort of cool breeze was coming through the screen, but no noise. So it was still like a church all empty, with maybe just you and like the candles that people have lit for offerings, sort of flickering in the red-glass holders, and maybe, off somewhere where you can't see, somebody with a footstep making an echo, and then coming closer, till there he was, which would be Jackie's voice.

He said, "Sometimes, Kev, do ya think about what, in your life, you're going to be?"

And like so many of the things you'd really love to do for your whole life don't turn out to be things you can be, so you just can't think of 'em that way. But I did have one that came close, which I told Jack was a sportswriter. "You get to go to all the games," I said. "And you get the best seats in the house. I mean this is for your job. And then I'd really love it, writing the stories. I'd totally love that." Then we thought about stories like the Joe Louis story. And about me, especially, being a sportswriter, JL said, "That would be really cool. That would be a great thing, Kev, for you to be."

And I don't know, I mean those words, stuff like his saying, "That would be a great thing, Kev, for you to be"—they right now put that shit pain around my throat like a rope. And it's not only the words. I mean Jackie said some cool stuff. But it's not just the words. It's the kid sayin' 'em. And the place. And the time. Which was like the last time I remember Jackie and me ever talkin' like this. I mean just the two of us and the whole world like cleared out and gone to sleep, which was so cool. But shit. It's like some bad dreams I've been having, how to think of this stuff hurts and like so fast it leaves me feeling totaled.

But I remember Jackie said then, "You know, Kev, if I could take Katie L along, I think it would be very cool to be a priest."

Of course I quick checked to see if Malone heard that one.

Jackie saw me, and was chucklin'. "Guess he's asleep all right."

"Oh, yeah," I said.

JL laughed. Then he said it again, I mean that he'd like being a priest for a job, except no way he could give up being married and having kids and stuff, and all that normal life.

And I mean when it's some simp shit like Lenny Feraro or someone like that, you know, born with his hands folded and like afraid of himself if he ever talked too loud and like every single day wanting to stay after school because if he couldn't give extra help to the sisters he'd have to cry himself to sleep at night, you go, oh jeez yeah, put the dip out of his misery, let him be a priest and be done with it. And Jackie was never gonna be a priest. But I mention what he said because he was never a bullshitter, either. So it tells ya something about him. And because it's a cool idea, JL as a priest, 'cause for one reason I'm positive of how you'd feel for *real* something like the *hoc est enim corpus meum,* and the *sanguinis meum* coming from Jack Leonard. And, for another, so you wouldn't ever get the idea that what God loves best is total simps with their hands folded all day long, lookin' like they wanna cry, which for some reason the penguins seem to love. But no way without the Katie Luce factor.

Speaking of which, Jackie said, "But I think," he said, "you know, the four seconds—it was a little too good."

Which got us laughing our butts off. And then Jack talked about maybe being a doctor. But then, too, about being an electrician, the way his dad was, and how his dad already said to him they could be partners and stuff, which was cool, even though it meant Jackie probably wouldn't be rich, because Mr. Leonard wasn't. You know, the Leonards lived over across the tracks on Paulina, where the rows of bungalows are.

"So maybe that's what I'll really be," he said.

"It's cool," I said, "you and your dad. And then after that maybe some kid of yours. That's cool stuff."

"Yeah," he said, "it is."

And that's like the last words I remember that night. It was late now. And Jackie was asleep next time I looked over. Him and Frankie, which kills me thinking of.

CHAPTER EIGHT

FALL OF EIGHTH

IN THE INVISIBLE CIRCLE

And I mean, down into the heart it kills me. But I *do* think of it, I mean this kind of thing that like so much gets to me. It's what I'm doing all along here, I guess. So why would I? I know one thing—I'd be ashamed as shit if it was just for some kick—I mean my telling this story about Jackie. 'Cause of course there's a kick in sadness, who doesn't know that? Or if it was because I wanted somebody to like me, or some other pathetic crap, because it makes me look like I really have a heart or something, or I need a helping hand, when I talk about a friend of mine who's not here anymore. But I don't want anybody to like me, or, I mean, I'm not fishing for it. I just want to think about, and not shut up about, Jackie Leonard, who died, in this bad way. And if it feels like warm or good to get stuff out, I can't help that. And it's like you're not to be blamed either for being curious, if you are—because if there weren't something that got ya looking, you'd never see that kid. And I know this—people oughta see that kid. I mean all the stuff, like the morality of him, besides that left-hand swing, and the way he saved me from gettin' killed those times.

I know, though, I said I'd mention some more of those. So how about the time in sixth when we were at the toboggan slides south of 87TH, which we'd ride our bikes down in the summer (really hairy—trust me). And these hoods from who knows where showed up. Like eighth-grade guys. And they came up to us and said what they wanted was to burn our foreheads with their cigarettes. And there was this one big kid who was missing a tooth who seemed like he'd really do it. And there he was now lightin' up a butt and then naturally blowin' smoke rings like some kind of a poison fish, working its jaws on its fish food, then takin' the butt out and pokin' it through the center of the rings like he was thinking they were our eyes. And I don't know where this kid was from. And after that day I never saw him again. But it could've been that I'd never be able to forget him in my life, even if I never saw him again, 'cause there, every day when I looked in the mirror, would be a white scar on my forehead like a brand mark that said I always belonged to his ranch—which would over the years do what to my thinking about things?

And here the kid comes, naturally picking me to start things with, with the butt held up like a dart. And maybe I told you the Joe Louis story, for one reason, besides just the fact I love it, because of what happened right here, which was Jackie in like a split second just steps between me and the kid and doesn't just jolt the guy but knocks him flat—and OUT. And I mean you take a national survey of every country in the world and find out how many sixth graders ever knocked out an eighth grader with one punch (or let 'em have a hundred punches) and I think what you'll find is JL. And I don't need to say how this put an end to branding day at the ranch. So what I think of this kid now, with his missing tooth, is that he's like somebody who cuts off the car you're in but misses ya rather than hits ya. And he's got a car that's got like a huge bash in its side, so you think if he crashed into you, it wouldn't have been his first bad accident. But he missed you, and went on, and you'll never see him again, with it not mattering that it was such a close one.

And, thinking of the morality, there would for an example be Jackie on the other side of that fence with the colored kids. Which, though, brings up another thing I've been thinking about a lot lately, too, because of where I am right now, which is up north: and that's that the reason we moved up north, truth to tell, isn't just because our family got too big for the house on Hamilton, which it did, but because we wanted to get to a place where the property values wouldn't go down because of colored people coming. And it's like you never say the word 'nigger,' but at the same time, when it's time to go, you go—even my dad, and my mom, who I'd kill you if you said weren't good people. But I think if like that feeling, of like having to move out when it's a certain time, were ever a sort of like *object* in your brain, you might want to find a surgeon to go in there and knife the thing out. And then maybe you'd be kind of goofy in a happy-go-lucky way, you know, like having to be grabbed by people off the street because you missed it that a bus was about to mow you down. But you'd have a better shot at feeling what Jackie and I felt (and how about we *weren't* goofy), when on that Fourth of July night we were crossing the ravine in the dark, before we met Frankie, and heard him growl—that is, a *not*-sacred-to-death-ness, like right down to our guts and bones.

But there's more stuff I need to say, before I get to stuff that happened later. And I'm thinking of it because of those kids with the butts at the toboggan slides and because of something JL said, or asked me, that Fourth of July night in the pueblo. And it was, "Did anything ever happen between you and Prizer? I mean that explains why he goes after you?"

I said, "Ya know, J, that's the really whacked thing. I mean like way back when, like first grade, I used to play with the kid pretty much. So I've been in his house a bunch of times. And then there was a time when we were in fourth that we hung for a while, maybe two or three weeks in the summer. After that, though, we didn't see each other anymore at all. But there wasn't anything that ever happened. The way I've thought of it is like, well, it grew to be *I'm me* and *he's him*. And so never the twain shall do anything but kick the shit out of each other. Though it's been one twain doing the shit-kicking, primarily."

Jackie was smilin'. But then he got serious. "It's so crazy, isn't' it," he said, "the way stuff goes like that. I mean, you think about all the fights we've seen, Kev. It's like there's never an explanation for 'em that you can really see. It's all just like you say, two guys who just aren't the same guy, and there they are suddenly starin' in each other's face and gettin' ragged off, or like deliberately bringing on a rag-off. But you don't see guys just stompin' on each other for walking down the street, once ya get older. At least I don't think so."

"Unless," I said, "you're talkin' about guys like that insane goon my dad hit with the iceball."

"Yeah," Jackie said. "There's really dangerous guys, incurable guys…. And, I mean, trying to understand a guy like Prizer…what makes him tick…."

I piped in. "Maybe he swallowed a clock."

Jackie sniffed a laugh. Then—and this is something again that hurts me with sadness now, thinkin' of it—he said, "Maybe, Kev, to figure a guy like that out…to see where he's comin' from, it takes a whole lifetime."

And the way he put this, too, which was really slow and thoughtful, is maybe why I asked him then, sort of out of the blue: "So tell me this, do you think I've made bad confessions, J, 'cause I didn't confess that I've for like days at a time thought about serious revenge on that jag?"

Jackie was grinning now, but he had his lip curled up, too, in a mock and was shakin' his head. "Yeah. And you could say while you're at it that you're like heartily sorry for hangin' on to your life, and, you know, for breathing and stuff."

Which, even though I'd definitely come to the same conclusion, for some reason made me feel good hearing it.

Then Jackie said, "I mean it's not like you're ever gonna forget the guy, Kev. But even still, you'll get past the guy. And of course it'll take a miracle and a half, but maybe with time the goon will just grow out of bein' what he is now. *Maybe.*"

"Yeah," I said, *"maybe.* But in the meantime, I've been wondering, what does a poor punk do?"

Jackie sort of grinned again, but then once more he turned serious, and got all of a sudden like really serious, like that time when he told us, you know (with what would you call it? dignity-guts?), that against the Vanderkells *the next time would be the same as the last time.* He said, looking at me now right in the eye, "In the meantime, Kev, you've got Little

Stu—and you know you've got me." Then he stopped. But he kept that stare right on me, so that I felt like, honest to God, of all the times he woke stuff up in me, this was gonna be the shit. I mean, he's eyeing me now like here it is, the real unknown secret of Jackie Leonard (which George P sort of called once, you know, as if he was capitalizing it, The Third Ball Of John Patrick). And then he says, quiet, his voice all un-trembly, "And you've got *you*, Kev. Which means you'll never be backin' down."

And this, I swear, was kind of like receiving Confirmation—I mean the outward sign instituted by Christ to give grace, when you become a soldier of Jesus in the Church Militant, and not just from some local bishop, but from Cardinal Meyer.

But every once in a while, too, I really *was* thinking, which is to say fantasizing, that maybe Prizer would like pretty soon just grow out of it. Or, talk about dreams, or call 'em maybe just pure chickenshit thoughts in me—that maybe the two of us would just get back to what we were when we were six, or to that time when we were nine or ten and like forgot for three weeks that we "went to different schools together," as the saying goes. But then I'd turn, hard, and I'd think for sure that the guy was straight from the real and true hell and forever and ever incurable. But then, too, up in the pueblo, I'd have sort of weird, superstitious conversations with myself about how maybe it just couldn't happen, ever, that Prizer and I would become friends again (which we never really were, truth to tell, Prizer always being pretty much a spook in my eyes), or that we couldn't even be friendly-*like* with each other, until the Rat's family performed a certain act, which would be clearing all the carcasses and cut-up animal parts out of their house.

Because all those head and feet and like tusks and teeth and ears and noses and stuff did was make *him* sort of forever braggy, and *me* pretty deeply shit-jittery. Because there he'd be saying, you know, while he was pointing to this full-boat decapitated rhinoceros head that was stuck up (and this too is no bullshit) on the wall of the landing half-way up their stairs (so you'd have to pass under the incredible horn and jaws if you were ever to get up to their bedrooms and stuff) was, "My old man bagged this fella while he was seven weeks out on the plains in eastern Africa. Took an elephant gun to bring the big boy down and a dozen natives to dress him." Which I thought meant, you know, put maybe some funeral clothes on him. Which gave Prizer a chance for a good chuckle while he told me it meant cutting out the rhino's guts, which they did to get at the meat, before they took the big boy's head off.

And there were these coins there, too, at Prizer's—all set in velvety sort of squares, like little jewelry boxes for rings, in these really, really smooth-sliding drawers, the kind that make you think that the guy who made 'em probably enjoyed for like days on end just sneaking around on tiptoes and not talking, just whispering and eating teeny bits of food with the tips of his fingers, going "Oooh oooh, tasty tasty tasty." But I do have to admit the coins, which were from all over the world and all through history, were really pretty cool. And the smooth-slidey drawers, too. But it was all part of this really spooked-up scene, the way Prizer sort of turned into Dracula's fetchit boy when he got the keys and opened the drawers and all sort of smiley-whispery told me about how there was an alarm in the room, loud as at the fire station, and about the umpteen-trillion-dollar *value* of the *collection*. And the way he said *value* and *collection,* I mean it was like he was suckin' on the words and eatin' 'em—and they tasted mighty sweet. And then—after the honor of seeing the coins—you'd have to make your way back down and out under the rhino's horn and its sort of brainless-lookin' and ferocious-as-anything mouth.

Which was all cool, of course, 'cause it was supreme never-forget-it stuff. But try to tell me there's not never-forget-it stuff that it's unhealthy as shit to live right under its nose—especially if that nose has a tusk which was built to like pick up lions by the gored-through guts.

And naturally the son of the Big-Game Spook (and, like I say, 'spook' fits because if the man ever set foot in America, it would be a bigger deal than Columbus) was not always in attendance at Thursten P Vanderkell, ditchin', sort of like Frankie M, when he got the itchin', and he'd just sort of haunt around, so that I even saw him once from our b-ball courts at CK recess time. But I swear t' God, wouldn't you think that after he left me for dead in the snow he'd be satisfied—if that's the word for what a guy like that feels. But no. Not even when I walked with Bobby Stu would the punk give it up. Which made me think like, shit, I really *do* need some kind of an explanation—you know, for like why particularly the guy would concentrate on me? I mean this was a classical why-me situation, if there ever was one. And, enough times, he'd hang right at the Murder Spot (his home away from home) and he'd sort of slime or hulk around while we were walking by and he'd eye me. I mean, *shit,* the guy would eye me. Or one time, just for reminders, he took a last drag on this butt he was smokin' and flicked it about sixty feet and acted like right where he landed it, there was exactly the fly he was trying to cig-burn. And the way he looked at me that time, it was, I swear, like he was some mafia guy driving by in a big black Caddy, all under that silent shiny glass, you know, the kind of a guy who'd be wearing the blackest undertaker's hat in America, only ya wouldn't give him shit about it, goofy as he looked, 'cause he likely had a machine-gun under his overcoat. And he waved at me from Reed's in this slow, spooked-out way that sort of made ya think of the slow way an A-bomb cloud goes up, right before ya hear the roar and you get hit with the last wind you're ever gonna feel.

But one time I wasn't just with Bobby Stu (who wasn't a bring-it-on kind of guy, just a prevent-things-from-happen-ing kind of guy), I was with Bobby Stu and Francis X and Jackie L. And I've gotta say, to talk about the goodness attached to the toughness again, which could be the real story of JL's life, there's this thing you truly love about a guy who never, never, brings it on at the wrong time, but when it's the right time, he surer than shit brings it on. And like one more time, I don't care if it sort of makes me start feeling my sadness like it's a pleasure. I'm gonna say it anyhow: the time Jackie took it to the Rat King himself was a time not long before he died—not a week, because he died on a Saturday and this was on a school day, just before.

"Well, well, well, well, if Kevvie boy doesn't have the whole CK punk brigade with him this time."

This was the way Prizer, when he came out from Reed's drive like something out of a bad-shit fairy tale, got things started. And, credit where credit is due, I've gotta say the Rat was pretty bold-insane bringin' it on like this, with not just the Bobby factor but JL there too. But of course he was nowhere near as nuts as Frankie, who first off started up by laying a kind of record-breaking, really hocked-out-of-the-schnozz, green-river quid—you know, the kind that you suck outa your nose so hard it looks like you just got stabbed in the back, then, after mixin' it with the spit, you lay it out, all quiet-like, and it's a true Loch Ness monster. Then Frankie says, "I heard you're maybe flunkin' outa even Vankderkell, Prizer, because—besides the fact you're a zit-puss jag, you're a total moron."

"Hey, you, fuckin' *punk-shit*," Prizer said, at the usual rate of speed working up the usual colossal rage. "I find you alone, I'll knock your teeth right down your neck. You remember that, if you're not stupider than your fucked-up, worthless brother. And remember this, too. I *will* find you alone, punk-shit. Just a matter of time. Just a...*matter of time*."

'Course these were the kinda things he loved to say to me, too (minus the Tom Malone factor, lucky me for not having that in my life). But Frankie's got his own special response-style, which is to say he goes full-out instant insane. But now a funny thing was how, 'cause of what Prizer said about bro Tom, Frankie took up the subject of family feelings. "FUCK YOU!" he starts screamin', "talkin' about my brother, you atheist shit-brain!" Then he just drops his throwing arm kinda down at his side and a little behind him, like he's got a hand grenade. But it was just his way of getting his fist ready for the wildest roundhouse throw he could give to it. And bang he starts comin' on like some kind of psycho shot-putter. Only he forgot that one of Bobby Stu's sort of life-jobs was keeping Francis X Malone from any extreme stuff. So, I mean, Bobby didn't clothes-line Frankie. He just sort of, I guess you could say, *abdomen-ed* him. You know, stuck out his arm and, uh, halted his forward progress, *play's over*. I gotta say it was kinda funny, too, seein' Frankie lookin' like sort of a really, really pissed-off midget, slung up now on Bobby's hip, goin' "God damn you,

Stupnicki!"—which Bobby paid no attention to—and "Let me at that pimple-puss spastic shit brain!"—which Bobby also paid no attention to. Because what Frankie wanted to be let at was of course his maybe most favorite thing of all (after, that is, BB all lewd, crude, and nude), which would be suicide.

But now while Stu's got Frankie held back at a safe distance, Jackie lets ya know that somewhere down inside him—and not where ya do your talking, or your wondering about Prizer's long-time future—he'd come to the conclusion that it was time again for some very necessary action. So out he steps. And he says to that shit-ass Rat Punk, "You like to tell people what's gonna happen to 'em, don't ya, Prizer." And I'm lookin' at Prizer's face now, and suddenly he's not saying shit anymore, just standing dead silent, right exactly where he'd been the world's leading spew king, that time he was pressing my neck down toward the dog dump and my veins nearly blew out. And you know how in the cartoons when somebody goes over a cliff and suddenly he's scramblin' with his arms and legs like he could climb back up on the air? Of course Prizer's trying to be as cool as possible. But I'm like seeing this going on inside him—I mean, how suddenly now he's wanting to scramble back up on the air and save himself after his bold suicidal troll-show.

And then I'm lookin' over at JL, who's, so to speak, gonna be carrying now the whole conversation. "You love that, don't ya, Prizer," he said again. "You love that, don't ya—telling people what's gonna happen to 'em." And I'm lookin' at that tough-kid face with the crook tooth and it's more like the face now of an archangel doin' a slow burn, or like the face of one of the Knights of the Temple (who I don't know anything about except that saying their name makes me think of iron-boned guys who will kick your ever-livin' ass). And now, with Val-boy still saying not first syllable number one, Jackie finishes up with, "But this time, I'm tellin' *you*, Prizer. You ever touch Frankie Malone or Kevin Collins or any of my friends, any place, any time, and you'll be wishing you hadn't. That's what'll *happen*—if you ever mess with any of my friends. Ever. Anywhere."

Whoa, shit. You know how sometimes when ya talk, it's more than you talking. Sort of like with singing, only here it's not music you're working with. It's like inspiration from some holy-shit-look-out-for-that-crazy-fucker kind of place. Well, this was like the ultimate of that I ever saw in my life. And I know that, mixed in with the cool, I've talked about some royal piss-and-vinegar seeming kind of stuff with Jackie's sayings, like his words here, and like "Go ahead and hit me and find out." Or like his saying, which is hard now for me to say, that he liked the sort of edgier psych that comes if you're not like all-powerful or you don't think you're gonna live forever. But still I'm saying, along with, once more, that I can't say where in himself another guy's kind of miracle-guts come from, that with Jackie it was like at the same time he was not pissed, or vinegar-ed, but that he was just, finally, cool.

Naturally, of course, Prizer's gonna still play it rock hard. So he lays out his own quid, tryin' as much as he could to make it look like what he's spittin' out of his mouth is a chewed-up, semi-liquified JP Leonard. But you could see plain enough how there wasn't any stepping forward on his part—just this kind of up-from-under-his-eyebrows, as he finishes his quid-laying, "Eat shit, Leonard. And you re-member November 5TH," (which, I forgot to mention, was the day we'd sort of throw-down-the-glove agreed on for the next Vanderkell-CK game, 'cause Big Joe Stupnicki and Entemann's brother would be free again that day). And I mean the Rat King's theater-work here didn't change—he was still playin' the role—but then off he goes, or slinks, back down Reed's drive toward Castle Alucard (which if you didn't see the movie in which Drac used his name backwards, it's his name backwards). And I'm thinking, too, of all those times Drac has gotta whip up his cape over his eyes 'cause he's like gotten a crucifix in the kisser, or seen the sun. And the music lets you know that good has set back evil. I mean it was the kind of deal that if ya didn't see it with your own eyes, you could maybe stay a Doubting Thomas for a very long time.

But I think what I'm saying, too, is somebody's gotta make this kind a thing happen, actually *happen*, before it goes deep enough into your heart and guts to like be a turning point in your life. As, though, I'm standing there with Bobby and Francis X and contemplating what JL just did make happen, taking in the actual slink-off, I mean I'm thinking that my life *might* have just changed.

But actual happenings or not—I know now you shouldn't get like over-excited about the kind of courage that comes into ya just from, you know, seeing something, which is still a huge deal, and crucial, but can sometimes last ya just until the next time ya get clocked.

How I know that, I'll tell ya later. But that night up in the pueblo, with the moon once more extremely cool, trust me, and my room really quiet and dark but covered over with cool silvery-ness and The Woods all dark and covered with silvery-ness, I was loving my friends more than I ever did. I mean with Bobby keeping Frankie (whom if you can't somehow figure out how t' love, I think you're dumber than SMM) from killing himself, and JL stepping out there, zero hesitation versus the Rat King and looking like one of the archangels on fire or a Knight of the Temple with his armor shining all right. And I was thinking how kids do know some real shit—I mean that adults (who maybe think stuff but don't do it) would never know. Like Frankie and that kid at the fence, which was something I was still going back to for some reason, sort of over and over. I mean about how being polite about stuff keeps ya semi-fake or something. But then, on the other hand, there was the way JL and I had that whole long extremely cool day in The Woods with Toby and Laetitia and all the others, which Frankie didn't get. But on the other hand again, JL was, 'cause back and forth we go, about as polite as a world-championship knockout punch when he stepped out against that rat punk Prizer. And when I was thinking about that, that night in the pueblo, I was thinking that I was out there that day where kids, all right, do whomp the shit out of each other rather than just think stuff but because I was out there I had a pretty no-bullshit understanding of what Joe Louis meant to George Johnson, which if you don't get the point of, I feel sorry for you. Which makes me think, too, for some reason, about that way I liked to move times around, and places, for maybe what? making better the point of stuff? Or how in the pueblo I'd just shorten stuff into like a private language and say stuff like *afghan wings:* that's what Joe Louis gave George Johnson.

Anyhow, there I was, feeling a very cool happiness, almost laughin' out loud to myself, when I thought about Joe Louis and JL having the exact same initials. And I got into stuff like how I'd love to go on this detective search all over Chicago to see if I could find George Johnson, to talk with him about coolness, which he would know about, and maybe introduce him to my friends so we could listen to him tell stories about his life. But I worried about it being 1961—and how the last time George Johnson was seen by anybody I knew was about 1935, which would be a hard time to change around, and that, back at that time, he had a loaded gun in his hand.

But right now as I'm up north here telling you about all this stuff, I'm thinking about a tattoo (which the forever-ness of kinda fascinates me)—one I could have put on me somewhere with a 'J' for Johnson and for Joe and for Jackie, so there'd be like powerful memories written on me in a secret place forever, and it would like motivate me, sort of like actual grace, and also the 'J' would be for Jesus (who, being the true CK would be on occasion, I guess you could say, a bit different from our version). And I'm thinking if you like cram all these cool meanings into a thing like that, the tattooed letter might even for some cool-spooky reason start beating on your skin like a heart.

But for people still alive, maybe you wouldn't have a tattoo, because things change, and you part ways and stuff, like me and all my friends, which is so weird how fast it gets *un*-weird to talk about. And with Patty, too, because, I don't know, it's just so embarrassing to like all-the-way-across-Chicago call somebody you're never gonna see in your life again. It's just stupid. But just dreaming about somebody is really stupid, too. I don't know.

But I'm specially thinking of Patty now, because it makes me know that, with it the last few days he was here, I mean on earth, it had to be on a Monday that JL (or should I just say 'J'?) sent the Rat back slinking into his rat castle. I know because I collected at Conlons' on Tuesday, and Patty was there, and I told her all about it, because now she and I could actually get out words without choking on 'em— but still not like we were pals, 'cause still, somehow, we didn't either one of us want any part of being like the guy and the girl who are friends, which would be really pathetic and lame when you're talking about the girl who when she touched with you, it like killed you, in the good way.

It was her mom who answered the door. And I've gotta say I love that. I mean that it wouldn't be Patty, rushing out to meet me. Sort of the way Scotty McKinnon asked me when Mary Monaghan wrote *I love Scotty* in blue ink all over her white Keds, "What's a guy supposed to do, Kev, besides, you know, heave?" Which was a question that I could not answer.

And then Patty's mom, when she paid the bill and gave me the usual embarrassing humongo tip, said, "I think Patty's in the kitchen, Kevin. Would you like to see?" Which was a question that no matter how many times I'd seen Patty Conlon in this world was like asking a blind man that you were offering an operation to, to bring him vision, "Would you like to see?" And then there I was, you know, unwrapping the bandages, slowly, slowly, and like then there's light, and I'm starting to make something out. And I've got my fingers crossed so tight I'm gonna break 'em. And then I like blink as I'm walking through the kitchen door—and it's Patty, sitting at the table again. And it was like she was all surprised, too. 'Cause of course, which you can trust that I love, she was totally lost in a book (or maybe she was just fakin' that she was). And when she looked up—it was me.

She kind of went a little speechless for a second, and then she just kind of smiled (not enough, though, to blow her cool, which is solid, trust me), and then in this incredible girl-soft voice, she just said, "Hi."

Just "Hi." Nothin' else. But one of the amazing things about her being so cool is that like any little change in the routine is the hugest thing in the entire universe. So naturally I'm ripped by the ache. Because the way she said it—it had just this one ten-ten-thousandth of a new sort-of warmness in it. And the amazing thing is, that's enough, I mean one ten-ten-thousandth. Which says something about something, I don't know. But naturally while I'm saying to myself *Don't stare, don't stare, don't stare, don't stare*—I'm, you know, staring the crap out of the deal. But then by a miracle, about a thousandth of a second before I lost all cool to fool, as George P said once, I managed to find my voice somewhere down in my throat (after I cleared the pipes once or twice, to the point of, like, *call St. Blaize!*) and I got out my own "Hi."

Of course, as I just-awhile-ago hinted at ya, the slink-off of His Rodentness would turn out to be only a fake turning point for me. Still, I was only twenty-four hours past that slink-off at this point, and I was almost feeling that my imaginings about clocking the King of Punks (and, glad as I might've been about the no bad confession, I had a million such imaginings, trust me)—that these imaginings could actually come true any old time I wanted, and that all by myself I could make a royal, yellow-bellied rat-slink happen. I swear, too, that right out of the St. Blaize choke deal (and is it not weird how ya can go from one thing to the total opposite?) comes this opposite desire to speak up—I mean, even to say some bold, this-is-what-I'd-like-to-do stuff. So I said, "Wanna go outside? It's like the most beautiful day ever." Which happened to be true. But you know how it is, when your heart-guts-brain, or whatever it was I called it before, gets really humming, which it was, after I got the fishbone out. I mean—you're gonna find what you need no matter what kinda day it is.

But of course, now, that's why we don't say too many words. Because when we finally do say 'em, we don't know if any, like, *things* are gonna happen because of 'em. And this truly was a first for me, I mean saying something like what I just said. 'Cause even though Patty and I had been talking about stuff in a pretty good flow these last times— that is, once we got past, each time, all the embarrassed-to-deathness—and even though we'd even like laughed our butts off once or twice about stuff (which like with Toby and Franklin and Theodore, I mean the laughing, it's this really excellent cure for stuff like excess coolness)—I mean, even though we'd done all this stuff together, we'd never really *done* anything together.

But now my words were like hangin' out there, waiting to see what time would bring. And of course I'm all instant-ly prepared to fake like it didn't really mean diddly to me, one way or another, if she wanted to go outside or not (and does it not eat dirt that there's like an anger sort of sliming around and getting ready in ya too, when it comes to real-ly badly wanting something that you might not get?), but now she like sort of smiles at me, and she closes her book and puts it down, like not even marking the page or any-thing, and she says, still all girl-soft, "Okay."

Just "Okay." But you know what I said before.

And while now I'm of course faking like her saying yes— that *that's* not diddly to me, I'm thinking like oh, yeah, there's been a turnaround all right—in my life. And I'm thanking Jackie—but not just because he sent a certain, shall I say *mouse*-punk packing—but also because of an idea he was giving me for a certain...very secret...four-second deal. Not to say I was working on any kind of a definite plan—and I gotta say in certain situations, like this one for instance, definite plans would leave me not just feeling cold, but like I deliberately hurt my mom or something. But my heart-guts-brain was definitely up to something, no doubt about it.

Then when we got outside, there it was. I mean that trail in The Woods that, you know, was the scene for that movie in the foot-deep snow called *The Ice Tree* or *The Worst Day of a Kid's Life,* which got made like moments after I'd starred in *The Best Day of a Kid's Life.* But I'm thinking, too, looking toward the trail, of how Jackie laid that very real threat on Prizer (not like Susie Shannon's, though I'll be always grateful to Susie for hers), and how when Jackie Leonard said something—like the next time would be the same as the last time—he meant it. And also I'm feeling this kind of cool-warm courage (which I know is a stupid way of saying something, but maybe you know what I mean)—this courage, that is, that ya feel when you're with the girl.... You know. I know you know. And I'm not going to add anything sugary-stupid—so don't expect it. And, lastly, there was the heart-guts-brain thing, hummin' on in the dark, giving me a shove, too, from the inside. So I pointed and said, "There's how I head for home. That trail there. Do you ever walk down it, or anything?"

"I used to, kind of a lot," she said. "I mean with my dad. We'd walk The Woods on the trail."

I nodded, because it was like instant deep respect I was feeling. And I was thinking, too, how much a place like The Woods looks one way if *this* happens in it (like a shit-beating), and then another way if *that* happens in it (like a walk with Patty Conlon), which, as we started kind of drifting toward the trail's beginning, had my heart-guts-brain all buzzed up into becoming some kind of magic wand that would truly have the power to turn a bad place into a very, very good one. And it was deeply cool, too, to think of Patty out there walking with her dad on the trail that was my way home.

And today wasn't winter. It was the 26TH of September, 1961. Funny, I remember once braggin' to my cousin Rick that I could remember what I did on every day of my life. And he's comin' up with days, like "Okay, butt-hole (which is not a day, I know). What'dya do on April 10TH, 1958?" And of course I'm bullshittin' up a storm—but I'm actually fishing for big days in my mind that were close to the day Rick picked out, and then backtracking or shooting forward from those days and kind of giving things a look like I really did remember the exact day Rick said. I mean, for example, I'd of course know my birthday and remember, sort of, what I got that year, like maybe a jacket. And if the day was close to that birthday, I'd say I went with my mom to For Men, Jr., and we bought this jacket for me (which was kind of a ritual actually, a lot of times on my birthday—comin' the way it does when winter is finally over and ya don't need your coat anymore). And then I'd describe the jacket and get into all kind of detail, I mean about the store guy and all the bullshit. And it was cool, because I was driving Rick right up the bejeesus-tree.

But I do know what happened on the last day of September, 1961. And, while I'm getting this feeling that it would be better somehow if we could name no days, no matter what I mighta said about the point of stuff, I'm glad I can go back from the 30TH four days and put the exact day I walked with Patty on a calendar in my brain (like a secret tattoo), so whenever the 26TH of September comes around I'll remember, because if it seems pretty stupid to call her, it seems like the stupidest thing possible in my life to ever forget her.

And I can tell ya a lot about that day. About the sunshine. The beautiful weather, which sort of softened ya the way not a big but a little fever will, when you're not like really sick but still you don't have to go to school and you're lyin' warm in bed and there's maybe a cool song playing on the transistor and you're looking out your window up at the sky and thinking that if they keep playing cool songs like this one, you'll feel 'em even down to where the old wet-blankety voice says *this good thing is going to end*—and that the songs will be cool enough to like lullaby that voice to sleep. So I was softened up that way, when I said, "Did you and your dad ever, I mean when you were out on the cindery path, see a horse or anything?"

"I never saw a horse. I didn't think they had them anymore in The Woods."

I felt even more relaxed now, because I had a little story to tell. Or a picture to tell, if that makes sense. So I told her, as we were walking on into The Woods, about the horse coming out of the fog with the lady, who I said was like the first lady I ever really noticed as beautiful. And I told her about the hugeness of the horse and how it shook the ground and dug out the cinders. And, so she would know it was real, about the jingling of the bridle and saddle stuff. And about the clothes the lady wore. And then about how the lady and the horse disappeared again into the fog. So there was this beautiful thing and this huge, powerful thing kind of with you for just that second, then gone, which made it, though, something you remembered.

But now Patty was kind of like smiling at me. Then she teased me. "You're sure you didn't dream that one up, Kevin Collins?"

Of course I liked the tease, especially 'cause it came all sugar-coated, which is to say smile-coated. And I woulda given her a "Patricia Conlon" for that "Kevin Collins" she threw my way (and, yeah, I loved that too—for have ya noticed there's been like zero of me calling her Patty or of her calling me Kevin, when we were with each other). But I had this whacked thing going suddenly in my head like I honestly for a second couldn't tell—I mean what was real and what was dreams. "I don't know," I said, kind of fake-arguish-sounding, but actually kind of meaning it, "I suppose if you were in the mood to keep up your little *number* on me and told me like five straight times I was dreaming, I might fall for it."

And now she does this thing which I almost don't want to tell you, it's such a secret in me. But she looks up at me— and I swear to you if I ever told a truth this is it—she had the most beautiful face I have seen yet in my life, with her light-brown-blondish hair and her lips all, I'd say, rosy and soft—with this slight shine but not yet because of lipstick or anything, and her eyes soft-shiny too, soft and shiny blue—I mean of the one-look-and-it's-right-down-into-your-heart kind. And now it's *another* smile, which I swear in my mind was a notch warmer even than the kitchen smile. And she says, her voice going all girl-soft again, but now kinda slow, too, exactly five times to me—"You're dreaming. You're dreaming. You're dreaming. You're dreaming. You're dreaming."

And it was like she fully knew. I mean I felt kind of like a complete idiot, as well as serious jerk-water, for being maybe gross-obvious. But it was like she totally and completely knew that the reason I'd wanted to go outside and stuff—and why I wanted to like talk about the path so we'd of course sort of gravitate over to it and then start walking down it—was—so I could kiss her. But it really *was* like I was dreaming now, because, I mean, she didn't break out laughin' or anything, or look disgusted and like she never wanted to see me again as long as Earth was a planet, even though she knew what I was up to, I think. She just kept kind of smiling, in this warm way, and now a little shaky, too. Sort of a shaky-warm smile. Which had me flat dyin', because it said when you try to kiss me—Kevin Collins— I'm not gonna like shut down, so to speak, any window shade on ya. And so now, which was also extremely cool, we had sort of a second thing that we knew, without saying a word about it, just like the way we touched together our forearms in school, and never said the first thing, not even to that day or ever after.

But now, I don't know, speaking of gravitating, I had suddenly this weird other desire for something. And that was to walk with Patty down the path right to where I got the holy livin' shit beat out of me at the Ice Tree, and if there was going to be any kissing done, to do it there. One thing I know is that you can't ever *make* true power-magic stuff happen and you can't *make* remember-it-forever stuff happen. But if you really are gettin' shoved by some feeling, I mean really SHOVED, then it's not like you're the one trying to make anything happen—so for that reason, keep your fingers crossed, it *might* actually happen. And like I say, I was—I mean getting shoved. And all of a sudden, also, it was like I got really superstitious. I mean, it was like I was becoming dead positive that Prizer was gonna know my moves—and *appear,* or something—right now. But then (with Jackie's dead cold knight-in-armor and archangel-on-fire warning to that shit-punk moving like a warm feeling in my heart and guts) it was like all this desire-feeling running up against the fear-feeling suddenly made The Woods kind of the cool-craziest place I've ever been in. Like *This Is Your Life, Kevin Collins*—only the trees were doing the talking. And I mean I really could hear sounds like I was all alone—even though I wasn't alone (lucky me)—or sort of like the night we went to see the Hanged-Kid Tree and Terry was so scared (and not alone in being so). And I was like some kind of hero, only about fourteen different ways scared shit-less-insane. But I was feeling SO GOOD, too.

So there I was, walking with Patty Conlon—in The Woods (and though we were both too gutless to hold hands, I know this, we were both thinking about it—I know we were—I mean to the point where the thought was jumpin' in our fingers). But there up ahead, not far now, was the Ice Tree, which believe me I'd be able to pick out of a jillion, winter or not. And yet, believe it or not, I'm calming down some, with the walking. But now, after another shove job, I guess, I for some reason start figuring I've gotta talk to Patty and tell her stuff—I mean *tell her* about the Ice Tree and stuff. I hope the reason wasn't that I wanted to sucker her into any feeling sorry for me, which I swear to you is a thought that makes me crank out of this like deep well inside me a healthy puke bucket. But somehow just to like tell her my secrets and stuff. Because if she ever told me a secret about *herself,* I'd go full-out ache, from the heart right through the guts and up into my brain—full ache, total. And you tell me the reason for that, which somebody oughta know, I mean when a thing just *decks* ya with the everlasting truth of it.

And then, 'cause it wasn't far, there we were. And (though I really hoped now I wasn't looking like I was up to something—I mean of the four-second variety) I stopped, and looked at her. And then, bang, it was another one of those moments when you grow up and become a lot older in like a single second, the way I said, "Do you know Val Prizer?"

Of course she was right with me, because she's bar none (except for the Stu-ball, in mathematics, which makes me laugh so hard) the smartest person I ever knew. So now she talks, too, like she's instantly older. "Yes, I know him," she said. Then, "He's not a friend of yours, is he? I mean, you're not sounding or looking like he is."

"If I sounded or looked like he is," I said, "I'd have to be somebody other than who I am."

She gave me, now, this like quiet little nod, like she got what I meant. And she was looking very thoughtful herself. She said, "I mean, I don't know why you're asking me if I know him." Then she smiled again, or sort of grinned a little, and said, kind of questiony-like, or like an invitation. "I'm guessing I'm going to hear, though?"

I grinned kind of a stupid grin back, or like I'd just put something in my mouth and I was tryin' to hide it. Then I said, "No. You tell me first what you think about the guy, or what you know about him."

She changed, took a breath, kind of thoughtful-like, you know, as a way of saying *okay*. Waited a second. Then, "There was this time," she said, "this time…when I was coming home from school. And I was right out where our street turns into The Woods, at 91ST. I was still talking to Gina. The two of us usually end up walking backwards for about a quarter block, still chatting away, after she goes her way and I go mine. You know girls...."

I sort of sky-eyed it now, like I knew girls all right, and, you know, investigated it and reached the conclusion they were certifiable one and all. But I'm at the same time sort of picturing Patty and Gina Rochford, in their uniform skirts, saying good-bye to each other, walking backwards, still yapping away, and I'm like really liking girls—a lot. But I saw, too, that Patty was getting ready to sort of reveal to me something.

"And then," she said, "I turned around, and he was there. Val Prizer. So close I almost walked right into him. I mean, I guess I'm glad he's not your friend or anything—because it really creeped me, and scared me about half to death. I mean, he was just standing there, so close. Way too close, if you know what I mean. And not moving out of my way, either. And looking at me, too, like he was trying to really scare me."

Of course I'm getting this kind of cool, strange feeling now—besides wanting to fifty-miles-per-hour charge Prizer with a lance—like the two of us, Patty and me, I mean, are in this thing, without knowing it, kind of a team (which would be the Prizer-specially-selected-us-for-torture team). And I'm givin' her a *go on* nod. Or maybe an *It looks like the team'll have to do something about this punk, doesn't it, and, yes, go on* nod.

"I'd known him," she said, "from when we were in piano together, back in fifth, at this music camp in Evergreen Park. He was a good player. Actually, an outstanding player. But he was strange. I mean he seemed to be so angry all the time. Or sad, or something. But never smiling, except at the wrong time. And that way he looked at me when I almost walked into him, reminded me of that." She stopped now, and put her head down, half closed her eyes. "I shouldn't say this. I really shouldn't...."

"Go ahead," I said. "It's not like you're changing my opinion of the guy, believe me."

She kept hanging her head a little. Then, for a second talking with her eyes fully closed, "I think maybe he stole some things from our garage. There was a hubcap missing from our car. And a hammer from my dad's toolbox. The reason I think he was the one, is that he was there another time, on our street. And he asked me in this weird, creepy way, if I wanted to go and see his hubcap collection."

I shook my head, thinking there was more shit-weirdness to the 'collection-guy' than I even thought. And (with my old superstitiousness kicking in again) that he was like everywhere. "I guess that would be pretty good evidence," I said, meaning about showing her the hubcaps, thinking too that with a guy like Prizer what he'd really want to show you some day was that hammer.

"I guess," she said. "That and the feeling he gives you that he'd just be sort of happy to do something to you. For no reason, except that there's something about you that he doesn't like."

I nodded, 'cause needless to say, I got what she was saying. Then, "See this tree," I said, stepping over and putting my hand now on the prong that speared me, and looking high up into the tree, which was already getting yellow and brown, even though it wasn't quite October yet. "There was this time." I looked now at Patty again, and I don't know if you're a guy and you've ever had like a girl's like gentleness and beauty give you this feeling that sort of starts right in the center of your chest and from there it starts melting you all over your body—but I had now maybe ten jillion things going through me, like a thought too of Patty up on her toes for ballet and her eyes almost closed and holding her arms around some invisible person. "This day," I said, "that had been like really a good one for me—the best, which I won't go into. But then I was walking through here, 'cause like I say, this is my way home. And I'm feeling really good still, 'cause of my incredible day, even though it's dead winter and the snow's about a foot deep. I mean the snow's just seeming totally beautiful and quiet to me—when I look up, and just like you, I see Prizer standing there, just a little distance down the path."

And now Patty came up to me a bit, with her eyes and mouth, you know, kind of concentrating, saying, in so many words, *Go on, I'm listening*. And I'll say this for the punk—he's about as interesting as it's possible to be. And I'm very deeply grateful, too, because there Patty and I were sort of before-you-know-it settling ourselves on this fallen trunk of another tree there, and I'm *going on*, because *she's listening*—about Mr. Supremely Interesting. "And I don't know," I said, "if when he was standing there between you and your house, you felt like who are you to be blocking my way home. But I, well, it wasn't the first time with me and him either, I had that feeling like crazy."

"I did have it," she said. "Only it was later; at the time I was too scared and startled to think."

"I had time to think," I said. "But it's funny. I mean, when it's winter but you're feeling really, really good, it's like your eyes and your body kind of go half-sleepy and stuff. Ya know? And everything's all kinda soft and quiet. And that's how your boots feel in the snow, too. It's almost like you could go to sleep in the stuff, 'cause nothing feels cold.

It's like cold becomes warm, which is so *cool*. If that's not too many temperatures."

She smiled at me now, a really cute one. So while I'm actually beginning to think that with my words I might even conjure up the King of the Punks, I'm also thinking that something very, very good is coming my way. Or forget that. It was already there.

I laughed then the kind of sniff-laugh that sort of clears off the joke and gets things serious again. I said, "But then, like I said, I did have that time to think. But it wasn't like I had any strategy or anything. I just sort of had this whole new feeling about the snow and the ice and the things I was seeing. I mean like instantly I wasn't half-asleep anymore but all kind of wakened up like I got hit by an iceball right in the skull, so everything felt cold and miserable. So…so much for my great day. And there I was. And there he was. And I knew it was gonna be very ugly, because, like I say, I'd been through this."

"I can understand," she said. "I mean I think what we're talking about is a common enemy."

Which for me was this like very strange-cool thing to hear, 'cause hearing it makes ya all of a sudden—I mean like instantly really close to each other. And now, like a floodgate kind of deal, all sorts of stuff started suddenly coming out of me. I mean about that punk movie that I was like the sorry-ass victim in, and the shit-beating. And it's so weird. I mean I was like some actor who started with some serious bullshit, like *To be, or not to be,* but the words like woke up sleeping stuff inside him. So he wouldn't be really bullshittin' up on stage. And with my own mouth I was saying stuff, and, yeah, it was like I was up on stage, puttin' on an act, which, yeah, had some bullshitty aspects to it (because, yeah, I had feelings here and there like I was trying to soften Patty up—but then, get this, I had feelings too like I was sort of weasling on Prizer!). But this was like stuff that got stomped out, because all of a sudden I was all hooked in, if that makes sense, and it was like my own words were rippin' me wide open. And I went right on and told her about Bobby Stu with the wave and Jackie and the slink-off, so she'd really know how great those guys are. And it was so cool, I mean that she didn't put on even slightly any girl-type bullsh about how she was surprised because of course all boys are sooooo stupid. No, what she said is she knew Bob Stupnicki and she knew Jack Leonard, and she wasn't surprised one bit, which was so cool how she was not grossed out by guys and all their stuff. But there was more. 'Cause when you're with a girl, there *is* more, and it's something different. And so now all of a sudden I was like kind of trembling, and saying yeah, thank God for Bobby and JL because, truth, I was deep down scared that that big-time star of his own punk movie might do enough—I mean like enough to really damage me. Which confessing that I was scared, though—I don't know if this makes any sense—but I mean 'cause I was with Patty, I was like telling her this stuff so somehow, with her there sort of *being* with me, I'd get the scared-ness out of me enough so that bad confessions of the sacrilege kind wouldn't even like be an issue in my life, 'cause I'd be so un-scared I couldn't care less about Prizer, or for that matter, my own skin.

Which the way she was lookin' at me and nodding showed she got it. And with this showing me how she got it—it was, it really was now like a secret about *her* was getting ripped out, too. Which I could tell most when I finished because she didn't talk. She didn't say a thing. She just touched me.

On my shoulder, like close to my face. So (though I really couldn't believe I was alive) I thought it was okay, I mean to touch her face. And though I'll never know how my hand had enough guts—all of a sudden I touched the cheek of Patty Conlon. And still she didn't say anything. She just closed her eyes. So with my hand still on her cheek, which until you've touched it, I'd say you've touched nothing, I let myself listen to my heart-guts-brain when it said move your fingers back under her ear and hair (and if Patty never told me a single secret with words, what she told my fingers then about her, with the soft warmness of her skin back under her ear and hair, would be enough for like ten thousand years). But then when you're this crazy far, ya go the step. And I did it. I closed my eyes, too, and I kissed her, which would be the softest sweet taste that I ever even came close to, ever even close at all.

But a thing.... A thing I think, I mean I know, that I'm glad I never did was I never asked Jackie if he kissed Katie Luce more times than just that one. 'Cause I kissed Patty four times that day, each one enough to sort of give me the magic to wipe the blood from my head off that prong on the tree, maybe not so much from putting more guts into me as from making me feel so good I sort of forgot the past and like who I am (all OH-NO's included). But any way you look at it, if I went back to that tree now, I'd see enough stuff there happening all at once, good and bad, me and I guess you could say *Kevin Collins-in-a-good-way-forgotten-about*, that I could call it the tree where just about my whole life, at least so far, woke up. And I far-down-in-me hope that Jackie got to kiss Katie more than that one time. I hope it extremely. 'Cause even though Patty and I eventually broke all out of our trance there and like found ourselves embarrassed as could be, it kept getting better with each kiss while we were kissing, which wasn't like makin' out—it was just a kiss, then a kiss, then a kiss, then a kiss—until I had enough happiness in me so that even still I can think that maybe in Patty's mind, for a time in her life, inside that invisible circle she made with her arms, it was me.

CHAPTER NINE

FALL OF EIGHTH

BLACK CADILLAC

Even with the four kisses, though (which don't think that it makes me sad), it turned out exactly the same as with our touching ourselves together. Not the first word about those kisses, ever. I mean, you know I love it that not one second of one day did Patty and I ever become easygoin' with each other: that just like we had that unsaid thing going on in our fingers when we both wanted to (but didn't) hold hands, we had a kind of opposite unsaid thing going on about *not* wanting to be easygoin'. It's like both of us were sort of treasuring and protecting our not-easygoing-ness—because, like I say, we had a secret feeling that it was actually about a whole world cooler that way. I mean like go all the way and, even trembly, let stuff out about what your common enemy did to ya, or in Patty's case let me touch her hair and skin behind her ear—and then right away, af-ter that, scramble back into your separate corners and act like ya don't know each other. That was sort of our cool little embarrassment two-step dance. But I gotta say, too, I mean, I *know* it's true that embarrassment's the killer. I mean, it's the reason, or one of 'em, that I haven't called her (which, for the same reason of embarrassment, I never did when I lived on the South Side either, never even your standard have-it-ring-once-and-then-hang-up kind of sorry gutlessness, I swear).

I mean maybe, though, like I keep on saying, if I weren't *such* a punk. Fourteen and one month old—whoo. Look out. You know, if I really *could* drive. But, let's face it, even when it is sixteen-year olds, you don't hear about kids going back to old neighborhoods, not all the way across Chicago. Or maybe if you go back once, you don't go back twice. But something about it all fading away, I mean like my whole past life's fading away like to nothin'—it seems to me really unreal, especially when sometimes, I mean, I feel it in my stomach that part of me's like falling down this totally silent hole, and out of sight forever. And it doesn't matter that I'm making friends up north here, and they're good guys, I think—I mean I know they are. And that there's girls up here, too. I'm not blind. Really cute girls, especially one or two. But, I mean, it just doesn't matter that much, this new-friends stuff, when it comes to that feeling, which I know sounds crazy, but it's the feeling that you're sort of disappearing from your own sight, which isn't the same good feeling as Kevin Collins forgotten about, trust me.

But then—explain this one to me—I mean, that there's something so stupid and easy about it, too, I mean about not calling old friends and not having to say hello to 'em all over again. So like you're almost glad that there's no point in going back—and that every day there gets to be less of a point. It's all just sort of easy, like lettin' your eyes just go ahead and, yeah, look at the new cute girls. Or maybe sweet and easy like thinkin' only about a picture, you know, or like working with only a memory of a picture, like of that ballet picture of Patty, rather than dealing with her real voice, or the actual person of her. Or how about this one—I've imagined going back in secret some day to the Ice Tree, and all the places, the Hanged-Kid Tree, and the dance-building without walls, and where we played softball with the colored men on the Fourth of July, and the place where we saw that three-eyed lunatic with somebody else, and the place where we put out the magnifying-glass fire, and the place (which I haven't talked about yet) where we played the final Vanderkell game—and then going back up through the rabbit hole, into the Dead End, and standing where I could see the window of the pueblo way up there in the air, just so I could get back all the feelings—but then not looking anybody up—even, you know, kind of staying ducked out of sight. I mean it's weird watching what your mind does. And would there be a new kid I'd see in my window?

Which makes me think—I don't know—maybe it's that ya get the feeling that, even that fast, everything's really different now—and *you're* really different now, and not just 'cause your arms and legs and shoulders and stuff are really changing, but just really different. And that they, I mean your old friends, would be really different, too, even that fast. And that everybody'd be looking at, and even eyeballin' everybody else like *Who the hell are you*. Which actually is amazing, how fast that feeling comes. I mean I've already had the feeling, completely. And it's an officially *shit* feeling, so maybe no wonder ya'd rather just look at pictures in your brain, which by now you've turned into sort of a scrapbook of past times or something.

But then if I did just plain get to go back sometime, I'm for some reason dead positive that the stuff that would be absolute best for breakin' the ice, would be talkin' about the really goofy shit we said and did, ya know, when we were all in the same stupidity boat together, which, and I can hear us laughin' about this, would have been most of the time. And it's like even weird how sometimes the idiotic stuff just stands out, even if sometimes it seems wrong for it to do that, maybe sort of like old guys gettin' drunk at an Irish wake and laughing when they oughta be crying, or crying when they just oughta shut the hell up. But here I am, wrong or not, thinking, first thing—and it is about that worst day in not just mine but all of our lives that I'm gonna talk about now—of goofball Georgie P shoutin' out "ICBM! ICBM! ICBM!" (which every kid in America knows stands for Inter-Continental Ballistic Missile). But he wasn't shouting it because like suddenly he got a job working for the Civil Defense, or something, but because he suddenly decided to drop trou in The Woods and take a dumper. Or maybe I'll give 'm a break and say the need presented itself.

And of course then—seeing how we were in the forest and all—the word *log* came up. So we started comparing GP's log to the trunk of an old tree that had fallen down there. Which led to our all completely agreeing that GP's was by waaaaayyyyy-far the more humongified of the two, and to our like fako starting to 'see', as we looked it over, that, yes, indeed, it also had quite a few more toadstools growing on it and more fungus and old bark, which naturally led to our giving GP our sincerest congratulations, even Frankie, who occasionally would like shock ya because he actually did have what Mother Mad said he did not have, which was a "slightest grain of knowledge," which he showed by calling GP's deposit "the Sequoia" and saying that somebody, like maybe O'Connor, really oughta take an hour or so to saw it in half and count its rings.

But then Pete, who ignores the suggestion, goes, "If 'the Sequoia' fell in The Woods and there was nobody there to hear it, would there be a sound?"

Which of course made it very, very lucky Pete didn't get pantsed on the spot. But we actually, if you could call it that, *thought* about his question, after of course we'd all told him he could (to use a rhyme we got from this high school guy Jim Blunt, which we debated if it was Blunt's only contribution to humanity) suck every wang in the gang. And it was always so funny to hear Terry, still the littlest of us by a thousand miles, come in kinda late, all by himself, and say stuff like, "Yeah, O'Connor, you can suck my everlovin' *wang*." You know, all kinda hilarious like he's pissed as *shit* about Pete's even asking the old sound-in-the-forest question. And this kind of coming in late Terry was always doing deliberately now, because he'd discovered it could be his special contribution to the moronicity, which the perfecting of was pretty much at all times, like I've said, our number-one goal in life. And he got really good, you know, at getting the timing exactly right for hilariousness. And it's like if you get the *confidence*, you can actually find out about stuff like your hilariousness-timing, and, besides that, maybe not screw things up by being nervous and overdoing it but sort of just waiting till the right moment, which I give JL complete credit for, in Terry's case. And the reason is he always let Terry know he was covered when there was somebody, like you can guess who, wanting to use him as a punching, or goossage, bag. So sooner or later Terry found out he could like pipe in with stuff without getting ranked on or dumped on or biffed or pantsed or goosed till he was cryin' and couldn't breathe. So then all of a sudden, you know, he sort of flowered into being funnier than all get out.

Of course there'd be Bobby Stu, still at the opposite end of the world from Terry, size-wise, and Stu's just sort of smilin', all relaxed, which would be his at-all-hours-of-the-night-and-day *style*. And I'll get on to what we had to say about the sound of a log goin' down in The Woods when nobody's there to hear it, but I was thinking then, as I looked at Bobby and Terry, about if Terry grew to be as big and strong as Stu, would he find out he had inside him all along a relaxed person who was like already an expert at being relaxed, like a baby animal, say a horse, that's an instant expert at walking and all he needs is just to be born.

But now for Pete's question, which Frankie, naturally coming up with a question for a question, answers by saying, "If a nun does something sure-as-shit mortifying and I'm the only one to hear it, does that mean she's not still nailed?"

Which of course called for an immediate and full explanation. Which Frankie, 'cause he's been waiting all day, or all his life, to tell us, goes into now with about as total a happiness as I ever saw in the kid. And he starts out by reminding us that ever since he left us briefly and then returned, which George P said he never could believe didn't get him mistaken for Jesus Christ our Lord (who Frankie said Stenham did mistake him for), he'd had, *since he came back*, to sit right smack dab-ass in front of SMM's desk, 'cause SMM was also now our eighth-grade math and art teacher, worst luck possible for Francis. But of course no one in all of CK needed to be told where Frankie sat now, because he was a living CK legend and whatever happened to MALONE was, you know, important to the whole student body, all the way down to "the littlest, most impressionable" punkeroos; and sure as shit we didn't need to be told because, first, we were in the same room with the idiot and, second, because he'd about five jillion times talked about it himself—take, for one instance, the time he told us he was sittin' so close to SMM now that whenever he felt like it, he could up and give her a Bronsky, which I won't go any more into except to say that Frankie claimed he'd in fact heard SMM several times very, very softly and tenderly whisper the word *Bronsky* in his ear.

And now he says, going college-professory on us again, "You may recall…" (which gets Pete so sky-eyed he's like gonna fall ass-over backwards) "…that today was art day."

"Artsy-*fartsy*," Terry says, sort of like he was spittin' through a pea-shooter.

"Precisely, Mighty Mouse, precisely," Frankie says, which now had JL and me and George P about doubled over in laugh-pain, with that 'precisely', you know, coming from such an idiot. And then the Insane One lays on us the maybe all-time, number-one shit-eatin' smile, all slow and with an extremely, believe me, loopy kind of sly. "During art today," he says then, "while all you good little jags were busy doing your bullshitty little pictures (which, like I say, Frankie could say because of how great he could draw—and I'm thinkin' right now about this picture he did of the Armadillo with everything perfectly normal except he gave her an enormous right foot, which he drew as hangin' out over all our heads, ready to stomp, as we sat at our desks—

which drawing we ranked at the time as one of the Seven Wonders of the Moronic World) ... *And,*" he says now, "while you were all too jaggy-busy to notice that Her Humongousness the SMM was like bendin' over her desk, too, correcting papers...." And now, I mean if his eyes coulda made sounds, they'd a been whoppin' belly laughs, he says, "I was close enough to.... Juuust close enough..." he says. Then he stops. Of course to get our curiosity hummin' all the faster. Then he goes, "...close enough, boys...to hear the happy sound of a little *fart,* rappin' off the wood of a certain penguin's chair."

And what could we do but instantly die laughin'—especially when George P asks, you know, like it was a very important scientific question, "Was there *vibrato?*" and Frankie says, "I have to say yes to that. There was *vibrato,* if ever so slight." And I mean even Pete was dyin' now, especially while he was trying to talk again, 'cause what he had to say was that even though the sound of that poot escaped him, he was dead certain that it *had* existed. Which was like the second funny thing to come outa Pete in his life, the first, who could forget, being that blowin' up of the Trojan with his beak. And this second one came at a time when even a Pete joke was rip-you-up hilarious. So now we're really fallin' over, even Bobby, who usually, the funnier things got, just sort of smiled harder.

And there was more. Which we could tell 'cause now Malone just starts sort of nodding, and smiling, like he's got additional top-secret information. Oh yes he does. So we're splitting, but we're listening. Then he goes, "Like I say, even with the *vibrato,* it was just a little one. Which surprises ya, 'cause of course if ya ever do hear SMM cut one, you expect it to be very huge."

"And very *deadly,*" Terry said.

"Precisely," Frankie says.

And, I mean, I've got tears goin' now, and every one of my friends has got tears, even Bobby. And of course George P's got tears 'cause he has 'em about five times a day anyhow, just thinking about his own thoughts, which I gotta say I have never one time known not to be certifiable. Not once.

"But," Frankie said, "if you want even your little farts heard…."

And naturally we all started nodding and agreeing that yes, we did want them heard. Of course we did.

"Then I think you'll agree, there's no better way to get the job done than to pop 'em off the seat of a wooden chair."

There was some arguing about if this was the *absolute* best way, but nobody disagreed about it being a truly *primo* way.

"So," Frankie said, "I heard that little poot all right, clear as a bell."

"From *hell,*" Terry piped in, this time, obviously, steppin' her up to a little poetry.

"And a 'course," Frankie said, "I coulda been polite if I wanted to…."

"Nope," George P said.

"Well," Frankie said, "anyhow, I wasn't. So when I heard it, I kind of slowly looked up. And what do I see?"

And I need to get on with this story, so I'm not gonna bore ya with the fifty thousand or so guesses we had on what Frankie saw, except to say naturally they included smoke coming off the chair. But what Frankie said was, "No. No. What I saw, boys, was SMM just sittin' there. Just sittin' there—and still lookin' down at the paper she was correcting, like she was glued to it. And still for a good while just sittin' there, not lookin' up. And not lookin' up. And not lookin' up. Until finally, because she just couldn't *stand* not knowin' if anybody heard or not, she just this little, tiny bit—ever...so...slightly—starts to peek her eyes up from under her penguin brim. And a course not one person in the whole room heard it but the one who got put right in front of her. But there he was, goin' just like this, right at her."

And there we were, seein' Malone, waving this cutesy little wave like a bye-bye or a night-night to a baby, and wearing on his kisser the shit-eater to beat all shit-eaters, even loopier and more wicked-satisfied than the one he'd just showed us. And I gotta say there was no chance of life left. We all died on the spot. And there would be Jackie, too, who was pretty much always respectful about the nuns, laughing harder than just about all of us—and part of it I know was that, way far down in, he loved it, to see how Frankie Malone got such sweet revenge.

And there's this other thing I remember too about us bumblin'-ass along that day.... But, shit, Jesus...I gotta stop.... I'm not gonna cry. I'm not. I'm not. Fuck this shit. God damn.... I just gotta stop a second.... And breathe. And swallow the fucking pain outa my throat. Which you'd think I'd cried enough not to feel anymore. But at least if I close my eyes for a second and swallow it down, I can get it outa me for a time. And maybe shake off some of that feeling, you know, that's like I've been crying straight, from the day I'm talking about now, right up to this minute.

God I hate this. But it's like I've gotta say it. You know, to *somebody*, about this day. I do. And not just 'cause it's more of that kinda craziness that makes you keep *going*, or here, running at the mouth, once you've started something. There was a craziness that made me start talking in the first place. Or I mighta got some brain disease, I swear. I mean so much of this stuff I've told ya, sort of had to come out.

So I'll say that where we were *goin'* was toward that field in The Woods where I told ya about Jackie and me playing so long ago, you know, as those two little punks with the towels in their shirts for shoulder pads—because as it turns out that's where we had our practices for eighth-grade football, which sometimes, like this day, were just no-equipment touch games to like work on plays and stuff. But the thing that happened, as we were making our way there, was we actually, after a while, got back to Pete's question (and thinking about us goofing with that question, and other stuff, it's good for getting me smiling again, and feelin' happier—so I'm glad for that): I mean that question about the sound of a tree falling in the forest when nobody's there.

Of course we were laughing at how totally moronic a question it was. But then, *out* of *the* blue, comes this one, from Bobby Stu. "Have ya ever," the Stu-ball says, "walked along a beach someplace. I mean like in Grand Beach or Long Beach or someplace on the other side of the Lake, when the sun's goin' down...."

And like immediately we're pretty much blown apart by the fact that the big guy has said this many words, let alone that he's like sayin' 'em in a sort of serious voice.

And then he says, "And while you're walking along, seen how there's like a pathway of light going across the water from the sun to you?"

And of course who's even gonna think about pants-ing Stu. So, like, the logical response here was not getting suggested. So we're listening to the guy.

And on he goes. "And then ya see how when you move, the pathway of light moves over the water and follows where you go? And that what's light and what's dark out on the water depends on however it is you decide to move, so that you're making things light, or dark, as you walk? I mean, so it needs for you to be there, that pathway of light on the water?"

And naturally we're all starting to look at each other like the big guy's having a nervous breakdown or something. I mean even Pete was doing an eyebrow squinch like *What hath God wrought?* But then not really. I mean at least Jackie and me, 'cause the two of us weren't really thinking any smart-ass stuff at all, which not-thinking-like-smartasses we knew we'd see in each other when we looked at each other. And I'm bringing this time up, for one main reason, I think, and that's to tell you about one of the last things I'll ever remember Jackie Leonard doing—which would be his looking over at me when Bobby Stu was saying all this about the light on the water when the sun's goin' down. And it was the way he smiled at me then, about our friend, you know, which really was maybe what I told all this stuff for—I mean the stuff about all this day so far. Because, in my memory, Jackie's smile to me about Bobby, it was such a sort of like peaceful thing coming out of such a, you know, ass-kicker, that it seems like…. I don't know, I mean, to me, anyhow, like somehow he knew that this day would be the last time he'd ever see us, and that he knew he was heading that day for a place where it was peaceful forever.

But I can't say shit like that. I…. Not and keep talking. So fuck it. I mean, ten times over. But let me say that I hate fucking black Cadillacs, too. And I don't really think of stupid shit like premonitions as real, even though, shit, somehow you think, or you really want to think, that really good things are like getting whispered into someone's soul or something, right before they die. Or (and I hate lies, I *hate* 'em), maybe you really *do* believe this stuff, from the way the person looked—like Jackie, so totally and completely kind of generous all the way through him, smiling to me about Bobby. But sometimes, too, it's maybe because your heart really's feeling some kind of a spooked-out fear, that you believe it—I mean, that there's premonitions.

Which, if I didn't have that day, I mean any fear, when I saw the Cadillac pull into that parking lot, I would now. I have had it now—I mean, when I see those big black cars, with the fins like spears—I mean some kind of fear that something truly bad is gonna happen, which I'll get over, I guess, some day.

And you know the one I mean—it was that parking lot that sits just inside The Woods off 91ST, across the way from the Rock Island station. Ya know? Next to the field I just talked about again now…. The field that I said I see these days, sometimes, like from a helicopter, with me flying way up high over it and then turning off and away.

And, take it whatever way you like, but it was weird, the way the thing came in all by itself, with no driver we ever saw, and got parked all the way down at the field where we practiced, which was far from the train. And why would a car end up there, when, on a Saturday, in the whole huge lot there were mostly just empty parking places, all the way out to 91ST? And why would somebody back it in when there wasn't a single other car down that far—and so there wouldn't be the slightest trouble at all backing out? It turned out it was just some old guy who parked where he parked all week, and in the same way he always parked, even though that day was Saturday and he didn't need to. Just his old-guy habit. But you think when something's so weird and insane like that, that there has to be something behind it. I know that that's what we all thought, until after some days we just got worn out and gave it up, realizing that it really was all just stupid. Not, though, that you wouldn't still like to make that guy feel the blame down to his guts, the stupid idiot. At least until you think how bad he must feel, too, which Mrs. Leonard told me about. I mean that the owner of the car came to her and couldn't talk because he was cryin', even though he was an old guy, past seventy. But he finally got it out and told her that he just gave the Cadillac away like the very next day, because he never wanted to see the thing again in his life and he couldn't take money for it.

The grass cutters had just mowed the grass of that field, like that morning, maybe just before we got there. And I swear every time now I smell just-cut grass, that day comes back to me, in like no time. It's done it like five times already now. And then, from that, my mind jumps back, too, kind of like automatically, or at least a lot of the time, to when Jackie and me were little guys, having so much stupid but cool fun, acting like we were future pro players or something, playing punt and catch in that field, with our white night-game football, which we thought was so cool. And maybe it will be there forever, when I smell cut grass, which the cutters cut that day maybe for the last time of the year, 'cause it was the end of September, which I know I'll always know now has really green grass, and that when you see leaves fall in Chicago, it will be on really green ground that you see 'em. And then you put times and things together, too, even if you don't know if you have a reason. Like, for me, it will always, forever, be on green grass in late September that Jackie and I played, too, when we were little—though I'll be honest I can't remember what exact time of year that was. Just that it was only the two of us.

But that Saturday practice, there were more of us CK guys there, I mean more besides just Jackie and me and Frankie and Stu and Terry and George P and Pete. Jimmy Waldron was there. Tom Kearns. Mickey Grady. John Bayer. George Youhas. Rich Delaney. Andy Trout. Jim Roche. All the guys on the team. Dave Morrisey. And I can see 'em like coming in, from all the different directions that guys lived, or hung out in. Tommy Pelagi from up on the hill there on Longwood. And Robbie Bissette from over on 92ND. Of course we all, like in neighborhood kind of groups, and together with the friends we hung with, came in about at the same time, which was two o'clock, I know, 'cause it was Saturday practice. But the memory of it feels and looks in my mind like some kind of a procession or something. Or a ceremony, where every kid gets called up one-by-one. And the person up at the podium takes time with every kid's name.

It never speeds up, either. Even though, soon enough, that day, we'd be gettin' down to business. Of course there'd be the usual goofin' off and stuff at first. But before ya know it, because about football we cared, we'd be bending together in the huddle and then, just like that, clapping our hands for *Break!* and there'd be the lining up and then the snap of the ball. And everything would be kind of super high speed, too, because there wasn't any tackling. I can even see guys' shirts rippling, because, like I say, we weren't wearing equipment, just our shirts, and I mean rippling because of the high speed. But it all goes click to slow speed, then, in my mind. And I can see all those guys, who were in like that procession or that ceremony, with somebody taking time with each one of their names, all moving suddenly slow, like they were in a movie, or something, that somebody wanted to make out of a dream.

And I wish now—maybe five thousand times I've wished it—that I could say there was something really great that Jackie said to me. Some extremely cool last word, or like a message, that helped me not just to get things, but to get the whole deal of my life. I can't tell you how much more even than I tried to figure out why that car would be there, parked in that place, in that way, by that old guy—how fifty times as often as I thought about that, I thought was there some message Jackie left me. Or some cool last look in his eye, into mine.

But it was just an ordinary, average play. Just Frankie, who was our quarterback, making an ordinary call, which for us would be somehow trying the best way we could to get Jackie free. And I was the other halfback, across from Jackie—so we'd make a call like the one I'll be able to hear now in my memory for the rest of my life, which was Frankie saying, "X 23," which would be a fake to me in the three hole and Frankie rolling right on a bootleg to find Jackie deep in the corner.

Sometimes I can see us all just like normal. Mostly skinny guys, and then big Bobby standin' out like the Rock of Gibraltar—I mean all of us just wearing our shirts, no equipment, so you could see all there was of us, which wasn't too much. Except one look at Jackie and you said to yourself—that if you were ever gonna beat us, that that was the kid you'd have to stop, which if you had much sense, you wouldn't be all that hopeful about your chances. But it was all just ordinary, and that's how I see it. Except then sometimes it changes, and it's like I have an eye way down low, like on the ground, and I'm looking up into all the faces of us as we're huddled over and Frankie's calling that play.

Which would be like some photograph I've seen somewhere by some famous photographer, and you can see so clearly, with the camera looking up, each guy's face in the huddle and all the differences from face to face. And you stop, and you think about what this kid's life might be. And this kid's. And this kid's. And this kid's.

Then it was "X 23, on one...BREAK!" And for me, because there was no tackling, it was about as fast almost as the snap, faking through the three hole. But then what happens is ya let up and ya jog, because there's no contact, and because you know the pass is up and in the air. So you look up to watch it fly. And for me, and for everybody, it's not like with that old guy now, with all of us trying to find some reason to blame him. I mean not like it in any way, because our minds want never one time in this world ever, for as long as we live, to blame Frankie Malone. There's like stuff in your mind that's like puke, the way it comes up on its own. But you just get that hard hum going in your brain—the one that drowns out the sound of things with a nnnnnnnnnnnnnnnnnnnnnnnnnnn. And I'm thinking now—and I've been thinking for months—what all must go through Frankie's mind now if this goes through mine. What tricks, and noises, does he use? But I know that this would be exactly what no-bullshit prayers are for—I mean for Frankie's mind. Even though he meant nothing, which in the craziness that's in our heads doesn't matter. It's so crazy—it's like God didn't get this right, the way you blame yourself when there's no reason. When you're innocent. Like Frankie, 'cause he was just lettin' it fly. And Jackie could run under any pass you could ever throw—so why not let it fly deep as you can throw it. And who am I to say.... Who in the world am I to say? I should have yelled.

In dreams. I can't even yell in my dreams, no matter how many I've had, the same one again and again. It's always that my voice makes no sound. With afterwards, just the sound of me bawlin', which sometimes I wake myself up with in the middle of the night. And I see that ball, about every night, the way it went that day. And Jackie as always running faster than anybody I ever knew, or in my life I ever will know. Or most people ever would. I'll never see a shirt rippling on a running kid, without thinking. Or hear about an athlete, anybody that somebody thinks is great, without thinking I knew somebody better. I don't think now that I ever will. And I won't ever forgive that old man and his Cadillac. Fuck him to death.

But please, God, you've gotta help Frankie. He didn't mean it. He just let it fly. And there it was. And Jackie came under that pass at his top speed, the way it would always be. With his eye on the ball. Never one time in this world off the ball—not a chance. Because Jack Leonard wouldn't chicken-blink for anything, ever. So he never saw that backed-in Cadillac with its spear-fins. And he never felt it. I say prayers every day for my feelings, and like my mind, and for every kid's that was there that day, that Jackie never felt it. The doctor swore to us he never felt it, when the fin went straight like a spear into his heart. Because it went so straight, the doctor said, Jackie died instantly, with no pain whatsoever. The doctor promised us a hundred times.

But like a thousand times over I see that second when Jackie was making his last reach for the ball. You can bet your whole life ten times over that he caught it. He caught it clean. Tight in his hands. But then I see all his speed getting stopped in one second by that Cadillac. By the chrome-and-black spear. And how that car seemed like the incredibly heaviest thing that was ever allowed to exist, because it didn't move. It seemed so much like it should have moved, when Jackie hit it, because he was coming in full speed, and he was Jackie. But it didn't move. Only he moved, I mean that last slow sinking down of him as his body came to the end of its life. It was sort of like the world for Jackie shot ahead in one second to its final ending and there was, all of a sudden, right now, this slow, bending-over motion of some kind of last bow that he was taking, with his arms and his head slowly going down, and his eyes closing, and the ball, the last thing, dropping out of his hands. Which made I think all of us know like right that second, the second he dropped it, that he must have died.

With no voices, not from any of us, we all came up, slow, like it was toward the edge of some kind of terrifying high cliff. But we saw that with his eyes closed Jackie's face didn't have any scared look. But that there was nothing. No sound, anymore, when we finally called his name, which was all we could think to do—because, even though not one of us had ever seen somebody die before, we knew now that we had.

It was all these fast panic feelings waking up then out of feelings that couldn't at first move. I mean it was, in all of us, like the terror they must have been feeling in ancient wars. 'Cause that's how Jackie Leonard died—in total truth—from a spear in his heart. And, in front of all our eyes, there he was, bent over, with his eyes closed, and the spear gone through him. And the blood everywhere making his shirt all red.

I remember just a few things of the next minute. I remember Davey Morrissey, just running. Before any of us, Dave just broke and ran out to 91ST. And he saw people at the station and started screamin' at the top of his lungs what happened. And that men came running, following Dave. And that the first man to get there, who was that doctor who would promise us Jackie never felt what happened to him, did what we all were too petrified to do. He put his arms around JL, and he pulled him away slowly and carefully from the spear, which was all covered too with blood, so much, we couldn't believe. And he set Jackie down. Then, for a time, he put his fingers on his neck to check for any pulse. Then—I'll never forget—he whispered a prayer to God to take this innocent boy into his eternal care. Then he took off his coat and covered over Jackie's heart with it, and the blood. And that then we could just see our friend's face, with its eyes closed, with this dead look that made you think that the truest toughness you'll ever see was gone out of the world. And we saw the doctor, all covered himself now with blood, touching Jackie's hair back and then running his hand hard over his own eyes.

I remember George P, how he just sank down on the grass then and lay there face down and started wailing on the ground. And how Pete O'Connor had his face up, and was standing, but he kept wiping the tears off his face with his arm, again and again, and kept sobbing and looked like the saddest kid who ever lived. And how Bobby was crying, with his face all wet and like completely in pain—but that he had a job to do, because Terry just ran to him and held him like Bobby was his father. And how everybody was crying so hard, which you remember maybe even more because it was boys.

And I remember myself like shivering cold and on fire, and with my fists clenched so hard, just like hitting and smashing them together, again and again and again, while I hurt so bad it was like my whole life was in pain. And I felt like something was bad wrong with me, too, when I was just punching my fists harder and harder together, because I was just standing there and not going up to Jackie and holding him and putting his blood on me, the way it was on that doctor, and telling him good-bye and that I'd love him every day of my life. And not ever forget, ever. Not anything. Not ever. But I was just frozen in my legs, and just hitting my hands together, not wanting to make myself somebody more important than any of my friends.

Then there was another thing in me, a thought that I could think of suddenly, and that was where was Frankie? Where was he? I wiped my eyes hard with my arm and looked around, till I saw him, all the way across the field, looking back, but walking away from us backwards, looking so scared like he could trip. And then I saw him just turn away and run, high up Devil's Hill and back into The Woods as fast as he could go. And what good is anything if God didn't see the prayers in my eyes? If God didn't see what I had in my eyes were prayers?

I remember things from that night. How up in the pueblo I was so deep in like fear and sadness I was fever-sick from it. And how things in my sadness I was thinking over and over again, were things like Jackie saying to me, right there in the pueblo, how I had *me,* so there wouldn't be any backing down, which each time I thought it, it made me clench my fists till I was shaking with like promises I was praying I could in my life somehow keep. And I thought about, over and over, too, how Jackie told me that the kiss he gave to Katie Luce, which was only one kiss, was for four seconds, which every time I thought about it, it made tears come up so hard it was like I was back again at the field, and the parking lot, watching that second that he died, with no sound coming out of my mouth.

And, as time passed, too, I would think—it's so hard for me to say this—how my best friend…how he would never go beyond the time he was thirteen…that like day after day, and year after year, I'd be moving farther and farther away from a place that he would never get past. And he'd just forever now be like a picture to me, one that got older, and faded, but never changed, of a kid in eighth grade; and that nobody would ever see what Jackie Leonard became like as a man. I had to make a voice of his in my mind tell me I didn't need to be ashamed of this. I mean, that the one who got to go on would be me.

I remember I woke up in the middle of the night, with my heart like beating out of me, to find my mom there in my room, with a chair pulled up next to me. And that it seemed somehow normal for her to be there. And that she didn't say anything. She just held me until I calmed down. Then she kissed my hair and whispered that she'd be there, and that I should just try to sleep. And it seemed normal that I didn't even answer, but just sort of nodded and closed my eyes and did what she said.

CHAPTER TEN

FALL OF EIGHTH

THE FENCE & THE SCAR

Things got so blurry and melted, it's like strange I can even remember. But three days passed before the funeral. I know. And it was the eighth-grade girls who were the only ones who sang at Jackie's funeral mass. Not us boys, or any other of the kids from the school, which was the way the nuns had it. There was something, too, about our girls that day. I don't lie. They seemed to me like the most beautiful I'd ever seen in my life, with the saddest but the most beautiful voices I'd ever heard. They had just those little like hankies of white lace over their hair, bobby-pinned. All of them with the same.

And Katie, Katie Luce…. On her lips there was the secret that Jackie had kissed her there, a secret I knew about. And it made Katie seem even more beautiful than she ever did, especially when her head was bowed and she sang the Gregorian chants, which does something very beautiful to the way a girl looks, anytime. And maybe there was something somehow better about things, or that said that like the world isn't all for crap, or worthless, because of the way Katie looked in that incredible sadness.

And what, added to all the thousand other things, that day I loved about Patty (who if there ever was anybody who knew how to do things right, she would be that person) is that—if only for like a few quick seconds—she definitely broke our rule of coolness and made like a point to look over at me. And what her look was for, was to bring back again, up into her eyes, our time together at the Ice Tree and to let me know that she got it very deep down inside her, what I'd told her that day about Jackie, and his move against the Rat King, and that she knew how far down those things went into my life, and about what Jackie's and my friendship was, from so far back. And if you don't know how all of that can get said in like a look that lasts maybe just a second or two, then there was maybe no point in me telling you anything I ever told you about Patty Conlon and me. Or in telling you, either, that her wearing, pinned to her hair, the exact same small white cloth as every other girl's only made her seem more different from every other girl than she ever did.

Father G was the one they chose to give the eulogy for Jackie. Which was good because Father Garvey's words never gave ya like that crud feeling that the one talking about him didn't know much about the person who died, which I know from my grandfather's funeral makes ya think that maybe pretty many things are bullshit. Instead they showed how Jackie's deal was real clear even for adults, if they had their eyes open, like Fr. G, and guys like Doc Schwendrowski, and my mom and dad, and I gotta think some of the nuns, too, like—and I won't call her anything now except Sister Armida, who, this time not long after Jackie died, when I slipped off early by myself to the six, saw me after mass and called me over and she said to me, "You know, Kevin…in these days now…in your prayers… promise me you'll remember your friend Frankie Malone." The way she said 'Frankie', not 'Francis', the way it would be in school, or even 'Frank', I really and truly appreciated, and always will.

With Mr. Leonard there, and especially, no doubt, with Jackie's mom, I don't know how Father G even got out the words he said. And with Jackie's casket there, too, just like coffins at other funerals. Which was so completely unreal, with the flowers spread over it, and the smell of incense. But it was there. And Jackie was inside—with like no life now in his hands, or his eyes, or his mind, or his voice, so he wasn't even like a ghost, but would be like held forever right there in that casket, in the dark, where his body would decay down till it was dust. I couldn't look over at it. It was like, if I did, something would come back to me that would kill me—something from our life—his crossin' over The Woods from his house to mine or me from my house to his, so many times to hang out. We all of us were at times hard rippin' our sleeves over our eyes. But one time I saw that Frankie, who sat over with guys like Pelagi and Bayer and not with us, was looking—I don't know the words—maybe too scared to show any other feelings but fear. Which, for the second or two that I saw him, and it was so weird that he wasn't there with me and Stu and Pete and Terry and George P, made me think of Frankie as the ghost.

Father G waited like a long time before he started to talk. And his voice came out different, I mean than when he gave sermons at the nine-fifteen, which was the school-kid mass on Sundays. And all six hundred kids from CK were there now, too, with maybe six hundred other people, out to the vestibule and standing all up and down in the aisles, which included a lot of guys who'd gone on to high school, guys who'd got let out for the day from Rice and Ignatius and Carmel and Leo, which was pretty amazing to see them all, O'Grady and Brookings and Dietrich and Saccitello and Donovan and Big Joe, and all sorts of other guys.

And what Father G said was honest stuff about Jackie's being a leader—and I mean 'cause he got the deal. So his words, even like 'leader', which can make ya wanna spit sometimes when adults throw it at ya, connected truly and deeply to the person he was talking about, which truth you could tell in like your throat and heart. And he talked about Jackie showin' us without being conceited, with his guts, how you get past your fears. And he said sin, which I'll never forget he said has death as its shadow, was kind of like being stuck on yourself, which Jackie wasn't. And that sin is what makes a coward out of ya, all worried about number one, which Jackie wasn't.

And then he stopped a second—and he looked at us. I mean right at us—the eighth-grade boys. And he kind of smiled, in the way you do out of kindness when there's really nothing to smile about. And he talked plain, right to us. "He was so great, wasn't he, guys," he said. "Such a terrific friend—*your* friend." Then he said, "But now…he left you. Your great friend…. He left you. And you guys know how—how when we're all here together on Sunday—I'll sometimes stop and ask you a question. And maybe if this were Sunday mass, I'd stop now and ask you to tell me who it is that that reminds you of? Someone who showed us the way...and then left us? And I know you'd know the answer. But I'll ask another question now, that I'll want you to keep asking in your hearts. And that is, why it was, that once he showed us the way, our Lord left us, and left us in a world all still filled with trouble?"

Father G smiled again now, in that way that was for kindness in a bad spot. But this was a day when he'd have to answer his own questions—which was good, because his answers would have no crap or stupidity in 'em. So now he said, "Because, guys, in *the end*, the Lord's way is to leave things up to us, no matter how many times we might fail. Because He knows you never *really* know how to do a single thing—until you do it for yourselves. And that once you show people the way, and the life, then the best thing you can do, is to step out of the way and make them do things on their own. Make them fight their own battles. I said that Jackie made it easy for us to love him. What could be more true than that? I know that every one of you knows how true that is. But he made a lot of things easy for us, didn't he? He carried that ball for us. He brought that ball up court, and he shot it. And he hit it out of the park. But it's as if, maybe...*maybe*...Jackie wanted you guys to do things now your*selves*. I think you could think of it that way. I really do.... You know, that Jackie just stepped aside and said, 'Okay, I've showed you guys how to live your lives. And now it's your turn.'"

I kind of closed my eyes when I heard Father G say those words, feeling, sort of the way you do sometimes, that somebody just picked you out of a whole huge crowd to talk right at. And I kind of let his words, which, to say true, have been with me, sort of here and there, since I began all this telling of things—I mean, or what I'm saying is, I kind of let all Father G's words turn inside me into a hope that, in the right way, not stuck on myself, I wouldn't as I lived my life, be gutless.

There were other things he said. Cool. Not bullshit. And all of Father G's words made it, I promise, so that when we went to Communion, not with the usual thinkin' about how we looked, it was just sort of us, one by one hearing the *Corpus Domini nostri Jesu Christi,* and then all dedicated and even-inside silent, with just the Host in our mouths. And I know, for me, my head-bowed prayer after Communion was still mixed with those words about Jackie leaving it now up to us, to do by ourselves, after he showed us how to stand up in this life and then afterwards to keep our mouths shut about it, even the mouth that like all the time, inside us, says *me me me me.*

They buried Jackie at Holy Sepulcher, on 111TH Street. But I think maybe I'll leave his burial one of the only things I didn't talk about in all this talking—I mean, for other reasons, too, but because of like my memory that day of Mrs. Leonard, who explains a lot about Jackie by the way she is, I mean always so incredibly kind and good to everybody, but who broke down really badly at the grave, in like complete sobbing and sorrow, so they had to hold her and even carry her, Mr. Leonard and his brother, which is all I'll say about that sadness and pain—except, too, that Jackie's grave was like so close you could almost see from it my grandfather's, and my uncle's, my dad's brother, who was a fighter pilot killed over Germany—and that, buried at my uncle's foot, in the same grave, is my own brother Timmy, who fit in the same grave-plot because he died just a few months after he was born, from having a hole in his heart, which makes me think now, with like really hard sorrow, of even cemeteries on the South Side as places you might not ever get back to.

Because it's where our bikes were and stuff, we came back, after the burial, to CK. And after something like that, it's like you're only half awake—sort of like half-way out of a bad night-dream—but it's also daylight, right in your eyes. So I was feeling hot and worn out to shit, and didn't feel like hangin' with anybody, at all. But at the bike rack, when I was about to pull out my wheels and, like half-asleep, head off in that hurt-your-eyes sunlight, there would be Frankie, at his bike, and I have to say lookin' pretty seriously screwed up, sort of totally hang-dog and yet still really jumpy at the same time. Which is to say, like the kid a nun would make me promise just a few days later to pray for. And a few bikes over from Frankie, looking all bizarrely for his bike-lock key—kind of spazzing around in his pocket—and sniffing up snot that I promise had nothing to do with tears, 'cause he would be maybe the one guy in our class who didn't get the deal at all on JL, was Pin Flynn.

And Frankie, with his nerves, was in no more mood than me for hangin'. But when he for a second looked up and caught the Pin in his sort of sniffly jaggings around with his hand in his pocket, Frankie, outa nowhere, said, "What the *fuck* is wrong with you, Flynn?"

Then the Pin, and I mean with a like really quick, total pissed-offed-ness (because it seems he never forgot for like even a second about getting lit on fire, and also maybe about that time he was pissed on in the winter and his pants froze yellow—talk about your fire and ice), said, "Wasn't Leonard supposed to be your friend, Malone? Maybe you oughta try to be decent on the day your supposed-to-have-been friend gets buried."

"Shut your face, you worthless, snot-shit fuck. What

do you care what happens on Jack Leonard's funeral day? Hunh? What the *fuck* do you care? You supposed-to-be-human-but-aren't *shit bag.*"

Frankie, like I say, had been looking like he wanted to cut and run. But now it was like he decided just to come back instead and beat the livin' shit out of somebody and he'd just found the exact right goat. So now he like stomped this insane-man march right over to the Pin and put a hand up into the Pin's face and just shoved him back, really hard. "Shit," he said then, as he wiped his hand off on his pants like he was smearin' off maggots. "What am I touching you for?"

The Pin, sort of like half fallen, still sort of crouched over, said, in this kind of gross, half-cry-ey way, "Maybe you'd rather light me on fire again, Malone. Maybe you'd feel better if you saw me going up in flames and then melting into a pool of black burning blood and guts like from the tortures of hell or something, with my eyes melting out of my face. Maybe that would make you happy."

"What would make me happy, you Riverview-reject, would be if you never said another word that like told us what was in your non-human brain. It's like your mind's got puke-shit halitosis, Flynn. So keep your words inside your fucking skull, which maybe you oughta just tattoo some crossbones on, to let people know you're poison as shit to swallow."

The Pin stood up now out of his like weepy crouch but looked really weird standing there, like he was turning his face into not that smile-mask but the frown-mask, the one for tragedy. Then he shot it out. "You mean words, Malone, like *nice pass?*"

And I gotta say that I sure as shit wished I'd had Jackie's crook-toothed, kick-your-ass toughness to go along with it—but I did have, from knowing the JL deal, pretty much at least the knowledge of what to do here, because what was gonna happen here was Pin Flynn—I'm not kidding about this one slight bit—was gonna lose his life. So I just jumped in between Frankie and him, and I just grabbed Frankie, who was coming on to truly kill the guy, and got Frankie in like a full wrap around his chest. And over my shoulder I said to Flynn, who for some strange reason I called by his real name, "You go! You leave your bike here and go, David, and keep goin' and don't look back! Ya hear me! RUN! And don't look back!"

And I was—in one way of looking at it at least—luckier than shit because Frankie could have maybe killed just about any human at that time, including me—but he just sort of broke down now when I was holdin' him. His mouth and face started sort of going all trembly. Then suddenly he sort of jerked and spazzed all crazy and was screaming at the Pin, who was cuttin' out as fast as I told him to and getting himself out of sight, "Go hang a cat, you piece of shit! GO HANG A CAT!"

And Frankie kept like top-of-his-lungs screamin' that, right in the schoolyard, where there might be nuns: "GO HANG A CAT! YOU GO HANG A CAT!" But now he was like shaking again, even more, and not fighting to get through me at all. And I was still holding him, but now it was like fully for comfort, not at all to hold him back. And it was so, like *not the way I saw life,* to have Francis X Malone sort of shaking and trembling on my shoulder. And to have protected the Pin like that after what the groaty shit said, which ranked for sick shitty-ness, I mean it, right up there with anything I ever heard in my life, not that it would have ever come out of his mouth if Frankie hadn't, so to speak, lit the weirdo up again. But I was glad, thanks to Father G and JL, that I hadn't dither-shat around, even for a second. Because Frankie wouldn't a just goated the guy—like I said, he'd a killed 'm, or tried—and don't think he couldn't 've, I mean really damaged the punk. And now I had Frankie where, while he was by now trembling, I swear, like he was hangin' up on the edge of some scary-as-shit ice hole or something, I just kept trying to pull him out of it, whispering in his ear, "It's okay. It's okay. It's okay. It's okay.... It's okay.... It's...okay." Which I did, I swear, for a full like minute and a half, just holdin' him, before he kind of got a hold of himself again, a little. And then we were just sort of standing there for another pretty long time, sort of catching our breath. And then, you know, just to calm down a little, we kind of went over and were sort of sitting-leaning against the bike rack (Frankie having first hocked up and dripped a stringy green quid on the Pin's bike seat and then kicked the bike's tire so hard I thought sure he'd about break his own foot), after which we were kind of laughin', sort of the way you do when you don't know what you're laughing about except that it just seems normal after something very officially insane.

But then it got so it was time that I really knew I oughta try some other thing. So I started making this stupid kind of lecture-y speech, like I was a school marm on Bonanza or something, but with some of our terminology mixed in. I mean I was, or I sure hope it came over that I was, completely mockin' the idea of giving the kid a sermon, but, you know, still just slightly reminding Frankie that he did rank on the Pin and he did ignite the kid's ass once with a beam of light. Then I went from there to how ranked-on and ignited people are of course gonna think of the shittiest things they can say back, regardless of the truth factor, working basically only with spite and poisonous shit—especially if they're lepers to begin with, because all that lepers do while they're checking out their very famous scabby situation is think up poisonous, lepro-fied *sheist* to say—and if you asked 'em if they cared if it was true or not, they'd sort of in this sick way snicker till another body part fell off.

And I was goin' on, but now Frankie, good thing, told me to *shut* the *fuck* UP. But at least he was sort of smiling now, and he slugged my arm in the familiar Malone way, which was always with the old knuckle pronged out for a little spear and *way* too hard—but, when it was directed at me or Jackie anyhow, in fun. And then we kind of took a breath, laughing now. And then there was him calling me and me calling him, kind of stuff like "you completely adenoidal colostomy bag!" You know, in sort of an SRA language exercise, where they have stuff like "Use *colostomy bag* in a sentence."

And we kept working on these kind of moronisms till we'd sort of made things idiotic enough. So now chucklin' kind of hard, we mounted up, and biked off, with me cruisin' over Leavitt way with Frankie, rather than straight down Hamilton to home, just to kind of hang with him a little bit more. Because what was he going home to but the rages of bro Tom and to his mom's being extremely mortified beyond all possible hope, and to his dad, who was back, singing Irish songs one minute and bein' the father of Huck Finn the next, which home stuff was, no matter how bad, probably nothing compared to what he had on his mind besides home. So what could I think of my friendship with Frankie Malone as but unfinished business? And I mean maybe as serious business as this dream I had like three days after this, where no one other than Val Prizer picked out Frankie from this whole huge crowd to join a gang of vampires, and I was tryin' like crazy to get out the crucifix and it was like I barely made it in time with my heart bangin' away like insanity. Jesus.

And now I gotta say something about this time that, on top of all the other things, turned out completely shit-painfully weird, and in the real world, not dreams. I mean, too, it must have been weird and hard as anything for my parents, too, having made the move they made, which was, unbeknownst, to head way up north, out of the city, and buy this house they saw—for them to have to *tell* me about this, like right after the time Jackie died. I mean they actually bought our house up north here on the *day* that Jackie died and then, after some days passed after the funeral, because we'd be moving so soon, they had to come up to the pueblo (so I knew something not normal was about to happen) to tell me, which included telling me that my mom was going to have another baby.

"And if it weren't for that, Kevin," my mom said, "maybe we would just stay right where we are. I know that right now the thought of moving away from your friends has got to be so hard for you—with all you've been going through in this terrible, sad time. And, Kevin, I would never tell you, honey—even though there will be so many new people to meet up north, and even though your life will be very good and happy there—I would never tell you that you'll find, there, or anywhere, a better friend than Jackie Leonard. I would never tell you that, sweetheart, because it isn't true. There can't *be* a better friend than the one you just lost. There cannot be. But perhaps someday there will be some friend or friends just as good. And I think there will.

I truly do. But after the baby, Kevin, there really just won't be room for us here."

Now my dad said, "So, Kev, you see, we *had* to think about moving. And, you see…. Well, maybe even if Mom weren't going to have another baby, we'd still think of moving, because, the fact of the matter is, Kev, our neighborhood, well, it's going to change before too long. If we sell now, we might get out of this house not too much less than what we have in it. And pretty soon that might not be the case at all. But it isn't just money. I don't like to say this. But it's, well, it's safety. I really *hate* saying such a thing— but it's true. Very unfortunately true. When colored people come, trouble comes. Such a miserable, sad truth. But you can't be foolish and ignore it. Your Aunt Rita ignored it in South Shore, and she's really all alone now there in Papa and Nana's old house on Constance, in a basically all-colored neighborhood, and she's scared to go out. Houses and stores there, where I grew up as a kid, have iron gates over the doors, and bars on the windows, house after house and store after store, everywhere you look. We just don't want to live like that, Kev. It's not the fault of nine colored people out of ten, who are all as good as anyone white or black—in fact it takes *more* courage for them to be good than for us. But there's that one out of ten, who makes things really dangerous and miserable for everyone else around. Rita told me the other day she heard gunfire right in the alley behind the house—which wouldn't be for the first time. And it's coming, Kev. I don't know if Jackie mentioned this before he died, but a colored family just moved in on Paulina, not two blocks from Jackie's house, which means, I'm afraid, that the Leonards' block will probably change now pretty fast."

And it was like, I was sort of just nodding. Or like how much could you take, with Jackie just now put in the grave. So maybe I seemed like I was okay with things, when what I was, was goofed-up numbed to shit. Then when they went back downstairs again, it was for the first few minutes like I was someone caught in a battle or something—I mean like somebody over in World-War Europe, who had to grab fast whatever he could carry and then run to some place where you hid, which would be like just the first place out of a string, that would be coming for a long, long time, of places that you lived in without a house, or a room, or a bed.

So my bed was feeling like just this sort of cold rock of a thing. And the pueblo was this thing that I had to get out of in like twenty-four hours or else, because it had been sold to some sourpussed stranger I'd never heard of and who never heard of the past, or me, or anything that went through my mind. I mean like all the feeling of privacy of it, too, was gone, just like that, in no time. And I was thinking if I looked out my window, there would be Susie Shannon, back again after she hadn't been there in about two years, shutting down her shade on me, or something.

And it all was really strange because it was like a really terrific night, too. The pueblo was completely filled with excellent silver from the moon. If I looked out at The Woods, I knew what I'd see. I mean moonlight spread all over the trees, which had this way, a lot of the time, of making me think of my life as a kind of story with all these very cool chapters in it, which I could go over as I looked across The Woods—sort of the way you'd leaf through a book that you knew like the back of your hand. But when, with still a really *bad*, I-don't-give-a-shit-anymore feeling, I finally now got up the energy to sit up and look out, then on comes this *other* totally screwed-up feeling of like I was a guy with amnesia or something and somebody would have to tell me, as he walked me through it, that, "Kevin, this is Ryan's Woods," and, "This is the ravine that you shot the bridges of in a plastic boat when the rain made the stream go wild," and, "This is the way to the tunnel that crosses under 87TH to the toboggan slides," and, "This is the tree where you sat inside it and told your cousin Rick that if you listened hard enough you could hear God calling your name, which was something you made up but then started after a while to believe in yourself and had Rick going with, too, who said he could right then hear God calling him *Richard,*" (but I said as we were sitting hunched in the tree-hole that I actually thought I heard God say, not Richard, but *Ricardo,* which had us then laughing like crazy in that little tree-cave of ours). Which was all kind of stuff that I never talked about here, along with a million other things, most of them cool, and some of them remember-forever things.

But then I did start thinking of things I've talked about here, which there's no point in me going back over again, only I'll say that somewhere in my thinking I started going from *who gives,* anymore, about this place, to like a there-wasn't-even-time-to-feel-sorrow kind of instant teary eyes and choked-out sobs and stuff that I wouldn't have let anyone see but with no one there I just let out. And Bobby Stu's wave, it came to my mind like twenty times then. And it got so I had to grit my teeth hard as shit to stop crying, because I was thinking of Bobby's wave now as like this wave good-bye, or something.

Of course with what my dad said about guns and danger and Aunt Rita, which there was no denying, I thought, too, of all those saxophones blowin' through the night-time

Woods, and of Toby and Laetitia and the Fourth of July that Jackie and I had. I gotta confess, it made me mad then that Toby and Laetitia, cool as they were, would probably still be part of this like huge army of colored people that were movin' me out of my room and house, especially when I thought they might not give even the slightest shit-ball about that, but would be pretty much psyched up. And I was dead certain that there was *nobody,* Toby included, who could get a good set of thoughts and good feelings going in the pueblo the way I could. *Nobody.*

But I kept thinking, too, of that Fourth and how great it was—and so how bad it reeked that white people and colored people couldn't just *not* get into, like, *automatic* fear or raging, so everybody's automatically either pissed or scared or both, and moving away from each other (which could like maybe create a feeling of can't-remember-that-place amnesia all across the nation, if somebody didn't stop all the moving and moving), or getting ready to take each other out to the Ice Tree, like this really *was* some kind of World War we were all in, over you're not me and I'm not you. To which I guess I'd say I'm not Patty Conlon either, and she's not me, but look how that one turned out at the Ice Tree. Or if you wanna call it the Melt Tree, you might try that.

And I thought of Paulina Ave and if Jackie were alive how he'd be having to move—if the Leonards would move, which would not be the kind of thing *at all* that fit with JL's character, so I actually thought, when I thought of how even my dad could get into this *have-to-move* thing, that for some things it was maybe even better that you never got past being a kid and so never had the shit knowledge of it. But then I thought of Jackie as being like the last white kid on Paulina, but not holed up like Aunt Rita, instead hangin' out, ballsin' it, 'cause sooner or later *somebody* had to not move and just balls it, or the same old they're them and we're us would go on forever, logic proved. 'Cause without balls and guts, and without, too, what you learn from beautiful girls, it's the Ice Tree forever. Which it doesn't need to be, as Jackie and Patty proved it to me. But I thought, too, of Jackie maybe shot dead through the heart, out on Paulina Ave. But then, too, of like Laetitia holding him, cryin', getting the blood all over her body as she put her tears on Jackie's body. But then, too, of the 'Prize' as—for psychkilling terror—like organizing groups to sniper people coming into the neighborhood and collecting scalps that he wore on a belt and wearing war paint and burning people at the stake and preparing hot twigs to do the Isaac Jogues on their toenails and getting a nice full meal of hot coals ready for their mouths as soon as they got hungry. Which struck me as like, possible, because Dracula is maybe the dead cold perfect and total opposite of Jesus Christ, which they of course know when they make Drac movies.

Up here in my room up north, I'm looking right now again at the snaky scar on my thigh, and thinking of the way I got it, which I never said more about than that it was on the Ryan's Woods' fence. So I guess this is the time to say that when I got it was exactly the day after my mom and dad came up and first told me we were moving away, which I know was the 5TH of October, so not a week after Jackie died. I was feeling a little insane and just wanted to get out into The Woods. So I didn't bother with the rabbit hole down in the Dead End, I just hit the nine-foot cyclone where it ran along the end of our back yard. Which would be not too far from where we almost didn't put the forest fire out, or from where we saw the Nude Guy with whoever it was he was with. And there's not much you can get through to there, because up along the houses, they pretty much just let the brambles grow, so nobody will be coming up and like staring at ya from the proverbial outside looking in. But I went ahead and scaled the fence there anyhow, and got myself down into a place not too prickery and then worked my way out to the spot where we did end up putting out the fire. And under this huge tree there, I sat down.

I hunched my back against the tree and was thinking all of a sudden of that sick nude three-eyed smiley fucker and of statutory rape and spreading flames. I started looking for ashes but couldn't see any, so I thought, too, about how fast The Woods didn't really worry too much about that kind of deal, I mean, like, damage and destruction. Then I thought of the years of rings that must be inside the big tree I leaned against still, which of course just kept standin' there while the leaves it put out hung around for only a little while and then fell, the way they were coming down right then, one here, one there, then in a bunch, and then nothing, then more either by themselves or in numbers, because it was that time of year, when whenever the breeze came, the leaves like fell in ways and numbers that showed how strong the wind was. And then I looked up, because I knew I would see—and then I did see my window really clearly up there in the sky, because so many leaves had fallen. Which seeing my window made me think, too, now, for better or for worse, of private property and then of property values and then of that shithead Prizer's saying that a stolen broomstick was his property before Susie sent it clank-clanking to the dump of sewer-y hell and gone. And good riddance. But not good riddance, no way good riddance, to the pueblo, where Jackie told me, that time, that I had me, so there'd be no backin' down—and even though I felt like so incredibly bad in my heart that it was me hangin' on and Jackie now gone, I could hear him saying, I could, that it's okay…it's *okay*. And then I thought about him saying, that other time, how a sportswriter—that that would be a great thing for me to be. Which so got to my heart.

Then, outa nowhere, for some reason, I thought of Terry having a Stu-place inside him somewhere—and how it's gotta be important for us to know the places we have inside us, so we can have all kinds of hopes about what we could get re-born as without really even changing who we are. Or, so we could put ourselves in other people's shoes and things. But I thought then of the pueblo as my special, *totally* private place, where I was who I *really* was, which is the one place—I mean where you really are *you*—where you get the absolute, no doubt about it, number-one power of psych. So fuck you forever, Prizer, with your stick and all your troll-shows, keepin' me from heading my own way home.

But it's weird, too, if not maybe like the deepest weird thing I know, that, sort of again like looking at new cute girls (and there are some beautiful ones here, up north, to tell you the truth), you just sometimes don't really completely like fall into sadness when you move—because you're even sort of excited about leaving the past behind for some complete new deal, so that even if you heard that like all the pictures from your past got burned in a bum's trash barrel, you'd think it wasn't that much of a price to pay for the excitement of that new deal. And I've got to say that the new house up north, because my parents had naturally really talked it up—"Oh, just wait, Kevin, till you see the new house"—but which I've got to admit was a talk-up that it deserved—was something that I right then couldn't help being excited to go see. And—truth—right now I'm wondering even if Jackie hadn't died would it have made any difference about my ever going back again, or even calling.

But you know how I said that I think sometimes about sneaking back? I mean back to the old neighborhood, without telling anybody, and from some secret sort of lookout, sort of spying on all the old things? It's this thing that I'm understanding, about how, when you move, even if you don't want to go back, you *do* want to go back—which I don't know if it grows right along with you but I'm like positive is going to last as long as this snaky scar on me, which could be my identifying scar, all right, in fact will be, I'd say, no matter what else happens to me in the way of scars in my life. 'Cause maybe you could call my thigh-scar the like heartbeat tattoo of every forever-thing, good and bad, that I ever was as a kid.

And another thing I'm understanding is this: and that's that there's times when, all right, you might be focusing on just the best stuff, I mean like stuff about JL, but at the same time you're not lying one slight bit. And you can throw in this, too, which I was getting while I was sitting under that tree, and that's that my mom was right as it is possible to be, that night up in the pueblo, about, if maybe somewhere, sometime, I'd know somebody as good, I'd never in my life know a person better than the friend I just saw die, and his body getting put in the grave. And that, going from right as it's possible to be, to impossible as can be, there just isn't going to be any amnesia about the things you could call 'the best', or about people you, deep truth of it, really love, or maybe, either, about stuff you'd in real truth call 'interesting as hell.'

So now, as I sat under that big tree, it was fire in my mind,

all across The Woods, and JL putting it out, and us wondering whether or not to run, and the weird evil of that nude
maniac, and laughing till you peed your drawers, which was
more because of how scared you were than 'cause there was
anything funny about it (but then scary things do happen
to be hilarious as shit, for some reason)—and through all
these things the feeling now that I'd remember them forever, all right, to my grave. I mean, hanged kids and night-
time saxophones blowin' through the trees, and JL and
Frankie and Stu and Terry and Pete and George P. And the
King of Rats, alias the Common Enemy. And Patty Conlon, as beautiful, and as cool, as it is possible for a girl to
be on earth. So that when I looked up at the window of the
pueblo now, I had a feeling that, maybe even especially for
remember-it-forever stuff, there might never be times like
the times before I hit fourteen.

And that was me when, going back, I skipped the rabbit hole again, and went straight through the brush to the
outside-looking-in fence, at our back yard, and got myself
up on it, starting to think that from like right now already,
I'd have such a short time left here, 'cause off I was going
to that new life, and, like, world. And it was with all that
in my whirled-up brain, and me all straddled up on that
nine-footer, that my hand slipped and my thigh went hard
as shit down onto the fence prong. It went plenty deep in
me, too, the prong. And you know how cyclone prongs have
like a shoelace twist at the end, so it's like two prongs not
one. So when I say 'it', I mean they both went deep, like
well more than an inch. And yeah I just stayed there a second with the blood gushing because I didn't know what to
do about pulling the double prong out. And I swear, too—
talk about weird, but I kid you not—I did have enough

time, with that prong speared in me—I swear this is true—to think I'd stay there and feel the pain for Jackie. It was like something in my mind was squeezing this insane fist and gritting teeth and saying *Blood brothers till we meet again in heaven.* And then, when finally I pulled myself off that thing, it was slow, all right, because I did see the guts in my leg, through the bad rip in my pants. And you can trust that the blood was insane.

CHAPTER ELEVEN

FALL OF EIGHTH

"BYE"

But they say about puncture wounds, that they heal fast. At least that's what I was going with when I like strapped my leg with a towel and got back up to my room—because I wasn't gonna miss a single football game. No way on earth. And especially I wasn't gonna miss the Vanderkell game, which I had now like this insanity about—because if I was feeling, like for a while there, a *who-gives-a-shit-anymore* feeling about the place I'd lived in all my life, I had now this supremely crazed feeling of like I wanted to go nuts in that game, which would be my last one with my friends from CK.

At school, because I couldn't help limping, even if I didn't make anything abnormal out of it, I told people about the deal on the fence, or sort of—enough so they'd just kind of drop the subject. But I didn't say a word about my family's moving, which made things extremely weird—because everybody of course was treating me like normal, which made me feel like I was in possession of secret knowledge. But it was more like I was in a weird daze of being an unreal human being, like one of the living dead, except for the fact that my leg was hurting like a very much *not* dead person's. And I did all kinds of weird sorts of moving around and rustling-around-in-my-seat kinds of stuff when it came to my sitting next to Patty, because, besides the serious pain, I was feeling like this really crap feeling that I'd be like pulling a fast one if I came anywhere near touching her now, when I was outa there in like no time, and she didn't know it yet.

But the very next day was collection day for the *Southtown*, and I knew a couple of things. I mean, I knew that with my family leaving in just a short time I'd have to quit my route like right away, so that the *Southtown* could get another kid in there and that, cold truth of it, *that day* was gonna be the last time I ever made my collection rounds. Which turned out strange, too, because there I was in school with my best friends, a bunch of 'em friends for all my life so far, but I'm gettin' by okay (of course I hadn't told 'em word one about me moving). But now here I am with like the people I collect from, adults, and pretty many of 'em sort of old ones, and telling 'em good-bye, and I'm like getting choked every now and again.

And another thing I knew was that if I didn't *right now* talk to Patty about our moving away soon, she'd find it out from somebody else, and that I'd be really ashamed of that, especially after her look to me at Jackie's funeral, and all the other stuff we had as our secrets. But there I was, at the end of my route, heading down that stretch of Winchester that makes its way that one block into The Woods south of 91ST, and heading step after step toward Conlons'—and I'm thinking that as much as I hoped like a heart-pounding lunatic, all those times, that I'd be lucky enough to find Patty home, I wanted today maybe to find her not home. Because it would be the easy way out for me. I was thinkin', too, of that old idea that I'd be the Conlons' paper boy till past the end of time. But even as I was thinking how sort of stupid that was, I was pretty positive that the kid who thought it, was better than the kid walking down that street now, lookin' for some back-door way out of like being dead embarrassed by a good-bye.

So it was like plainer than day to me that it was time for a little bit of suckin' it up, like the kind Patty had pulled off for me at Jackie's funeral mass. And it wasn't my heart-guts-brain, all hummin' and pumping, that was going to make it happen that I would tell Patty good-bye. I guess you could say it was my conscience, which is a different thing.

And there's something about the way things go sometimes—like somewhere there's somebody plannin' 'em.... I don't know, but after I did listen to my conscience and went to the door and rang, and after I heard those sounds, in the house, of steps coming down the stairs to the door, and then after the door opened—of course it wasn't Mrs. Conlon who was there, home from her teaching at Chicago U. And it wasn't a picture, either. It was, no matter how many years it's going to be, till the last day I live, the face, that when I think of beautiful girls, I will always remember.

It was like she'd been practicing dancing or something, which I, now that I think of it, never asked her what it might have been, because there was a blushiness in her cheek and a kind of falling of her hair slightly down on her forehead. Her eyes were, too, not just incredible as usual but sort of showing something—I mean like sort of *showing* how cool the stuff that went on inside her was. And it was like I couldn't believe it was possible that I ever in my life got to kiss her—that's how glow-y soft and beautiful her lips were.

And then, about which I won't go on again, she just, you know, said, "Hi," and let me in, with this smile that said, "Infinitely cool as I am, I'm really glad, Kevin Collins, that you're here again," but, you know, saying it silently. Which they make sort of a joke out of a girl's being modest, like it's a fake and an act. All I'll say about Patty is two things. It was never an act. And if there's a way a girl can show a guy more of what he's really looking for, I'd have to have that proved.

Which, *still*, though, thanks to our coolness, I was thinking could have been instead a way of saying *Do I know you? Who are you?* I mean, because like my nervous thought of something cold like that still happening made her words come to me, one more time, like they were one stroke after another of real miracle luck. But there still was Patty, inviting me into that quietest house in the entire universe, which was, for me, like it was the House of Peacefulness, or something, and asking me on into the kitchen (where I forgot to say that her mom had, which I won't ever forget, these extremely cool flowers growing outside the window on a flower-holding thing and that these flowers, with this purply color, sort of came into the light in the kitchen and made this kind of very cool, blue color in the light there, which I guess you'd have to be there to picture—but which you can trust was, about that kitchen, a thing you'd remember).

It wasn't Hershey bars or anything. It was about Jackie that we talked, at the corner of the kitchen table. Which kind of immediate heart-to-heart still wouldn't be typical, because even after the Ice Tree Melt, we pretty much, like

I say, re-froze up, until there would be, very cool, trust me, the occasional re-melt (so yeah, I kissed Patty more than those four times, a few at least, each one like a complete new incredible secret forever). But, I mean, it would even have been weird and unnatural not to talk straight out about Jackie now.

"It's the way you're so positive," she said, "that it can't be true, and then you have to say that it is true—but even still while your heart keeps sinking, you still keep saying it can't be, over and over—until finally you have to say he really won't be coming back, not ever, to school again. It's that feeling of looking where he sat, and finally knowing…."

She didn't have to say she was thinking of her dad, too, along with Jackie. I (because I'm not dumb, no matter how dumb I sound) could tell this from the first second. But when she talked about Jackie's not being in school any-more, I had suddenly like this really selfish feeling about myself, like I was comparing me to Jackie, I mean over the not ever coming back. I knew it wouldn't be like a happy thing to change to how was Katie Luce doing. But it wasn't on the subject of me, or of not coming back—so I asked, "How's Katie L doin'?"

Patty took her hand, when I asked this, and with two fingers sort of took up that falling of hair over her fore-head and moved it back, which made me look at her hand and then watch her hair not fall all back again but fall back some, really softly.

She said, "I know this sounds like I'm maybe imagining things. Or talking about things that just couldn't be real. But I promise you, I think Katie thought she would marry Jack Leonard someday. I know that you don't really think about those things when you're talking about kids our age.

And there's so many things that come along to change things. But there was something about the way she never cared to think about anybody else. And she even *said* to me once that she wanted to marry Jackie Leonard someday. She wouldn't be the first girl our age to say it. But there's saying it. And then there's saying it."

I nodded. I said, "I didn't know all that. I knew some things. And seeing her in church. I guess…. Well, I know she'll be able to, I'd guess you'd say move past it, you know, as time passes."

"I know," Patty said, "and she will. There'll just come the time when she one morning wakes up and says, 'Life goes on.'"

I nodded, but now what I did was I sort of got lost in thought.

Which Patty saw as me thinking about JL and maybe Katie, which wasn't really right. But she said to me about JL, "For all your time at Christ the King, he was your best friend." And the way she said this was exactly like her look to me in church. Then she kind of lowered her eyes, and then after a second, she said, almost kind of emotionally, "There are kids out there who, like, enjoy making people frightened. Jackie Leonard, the way you told it to me, and the way I saw it, too, enjoyed making people not frightened, which was so wonderful. Such a sign of a good person, especially because I know you didn't mean, you know, that he had that baloney that sometimes gets called watching out for people—I mean that stuff that's just another name for bossiness and being annoying. I know that Katie saw that—I mean that Jack had this way of like making sure that things were okay for people, in a quiet way, but for real."

I was so afraid of like saying things out, but I wanted

right then to say something really crazy like thank you with my complete heart, Patty, for the way you looked over to me in church, which would have been deadly uncool—so I kept my mouth shut. And what she said about all my time at CK—it had me getting emotional myself. So I really changed off that, and said, about that other thing that she was so right about, "What you said about not believing that it could be true—and then you look over to where he always was and you know he's not coming back...." But it was like my mind secretly went back this direction, too, to make me really emotional and sad—so I was getting choked right in the middle of my sentence.

Patty let it go quiet for a bit. But then, because we'd like come to this place of emotions, she said to me, though she was really careful in the way she said it, "It must have been so terrible, being there, when it happened...."

Which I've gotta say, though, no matter where we were, caught me about one hundred percent off guard—because I'd been pretty much doing my best not ever to talk about that, even with as many times as I'd thought about it, or maybe you'd say had pictures of it like running scared through my head, lookin' for some secret place in my brain to hide. But after a while, I did—I started talking, and it was like I was, if you know what I mean, *listening* to what my own voice was just all-of-a-sudden saying. I said, "It was like I'd never seen anything stop him. And then you saw the ball and Jackie and that thing, that car, come all three together as Jackie caught the ball—and then he just stopped, and the thing didn't move when he hit it. And it was like we all knew, from the way that thing didn't move and the way Jackie was flying and then just stopped, and sank...and the ball fell...that before our eyes...he just died."

I swallowed, and shook my head hard, because I wasn't gonna get through with this. But I cleared my throat really hard, and shook my head again, and like breathed. And like being with Patty, talking no bullshit things with her, like was so powerful I was forgetting what was coming in my own future—I mean that thing that I had to talk to her about. So I just started saying, kinda chokey-whispery, "I mean, it's like maybe for your *whole life* you're saying this can't be true, I mean that you could ever really, truly die—kind of saying it all day long, every day, every year, in silence, I mean—but then like all those sayings—they all go quiet when you see it happen before your eyes. And then it's like that whole voice inside you just shuts up—I mean when you know you really *can* die, because you just saw the toughest kid you ever knew…in like one second…."

Patty couldn't take my hand or anything, like we were adults, or one of us was. She just nodded then, kind of over and over. And some time passed. Then she said to me, like the same voice or mind was inside her as was inside me that time with Frankie, after the Pin said what he said, "It'll be okay. You'll be okay. It's so hard. But you'll be okay. Trust me, you'll be okay."

And this struck me—I mean that it was the exact same words I said to Frankie. And I kind of smiled. But then after some more seconds, Patty sort of did this other kind of reverse, which in a way brought us again back to something hard and strange—strange as maybe what was it like to be there and to see it with your own eyes. She lowered her eyes, kind of, and said, "Sometimes, though…. Sometimes…are you angry at him? I mean…for dying?"

Which thought was beyond even something I'd ever tried to make go away. It was something that I'd never even thought of. So as I started answering her, I felt like I was completely making stuff up, but as I was making it up, I felt that I somehow *wasn't* making it up, sort of like it was coming to me word by word out of somewhere weird, now that she'd put the thought in me to get it going. I said, again kind of listening to my own voice like it was another person's, "No. I mean...I'm not. Not angry. I mean, I think, if I get what you're saying...'cause Jackie...with his life, he showed me enough good things to outdo any of the bad things I ever saw, or I ever will see.... I mean, for me, he did more than enough of really good things that I'll never forget in my life."

She smiled, with this kind of very soft coolness, and total beauty. Then she asked me, which somehow didn't surprise me, "How's Frankie?"

And I said, still in this mood that she'd gotten going with her soft words, which even, and maybe even more so, when they asked strange stuff and hard questions, were like word-miracles, "I'm praying, ya know, hard...that...you know... he'll see things straight. That...I mean...'cause you know, your mind can tell you you did wrong when you *didn't* do wrong. You didn't. Not at all."

She'd begun now sort of studying my face like it was a book. And she said, with this complete thoughtfulness, "I so truly believe—truly, *truly*—that it's the ones who really love people who see them right, and help them to think of *themselves* the right way. And this is so good. Otherwise, I mean there'd be people, maybe like including Frankie himself, who'd just mistake Frankie Malone for the kind, you know...who stole my dad's hammer." She stopped now a second, looked down, then up at me again. *"So,"* she said, "Frankie's a really lucky boy, because, as time goes by, he'll have such true good friends—who'll always see him the best way, and who'll help him."

Which when she said all this, I was thinking ten thousand things that were mostly all ripping my heart. And about how, although I was choking in all ways, I *had* to tell her soon what I'd be even more completely ashamed now if I let her hear it from anybody else. But it was even getting harder now, and I was feeling maybe as ashamed to tell her about the move as not to tell her. So I thought maybe still I'd come the long way around, change the subject and come back, the slow way, to what I had to say. Then suddenly there was this weird shitty, screwed-up thing in me— and it's amazing the shit that bubbles up in us lookin' for a chance to spew out—this incredibly shitty thing that just wanted to throw the news about the move right out there in like some cruel way just for the sake of seeing what would happen. I mean it's like you've got to keep an armed guard over your brain because of the crap it just might pull for just seeing what happens. But I squelched this stuff and talked about this and that. Until finally, though, I had to come out with it. Though I wouldn't be talking about any of that change-in-the-neighborhood stuff, because I was, I guess you'd say, not proud of that.

I didn't say, "Patty." I just said, "There's something I've been meaning to say…." Which was unusual enough, so she looked at me, naturally, like something strange had to be coming.

"I mean," I said, "I mean…this is going to be the last time I come collecting for the *Southtown.*"

She didn't go uncool or anything, like saying, "Oh no." She just sort of quietly said, and I won't ever forget that she let me know with her voice how she felt sadness, "So you're giving up your route?"

I had now this instant bad lump of pain in my throat, which it really hurt to swallow down. But whatever it is that makes us go through with stuff, made me go through with it. I said, "Yeah, but…. It isn't…. I mean it isn't just that I'm giving up the route." And like all of a sudden I so wanted to say her name. But I didn't. I just got it out—"It's that my family's moving away."

The second the sound of those words came out, I was choked really hard. But I just sort of kept looking at her now, with that choke in me like stopping my mind, too, or saying to me don't say any more words.

Patty didn't cry or anything, or lose her cool. She just sort of got trembly just this little bit in her face, and started to smile, and then sort of let her mouth just fall a bit. "I'm… so sad," she said, trembly again. "That makes me so sad."

And then we sort of looked at each other and didn't know what to say. Which I'll always be thankful wasn't "I love you." Because, even though we were in eighth grade, and so the words would have been dead sickening uncool, that's what it was.

I, like I said, didn't go into any of those reasons about the neighborhood, or property values, or Aunt Rita over on Constance Ave (which I think means maybe I *did* make a bad confession here, not letting that out, though it puts in me a very true contrition, I promise). Or really anything, except, you know, where we were moving and how soon it was gonna be. But I asked her, too, if she would keep it secret, 'cause I hadn't told anybody else—which seemed like, right as I was saying it, and she was just nodding, not saying any words, we both somehow knew could maybe be our last secret.

Then it was time to go. So I stood up from the corner of the kitchen table, which was our spot. And me getting up and backing the chair away would be the only sound in that quiet house. Then I just walked to the door to let myself out. But when I looked back at the door, I saw she followed me. So she was standing there, sort of under the dancing picture, with her hair fallen some still, and her beautiful lips, that I got those times to kiss, and her eyes. And I can't say what will ever happen to me in my life, but that time, with all that happened in that like week and a half, is right now the hardest I think I ever want to go through, which was I think in my voice, when I just with this kind of stupid sort of nod, said to Patty Conlon, "Bye."

The pain in my thigh was all of a sudden throbbing then when I, without looking back, made my way to the path in The Woods there. And I felt so weak it was just like coming away from Jackie's funeral in that half-asleep feeling, with the heat of the sun kind of letting me know what Hades might be like. So I thought sure as I started down the path that he'd be there. And that he'd be like smirking about my protector being dead or something, even laughing. And that by black miracle he'd have heard already that I had to tell Patty I wouldn't be coming back. I swear I almost turned around and ran out of The Woods. But there was that old insane and now pretty sad and complicated feeling about nobody stops me from taking my way home. But I had another feeling as I got closer to the Ice Tree, which made me not just step up the pace but start running top speed, right on by, when I got there. And it was the feeling that there were like thousands of men's voices and in some scary as shit way the voices made me feel like it was *my* funeral, or that any second now I could get killed, or murdered. And why me? No reason, just that death had me singled out so bad it would make a fortune teller close her eyes and say, "Seek to know no more."

It didn't happen, though. I didn't run into Prizer, and you can call him Death, in The Woods. And because we had ten days after I speared myself before our next game, I didn't miss a game, just the way I hoped. Can't say I did too much in the going-nuts-in-the-games department, but it wouldn't be for lack of trying. And without Jackie, we managed to get our asses pretty well kicked by St. Cajetan's, who had this guy Robbie Nieman, who Stu really Mack-trucked this one time, so it was like stars shining deep in his gray matter for sure. But the kid was tough as shit and even faster than he was tough, so with a basic AVOID-STU policy, which who can blame 'em for, Cajetan's took us 21-7.

We won our next game, though, against Margaret of Scotland, and then we beat Barnabas, too. So that was pretty psych, I've gotta say. And what was really psych was that—and so I'd say it's totally proved that prayers aren't any waste of our time—Francis X was coming back out of the grave with some very smart work, like a bootleg td against Margaret's and some passes on the money against Barnabas, which when we celebrated at George P's after the Margaret's game, Frankie broke all records by eating like an entire large pizza by himself, which of course had us all goin' "Where does it all go?" And you know how some people can belch for like a minute and speak out entire belch sentences? Well, naturally, this would be one of Frankie's primo skills, so out he comes with this answer to the question "Where does it all go?" And the answer is this incredible humongo belching of *"INTO THE BOTTOMLESS PIT."* And by the time he got to 'PIT', I'm dead positive he was bringin' up some serious by-product. I mean, it was really beautifully disgusting and, thus and therefore, outstanding for hilariousness.

So we all, as time was goin' on, were like feeling kind of back from the dead and stuff. Or sort of. Which was giving me this kind of hazy-in-the-head feeling that this time was gonna go on forever. Because still I hadn't told anybody but Patty, who, needless to say, kept her promise not to tell anybody else. And it was weird, but cool—I mean the way I felt.

But maybe besides prayers, bad superstition works too. Because I kept feeling as the Vanderkell game kept getting closer and closer and closer that for sure I'd run into him. The Murder Spot was always sort of jumping with some sort of devil-spirits for me—those men's voices sort of, I guess you'd say, brought down to a hum, but that gave you the feeling that if you listened carefully they'd start sounding like a thousand devils disguised as Capuchins with hoods in the basement of that church made outa bones in Rome, but now converted in my mind into a place for Black Masses. Only it wasn't in the Murder Spot. It was on the horseless horse trail, one night after practice.

May all your superstitions come NOT true would be something you'd wish for people you cared about, no doubt. Or *may you believe in your prayers as much as you believe in your superstitions*—especially seeing as how you really do get the feeling that if you (and pray is to prayer as what is to superstition?) *superstitionize?* enough, you sure as shit will make something happen. So it didn't surprise me that there he was, roaming his happy smokin' grounds. But there I was one more time, goin' suicidal, not dodgin' off from my way home. Only I wasn't thinking, the way I did after the great slink-off, that my life had come to any turning point, which seemed to me now to have depended about one hundred percent on Jackie's being alive. And I was thinking of how I could have about died that time in the snow.

"Well look who the fuck is here. If it isn't my favorite little twerp-shit." He said this with his butt still in his mouth, then took it out and cupped it, hard-guy style, 'cause just like that, we were back in that psycho feature film again. "And he hasn't got the friendly idiot giant and he hasn't got Mr. Jackie Superstar, who upped and went bye-bye. Fuck, Collins, I'll bet you were the saddest kid at the funeral. You and that psycho Malone. And say, Malone killed Leonard, didn't he? Throwin' up one of his shitballs? That's the word around town. Of course I'm sure you were every bit as worthless, standin' around with your teeny weeny peeny in your hands."

I was thinking a million things during this spew-time little theater—but like, which was sort of cool-insane, almost laughing, too, somewhere way down in my heart, about how predictable it was that this psychotic soul-mate for the Pin would try to make me and Frankie think Jackie died because of shit we did or didn't do. And talk about throwin' out shit like firecrackers, just for the fun of seeing what it would accomplish—it was this pervert's lifetime habit. But I thought of the slink-off, too; and even though I knew my life had *not* changed and any smart yapping would spell the grass-ify-ing of my ass, I couldn't help it. I said, "I'll bet you would have been the *gladdest* one at the funeral, you shit-hell punk, seein' how one of Jackie's last promises was that he was gonna kick your ass till it fell off and then hand it back to you on a butt sandwich, which promise as I recall had you slinkin' off like a rat to a sewer hole."

"You know, Collins," he said, "here we are, all alone in The Woods, and I could kill you. You realize that, don't ya. I could fucking beat you to death. All I've gotta do is do it. And I swear to God, something about you and your smart mouth makes me want to rip you apart. But I'm gonna let you go. I'm gonna give you permission, you lucky little prick, to live another day. And the only reason under the fucking sun is that I feel like it. Understand! No other reason. I feel like it—period! But in that game comin' up, you understand *this:* I'm gonna murder you. I'm gonna fuckin' splatter your sorry brains. And don't you forget it! Now trot along, you pathetic little fairy, before I change my mind!"

Naturally I let out a little spit juice, with a through-the-front-teeth shot, to let him know that if I were bigger or armed with a gun, he'd be the one dead. Which of course was a disguise over the fact that I was maybe as scared as in my not-all-that-different life I could be. But I hard-guyed it and walked, even slow, rather than ran.

So he put his cupped butt back in his mouth as I walked past and smacked the back of my head hard as shit, not with his palm but his fist. "GET MOVIN'!" he shouted, "before I fucking CHANGE MY MIND!"

I didn't run. But I didn't stand up to him either, or tell him to fuck himself. Because I like believed it pretty much to be true that he could actually kill me. It's funny how there's something in ya that says, "Go ahead, kill me!" But then there's something too that keeps on walking away, the way I did, listening to him laughing, saying, "Fucking fairy, you're dead in that game! You're *dead!*"

In the pueblo that was less and less mine by the minute, I'm thinking that night that I've got no honor or something, you know, because I didn't stand up to that Rat Shit.

I'm thinking that what Jackie said about I've got me and so there won't be any backing down was already like a curse on my head or something. But I decided that at least I could tell my friends the next day about the move, because walking around with secret knowledge gives you a sort of sneaky and chickenshit feeling, which I was getting tired of. So I at least could get that off my chest.

And naturally it went like completely idiotically. I mean, I waited till we were all together, that is, me and Frankie and Bobby Stu and George P and Pete O'Connor and Terry, kind of walking along after school out on Hamilton, past the Priests' Yard toward 92ND. I said, "There's something I've been meaning to tell you guys." Which of course was a huge mistake on my part. Because naturally the guesses started exploding from the first second, which included George P saying I was leaving home to become a dancer and Frankie's saying good, good, good because I was a natural dancer—then Terry saying, all sort of fako pissed off, "a natural *prancer*," which got us laughing hard and which was good to see, because after Jackie died, Terry had sort of been getting all quiet again. And needless to say there was a nice steady flow of more and more stupidity, which I was glad for, 'cause finally it did enough of a stupidity job on seriousness so I could just get it out and say, "I mean, what I meant to tell you guys was that my family's moving away."

We were standing on the corner at 92ND and Hamilton, which I'll always connect with Frankie's mortar-shooting that old guy's car with the iceball. And this was where we usually split, too, with Frankie heading off toward Leavitt, and Pete and George P over toward Hoyne and Terry on past that to Damen, and me and Bobby heading on down Hamilton. Which place now I'll always connect too with this time I let my friends know I was leaving. And in my memory now—I mean when they all kind of at the same time asked "When?" and I said, "In two weeks," and then it was like my thinking of the way everybody came to practice the day JL died, sort of one by one in a kind of ceremony—I mean that's how they said 'So long' and 'Good luck' and things like they'd miss me and no they wouldn't, only now it was like kids in a school play (only it was George P and Pete and Terry) taking their last bows and then sort of disappearing and then when everybody had their bow, all the clapping going quiet. And then it was like the way you might run into somebody still in the theater with it all almost dark and only maybe you and that one other person there, I mean that's how I'll remember Frankie, 'cause he didn't really say anything, he just sort of waited—but then there was this other unusual thing, which was he pulled way down hard over his eyes his Sox cap, and then, before he walked away, just gave me a sort of wave, which in the end turned into this slight squeezing tighter of his hand.

Stu, when we made our way down Hamilton, didn't say anything, which wasn't too unusual. But then he asked me, to make sure, "You'll be here still for the Vanderkell game?"

I said, "I guess I don't like our chances. But I wouldn't miss it for the world."

He nodded. Then he said, "I'm glad, Kev, I mean that you'll be here. 'Cause I've got an idea. I mean something we could do if things start going bad. I won't spill it now. We'll just wait and see how things go."

I was thinking Stu maybe had some strategy of plays or something. I mean I didn't really know what to think. But if he didn't want then to spill his big idea, I wasn't going to bug him to spill it, especially since I out of respect sort of generally preferred never to bug Stu (not that the big guy *ever* got pissed). And I was glad, too, that Stu had started up this, I guess you could call it, little mystery about the Vanderkell game—because when I left him at his house and headed on down to mine, we had something else going in our minds besides the fact that I wouldn't be doing that, I mean heading on past Stu's to my house, too many more times.

And what a good, *good* guy Bobby Stu is. I mean, I'm thinkin' about it now up north here in my room, and it still makes me really happy thinking he's gonna be maybe an incredible doctor or scientist someday. And it's best because like nobody would expect it. Sort of like, "See that truck driver over there? The one whose hands make his coffee cup look like some little girl's plastic cup out of a play tea set? Just go ask him to do the hardest algebra problem you can think of—and see what happens." I don't know. I just sort of love shit like that—it makes me happy really far down in. But no, ya scoldy bastard, I haven't called Bobby either. And I'm not going to. And I'm not gonna call Frankie. Because ya wanna know the reason? Ya just don't. That's the reason. And that's all there is to it.

And I've gotten happy up here, because that's the way that goes too, even if I never do get over black Cadillacs in all my life. I've got a great room to think in, which I should add—because I haven't talked about my little brothers and sisters lately—is entirely punk and punkette-free. I mean it's no third-floor deal like the pueblo, which was unmatchable. But it's bigger—and really cool. And speaking of the punks and punkettes, I've just had a to-me funny thought, which I'll share with ya. I mean, it's that I'm talking to one of my mom's new friends, you know, like Mrs. Broderick or somebody, who says, "Oh, Kevin, I'm so sorry to hear that all your brothers and sisters…that they are *all* punks. Is it really true?" And I say, "I'm afraid it is, Mrs. Broderick." And she says, "Even little Peggy, she's a punk, too?" "Well, Mrs. Broderick, would the word *total* mean anything to you?" "Oh, Kevin, that's really such awful news." "Well, yes it is, Mrs. Broderick, no doubt about that." "But, Kevin, I'm sure that you're a great, great comfort to your parents, being of course the complete exception to the rule in your family." "Well, Mrs. Broderick, I have heard them say *Thank God for Kevin*." "I'm sure you have, sweetheart. I'm sure you have." I don't know. I just enjoy thinking of stuff like that. And yeah, I enjoy thinking of the girls up here, too, which would be inevitable, I guess you'd say.

CHAPTER TWELVE

FALL OF EIGHTH

LAST PLAY IN THE WOODS

But let me go on now to the Vanderkell game, which would be the last thing that my CK friends and I really did together. Because I think it says something about something, though I'll leave you to figure out what it was.

Big Joe Stupnicki had a day off from his practice at Leo, where he was already a star tackle, even though he was only a sophomore. And Entemann's brother, who, truth to tell, was a really good guy, wasn't playing anymore at Morgan Park, so he was free to ref with Big Joe, which they did really well together, if you ask anybody normal, which of course there would be exceptions to. And where we played was I'm glad to say not off 91ST over near Longwood, but at the field at 88TH and Leavitt, where it was really cool, because the big trees of The Woods sort of opened out just about in the shape of a football field, so it was like you were in a pro stadium with the big trees as like a huge surrounding crowd, only they were trees, so they were a really shadowy and quiet crowd, which was also very cool. And even though this was a game which the Vanderkells and the CK guys just arranged by themselves and got their own refs for and was no league game, still it was the biggest game of the year by a mile, so even though the girls didn't come when it was sixth or seventh, now that it was eighth grade, they did, both ours and theirs. And it was cool to see the girls, not just like normal, standing with their pom poms along the ordinary sidelines, but instead standing there with them in The Woods, under the huge trees. I suppose somebody could write a book about what makes stuff remember-it-forever stuff, but what's like all around and does stuff like make a cool, lit-up stadium out of a place with like deep-shadowy sidelines ought to be part of it. And the difference between sound and no sound.

Of course we were hackin' off and laughing, but it was mostly because without JL we were definitely lookin' like a case a little too hopeless even for St. Jude, not that he'd become our patron saint or anything since Jackie died. But I mean there was Entemann and Pateo, two serious kickers of ass, and Pete Fox, such a good athlete. And they had this new guy named Carruthers who looked, you know, like he had a family and five kids or something. And their linemen would be dwarfing our guys all down the line, until, of course, the train screeched to a halt at Stu-ville.

But I'm thinking that with Big Joe around and Bobby, too, and all the rest of the world, that Prizer's saying he was gonna end my life would be just a manner of speaking. Still, I'm thinking now that this game could be like another word for very serious pain, despite all my thinking earlier that I was gonna go crazy in it. Something, one more time, about the difference between what you think up in your room (even when it's not your room anymore), and what you run into in the actual world. So I was just like George P when, with us hacking around together, he said, "You know, I gotta be honest: I'd say we're completely screwed."

"As Bardot said to her sister after they met me in Paris," Frankie said, in one of his lines that got its excellence from his dad, who wouldn't talk about Bardot and stuff like that in front of kids, but was always coming up with lines just like that one, I mean when he wasn't red-eyed and Huck-ifying Francis X around the house, or giving language lessons to the myna (which naturally we now called the Malona Bird), which by the way turned up, as Frankie put it, stiff as his early-morning woodrow, about a week before, with Frankie saying *good riddance to bad shtank*. And there was this drawing he made of himself lying there with a stiff myna bird right where his wiener would be. Which I mention so you can get some idea of what all I mean when I say the word *Malone*.

But even though we laughed our butts off at Frankie's line, we I think all agreed with George P, all the way. And I was lookin' over at Terry then, and I mean he looked so small that I thought maybe we should hide him (you know, like under a leaf or something). But then—I've gotta put it in, that—there was actually one exception to the way we were all feeling. And that would be the way Stu was feeling, which would be I'd say, even less worried than his usual not worried in the slightest. I mean, there was Bobby, just sort of smiling, all kind of peaceful, like that Chinese statue of Buddha with the big gut. But I really couldn't think that even if Stu had a strategy, it was gonna help much. I mean it was us against all those guys who *no way* didn't flunk or fake their birth certificates or something. I mean, even Johnny Gibbons, or Shakespeare the Atheist, would have been kind of big guys on our team now.

Of course we were all acting tough and telling George P to pull it together. To which suggestion, naturally, he had a quick and pretty funny answer. So we were kinda laughing, at least, or mostly fako laughing, when Big Joe blew that whistle and told us it was time. We sent Pete O'Connor out for the toss, which of course we blamed him for when we lost. Which was kinda funny, too, but I swear there's something goofed-up serious about the way you do stuff like that, actin' like somebody shoulda had the magic to make a coin fall the right way. But no matter anyhow—there we were. And if you never played football and stood there for an opening kick-off, trust me, especially against a gang of brain-bangers like the Vanderkells, you might think you do, but you don't know to jack-point-one the meaning of the word *butterflies*.

And of course, right off, the King of Rats has me in his sights, because there he was, with us all lining up, and CK being the kicking team, pointing at me like the end of his arm was a gun—or like out of his mouth was gonna come a voice like God's, saying, or thundering, "Behold ye, the gutless little twerp-shit." But instead then it was just the actual whistle that sounded. And Bobby Stu was our kicker, so the ball took a very healthy lump and went sailing all the way over Pateo's head and was rolly-polly-ing around behind him. So we had a chance to put 'em way back. And off we were flying (with the noticeable exception, as always, of George P).

But there's this thing in the pre-mustache phase of your life that you learn from football—and that's that for every un-mustache-ed action there's a completely *un*equal mustache-ed reaction. Which is just a goofball way of saying that when, with him comin' at me like a humongo east-African animal his old man would be ever so happy to bag, I hit Prizer as hard as I could—he stopped my forward action in a way that you generally think of with like dropped transmissions. And because it was a while before our guys even got to Pateo, let alone brought the kid down, Prizer had time to pop me again, twice, so I looked like a jerk in a cartoon, you know, too stupid to figure out that the tunnel on the brick wall was painted by Bugs Bunny. And Prizer of course had time to ask me an old familiar question or two, like, "Where ya goin', punk!? Where ya goin', hunh!? Why ya goin' backwards, hunh! hunh!, ya dead piece a mouse shit!?" Which private little conversation with me, spiced up then with a third solid slam, he finally stopped just a little too long after Pelagi tripped up Pateo and the whistle had blown. So now the whistle blew again, and Big Joe (obviously knowing that Prizer was a disease ya had to prevent early) right then and there hit the Rat with a flag, which I've gotta say, I mean it, I wanted to be Prizer's lawyer for and get him off, 'cause there's something about getting your ass kicked royal on the first play of a football game that makes you want to throw up the white flag and *just be friends*. But there was Big Joe, wasting no time, and Entemann's brother nodding his head like no way Big Joe was wrong about this one, and Big Joe then stepping off fifteen big ones, with everybody on both sides kind of slow-motioning on behind him, which of course gave you-know-who, who naturally didn't give a *sheist* about what he just cost his team, an opportunity to whisper to me one more time, "You're one dead punk." To which I came back with like the most pathetic anti-spew of all time, which was, "We'll see about that." I mean, even still, with whatever else happened in that game, it gets to me that that ladyfinger was all I was able to come back with. And naturally it had the 'Prize' laughin' his ass off, or more like snickerin' his ass off, for better haunting effect.

But anyhow, with me feeling like I'd gone silent everywhere except my chestnuts, which you might think of as sort of whispery-crying, "Please, please, take us home, we're oh so very very cold," we did have 'em pushed back pretty far now, after the fifteen-yarder. I mean there were no yardlines in The Woods (what we did, for the game, was mark the sidelines and end zones with stakes, and, for first downs, Big Joe or Entemann's brother would pace off ten yards and put down another stake)—but I'd say we had 'em back about on their own twenty. And so, with of course those two whispery exceptions, oh so cold even scrunched up in my jock, we were feeling pretty good. You know, comin' out of our defensive huddle with a nice crisp, "BREAK!"

But I mean the very next play, with us being the bowling pins and them being like a gigantic Buddy Bomar, they go the full eighty yards in about three seconds. I mean it was like all eleven of 'em got bored waiting for us to pick ourselves up and get down there for the extra point, which of course they picked up like Buddy B clickin' off a one-pin spare. And so now we're having that really bad feeling of what a stupid, idiotic thing it was for us to have been thinking, even for one second, good thoughts, or even like that's what we just got punished for, I mean even *having* good thoughts in the first place. And another thing, which I was learning from football, was that, before, when they avoided Stu, what they found was Jack Leonard, and now when they avoided Stu, what they found was the rest of us, which was, sorry Father G, but, a little bit different.

And it was really dawning on me, too, that one thing you need when the other team is like Russia and you're like Hungary, which would be pretty much how I felt, babushka and all, (I mean, if you don't have a Molotov Cocktail or anything) is to keep the ball out of their hands. Kill the clock with some first downs, anyhow. But first possession after the kick-off, we got stopped once for no gain (me carrying) and then stopped again for no gain (Pelagi carrying) and then stopped a third time for a ten-yard loss (nobody carrying, 'cause they were in on Frankie before he could hand the ball off, which would have been to somebody who didn't particularly want to carry it anyhow). So, like so much for killing the clock, 'cause in zero time whatsoever, it was drop back and punt. Which turned out of course to be one of those punts that if you were playing a crum-bum team never happens in a jillion years but when you're playing a killer team the actual muscles go out of your leg so bad it's like you punted the ball with your knee, and the wind somehow, with like a huge belly laugh, makes the punt go so completely nowhere you actually think it's goin' backwards, which speaking of belly laughs, brought on one of the royal satanic version in the King of the Rats, who when he was chokin' on it, still was sort of busting, laughin', spewing, "What...*pathetic*...punks."

But I gotta say it again, there was Stu, and he's still got the smile of that Chinese Buddha. Which makes me think, though, I've gotta confess it, that the big guy was maybe, after all, like an idiot savant, which would be very cool, except for the fact that, you know, you're an idiot.

But then the next play from scrimmage, Entemann—and

I mean you just don't expect any dead-cold football brain-deaded-ness from Stanley Entemann—but there it was—I mean, Entemann deciding he'd give Stu a try. Which was maybe him thinking that if we can beat Stupnicki right before their eyes, the game is over before it's begun. Which was a good concept on the drawing board, I guess. But the connection that clicked in my mind the second that Stu hit the kid was with the jaw of that giant who Joe Louis beanstalked in that warehouse gym on Indiana Ave. I mean it was scary, as well as like sending echoes through the trees, and the ball popped right out of Entemann's mitts into the hands of Pete O'Connor, who, though, naturally proved he was the brain-o bookworm of our class by running the wrong way with the ball for about fifteen yards before Frankie called him a jag-brained idiot enough times so that, you know, Pete realized Frankie wasn't just working on a daily reminder.

So around Pete turns. And then of course steam-rollered Pete was. But at least we had the ball again. Frankie, of course, in the huddle, told O'Connor that maybe next time he went to the Bookmobile he oughta try the football section. Which, and this tells ya about Pete's brilliant sense of humor, had Pete like all of a sudden laughin' like crazy, saying, "There isn't a football section!" Which George P would usually, you know, about this kind of thing, find something really hilarious to say. But he was so one hundred percent at a loss 'cause of Pete's brain-o-pathetic-ness, he just hard-whacked the kid's helmet, maybe, you know, in an effort to knock some 'semblance,' as SMM would say, of a sense of humor into him.

But it wasn't just Pete. We were all, every time we tried to move the ball, lookin', you know, like Japanese guys in a tidal wave movie (and maybe it would at least have had some hilariousness if we all started making fako-Japanese language sounds, which we did once for about ten days, which was one of our really pretty decent stretches on the stupidity-calendar). And yours truly was really cremated once by Fox and Carruthers and then, two plays later, met one-on-one by you-know-who the Rodent, who had of course like that special love of whispering little messages through the little round earhole in your helmet. So you could think of him as like under your skin, and right up against the soul inside your body, where he whispered, "Remember my promise, *punk.*" Which of course was (manner of speaking? or not?) that very Dr. Death-ish "I'm going to murder you."

And, you know, you do NOT want a girl to pay attention to you more than once in your life because you got your butt kicked. Lettin' go and telling her stuff once is weird enough, even if it felt incredible, and was maybe the best moment of your life, followed by kisses which were better than the best. But I mean if guys like girls to be gentle and beautiful, all graceful and stuff, girls must like guys to have some serious guts. So even though we had our enemy in common, I especially, because here he was whompin' on me again, couldn't look over at Patty. And *man* am I thinkin' now about what a difference there is between the stuff you dream up, up in your room, and the stuff you run into on the so-called street, which here would be The Woods. And I'm like listening still to the twerpy little twins in my jock, who are really talkin' it up today, sort of sounding now in my head all high-pitched and high-speed like Chip and Dale, "Turning point in your life nothin', you moron! We're cold and we wanna go home!"

And on the kill-the-clock thing, you know, that was pretty funny. Because there we were punting again, though this time Pelagi got a little more leg into it. Not that the punt made it back to Entemann and Pateo, who were the receivers. But this was just as well, because it was Shakespeare the Atheist who fielded it, and we all were pretty determined to show this goof what God thought of his bullshit, so we gang-tackled the—I guess you should say—*hell out of him.* Good thing, though, that we didn't get too whoop-de-doo, because *next play,* bang, it's 13-0, as Pateo runs their 'Where Stupnicki Isn't' play around Frankie's end, with Carruthers taking out Pete and the Rat King hitting Frankie so hard you'd have thought he was me. I mean it was pretty much of a complete joke, with, ditto, the extra point. So it's 14-0 after about five minutes, or less. And I've got visions of 80-0. Which is making me think, whoa, was Jackie even better than I ever thought. And when I tried to work with that "You've got you" he told me, and so "there's no backin' down," it wasn't doing really anything more than making me wish like crazy that he was there. I mean, the thought that he could just look at us all and, like it was nothin', say the next time will be the same as the last time—I mean things were really dawning on me now. Not that it helped, or did anything but make me think that Father G's sermon was, if it was maybe better than the *clearly he didn't know the guy* sermon my grandfather got, still the kind of words that make ya wonder if they ever hook up with any real things, instead of just wishes and bullshit.

But after the kickoff (which I received, and which—except to mention that it got me another really serious personalized hammer job—I won't say much more about than that at least I didn't fumble, at least not before my knee hit the ground, which I hope wasn't "a mercy call," the way the

Rat whispered in my earhole that it was)—but—as I was just about to say—after the kickoff, with us already about dead full outa luck, Bobby Stu, all of a sudden, shuts up Frankie in the huddle.

"SHUSH IT," the big guy says. "Let me talk." Which would be the perfectly exact *last words* you'd expect from Stu, if you expected any words at all, which you wouldn't. So we were all kind of blown over. Then he said, in the kind of weird sudden quiet, "This isn't a league game. There's no rule about what a ball carrier can weigh. Entemann and Pateo would never get to carry the ball in the Southwest Conference, same as me. But they're carryin' it here. Let me carry it."

So there it was: Stu's plan. And, you know, because we never even like thought of Bobby becoming a fullback, 'cause of the league rules where we played, we all just sort of looked at each other, until, after a moment or two, we all just started like bustin' and going, "Yeah! YEAH!" So Pelagi goes to end, and Pete O'Connor moves over to Stu's spot at tackle, and all of a sudden we've got a brand new—whoa brother!—FULLBACK. And Frankie isn't wasting any time, or in any mood to let Vanderkell take, you know, comfort by thinking that Stupnicki was in the backfield just to pass block for a special play or something. So he calls on Bobby first play, off left tackle. Which tackle would now be Pete O'Connor—but trust me, it could have been Terry Thillens and it wouldn't have made any difference. Because you shoulda seen it. I mean, it was like all we needed was Faye Ray and the Empire State Building to complete the picture. Only of course, Bobby's no speedster, so it's not like he's breaking away. It's more like he's the five o'clock Rock Island with everybody in Beverly hoppin' on board, and you know, like kids laying pennies down on the track just to see how flattened they'd get. Which had to be a question the Vanderkell guys had whenever they did start to bring the big guy down. Because that's how it went. I mean, because Bobby couldn't break away, Vanderkell would, eventually, bring him down. But not till—well, I mean honest to God it got so Entemann's brother wouldn't even really set in the first-down stake, because he knew he'd just be pulling it up again, and again, and again.

"This is fun," Bobby said, in the huddle, as we were actually movin' in to make this game 14-6. And there would be a classic Stu-ism for ya—though you can bet he'd have like to've gotten his three words down to one. Only if he'd just said, 'THIS'—you know, what would that have meant? I don't know. All's I can say is—"Ask Vanderkell what it meant!" And there we all were now, goin' "BREAK!" outa the huddle, with a lot more psych. Even Chip and Dale were gettin', so to speak, a little gutsier, like this wasn't any pueblo dream. Which it sure wasn't. I mean the way the next play, Bobby just slammed it over for the td. And then slammed over the extra point, which ya only got one point for, but ya had to run, because there were no goal posts in The Woods.

So like, oh yeah: Kill the Clock, and *then some!* But of course we had to stop their offense to complete the picture, which wouldn't be easy. But we weren't what we were a few minutes ago, which is so amazing. You know, like, not to be what you just were, especially when what you were was like the number-one joke in the farce of a lifetime. And so on the kickoff this time, somehow I ran into a tunnel that was an actual, not Bugs-painted...tunnel. And I got down to clip Entemann by the ankles before he really got goin'.

And the next play from scrimmage, George P got forgotten, and then, whoops, remembered, as he met Pateo at the line and turned out to be an obstruction long enough until, you got it: THE ROCK ISLAND ARRIVED. And then, oh man, Vanderkell had to be thinkin' *FAAAHHHGGG—WHAT WERE WE THINKIN'*—I mean about the cream job we were gonna be doing on these CK punkettes. I mean it's like there are all these places that are invisible. But they're completely real—and you're in one place, say the one called SCARED OUTA YOUR BRAINS. But then you can move into another one, say GUTS FOUND AGAIN. And it's like you become a different person, only you're still you. And you can see the other guy, depending on what you do to 'm, going to one place or another. Which all is another thing you learn from football, I mean about all the invisible places that are still very true and real, which ya find out the second you get in 'em, even though sometimes you might not've ever been there before. And with Bobby putting guts back in us, I was going to a place where—and you know me on fako, bullshit, lying ways of kidding yourself, how I hate 'em— but that I was like going to a place that felt like I was nearby where Jackie was, so that if I like poked my arm through some kind of wall all around me, I could see JL, and talk to him. And I mean football is pretty amazing, with all these places it can bring you. Though one of 'em, unfortunately, would be right back to earth. Which is where I got brought the next play, when the Rat King was running interference for Pete Fox, and Bobby was tied up, and the Rat and Fox were flying my way, with the result that I got a helmet full of serious bang and an earhole full of spew.

"I guess your name sure isn't Leonard, is it, mouse shit? But don't worry, you're gonna be payin' your hotshot pal a visit, because you're gonna be just as *dead*. And did ya notice? 20-7. Rhymes with mouse-shit heaven, which is where you're goin'."

Then, do you believe this? I mean do you believe it?—he spit in my face, while he had me down. And I was afraid it was gonna be nothing but my twerpy little nuts that were gonna make any sound, you know, in a sort of sorry little peep. But while I was ragin', wiping the spit off my face, my voice actually said, without cracking, "It's a good thing for you, Prizer, you punk, that Jackie Leonard's not here. Because if he was, he'd have you slinkin' off like the shit-chicken you are. I've *seen* you slink, you shit-chicken. I know what you're really made out of. And it's liquid chicken shit."

Which was decent spew, coming as it did, out of my kinda fuzzy brain—especially with that 'liquid' thrown in. Which, though, the Rat answered by puttin' an iron grab on my face mask and spitting straight in my face *again*. And neither Big Joe nor Entemann's brother saw it, though naturally I was thinkin' that Patty must have seen it.

And of course the extra point was like the old hot knife through warm butter. So now it was 21-7 (still rhymes with mouse-shit heaven). But Frankie actually made a decent scoot with the kickoff return, and we were about, I guess you'd say, on our thirty, when back our way comes MO-MENTUM, who would be disguised as a Polish giant who wasn't too much for words but when it came to numbers and math would, trust this one, bub, kick your ass. And as I'd shaken out the fuzz and I was pretty happy with my spew, I was feeling the psych, all right, as Bobby was pickin' 'em up, and layin' 'em down. By which I mean all eleven members of the Vanderkell Cavalcade of Punks. And I mean it was almost worse for them that they did bring him down every ten yards or so—because, I mean, it was like they should have had a twelfth guy, in a lumberjack shirt, goin' TIMMMM-BER!—just to get 'em outa the way in time. And it was so cool, the way Bobby's running was getting us all coordinated. I mean, Pete was blocking like he never had in his life, and, you know, not in the wrong direction. And George P, who I forgot to say was our center (but I guessed you could just sort of have pictured that) was becoming, after he snapped the ball, an actual moving obstruction. And Frankie, which was no doubt the best thing of all that I saw since Jackie died, was calling the plays in like this cool rhythm, that made ya sort of hop and come down again with a cool rhythm, too, when ya clapped and broke huddle, which rhythms were going right with our momentum, which—play after play after play—was headin' right straight for the goal line. And there was even a play or two, which Frankie called without anybody peepin' otherwise, when we faked to Bobby and gave it, one time to me, and the other time with Francis X bootlegging round end, and those plays worked, too. Because of course the Cavalcade of Punks was very taken up with THIS. And when the play was to me, even though the Rat went completely and totally mouth-foaming insane diggin' after me and then spearing me and driving me right off the field, which resulted in a pretty solid whole-body bounce for me, it was like *football* with the way I didn't listen to my shivering chipmunks but just sort of dusted myself off and liked it watching Entemann's brother, oh yeah, takin' up that first-down stake and pacing out another ten.

So it was like guys in the North Woods sawing and sawing as Bobby was grinding out the yards. And then the guy in the lumberjack shirt goin' TIMMMM-BER! Until, like just before half, we (by which I mean Stu) slammed the ball over and then slammed over the extra point. So it was 21-14—does not rhyme with mouse-shit heaven.

And as we walked over, helmets under our arms, to this huge tree where we sat under it for our half-time confab and rest up, we all, I know it, had that extremely cool feeling, one more time, of this was a real *game*.

And, no, I didn't like get into a cocky maybe-I'll-take-a-little-look-over-at-Patty kind of feeling, you know, and give her any cool sort of nod—because first of all we were still losing, and second of all, because that wouldn't be mine and Patty's style even if we were winning 50-0. But, yeah, I sort of sneaked a look out of the corner of my eye. And what I saw was all the girls sort of getting as fast as they could into their girl thing, which would be to like pretty much forget there was a field there and to pretty badly fail a quiz if the question was that famous tough one: "What's the score?" Because, you know, guys have their kind of stupidity and girls have theirs. Only guys are pretty much more famous for theirs. But what I saw out of the corner of my eye, too, was Patty, one more time different from all the rest, sort of standing by herself, looking out at the field, even though it was empty now, and without any bullshit, or thinking of what she was doing, showing the world what not-ordinariness was, and what coolness was, and what beautiful was.

Of course our second-half game plan was keepin' up THIS. With of course our all having to play maybe better defense than we ever did in our lives. Which we talked about. But which we were feeling we could do, because of that rhythm feeling that Frankie was putting into the huddle breaks, which came out of the confidence that Stu put in us. And we were all kind of like serious and quiet and telling Bobby what an amazing great game he was having, which was a natural way of giving him back what he was giving us (which reminds me now how Father G said once in a sermon that 'confidence' came from the Latin, meaning 'with faith'). So it was cool. Not, of course that we weren't gonna hack around at least some. So George P kind of breaks the seriousness by starting to sing *Old Stu-ball was a racehorse/ And I wish he were mine/He never drank water/He always drank wine*—which ended up with Stu knockin' him just about over with a nice shoulder bump, which, since this time no words were involved whatsoever, was truly perfecto Stu.

So when we heard Big Joe's whistle sayin' it was time to hit the field again, we were laughing again, 'cause of course George P (Bobby not hittin' him very hard, in truth) does a pretty fine pratfall. But this time it was different, 'cause we were different, with the butterflies knocked out of us and a feeling like, much to the shock of everybody, we were *not* completely screwed. And now the kickoff would be comin' our way, and everybody was feeling like let's put an "Ah-hhhh Soooooo" to the old Japanese tidal-wave movie and punch a hole through these flunkie punks. Which kind of thing you can feel when you strap your helmet back on and the ammonia shtank actually smells and tastes good in your nose and mouth, the way beat-to-shit muscles can feel good after you've played a long but extremely cool game. And if you've got cuts, which ya do, you don't feel 'em. I mean it's like pain takes a way-back seat. And you're stiff as shit, but you're about one second away from coming back to life and bein' limber like crazy. So strap it on!

And when the whistle blew, we were rippin', after Tommy Pelagi caught the ball, on the fly, and not too deep. And Tommy was smart enough to ride the old Stu-ball Express, following the big guy straight up the pipe. And *yep*, I did go as crazy as I could and took after that Rat to stick 'm with the most lunatic block I could throw. Which was of course pretty much Bugs-Bunny-ed again. But at least I didn't drop two trannies in the same day, and the punk didn't make the tackle. Though naturally he told me, "Just ask 'em to let you carry the ball, you sorry little shit, and see if you're still movin' afterwards."

And you know how it is with insanity. Somebody says that, who you know can kill you, manner of speaking and not manner of speaking, so what do you do? Ya probably say stuff like I did, which was: "That punk Prizer says to me he wants me to run the ball so he can kill me. I'd like the shot. Maybe pop one of his zits and see if he melts into a puddle."

"Run it around end. I'll run in front," Stu says.

"No," Frankie says. "We'll fake right side to Stupnicki, and come back left side to Kev. On two."

And Frankie hopped and we clapped and broke in that rhythm, but somehow it just didn't feel like there was a lot of music in the air. Which was pretty much proved when like only a few of the Cavalcade fell for the fake. So I mean there would be Bobby, kind of whackin' away a bee or two instead of the usual hive. And there would be me, seeing my blockers go down and the curtain going up to reveal the supreme RODENT, who was like happier than Hitler when he heard the word GAS. And I mean he probably had echoes goin' through the trees, too, saying "Kevin Collins. RIP." And he not only straightened me up but bent me backwards, so I thought my knees might bust. And then he just drove me over and rammed my head into the ground. So I was really stunned. And I had trouble breathing, with him all over me. Which I was still choking from when he was up and standing over me—and goin' "I told you I'd fuckin' kill you, you punk! I told you I'd let you have it!"

Of course the whistle was blowing from about the second he hit me, with the question of forward motion bein' pretty quickly answered. So the play was over. And maybe the one guy on our team never to get a single penalty in any game he ever played in would be Stu. But of course *there's a first time for everything*—which, I'm happy to say, would be the words tattooed on Prizer's pimply butt about two seconds after he started his satanic glory spew, 'cause he found out that unbeknownst he'd been spewing in a Rock Island crossing. And like the ensuing clobbering sent a different bunch of echoes through the trees, like ding dong the jag is dead, the flunkie jag is dead.

Of course Big Joe has to act like he's got no patience whatsoever for Bobby's action here. And he couldn't do anything like wink to his brother. But if there was ever a wink wanting to happen, I got the feeling that it was in Big Joe's face as he was walkin' off fifteen now against us. Or I should say was walking it off after I finally got up out of the dirt, which took awhile. But not too much longer than the rising of the Rat, whose nuts may have been having a little word with his brain, too, only I think they spoke in Transylvanian.

But maybe now Bobby was gettin' a little tired. Because even though we moved the ball, and I mean we took up about the whole third quarter moving it, we didn't get it across. We got it about to the ten. But with fourth and four, the big guy only got three—so there we were. Stopped. And if Vanderkell got a slow drive goin' now, they could take it so far into the fourth quarter, that with our style, we wouldn't have time, even if they didn't score and get a two-touchdown lead. But this was amazing: just before the quarter ends, they run two plays, and we stop both of 'em, even though they were run away from Bobby. And first play of the fourth, they try a pass, which Pete Fox, who has the best arm Vanderkell ever had, just plain overthrows. So they're down on their like fifteen, and they've got to punt.

Which situation brings in Terry. Because, I mean, we'd never put 'm in there for regular scrimmage plays. But for a punt by them, we'd bring him in because he's really quick and has what George P called *the element of invisibility*. Anyhow, it's like God is a Catholic, or the Pope shat in The Woods, or something, because what happens now but Carruthers, thinking just because he's got a better beard, that he's better than Jim Ringo, snaps the ball about five hundred miles an hour right over Entemann's head, and so off the ball is heading toward the end zone, and it's rolling around and playing hot potato, so Entemann has to sort of chase it all kind of stoopy, stoopin' around like he's an old man chasing a piece of paper with the things on it that he wasn't supposed to forget. And when he finally gets to it, in comes, you guessed it, *the element of invisibility*—and, as Frankie said, he *toenails* Entemann and actually trips the kid up for a safety! So we were goin' nuts, of course. And, with Big Joe holding his arms up together to indicate *Safety!* there's Terry in the end zone, with everybody jumpin' all around him, sticking his head out and looking over at the Vanderkell guys and with, you know, that little garter-snake hiss, spittin' out, "Check the grass on your ass!" Which got George P to congratulate him for poetry even in the heat of battle.

But of course we were still losing, 21-16. And it was the fourth quarter now. And when we did get the ball back after the safety, we didn't get far, because no doubt about it now, the big guy was running out of gas. But we were in this place where there was guts and psych, and we were pla-yin' *football,* which is this unbelievable game, if you never played it and don't know. And you can believe it, how it was so cool that the ammonia was tasting and smelling really good again in my mouth and nose and that the friendship with my friends was so incredible, with all of us feeling no pain, though every play had in it a serious kinda hammer job. And, you know, that thing I said before about how I felt—that if I like punched a hole in some wall around me, there would be Jackie. I swear it was so strong, as like all the pain was out of me, and all the butterflies long gone, and my life in this place where the game puts it (which is the whole point of games, I think)—I mean the place where you feel you're right *there* where remember-it-forever stuff all the time, like, lives. It was so incredible. And one time when I was about to bend down into the huddle and when I was trying to psych myself to the limit, I felt this feeling, all through me that the most remember-forever things I'd ever known were Jackie's toughness and guts of morality. Then I looked over into the huge trees, all shadowy all around. And what happened was, it *was.* I mean, it was like I really did see Jackie there, *clear,* in the big trees of The Woods, on his bike, tough as shit, leaning on his handle bars. He was wearing the crook-toother, lookin' at me, and like saying all over again the thing he'd said to me before, adding in that it was *okay* that I was the one who got to keep on playing.

Which place of seeing things, which I'm pretty sure isn't certifiable, I swear football can bring you to when you're like beyond pain. And it was like Jackie knew it was time. 'Cause like I say, Bobby was run down so bad that he just wasn't going to be able to get us there. And what was happening was that we'd go a little, and then punt. And then they'd go a little, and then punt. And the middle of the field sort of right before your eyes was becoming dust. And all of it was cool. But now the time was almost gone. Down to about a minute and a half. And we had the ball, but weren't going anywhere. And we were still losing, 21-16. So we had to try something.

"How about a pass," Pete said.

Which showed maybe that the smartest guy isn't in every single case also the most moronic guy. But there was a problem. And that was that Frankie had tried like only two or three passes all game and they were pretty serious, big-time wounded birds, and way off, except for one that went right to Gibbons, who naturally dropped it, lucky for us. So Frankie, and of course he's got that pass he threw to Jackie on his mind, deep (which I'm hoping won't be for life), tells Pete to shut up his yap and calls another run to Bobby Stu, which, though, doesn't make it out of the dust. So next huddle Frankie hears it pretty much from all of us. And what else he's hearing is, from Big Joe, "ONE MINUTE."

And there's something about the clock, when it really kicks your butt, that like stops your hemming and hawing and makes ya just *do* stuff. So Frankie's got to clear his throat and it comes out kinda twerpy-voiced, but he calls a stop and go to Pelagi. And Tommy's pretty much clever as all get out. So there he is all open. But Frankie throws another crippled duck, that Pelagi came running back for—but luckily, truth to tell, it was near nobody, 'cause it was interception material all the way. So Frankie's now going pretty much back to hang dog. And the piss and the vinegar of him, which would be two of his middle names, with the third one being psycho, are all going quiet, and Francis X is seeming like being lost is gonna be this thing always right around the corner in his life. But it's like third and nine now, and the clock is stopped but there's about nothing on it. So he calls me and Pelagi in a criss-cross. Which didn't work, 'cause we were covered like glue. But just before he gets creamed, Frankie like shovels the ball over to Bobby. And there's room, 'cause it was an unexpected accident, but the play started working like a perfect draw-play. And it's like Bobby's last gasp, but he gets up some real mean steam anyhow and he sort of freight-trains right out of the dust. And it's the forty. Then the thirty. Then the twenty. With guys ridin' his back, but they haven't hit his legs yet. And then finally, about the fifteen, they bring him down.

So we got that first down, all right. But now it's Big Joe saying, "FOURTEEN SECONDS!"

So we called our last time. And we're thinking maybe we're close enough, so that Bobby could run it. But Bobby looked at us, and he just shook his head no. It would have to be something else. And now Big Joe is lettin' us know that time out is about to turn into time in. And the way we all start lookin' at Frankie pretty much kills all the other choices—but pass. So out of his mouth comes this sort of semi-lost kinda croaky call of Pelagi on a hook and me on a post. And this is it. So it was like too nervous for the rhythmy clap and jump at the break. It was all just no pain, but nerves. And quiet. And I thought maybe if I looked up I'd see Jackie again, so I did. But there was nobody there.

And it's another thing about football that about fifteen times out of sixteen, if it's a true, great game, it comes down to the last second on the clock. But I couldn't be thinking about that. I just saw this crowd of Vanderkell backs and linebackers in front of the end zone, 'cause it gets really crowded when the field's all shrunk 'cause you're down in close. But there's no time for worrying about that. And when the snap comes, there's no thinking, just doing what you do.

"HUT ONE. HUT TWO."

Which sounds made it happen. I mean the snap of the ball from George P to Frankie. And it was no pain, but all nerves. And all too fast to be quiet. But quiet. And I was angling to the post, even though there was a crowd. But because there was a crowd, with linebackers all there in the end zone, too, who'd I see drawing a bead on me but the King of Rats, who was gonna be there, sure as things in a game like this would come down to the last second on the clock. 'Cause it happens like that, in all truth. And when I looked back, what'd I see but Frankie lookin' right at me. And then his arm winding. And then that ball coming. Sure as the Rat was coming. All of us to the same place, at the same time. 'Cause by some miracle of football, Frankie laid it in there. And in it came, with my arms reaching for it, and my hands stretching. And it hit my hands—just as the Rat, whose face I could see like this picture of complete killer hatred, hit me as hard as he like really, in deepest truth, wanted to end my life. And it was one boom-lowering outa hell that he laid on me, if there ever on earth was one.

But then it was noise I heard. Big Joe's whistle blowing. And then blowing again. And again. And then there was Big Joe coming up and pushing people away. And Entemann's brother, too. And then it was Entemann's brother—he's the one I saw—shooting up his arms—for *Touchdown!* Which was a word I heard, too, as I looked down at my hands, and saw that the ball was still there. And what

Big Joe's whistles were for now was that the game was over. 22-21 CK. And that *that's* the kind of score that comes a lot in great football games, I mean a one-point difference in the end, says something cool about something, no doubt. Like an election of maybe a hundred million people, I mean a whole nation, that came down in the end to like just ten votes. And what Big Joe was doing, I saw now, while he kept blowing his whistle, was pushing away the Rat, sort of blowing the whistle smack in his face, till he was gone, 'cause you do not, under any circumstances on the livin' earth, mess with Big Joe.

Then it was everybody from CK all around me, sort of like maybe people in heaven would be, when you just got there. And you're rubbin' your eyes and stuff, after being dead. Only what I was doing was getting up and kind of dusting myself off. And there was George P, smiling, goin', "Yeah, Kev!" And Terry saying, all spitfiery, just like himself, "That's right, Kev. Way t' be! Way t' *be!*" And Pete O'Connor, clean as himself, saying, "Ya did it, Kev!" And Bobby Stu, with guys jumping all around him, because if I was Mr. Hero of the moment, Bobby was THE Hero of the day, if there ever was one in all of time—but he was looking over at me, and he shook a little triumph-fist, which was seriously cool, and quiet as Stu.

And then, walking through a kind of like gauntlet of back slaps, up to me, it was Frankie. And this would be one of my count-'em-on-one-hand favorite things of my life so far, 'cause FX comes up to me with a true, excellent little grin, just sort of barely there, and kind of nods, and goes, "Nice catch," and right outa everything in me, I get to give him a sort of small grin back, and say, "Nice pass."

But it's funny about even remember-forever football

games. 'Cause it's so fast, truth to tell, that you just sort of all melt away back into the ordinary world again. And like in no time, you know, people were just sort of heading off—like I looked up and saw the Vanderkell guys already moving off through the big trees, with their helmets under their arms, with Prizer already off in the far distance, jumping on his bike and tearing away, with good riddance, as Frankie would say, to bad shtank. Which to make a better confession, maybe I'll let the years of my life turn into a better understanding of that guy. But not now.

Then before you knew it, which got to me in the heart even right then, 'cause it was like only a few more days now till I'd be leaving, it was George P and Terry and Pete, heading off, too, with their helmets under their arms, through those huge trees. And Frankie Malone, which was how Sister Armida said his name, which I'll always like her for: I saw Frankie, walkin' by himself, a little pigeon-toed, which was a trademark, off into the trees too, and the shadows. And I hope still and always that prayers aren't bullshit. Because Sister was right. I mean, maybe all through his life, I think it's true that Frankie is going to need 'em, so he won't mistake himself for somebody else.

And our girls were being stupid, of course. Walking and giggling, doin' a little of that screaming that they do, which what a puzzle that one must be to, for instance, a guy like Bobby Stu, or maybe any sane human. But—truth forever and all of time—CK girls: extremely cool. Even though of course, probably even after this one, they'd have missed that question on the score. Except not all of them. 'Cause there was one, whose name I don't need to say, who knew it all. Girl stuff. Guy stuff. 'Cause there's people who live, a lot more regularly than most people do, where the things that last forever are. And she was with the other girls, Katie L, and Gina Rochford and Mary Stenham and all the others, but different forever. Which puts a pain in my chest right as I'm saying this, thinking that somebody else some day is going to get to kiss her. But there are things you shouldn't ever let yourself get over, and there are things you have to.

Bobby and Big Joe, 'cause we lived so close to each other, waited up for me. I told 'em thanks, but that I kind of felt like takin' a cut through The Woods, which is the kind of thing, along with anything else you might have to say, that you'd never have to explain to the Stupnicki boys. So Bobby and Big Joe headed off together through the trees, too, toward 89TH, where they'd cut over from Leavitt to Hamilton, where their house was right around the corner.

And it was kind of amazing how fast it happened, but there it was—just me. And I had my helmet under my arm, too, and was walking through The Woods. Only I didn't head toward 89TH but down instead toward the stream and the ravine. 'Cause you can be sure I wasn't going to try the nine-footer again, but I thought that I'd strip my equipment down, you know, so I could fit, and go, one last time, through the rabbit hole in the Dead End. And The Woods were all beautiful, with the wind coming through, with just the kind of breeze you'd order up to take the sweat off, and which put a good feeling into the aches and pains which were coming the way they do after football games, but which are like signs of how cool things were, which for me of course included the catch. And I mean, no doubt, this day was on that list of days I talked about, tied for second best, with first best still my time with Patty at the Ice Tree. Funny, though, how really and truly you don't, 'cause you shouldn't, make too much of things like a catch. I guess you hope always that you make just the right amount out of 'em, 'cause you do need 'em, for confidence, which would be the thing you need for, I guess you could say, Rat Kings and black Cadillacs.

And I was feeling it—I mean, like, thanks to my big moment, at least for now, the confidence that you're gonna need. And it started to feel so warm now all through my bones and aches and pains that I had that feeling again that honest to God I might see Jackie, that, somewhere out of that box in the grave, he was right around the corner. I know that sounds like bull. But I really did. Which is something The Woods can do to you. And The Woods in combination with football and being by yourself in the quiet is very potent. So it was like one punch through that wall, and JL and I would be talking. Especially, you know, when I was walking past all the places where we did stuff—which I won't talk about anymore, 'cause you know 'em. But as much as I thought it, he never came. And The Woods stayed quiet. Jackie bein' there with his crook tooth, on his bike, didn't happen, the way phone calls back to places you leave when you're a kid, which I guess we knew all along, are never going to happen. But when I got myself through the rabbit hole, and I was standin' in the Dead End, looking back at The Woods, there were some things I knew. I mean, I knew because of the way she woke up in me this understanding of what all it means for a girl to be beautiful, that whenever I see beauty, it will always in some way be Patty. And that whenever I see heroes, even though he died when he was just a kid, it will always be Jackie, like a knight in shining armor.

ACKNOWLEDGEMENTS

Sincerest thanks to Jay Amberg, John Manos, Sarah Koz, Jody O'Connor, Petie Avery, Natalie Phillips, and Francie Bala for all the help they gave in making this book possible.

ABOUT THE AUTHOR

Patrick Creevy grew up on the South Side of Chicago, moving to the northern suburbs at age fourteen. He graduated from Holy Cross College in 1970, received his Ph.D. in English Literature from Harvard University in 1975, and has taught at Mississippi State University since 1976. For the last seventeen years he has divided his time between his farm in Mississippi and his home in Evanston, Illinois. He has five children and eight grandchildren and has been married to his wife, Susie, for forty-two years.